Deadly Relations

By the same author

WATCHMAN
THE GREY REGARD

Deadly Relations

D. G. Finlay

C

CENTURY PUBLISHING

LONDON

Copyright © D. G. Finlay 1986

First published in Great Britain in 1986 by
Century Hutchinson Ltd
Brookmount House, 62–65 Chandos Place
London WC2N 4NW

ISBN 0 7126 9507 9

Photoset by Rowland Phototypesetting Ltd
Bury St Edmunds, Suffolk
Printed in Great Britain by
Anchor Brendon Ltd, Tiptree, Essex

For Juliet
who, with Katie, spent
some summer afternoons
clearing the weeds and
ivy from the graves of
many of the characters
mentioned in these pages,
in the graveyard at
St Mary's Church,
Apuldram

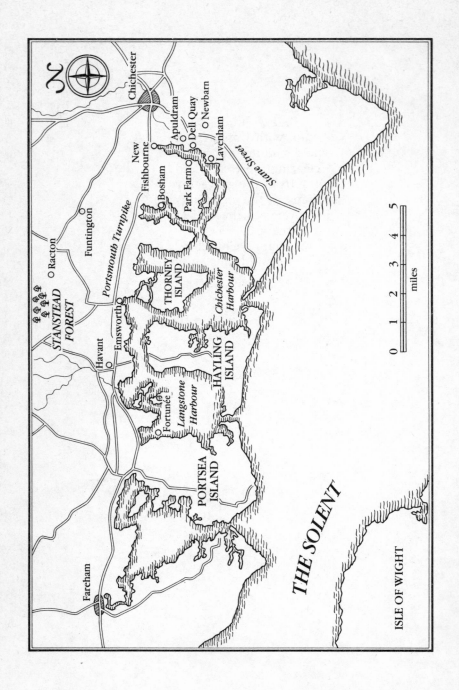

Chichester

New Fishbourne

Apuldram

Dell Quay

Newbarn

Lavenham

Bosham

Park Farm

Slane Street

THORNEY ISLAND

Racton

Funtington

Chichester Harbour

STANSTEAD FOREST

Portsmouth Turnpike

Havant

Emsworth

HAYLING ISLAND

Fortunê

Langstone Harbour

Fareham

PORTSEA ISLAND

THE SOLENT

ISLE OF WIGHT

0 1 2 3 4 5
miles

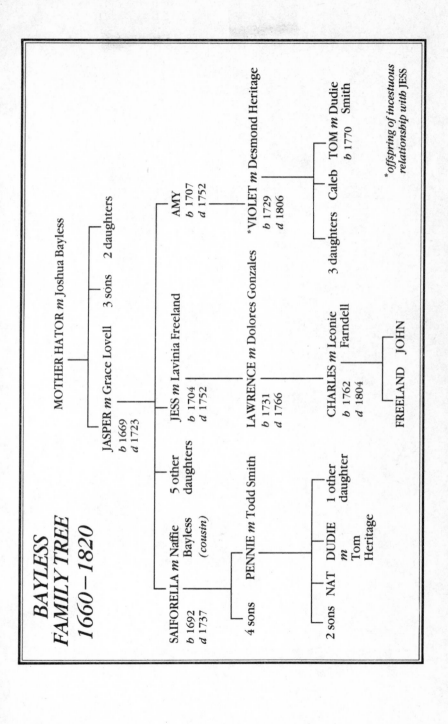

BAYLESS
FAMILY TREE
1660–1820

MOTHER HATOR *m* Joshua Bayless

JASPER *m* Grace Lovell
b 1669
d 1723

3 sons   2 daughters

SAIFORELLA *m* Naffie Bayless
b 1692   *(cousin)*
d 1737

5 other daughters

JESS *m* Lavinia Freeland
b 1704
d 1752

AMY
b 1707
d 1752

*VIOLET *m* Desmond Heritage
b 1729
d 1806

PENNIE *m* Todd Smith

4 sons

LAWRENCE *m* Dolores Gonzales
b 1731
d 1766

CHARLES *m* Leonie Farndell
b 1762
d 1804

FREELAND   JOHN

3 daughters   Caleb   TOM *m* Dudie   Smith
b 1770

NAT   DUDIE   1 other
m   daughter
Tom
Heritage

2 sons

*offspring of incestuous
relationship with JESS

Prologue

In the event, it was easier than he had imagined to detach his mind from the pain of having the dressings on his hands changed. The removal of pus-encrusted lint and bandages was an agony which he discovered could be forced to the back of his concentration – as long as he kept the centre of his attention upon the other, even greater, issues of the moment. He struggled with them now, eyes tightly shut against the sight of the District Nurse's solemn young face bent over him, a tiny frown creasing the smooth area between her eyebrows. She was good at her job, deft and swift and the tenderness with which she worked on the burns across his palms was no more than she gave to all her patients, he knew that.

'Try not to twitch. I'm being as quick as I can.'

He veered away from the pain and concentrated on the cause of his situation.

The stone upon which he had spread his hands in the moment of its discovery had been red hot. It was impossible to take that in, for it was just a very ancient boulder embedded in the hard-packed earth beneath the House's foundations. But it had been *red hot* . . . enough to strip the flesh from his palms. The shock was almost greater than the physical blow the stone had dealt him and now, even after half a day in which to come to terms with himself, he could see no glimmer of explanation for such an apparent impossibility.

FACT . . .

Lavenham had been built in 1726 on the site, so tradition had it, of some pre-Christian place of worship. How far it had preceded Christianity had never been ascertained. He would have to go into that very closely.

Since then, the Bayless family had repeatedly tried to live in the House, for it was beautiful and its land rich pasture. Those attempts had on each occasion been terminated with violent tragedy. Two generations had dwelt there and a child of the third generation had attempted to set foot across its threshold – only to be beaten out of the place by killer bees.

FACT . . .

He was here now at Lavenham – the Bayless blood beating strongly in his veins, unwilling custodian of a Power that had destroyed many of his forbears and set one branch of the family against the other. He checked at this point. He had had no inkling of that Power during his youth and nor had any other member of the immediate family, as far as he could recall. Mention of it had always been accompanied by an element of disbelief, though the traditional history of the Baylesses of Lavenham was strongly supported. That killer Power which the family diaries, written by Thomas Bayless Heritage, had referred to as 'flaming' had only manifested itself here at Lavenham.

No . . . maybe even that was wrong. It had broken into his soul a long time before, that very first visit to this House when he had been brought into the hall after crash-landing on the airstrip. At the time they had put his terror and confusion down to the damage that had been done to his skull. He had only been vaguely aware of Lavenham for an instant then, for he was whisked away to St Richard's Hospital in Chichester and the terrible bursting rage in him had soon evaporated. But he had never quite forgotten the sensation of being out of control with a strength of such magnitude that he was almost unable to contain himself. It lay out of sight, not quite recalled but never quite forgotten, and in the intervening years while he struggled to come to terms with the aftermath of his injuries, Lavenham itself slowly began to assume a fascination which grew until he had finally given way to it. Now he was here with a three-month lease on the place, living like a tramp in a near ruin. The villagers viewed him with silent suspicion, for there had been little opportunity of discussing the place with anyone so far. He was just one of those wartime Yanks, come back to wallow in the scene of their glory.

FACT . . .

He might not survive but he was set now upon an irreversible course of discovery into why all this was happening to him . . . why this had come upon the family in the first place. Why, and this was the big one – why the Baylesses had been singled out for such a trail of destruction across two and a half centuries.

He had given himself little rest during the last five days and nights. God . . . was that all it was since he had opened the oak door carrying a rucksack and a box of stores and walked straight into a terrifying kaleidoscope of personalities that bore his own genes imprinted upon their faces.

There was such a tangle of events to unwind, some of which were familiar to him but most of which had long been buried in the memories of men and women dead for decades. He would have to write down the details lest he forgot any small piece of the jigsaw which might prove to be the vital key before he could even explain himself to himself. It just might release the pustule of hatred and horror which had turned this lovely old House into a nightmare experience – or at least remove from him the weight of everything which had gone before.

'There we are. All done. How do they feel?'

The Watcher opened his eyes and looked up into the girl's face. 'Better. Much better.'

They regarded each other for a long moment which seemed to stretch . . . stretch and he said with sudden surprise, breaking the fragile spell, 'For such a typically English young woman in every other way, ma'am, you have remarkably foreign colouring.'

She grinned and drew back, turning away to gather up her tray of soiled dressings. 'Oh yes, I'm afraid I'm a terrible giveaway of the skeleton in our middle-class cupboard.' Her voice was light, making polite conversation to relax him. The blue and white stripes of her uniform reflected the sparkle in her straight-browed eyes. 'There is a strong element of the

3

gypsy in our branch of the family which we aren't supposed to admit to – but how can you hide jet black hair and an olive skin like mine when the rest of us are all fair or mousey? I'm told by our old cook whose own grandmother used to know them both that my great grandfather married a gypsy called Demeris. Isn't that a beautiful name?'

Her straight, strong features floated before him and he lay back on his sleeping bag, studying her carefully.

'I suppose it's part of my delusion,' his voice was little more than a whisper, 'but, since you're from these parts . . . and admitting to gypsy blood . . . you wouldn't be connected with the Baylesses of this old House, by any chance?'

She flicked her little watch out of her uniform pocket and put her fingers lightly on his pulse.

'There is a connection,' said Frances Ayles. 'That gypsy Demeris was a Bayless, so the story goes.'

PART ONE

Tom and Moses

Chapter One

After the first terrible months of his captivity, when every new moment was a nightmare of utter degradation and hunger, the daily act of waking followed a familiar pattern. An inexplicable timing mechanism in his head seemed to set up a chain reaction of warning, moments before the hatches were flung open and the night guards' hoarse bellows dragged him back into the unwanted presence of another day. Sleep was rarely enjoyed as a haven of rest – of forgetfulness. Sleep for most of them was another kind of nightmare, often as violent and uncontainable as the realities of each day. Between the flashes of remembered torture, of the degradation where man was brought lower than a sty full of pigs so that some behaved like them, of seeing a companion with his guts spilling out of his breeches, of the hunger that ate into the soul and made walking cadavers of them all – between the crests of stark reality came dark troughs of oblivion and it was out of these sightless suspensions that awareness grew.

It was a gradual procedure, the seconds stretching as he hung back, pushing his fear against a force which propelled him, like a leaf on the surface of a stream, inexorably towards that chink of light which was consciousness.

He was, as usual, aware of his own body before the senses acknowledged the enormity of his surroundings.

His bladder was full.

His stomach was empty.

The lice were once again breeding in his crotch.

*

The sudden screech and grind of the iron hatchbolts being drawn back brought movement into the reeking air below decks. Dawn was still two hours away but the guards' raucous urgings spelt the beginning of another featureless day for six hundred and thirty men, prisoners of war aboard the mastless frigate 'Fortunée'.

'Two bells of the mornen' watch. Turn out yer hammocks . . .'

An icy shaft of frost-laden air drove down from the open hatches through the slats of the deckladders. Men stirred and rolled, groaning, from their hammocks. Moving blindly in the pitch darkness like maggots in the rotten heart of the old hulk, they groped for whatever extra covering they might be fortunate to possess, too tired and demoralized to care for the elbows that jutted into each other's ribs, the stench of their night breath and body odours.

'Off yer butts, ye stinken' buggers . . . On deck at the double or ye'll feel the warmth of me boot up yer funnels . . .'

The rasping voices, the foul language . . . the debasement slid off Tom now so that he scarcely heard the message of contempt in them. Twenty-six months of it had created a defensive shell about his mind and body so that only deeply within himself would he admit to the private but continuing survival of Thomas Bayless Heritage, Individual.

He wrapped his thin wisp of blanket about his shoulders, crossing the corners over his chest and securing the ends in his string belt. The trailing corner would cover the flapping rent in his breeches until he could persuade one of the *Rafales* to mend it for him in exchange for the week's soap ration.

The reeking air was cold and his teeth chattered like castanets. February was even colder than January this year and it seemed that English winters went on and on until it was almost halfway through the year before the sun came to warm the slimy timbers of the old frigate.

There was general movement now towards the ladders and Tom let himself be thrust along among the press of bodies until his bare feet snagged against the bottom rung and he put out his hands and pulled himself upward and out into the pure and freezing air.

8

A hand gripped his shoulder and thrust him forward impatiently among the gathering swell of men on the windblown main-deck. Teeth chattering uncontrollably in the seering cold, they stood hunched close together for warmth, blowing into grey, cupped hands as the dirty tide of ill-clad men continued to erupt from the open hatches.

The Dawn Muster of prisoners on deck: a shifting, pathetic sorting out of spiritless souls who had once been men fighting proudly under their country's flag. Tom no longer felt the old repugnance which had threatened to blow his sanity when he and the others from his ship had arrived in Langstone Harbour following their capture. He and his nine companions had been thrown amongst ravening creatures who had once been men; some of them had already been confined in this and other prison hulks for ten years and more. There were few among them who still resembled self-respecting human beings for there was little of the human left to respect in many of them. He had shrunk from the ragged, menacing scarecrows with their comical, moth-eaten beards, afraid of the knowledge that he too must soon wear the hollow-cheeked uniformity of their despair. There was such desperate depravity in the rotting and shredded humanity whose only remaining motivation was in sustaining life itself at its lowest moral level.

Death became a close companion as dropsy and scurvy and those mortal ills that went hand in hand with overcrowding and disease took their toll – and many sought it as the only escape. Others, like Tom himself, devoted themselves to the very science of survival. More than two years later he stood shoulder to shoulder among them, with almost complete indifference to filth, insanity and constant humiliation, still able to recognize beneath the matted growth of lice-filled beards, the tiny differences between each bag of bones. Some were Americans and others French and Dutch, and there was even a peppering of mercenaries from Sweden and Africa.

Peering down the shuffling line, he caught the gleam of white eyeballs set in ebony and winked under the bulkhead lamps at Li'l Moses across the deck. A dim toothy flash signalled the answering grin and both men straightened their backs and knuckled their fists at their sides.

' 'TENSHUN!'

The hoarse cry echoed thinly through the ranks. The rattle of leg irons shifted and dragged and was still.

The Master of 'Fortunée' was beginning his inspection.

Herbert Furze paddled slowly between the lines of slouching, shivering men with the First Mate at his side and a pair of red-coated Marine artillerymen bringing up the rear with upraised lanterns. This was always the worst part of the Master's job, the Dawn Muster, for he had but lately rolled from a warm bed and breakfast was yet to come. His baleful glance bounced over the ranks, left . . . right . . . left again like a mouse caught in the bread locker. His gross stomach rumbled anxiously. Suddenly angry, he stopped before a Frenchman who slumped half-naked against his companion in a futile attempt to protect himself from the bitter dawn wind.

'Where is your jacket? Were you not issued with one just last week?'

The little Captain's nasal voice echoed down the lines but few bothered to crane their necks and watch. The *Rafales* were always in trouble and small wonder, for they gambled away their possessions with such fanatical zeal that naked Frenchmen were becoming a serious problem to the Authorities, or so it was said. When clothing was put upon their backs, they promptly gambled it away once more until the winter weather finally laid them out. There were few old hands among the *Rafales* but those few were the toughest and most vicious men aboard. The skeletal creature grinned back at 'Fortunée's' Captain, his sunken pebble eyes roaming insolently over the overstuffed figure of his gaoler.

'*Allez vous f'foutre, Cul,*' he said softly through a wisp of drooping moustache, making the insult sound like a caress. Furze stared back at him suspiciously. He had few words of the French language and certainly none of the sort that these animals used.

'Get yourself covered or I'll have you put in the Black Hole while you contemplate my orders . . . and get your hands off that man. I will not have your disgusting wickedness on show before my officers.'

He moved on before the Frenchman's hot eyes could

scourge him further. They were little better than a pestilence, these morally corrupt *Rafales*, and he thanked his good fortune that there were only a handful aboard now. The Colonial Rebels, of which there were many, were a much more orderly and controlled group, in spite of the high mortality among them.

He paused once more, beside Tom this time, and turned to the First Mate.

'This is the man I was speaking to you about. You fellow. They tell me that you are an educated Rebel and have been giving lessons to some of your less fortunate colleagues.'

Tom bowed his head. The intense cold brought tears to his eyes which irked him. The fool would probably think that he was moved by being spoken to by his Master.

'A little mathematics and astronomy, sir,' he said, looking at Furze from a height. The ship's Captain was a clear head and shoulders shorter than he and almost as wide as he was high.

'They tell me that one of your pupils is a Negro. How can a simple African, less intelligent than the dullest European, possibly comprehend either mathematics or astronomy, especially one as brutish and ox-like as this one?'

Furze turned his head and peered further down the line to where the vast bulk of Li'l Moses towered above his fellows, a fine crowning of morning frost already whitening his curly head and goatee beard.

'Sir . . . I am helping nine of my compatriots in these subjects and Moses has the swiftest comprehension of them all. I suspect that the Lord has blessed him with a far finer brain than my own. One day, sir — when hostilities are over between our two countries, I very much hope that Moses will come and work in partnership with me for I have the greatest respect for him.'

Furze turned away with a shrug. There were a few pet Africans in Court households, he knew — but they were pampered toys only. For the most part they were odd creatures with less intelligence than his own lapdog. No-account work donkeys, that's how *he* rated them — and the black giant who played at learning to appease this toffee-nosed Bostonian was no different from the rest. He shifted the weight of his grotesque body from one stout leg to the other and broke wind ponderously.

'Report to the Orderly Office after Muster and get yourself shaved,' he said to Tom over his shoulder, leading his party onward down the line.

'The man I have in mind is as presentable as he can be in the circumstances,' he said later to his wife across the breakfast table. 'I suspect that he fancies himself as being superior to the rest of us, in spite of his present situation. His papers show that he served for some years in rebel vessels, including two owned by his father and he was captured West Sou'west of Cape Cod while carrying dispatches. It was in my mind to offer his services to you after he is fumigated, should you feel inclined to make use of his education. What think you, m'dear?'

Mistress Furze's plump goodnatured face lit up and she smiled her pleasure across the white damask cloth. 'The children and I would be delighted with such a thoughtful idea, sir,' she said, heaping a generous spoonful of peach preserve onto her bread.

She would never refuse such a rare offer, even though she was unsure what actual use might be made of the poor man. She was in great sympathy with those pathetic wretches so cruelly herded in the hulks – and had been the mediator many times between her husband and the Prisoners' Committee, as they liked to call themselves. Living in comparative luxury in the Master's suite and being a constant reader of her Bible, she felt the deepest anguish at conditions below decks. She had no official voice to raise and certainly Herbert Furze, with his bullying nature fuelled by the small man's demand for assertion, had little inclination to heed any advice she might offer him – but there *were* ways and means of making herself heard now and then and none of these moments had been wasted since she had brought the five children to live aboard 'Fortunée'.

This man Heritage could tutor the boys and it might well be that, because he was bound to be a more interesting person than their present schoolmaster (his home after all was in such an exciting, faraway place as New England) he might be more successful than was Master Dalby in keeping their attention *and* din a little learning into their resistant young skulls. Yes, the more she thought of it, the better it seemed all round.

'What they talk to you 'bout during Muster?' Moses asked as they swabbed down the orlop-deck.

'Nothing much. Something about reporting to the Orderly Office after this and getting a shave. Reckon they might be going to fire our little cannonball at the Frenchies as their latest secret weapon and offer me the command of "Fortunée".'

Moses sniggered through clenched teeth. 'Ooh Jericho Jeeezuz, he don't need no cannon! The way he bin manufacturing natural gases lately, they jus' gon' point that li'l old man at the French Fleet, fill him up with kidney beans . . . and man alive, just listen to him GO . . .'

They laughed, heads down, their shoulders shaking till chest cramps stilled them. They finished sluicing their deck area and Tom threw his bucket and cloth into the slop locker. Somewhere further along the lightless deck a man groaned as his bowels vented themselves. There were too many dropsical men, too many suffering the first symptoms of scurvy, for attention in the little sick bay. Mostly they lay in their hammocks until the last life flickered out. Five more had gone during the night.

'I'll go and get it over with now. See you this evening. You're going with the Havant Warehouse work party this week, aren't you?'

Moses nodded. Despite his emaciation he was still the strongest man aboard and as a result had the greatest variety of daily jobs where brawn was the most valued commodity. He assumed his most vacant expression – always a master of such disguises – and wagged his crinkly head from side to side, eyeballs rolling alarmingly in his head.

'Oh Yas surr, sure surr, dis cotton pickin' nigger's jus' goin' to roll dem li'l ole sisal bales all roun' de Warehouse jus' like dey was Miz Pollyanna Peckinpaw's playhoop.' He tugged at his fuzzy forelock, rolled his eyes and assumed an expression of such blank lunacy that Tom was convulsed anew. It needed so little to make a man laugh or cry. He gave Moses a thump in the stomach.

'Save your clowning for our porcine friends. See you later.'

He did his best to make himself presentable. Put the comb he had fashioned from a ham-bone through his hair and fastened it tidily off his face with a piece of string from his belt. The orderly would see that his stringy beard was shaved before his audience with Master Furze. A pity for, scrofulous as it was, it kept a little of the frost off his face. Tightening his breeches and straightening his hopsack shirt, he tucked the tail neatly into the breeches belt. No stockings to straighten. No shoes to polish. No jacket to check for food stains. He arranged his shawl more closely round his shoulders and made for the Orderly Office up on the half-deck.

'Ha, it's you.' Furze was sitting behind his desk, a self-important gargoyle, with one square foot resting on a pile of ledgers, busily engaged in exploring the holes in his tobacco-stained teeth with an ivory pick. 'Took yer time, didn't yer?'

Tom looked at the Captain's brown and mottled face with inward disgust. The man was such a hideous individual, handpicked for this thankless job, no doubt. Thin gingery hair, receding off a broad forehead, red-rimmed eyes of an indeterminate blue, an angular hooked nose and a gash of a mouth which seemed to rip his head in half, the thin lips constantly agitated by a nervous twitch.

'I came as soon as I had finished deck duty, sir. Gotten a shave, like you said, too.'

He stood across the desk from Furze and submitted to a long silent stare from the baleful, deeply pouched eyes. His lower face felt indecently naked. There was a broad area of white chin and jaw that had not felt the chill air for a very long time.

'All right . . . so tell me about yourself. I'm considering you for certain duties which will be more to your liking and education than your present situation. Hence the need of a shave. Name first, then age and background with qualifications. Speak.'

'Heritage, sir. Thomas Bayless Heritage. Thirty-two years old and unwed. Seaman by profession. Born and brought up in New Midhurst by Boston, in the State of Massachusetts, Continent of North America. Three older sisters and one brother, sir.'

'What nationality are your parents?'

Tom gazed at Furze's hawk nose. There was a dewdrop forming on the tip. Others had formed and fallen before it for there was a damp patch on the left lapel of his blue jacket.

'Why, they are Americans of course, sir.'

Furze banged the desk with a pudgy fist. 'We are not here to have a political discussion, Heritage. Give me a straight answer. Where were your parents born?'

Tom smiled at the man's antagonism. He was a person of limited intelligence and they were both well aware of who was really in charge of the interview.

'Well, sir, it depends on how closely you wish to refine their ancestry. They were both born in Sussex not far from here, in fact, but my father has lived in New England for near on fifty years now. My mother — well she was born close to Langstone but she was a gypsy and they have a mixture of foreign bloods in them too varied to learn much about. I always reckoned my mother was more continental than English.'

He watched a series of expressions chase across the Captain's stolid face. A drop of moisture was forming in one ginger-haired nostril. It dropped onto the damp stain on his lapel.

'Thomas Bayless Heritage, you say. Is the Bayless your mother's name by chance?'

Tom nodded, suddenly wary.

'Well, well, well . . .' Furze speared a thin string of chewed meat from a newly-discovered cavity in a back tooth. He gazed at it for a moment before flicking it off the point of the toothpick onto the floorboards. He changed the subject abruptly.

'I wish you to attend Mistress Furze and my sons each morning after your deck duties are completed. You will ensure that you are clean and free of lice and then make yourself useful to her in any way she sees fit to employ you. You will cleanshave yourself daily and be neat and respectful at all times. She will receive you in my stateroom immediately. Go.'

Tom bowing, withdrew and stood outside the office door for a moment to collect his thoughts. He had long hoped for this position. Service in the officers' quarters was the job most sought-after amongst the prisoners for it meant working in warm rooms, in a greater state of cleanliness and there was food to be gleaned from the Captain's lavish table. There were already two prisoners acting as mess stewards to the officers but to be with Mistress Furze meant kindliness as well as the possibility of little gifts of meat and fruit. He took a deep breath, straightened his shoulders and made his way down the passage to the stateroom, putting from his mind that odd reaction of the Captain's to the name of Bayless. That could be mulled over at length later when he was once more sealed into the darkness of the orlop-deck below hatches.

Mistress Furze was no more comely than her husband but there was about her such an aura of good nature that it stood her in good stead of beauty. A round pudding face was accentuated by the bunches of fat, mousey-coloured sausage ringlets bunched on either side of her red cheeks beneath her pinner. Her eyes were small and struggled to do their job from between the twin bulges of cheek and brow. There was a large brown mole sprouting a couple of strong black hairs beside one nostril. She was taller than her husband but had spread nearly as widely and the wrap of her fichu and the whale-boning in her corsetry were hard put to keep her body in a recognizable shape. At the same time there was a comfortable easiness in her manner to which Tom warmed as he stood inside the stateroom door, respectfully attentive.

She had been quite excited at the thought of having a servant of her own. Herbert had kept the family in the little house at Nutbourne for three years after his appointment to 'Fortunee' and she had seen little of him. Then, without giving his reasons, he had gathered her up with the five children and brought them aboard and they had been living in comparative isolation in the draughty Captain's quarters for the last three months.

She had forgotten what an opportunist her husband was. There seemed to be some strange deals made at the dining table, when, late at night she had retired from the company. She had had no servant other than the officers' cook who served indifferent food with undue wastage which no doubt found its way into the prisoners' quarters with great regularity. There was graft at every turn. The prisoners bought from the cook and the table stewards. The stewards stole from the officers' mess, the officers made financial profits out of the cheap manpower they sold to local merchants – and the Captain took what he wished from everyone.

She was impressed by the look of the gaunt, dark-haired man standing quietly beside the door, one shoulder leaning against the lintel. In some prisoners this casual stance might have inferred a certain insolence but she saw none in this man's pinched but serene face.

'Come over and let me see you better,' she said, motioning him forward. He smiled and came across the room and stood with his hands holding the top of a highbacked chair, relaxed as though he were in the presence of someone known to him.

He was older than she had imagined but then, maybe it was simply the privations of his existence that had laid those extra years upon once young shoulders. He was tall and despite the wasting in him, she could see that his was a lightweight frame with broad shoulders and legs as long as a grasshopper's. His blue black hair was neatly tied back into the nape of his neck and the pale-chinned face that returned her perusal with quiet courtesy was filled with a private strength within its gentleness. The eyes that regarded her from beneath straight brows were the colour of the sea in winter but there was no chill in their expression, only a calm dreaminess that was content to await her command.

The interrogation began again but the questions were about himself and his interests and capabilities and he gave her the answers willingly, knowing that they held no traps.

'I can teach your sons mathematics, ma'am,' he said, seeing that she wished to use his mind while appearing to utilize his body. 'I can teach them to navigate by the stars and, were we living on the shore, I could show them the ways of the small wild creatures that live in the undergrowth. As it is, from here

I can only tell them of the birds that fly overhead and of the fish that live in the seas beneath us.'

'That would do very nicely for a start,' she said quickly. 'My children are not making progress with Master Dalby in Emsworth and it will be much easier for them to have lessons with you for four hours each morning than for them to be taken ashore in all weathers, as they are presently doing. I shall be going to Portsmouth tomorrow to visit my mother and will take the opportunity of equipping the children with slates and chalks. They will be ready for you to commence your duties on the third day from today.'

She stood up from her chair and moved round the table towards him. Her gown was covered in a pattern of fat pink roses unsuited to her girth.

'I hope that you will find some relief to your troubles in these mornings with us,' she said with a little hesitation. 'Before you begin, I shall give you some of my own shampoo to get rid of your unwanted passengers.' Her eyes twinkled at him.

He looked down at her shiny red cheeks with the bunches of ringlets framing the kindly face and the very tenderness in the light words smote him.

'I thank you most kindly, ma'am,' he said gruffly and turned from her, bowing his head.

A bitter wind lashed his face as he emerged from the Master's quarters. He felt nothing, his mind already sifting through the events of the morning. He tucked his freezing chin against his chest and, butting through the icy gusts which scoured the main-deck, scrambled down the main hatchladder in search of his companions.

'Apple pie for luncheon from now on, my brave fellows,' he said, coming upon the little group, heads bent over roughhewn dice. He squatted down as they made room for him, expectant faces turned eagerly towards him.

'I'm to teach our toad's little tadpoles in the mornings. Mistress Furze is a good, warmhearted woman and I foresee some tasty little titbits coming the way of the "Free States" crew in the very near future.'

A wizened face peered round the bulk of the capstan. There was something in the sunken eyes that was not quite envy, not quite hunger.

'Judgen' by the size of that one's titbits, reckon you'll soon find you've bitten off more than you can chew, Brother.'

Tom turned his back on the man.

The class of nine was only six this day as two were working ashore and Seneca Dillon was laid in his hammock with stomach cramps. When the weather curtailed the use of the deck and the daylight for recreation, candle wax was grudgingly used for studying. Now the lantern was lit and the daily lesson began.

A space was cleared and the men squatted round Tom, shoulder pressed to shoulder and necks craning the better to see the diagrams that he would chalk upon the deckboards. Each man there, as he strove to take in the numbers and equations of his mathematical lesson, nursed in the pit of his stomach the happy and secret anticipation of small succulent morsels soon to come his way, presented graciously to Tom by his new Mistress. It created an exciting area of hope in the apathy of their existence.

It was only much later that the thought occurred again to Tom. Why had mention of Mama so interested the Toad?

The question kept nibbling at him, burrowing deep – hurting. It still hurt to think of home for it conjured up a haven of peace and plenty where Mama ruled supreme in the house and Papa governed all beyond. They were a united family – Jane and Phillipa married now with children of their own and dear Catherine, long promised to Caleb's best friend. Caleb would be wed by now for arrangements had been underway before Tom's capture.

Letters . . . if only there was some way of making the tenuous postal arrangements more secure, the men would have felt less abandoned even by their own Revolutionary Council. Letters kept them alive in their dungheap of a prison, kept their imaginations filled with hope and their tongues

19

wagging. But letters were such infrequent treasures and there had been no news from home for several weeks now.

There was great closeness between those of the crew of the 'Free States' who had remained in one group. The rest of their crew, including their Captain, were scattered between Forton Prison at Gosport and Pendennis Castle in Cornwall, where all American prisoners were taken, immediately after capture, for re-distribution.

The men in 'Fortunée' acknowledged Tom Heritage as their First Mate and Leader and had a healthy respect for one whose father was a member of the Revolutionary Council. It had, after all, been Desmond Heritage's persuasive arguments which had inspired many of them to volunteer their lives to free their country from arrogant and distant Georgian misrule. Tom's authority and good-humoured guidance had done much to lighten the appalling conditions of their seemingly endless incarceration. Sickness was the gardener of their days for it claimed a cruelly high mortality. Scurvy, diarrhoea, gangrene and dropsy — these were the executioners which stalked among them, culling their numbers and making room for more.

Prison had not, they discovered, made equals of them all, even if their sufferings and humiliations were shared equally, for there were a few who resisted the fall into insanity or sickness and they were the rocks to which the others clung. Tom Heritage was one. The giant African Moses another. The two men, instead of competing with each other for the men's support, closed ranks together in friendship and mutal respect. One day soon the Parole Board would register their existence and give a little more freedom to some of them. One day soon a more fitting Captain with kindlier feelings for American Rebels would replace the Toad. One day soon . . .

'Ooh man, I heard the sweetest li'l tale today you ever did hear,' Moses said to Tom after they had been battened down for the night and most of the lanterns had been extinguished.

'Me and Osgood were a bowlin' our bales into Hayling Warehouse and came to rest to hear talk between two over-seers. It seems that our very own li'l old Toady is being prosecuted by a local farmer. Remember those sheep he had us round up in the marsh a fortnight back? Well, we thought he'd bought them, didn't we? But oh, no'dy no . . . he just up an' took 'em all without so much as a "Please, sir" to their owner . . . and when he came to present them at market for to gain the full price, rumour led the rightful owner straight to Master Furze and there was a fine scene . . . and now he is to pay dear for his greed.'

Each man who heard the whispered tale slept well that night, knowing in his heart that he slept, for once, a deal easier than did the Captain of the 'Fortunée'. They hugged themselves with glee in his discomfort and plotted in the reeking darkness to contribute to it further.

Muster the next morning was a livelier affair than usual. Furze sensed an unusual anticipation in the silent men as he came out onto the main-deck in the biting dawn. Another heavy frost rimed the ugly clutter of wooden shebangs growing like warts from the upper decks; they housed the galley and sickbay and gave the old hulk the grotesque, top-heavy appearance of a hunchback. He had completed the length of only one row and was halfway down the next when an odd commotion made him pause and cock his ear. Far away at the very back of the ranks a muffled bleating filtered through the packed rows of men. The corners of his mouth turned chinward and he frowned thunderously as he passed slowly on down the lines. There was, he saw, a growing insolence in the wolfish faces on all sides of him. He quickened his pace.

The sound grew until it seemed as though a flock of monstrous sheep had invaded the 'Fortunée'. Furze's nervous tic fibrillated his lower lip furiously as he moved deeper into the lines.

Now the scarecrow men were openly *Baa! Baa!ing* around him and he turned on his escort in fury.

'Stop them immediately!' he roared, bouncing up and down on the balls of his feet with rage, in which ill-disguised fear now played a keen part. The Marines shouted round him at those men within their reach, threatening them with raised muskets.

The prisoners took no notice except to increase the volume of sound. Weary and dispirited throats suddenly caught fire and were uplifted and the message of their contempt broke from them in exalted howls, catching the heartbeat of the next man and then the next. *BAA! BAA!*

'Silence!' roared Furze, a dark flush turning his pumpkin face into beetroot.

BAA BAA . . . BAA BAA . . .

With horrible dawning embarrassment he realized that they had learned of his Summons. Almost beside himself with rage and mortification, he puffed his chest out until he seemed in danger of exploding.

'Back below decks all you maggots! Go on, get down there – NOW!'

The guards were frightened by the sheer uniformity of the revolt and all too aware of their inadequate numbers. They laid about them freely with the flat ends of their muskets, the toes and heels of their boots, with elbows and balled fists. Frail bodies fell beneath the blows and trampling feet and were swept back down the hatches into the unaired miasma of their night's expulsions. The Pen, wired off from the deck-ladders to other levels, was suddenly empty. When the last man was down, the hatch covers were slammed shut and bolted – and the *Baa . . . Baa . . .* continued, a chorus muffled and contemptuous below the damp deck planking. The din continued for the rest of the day and by four o'clock in the afternoon a boatload of Port officials, alarmed by the distant sounds of rebellion, arrived with complaints from the Authorities.

Six hundred and thirty men were put on half-rations for the following two days. It did nothing but emphasize the ache of hunger in their stomachs and increase the mortality rate but there were no complaints. It had been well worth it just to see the rage and fright on the Toad's face and the worried consultations of concerned Port Officials.

Five days after the 'Sheep Revolt' a new supplies contractor for Langstone came aboard to inspect the 'Fortunée'. It was a day of watery sunshine, the first of that year of 1802, for January and February had been filled with icy snowstorms. Now, as the end of the month slid into March, a lull brought sudden clear skies washed clean and pearly to silver the harbour's slate waters lapping the weed-choked hulls of the four decaying hulks.

'The new contractor is on his way,' Mistress Furze said to Tom as he prepared the day's texts for his five pupils. They were dull children but clearly found him more personable than their previous tutor and did their best in order to ensure that this one stayed with them. Their mother always looked into the schoolroom at the beginning of each teaching session and sometimes during the morning, to reassure herself that they were not misbehaving.

'Let us hope that he is of a more generous inclination than was his predecessor,' Tom said to her with a rueful little smile that took the sting from his words.

She put a hand on his wrist for a moment. 'I am doing all I can for you men,' said the little squeeze of her fingers. He looked at her plain pink face, acknowledging her support and she turned away, closing the door of the schoolroom with a sharp click.

'Poor woman,' he thought. 'She is as much a prisoner as we are – and her conscience gives her a lashing every time she puts food in her mouth or clothes on her body.'

Captain Furze brought the new contractor into the schoolroom an hour later. He opened the door and ushered the visitor into the room as Tom stood behind the chairs of the two eldest boys, looking over their shoulders at the sums being wrought so painstakingly upon their slates.

'Here are my sons, sir, hard at work as befits their years. Their tutor is an American prisoner being put to good use, as you see.' His mahogany face was like a polished turkey cock's and the tic in his lower lip trembled furiously.

'What's eating him, all of a sudden?' Tom thought, his mind upon the boys and their work.

Furze seemed to swell, as he often did from both anger and extreme personal gratification. 'This man's name is somewhat similar to your own, Master Bayless. Did you not tell me that your mother was born in these parts, Heritage? That her name was Bayless also?'

Tom's head lifted from the perusal of a slateful of bad spelling. He looked across the room at the tall figure standing behind the little Captain, doing his best to appear unconcerned.

'That is correct, sir.'

The new contractor was elegantly clothed in plum brocade, bringing a welcome splash of colour into the little school cabin. His head was proud and wigless and crowned with a fine thick growth of clean crimped hair the colour of a new guinea. There was something a little foreign about the palely aquiline features but as the two pairs of eyes met, silent recognition passed between them.

'How interesting. I'm afraid I must hasten on now, Master Furze. Be kind enough to continue our perambulation.' He inclined his head at Tom and turned away and Furze followed, disappointment turning his face into that of an unhappy gargoyle.

Bayless.

Furze had called the new contractor Bayless.

Something suddenly lifted in Tom's chest and fluttered there like a bird caught in cupped hands.

They had looked at each other with Violet Bayless' great grey eyes and the instant shock of their recognition had been mutual.

Chapter Two

The acute discomfort of 'Fortunee's' Captain over the heavy damages awarded against him for purloining marsh sheep brought unexpected benefits to the prisoners. They lost no opportunity in poking fun at their gaoler by literally bleating him off the vessel if he issued orders that their Prisoners' Committee thought to be unjust. The result during the following weeks was a definite easing of the pressure upon them by the guards. A further improvement in their misery, which had nothing to do with the Toad, went unnoticed by most, however, and that was that the new contractor, while cutting down the spending of the officers' mess, was definitely delivering bread, soap and victuals with more regularity than had any of his predecessors.

Charles Bayless' dourly elegant appearance quickly earned him the nickname of 'Snake' among the prisoners. There was something slightly repellent about his gaunt countenance with its bloodless coldness and the washed-out grey blue eyes, deepset in shadowed sockets. His tall, slightly stooping figure was always impeccably clothed with no hair on his head out of place, however windswept his passage out to the hulk may have been. He made no effort to engage Tom in conversation; indeed he ignored him completely on the few occasions that they met. Although it was certain by June of that year, after receiving an affirmative from his father, that the new contractor was actually his first cousin, there seemed little chance of claiming this relationship. Out of the deadly boring existence he was living, where physical duties were few and exercise of the mind almost the only occupation, sudden small doubts and frustrations took root in Tom's head.

For all his patriotism, which had always been proud and strong so that he had never thought to plumb its depths or question any part of it, he suddenly found himself within a few miles of his family roots, in the heart of enemy country – and actually coexisting with the English genetic evidence of those roots . . .

Mistress Furze was not slow to notice Tom's interest in Master Bayless when he was aboard, doling out the weekly soap ration or spot-checking on his officiating clerks. After his duties were completed he could usually be induced to take a glass of claret in the stateroom and the pleasantries of polite conversation would naturally include courteous enquiries after the health and well-being of the contractor's family. By such casual means she was able to give Tom what became, to his new way of thinking, the most precious gift possible, other than his own freedom.

'I have just been taking tea with Master Bayless,' she said to him one afternoon as spring warmed gently into summer. He was in the stateroom, squatting on the floor beside an open casement, mending a chair whose leg had buckled under the unreasonable weight of its owner. He looked up quickly and for just a moment his eyes were filled with such eager anxiety that her heart bled for him.

He dropped his head again and addressed his attention to the pot of evil-smelling fish glue beside him. The contents were beginning to congeal and would have to be reheated again.

'Quite a frequent visitor, isn't he, ma'am?'

'More so than Master Stone was, I recall,' she nodded. Master Stone was a rogue and a charlatan, for he short-shifted the rations and clothing allowances of the prisoners nearly as badly as had that iniquitous first overseer of the hulks, Duncan Campbell.

'He tells me that he has two sons. His home is in Chichester, you know, so he is not greatly inconvenienced with travelling to Langstone.'

Another time she said, 'Master Bayless spoke of his elder

26

son's twelfth birthday this week and that he shared a tea party with the lovely young daughter of Lord Lennox at Goodwood House.'

She sighed and smoothed her hands across the flowered taffeta of her gown. 'How pleasing it would be to move in such refined circles. Of course, it is clear that Master Bayless is accustomed to such company for he is so cultured, don't you think? How much my boys would enjoy the freedom of a property such as Goodwood – but, to be sure, I'm talking to the air here, am I not, for you have not been there and cannot know of the sumptuous new mansion the Duke of Richmond has built from the old place.'

Slowly, Tom gleaned the beginnings of a picture of Charles Bayless. He was about ten years older than Tom which surprised him for he looked more, his parchment skin already etched with a tracery of fine lines. The two Bayless boys, Mistress Furze told him, were close together in age and their mother was always in delicate health with lungs that gave cause for concern in the winter months. Charles' primary business interests were concerned with the transportation of freight between the south coast towns and ports and so he was a natural selection for the additional post of contractor to the Langstone prison hulks, a post which he seemed to be executing with great attention. It was not an arduous appointment for there were only four vessels at that time anchored off the marshlands of the inner harbour. There were no less than ten languishing in Portsmouth Harbour, and more, maybe sixty in all at Woolwich, Plymouth, Maidstone, Chatham and other south coast ports. All were the subject of outraged objection concerning their administration, from both the Revolutionary Council in Boston and of certain Government enquiries and select committees like that headed by Master John Graham. Maybe this was why Charles gave such attention to the letter of the Law.

By mid-June of a summer that was already too hot for comfort, Charles Bayless and Tom had still not spoken although Charles had nodded at him on a couple of occasions.

*

27

It was while Tom and Moses were sifting out the 'burgoo' ration of stale cheese and oatmeal for the following day that Captain Furze approached them one morning. He was beaming from ear to ear, a sight which did nothing to soften his froglike looks. The two men paused in their work as he came waddling along the deck towards them, picking his way through the groups of prisoners who had emerged from the sour gloom of the lower decks to warm their scarecrow bodies in the pale early sunshine.

'Ha, Heritage . . . glad to see you with this man. Got a little job for him on Saturday. Is he in good health, would you say?'

Tom frowned, looking puzzled and turned from Furze to Moses who straightened his back and stood like a carving in black marble, wearing his most vacant expression.

'Well, sir, none of us is what you'd call fit, due to our situation and diet and Moses is much the same as the rest of us, by the looks of him. But why don't you ask him yourself? He's the best judge of how he feels and he's neither deaf nor dumb. How ya feelin', Moss?'

Li'l Moses rolled his eyes and thought. Then he rubbed his stomach gingerly. 'Feel a lot better with somethin' more than tatts in dis body, Boss. Cain't seem to know whether dees here cramps are hunger pangs or somethin' real bad,' he said dolefully.

Furze clicked his tongue impatiently. Every manjack of them suffered the same. This man was in good shape, whatever his complaint. He reached out a pudgy hand and gripped the bicep of Moses' upper arm, digging his bitten fingernails into the hard sinews. He grunted, well satisfied.

'Feels good and strong to me. Now if we were to feed you up for the next three days, how would you feel about fighting a challenger?'

Moses' eyeballs rolled alarmingly. 'Oh Lawdy me, Boss. I could fight Goliath himself an' all King Georgie's armies with a pot of good beef stew and summer squash in ma belly.'

'He certainly could, sir,' Tom agreed, tapping Moses' ankle with his toe – 'Come on, sell it to him,' – said the message.

'Why surr, back home in Virginny, I's a free man – an' many's the time I've had to defend that freedom. No man

28

makes a monkey of me, surr, for Li'l Moses is the greatest grip fighter in those parts.'

'Good . . . good . . .' Furze rubbed his hands together, the light of profit in his pink-lidded eyes. The man was definitely an engaging rascal and would be worth the admiration of his visitors, even if he had no chance in beating his opponent.

'Now, here is what I have in mind,' he said sharply, before Moses had time to say more. 'Lord Tankerville is to visit the ship on Saturday with his party. He has informed me that he will be bringing with him a member of his Estate staff – a cowherd, I believe, who has won several purses and a lot of money for his Lordship in the wrestling ring. He wishes to wrestle this fellow with the strongest man aboard and offers a purse of twenty guineas to the winner. You will do very well. No doubt your opponent will bring you down but at least you will give him some sport first, eh?'

He rolled away without waiting for further comment, well pleased with himself.

'You can see who he'll put *his* money on,' Moses said with a grin. 'There's a real sense of loyalty aboard this wreck.'

'Then let's make sure they all wager that the other fellow wins,' Tom said drily. 'Long as you know your manners and shake the man by the hand first, the best man will surely win.'

They rocked with secret glee as they made their arrangements. Oh, what a fine show this was going to be! The *Rafales* would have the time of their lives gambling for and against the great African. No doubt their bets would result in more broken heads, more stabbings and death, more retribution taken by the Authorities. It was an Event, all the same. Something to break up the soul-destroying monotony of each long, featureless day. And the best part of the whole thing was that only the crew of the 'Free States' knew what that English wrestling champion was heading into.

Parties of sightseers had several times visited 'Fortunée' – as they had the other prison vessels with the exception of the hospital ships. They usually arrived in parties of up to a dozen, and the only thing that raised the prisoners from deep feelings of degraded resentment to be viewed in the Pen as though they were animals in a menagerie was the pleasure of feasting their eyes upon women once more. Of watching the reaction in those dreamed-of faces . . . horror, pity, disgust . . . fascination. The day of the fight was no exception.

The large Tankerville party came aboard just before midday, clearly in festive mood for the ladies were brightly dressed in *décolleté* gowns more suited to their withdrawing rooms and wore on their heads the latest outrageous creations involving hair and feathers wired up on a tall frame with all manner of ribbons, flowers and even small stuffed birds. They twittered and giggled behind their gloved hands as they stared through jewelled lorgnettes at the prisoners, crowded close together in the Pen below them, and clung to their escorts in mock fear as the half-human rabble stared back at them beyond the wire.

This day the prisoners were astounded by a sight of extraordinary bizarrerie. They had feasted their eyes hungrily upon the ladies in other visiting groups but had never before come across such exotic creatures as these. Even the *Rafales* were, for an instant, lost for words.

'What in God's name are they dressed like that for?' someone muttered behind Tom. 'They look as though they have escaped from a masque . . . maybe they have.'

'I think that they are wearing the sort of clothing that pleases that fool of a Prince Regent,' Tom said, drinking in the posturing creatures with the same fascination as he was being regarded.

The party climbed up to the quarter-deck, laughing and chattering among themselves and finally disappeared into the Captain's apartments and the prisoners began to rope off an area for the coming fight.

Li'l Moses stripped himself down to a single cloth tied round his hips and brought up between his legs to be secured in a knot just below his navel. From somewhere he had gleaned a nob of pig fat with which he had covered his body, rubbing and polishing it into the skin until he shone like ebony. Had he been fit and not wasted and bony with lack of food and exercise, he would have presented a magnificent challenge to any opponent. Now, he waited quietly to be summonsed, squatting on the deck with his back against the stump of the old foremast, surrounded by those of the 'Free States' who were well enough to attend him. Dysentery had broken out in the vessel with the arrival of a hot summer and three of their number were among the sixty-four prisoners presently laid low with the infection.

There was a stir from the men leaning over the port side.

'Here comes Sholto the Cowherd!'

The man climbed from the bumboat and came, hand over hand up the rope ladder, leaping over the side with the agility of a great cat. He stood on the deck looking about him as his two companions followed, bouncing gently on the balls of his feet as he surveyed the company. He was hard and broad, his torso of such Herculean proportions that the *Rafales*, who had gambled heavily on Moses, were dismayed and began to murmur angrily among themselves.

The Marine guard stood closer, hands tightening nervously on their muskets.

Sholto was naked from the waist up but wore scarlet breeches and stockings. His feet were bare. He was quite bald. In fact, there was not a hair of any kind on his body and the muscles of his shoulders and arms and chest stood out in bulges like blown-up pigs' bladders.

He surveyed the tightly packed deck of half-naked, emaciated men with extreme indifference and slowly began to limber up. It was a most impressive performance – and clearly one that he was accustomed to doing before an audience. He was not as tall as Moses but there was not a wasted inch in the vast width of him, every part knotted with sheer iron muscle which rippled and jerked ominously as he went through the motions of flexing and tightening them.

Moses had seen Sholto come aboard but the two were now hidden from each other by the waiting crowd. Those near to Moses were disheartened to see that the only limbering up he seemed to be doing was with his fingers, wrists and hands – shaking the circulation into them, stretching and tightening his fists. Scores of eyes watched this unimpressive performance gloomily. It would need a better show of strength than that to top that vast rock of seasoned muscle whose arms were larger than a man's thighs and whose chest was greater than the chest of two normal men.

The Tankerville party were alerted to Sholto's arrival and it only took them a short time to refill their glasses and come streaming out onto the quarter-deck. They crowded the deck rail where they could look down in comfort upon the proceedings without having to rub shoulders with the prisoners in the packed Pen.

Furze pushed himself forward to the rail and cupped his hands to his mouth. 'Make way there for the contestants. Let's be having you both in the ring where we can see you. Jump to it . . .'

Sholto and his seconds moved forward and the men pressed back from him, clearing his way. He stood in the centre of the open space and the ladies in the party sighed with admiration, laughed and clapped, and the gentlemen followed suit, whispering to each other behind their hands. Sholto bowed low and swung from side to side with a broad grin, waiting for the applause to spread to the ragged ranks of the prisoners around him. Not a man stirred. They eyed him in stony silence and scratched absently at the lice in their crotches.

There was a movement within the crowded Pen and Li'l Moses strode forward, through hands outstretched to pat his arms, his back, through a murmur of muttered good wishes. He broke from the tight throng at the ringside and stepped over the ropes into the open space opposite Sholto – and the murmur among the prisoners rose to an angry growl. Tall he was – he would overstand Sholto by more than a head – but despite his youth and handsome features and the dignity with which he held himself, Moses' emaciation was all too evident. He was going to be no match for the mighty cowherd. Incarceration, bouts of sickness, lack of meat and fresh vegetables had all taken their toll. Beside his opponent, Moses looked like a stallion matched with a buffalo.

Furze had had an extra twenty Marines deployed to 'Fortunée' for this occasion, and they closed in now and raised their weapons, eyes on the little froglike figure on the half-deck above them.

The visitors were betting vigorously amongst themselves – not, it appeared, as to who would be the victor, for that was

32

a foregone conclusion, but how long it would take Sholto to defeat Li'l Moses.

The prisoners began to stamp and shout their objections and for a moment Furze thought that they would return to their bleating.

'*Silence!* I will have silence now,' he roared. 'If there is not immediate quiet so that these two can proceed, you will all be stowed below for the remainder of the day and the contest will go on without you.'

Slowly, the angry rumblings subsided and the men pressed forward and prepared for the unequal spectacle of a well-fed, perfectly-exercised pugilist annihilating an underfed, wasting giant whose only strength was his calm appraisal of the scene.

The sun shone remorselessly down on the crowded deck, burnished and boiling, to dazzle and fry the packed throng, drawing the last body moistures from the weak so that the noon heat was soon claiming victim after roasting victim. A hot breeze lapped the upper-deck, setting the ladies' bright plumage dancing.

Tom, standing at Moses' side, suddenly saw Charles Bayless in the group above, talking, head bent close to an elderly spectator. Was his wife one of the foolish, simpering creatures fluttering excitedly above them? It somehow seemed unlikely.

A small figure clad in yellow and blue brocade separated itself from the visitors and came quickly down the ladder to the deck. He pushed through the crowd and stepped into the ring. There was little of the fop about Lord Tankerville though there was a dusting of powder on his face and even a little rouge about his cheekbones. He stood in the centre of the ring and held up a red suede purse.

'I have laid down a challenge,' he shouted over the heads of the crowd, 'between my man, Sholto here, and the strongest man aboard this vessel. The winner of the contest will be the richer by twenty guineas and I daresay that certain ladies and gentlemen will be a great deal better off than that, judging by the enthusiasm of their wagering.' He turned towards Moses. 'You are the man accepting my challenge, are you? Have you fought in the ring before this?'

Moses regarded Lord Tankerville with extreme goodwill.

He smiled the smile of a happy child who has just been offered a lollipop.

'Surr, I's fought with ma brothers an' fought with ma messmates but I's neva fought with a man THAT size, no Surr . . .'

He rolled his eyes until they threatened to fall out of their sockets and the visitors were vastly amused at the drollery of this rangy black clown who seemed already to have taken fright at the sight of his adversary.

Tankerville smiled also, sorry for the poor creature. 'Take your stance then,' he said kindly to Moses. 'And may God be with you.'

He turned away but paused as fresh laughter sprang up over his head, making him turn. Moses had assumed a pugnacious attitude, fists raised before his face, and had begun advancing across the ring.

'No, sir. That is not the way we begin fights in this country,' Tankerville said patiently.

Moses looked surprised and lowered his clenched fists.

'Before any fight, it is customary to shake hands with the adversary to show that there is no personal animosity between the contestants,' Tankerville said, his poet's face amused and exasperated in turn.

Moses' face cleared and he turned a beaming smile on Sholto who now stood two paces from him. The wrestler held out his hand and there was no smile on his face.

'Shake this hand with respect, Nigger,' he said. 'It has already crushed a score of your Rebel brothers and is itching to double that number.'

Moses said nothing but moved close to the cowman and gripped the outstretched hand. There was suddenly no more laughter or buffoonery on his face. The hands rose vertically, wrists entwined and the two men stood rooted to the centre of the ring, eyes locked. There was complete silence as it became apparent that the contest was to begin even with the handshake.

The two figures stood together as still as rocks but slowly each slid a cautious foot away from his body the better to create a leverage. A slight tremble was discernible in the mighty muscles of Sholto's frame but Moses remained impassive, save for a fine perspiration which spread across his brow. Sholto's face became suffused and his neck seemed to swell, the veins standing out from it like thick ropes. It seemed that he was in pain for his lips drew back in a snarl and small gasps were forced through clenched teeth. The seconds trailed and there was no sound but the screech of gulls overhead and the grunts of Sholto's pain as the quivering in his body increased.

Movement came suddenly.

Sholto threw back his head, hunching his great shoulders as his whole body started to tremble. A huge groan slammed out of his body and it seemed that he was attempting to withdraw. Moses stood like a statue with his opponent pulled in onto his chest, immovable, dominating.

'Let me go, damn you . . .' Sholto gasped at last, his eyes bulging in a scarlet face. 'Concede . . . concede . . .'

Delight stirred the ranks of the watching prisoners as it dawned on them that they were surely looking at a clear victory for their brother.

Moses remained motionless, his eyes expressionless, lips compressed. There was a sharp indrawing of breath from those standing against the ropes. Blood was trickling between the clenched fingers. The visitors watched with mixed fascination and horror as it fell in a scarlet fork down the cowherd's quivering arm and dripped onto his knee, his foot and finally the warm oak of the deck.

'Enough . . . enough. Can't you see . . . I am beaten . . .' he hissed, now in such pain that it seemed that only his opponent held him off the deck. He slid downwards and Moses, not for a moment releasing his grip, knelt with him until they crouched together, the one kneeling – the other sprawled at his feet in a slither of bright blood – the whimpering animal sounds of his pain echoing up to the elegant visitors with bell-like clarity.

Moses' rumbling voice filled the hushed moment. He spoke quietly, almost as though he was musing. 'This hand which has killed my countrymen will not be worthy of your boast any more, will it? Not after today. Nor, white man, will they call you Sholto the cowherd from today but rather . . . Sholto the coward – who never shook a man's hand in honour.'

Sholto's head rolled forward onto his chest and, unconscious, the man sprawled out on the deck at Moses' feet.

Moses sighed. He released the mutilated hand and stood up, wiping his right hand on his loincloth as Sholto's companions hurried forward across the ring with water bucket and cloths. Tom came up beside him and the murmur of the prisoners lifted to a sudden joyous roar.

'He's won . . . Li'l Moses WON . . . Hurrah for Moss . . . *Huzza le grand nègre . . .*'

English, French, Dutch — the babble of voices thundered about their ears. Moses stood among them like a glistening black pillar, a head and shoulders taller than most of his wellwishers. He raised his head and calmly surveyed the excited visitors up on the half-deck above him, seeing little repugnance in their expressions, but bloodlust and gratification mixed with a new lustful awareness of his male domination.

One of the ladies took something from her head-dress and threw it down to him. Tom stooped and picked it up. It was a small brooch set in gold, the spray design picked out in agates and diamonds. He handed the precious trinket to Moses and smiled up at the preening woman. Over her head he found himself looking straight at Charles Bayless.

For a moment, it was as though two lovers touched. Other eyes pierced the distance between them, raking each other's souls with a familiarity that held joy, pain — and fear. Then Charles moved. He smiled and lifted his hat in greeting behind the shoulders of the other onlookers and then his figure was blotted out. He had turned away.

It had taken only seconds. Tom looked round him at the press of jubilant gamblers all bent upon showing Li'l Moses their admiration and heard the big man say quietly, 'C'mon, man. This is too much. Let's get below before some sneakthief has my fortune off me.' His bloodstained fist closed over the delicate little brooch. It clearly meant a lot more to him in that moment than did the purseful of guineas which Captain Furze would retain for safety against a written receipt. He tore a strip of material from his shirt and carefully wrapped the little brooch in it and stowed it away in the pouch hanging from the string belt holding up his loincloth. Eyes followed every movement he made and knowing what such a treasure represented to some, he raised his eyes and scoured the throng surrounding him. Eyes were lowered before the look. But not before he had noted the mixture of admiration, jealousy and hatred he had read in some of them. He had won some prisoners a lot of reward this day. Equally, he had lost much for those who had not trusted him. He would need to look to his back after this.

Chapter Three

Lessons with the five Furze children ended each day at two o'clock in the afternoon. Tom was then given meat and pickled cabbage with his bread and sometimes there was even an apple, a rare delicacy. He ate in the schoolroom after the children had gone and it was an hour that he enjoyed for he had the peace and privacy of the little cabin to himself while he ate and slowly corrected his pupils' work.

A few days after the fight he was sitting at one of the children's desks after school, busily swabbing up the meat juice on his dish with a crust of fresh bread. He looked at the long gash on the back of his hand with grim satisfaction for through it another of those creeping French varmints was laid out in the sick bay with scant hope of survival.

Life had become so cheap. His whole attitude to the sanctity of life and death had altered during his confinement. He wondered without greatly caring, chewing the gravy-soaked bread, whether he would ever again feel the guilt and regret of terminating the life of another human being.

He had not intended to maul the little rat quite so badly. It had all been too quick for rational behaviour. One moment he and Moses and Dick Sturdee had been leaning against the deck-rail, watching the shadows lengthen over the distant shore and then he had sensed movement behind them. He whirled round just in time to see the man put skeletal fingers deftly into the pouch swinging at Moses' hip. Something welled up in him and he took the man by the throat and swung him round. The Frenchman gasped and twisted like

38

an eel in his grip. There was a flash of metal and the little knife which was suddenly in his hand flicked upwards and across Tom's knuckles. Blood flooded out of the gaping cut and streamed across his wrists and down onto the man's thin neck. The sight of it had an odd effect. Something seemed to well up in him and he took the skinny body with a strength he had not guessed at, and slammed it again and again against the deck-rail.

Hands sought to part them but he had a two-fisted grip on the Frenchman's throat and he gritted his teeth and squeezed, hearing the rattle and seeing the terrified eyes bulging in their sockets. *'Kill him . . . tear him apart . . . blot out that filthy little life'*, something raged in him. Hands grasped his rigid fingers and prized them apart. The man fell away from him and he was pushed aside.

'C'mon, Brother.' Moses' voice in his ear was soft, persuasive. The adrenalin faded and the red glare in his eyes drained away, leaving him weak and trembling and filled with confusion.

'Don't know what got into me there,' he had muttered as the three of them left the little crowd grouped round the crumpled body of the Frenchman. 'I saw the little runt go for your pouch. After that damned brooch, I expect. I was just going to give him a good hiding and then something seemed to make me want to squeeze the life out of the little sod.'

'Should've let 'im get on with it too,' Dick Sturdee grunted. Those filthy French bastards were a constant danger to any God-fearing man aboard. Nothing was safe from them for they were always putting their rascally hands on your possessions or offering their disgusting bodies for a moment's paid pleasure. There was no one safe from the vicious morals and one less of their number meant that the air below decks was that much less contaminated.

The incident was only one of many but Tom had not been involved before. Now he was shaken by the memory of the event, not because of what had taken place but because of the ferocity of his own reflexes – and the extraordinary pleasure that had, for just an instant, lapped through him as he had squeezed the man's throat and felt the life jerking out of him.

The door opened behind him. He turned, thinking that it was Mistress Furze coming in to discuss the children's progress with him – but it was not.

It was Charles Bayless.

Tom sat very still, waiting for the 'Snake' to close the cabin door. All thought of his extravagant temper drained away in his surprise.

Charles turned and stood with his back against it. 'I hope that I am not disturbing your meditation,' he said with unaccustomed diffidence.

Tom shook his head. 'I was just finishing the food which Mistress Furze kindly provides.' He waited for Charles to explain his presence.

'Well, Cousin . . . I thought it was time for us to have a quiet conversation, for it seems that we *are* related. I had doubts until I discovered that you are the son of my Aunt Violet. It is regrettable that we have to meet as our countries' enemies rather than as blood brothers. May I join you?'

He unbuttoned his coat and sat himself down across the schoolroom table and they inspected each other, taking in the facial lines, the contrasts in colouring which divided them – the grey eyes that betrayed their bond. Tom still said nothing. In truth, he suddenly felt an unexpected mixture of fear and attraction for Charles. The washed-out colouring was the antithesis of what he might have expected from any relative of his, knowing that the Baylesses were all dark with an almost Latin look to them. Since Charles had also had a Portuguese mother, it seemed inconceivable that this very blonde, almost foppish English gentleman was so closely related.

'You don't much resemble any of us,' he said at last, embarrassed by the drawn-out silence.

Charles laughed and with the laughter came a softening to the coldness in him and his face warmed into an almost shy pleasantness. Tom felt himself relax a fraction.

'I'm told so,' Charles said comfortably. 'It seems that I am a throwback to my grandmother, Lavinia Freeland who was very blonde and fair-skinned, much more so than was my father. All my Freeland relations are on the fair side. I have bridged the gap in my own sons, it seems, for one is as dark

40

as my mother and the Baylesses and the other is Freeland again and very fair. Are you wed? Do you have a family of your own across the seas?'

The eagerness in his questions echoed Tom's for he seemed to possess the same hunger for details as Tom had had about him.

'No,' he said. 'I have been at sea too much. There was a girl but . . .' he shrugged and grinned ruefully. War had been his only love since he had been old enough to offer himself to it.

'I have three sisters as well as Caleb. They have been women enough in my life to make sure I kept well clear of matrimony as long as possible. All that squabbling and tale-telling. I miss it now, though. I reckon I shall surely settle down and be the quietest of husbands once this strife is resolved, and make me some sons – all the better to defend our country in the next generation.'

Charles leaned back in his chair. Bright daylight, slanting through the cabin window, etched small pockmarks along his cheekbones. 'How can you honestly justify making war upon the country that sired your own parents?' he said, shaking his head. 'I could understand if you were a poor immigrant who had made money over there but your wealth came from England, from these very parts. Does that not tug at your principles?'

'Don't let us talk politics, if you please,' Tom said shortly. 'You have not seen my country, have you – and so you cannot judge fairly any of the dozen excellent reasons for wanting to defend its future. I surely do have many yearnings to see where my parents came from, for England, the Mother Country, is always spoken of with affection back home. It is not the country with whom we fight but King George and his Government. He is an absentee Ruler – and appreciates little of the problems we have tried to iron out with his ministers.'

'Well, America is not alone there . . . for the Georges have tended to be absentee Monarchs in this country also, as their hearts are all wedded to Hanover – and that is where they have always preferred to spend much of their time.'

'Sir – I have too many hours of each day in which to argue with myself upon these matters so let us not, I pray you, talk

41

of them here. We surely have much more intimate things to discuss.'

There was such a flood of questions to ask each other, for who knew when another occasion like this would present itself?

'You and I may not admit to our relationship before others for it would lead to suspicion and trouble for both of us, but here and now we are alone, sir. Pray, tell me more of yourself. Do you not live at all in the family home now? Mistress Furze tells me that your home is in Chichester.'

He watched a guarded look leap into Charles' face. Here it was again. The same look that his mother had worn if questioned about Lavenham. The same expression on the face of his father. 'Look,' he said hurriedly as Charles opened his mouth to speak. 'Just tell me about that place. What in heaven's name is the matter with it – for I see the same expression on your face now as my sisters and Caleb and I have seen on our parents' faces if ever we tried to question them about Lavenham – and we did as children – often.'

Charles rubbed one side of his long jaw as though he was trying to erase something from it.

'Lavenham is a cursed House,' he said finally. 'I was brought up within sight of it but I have not been there. My mother promised my Great Uncle John Freeland that neither she nor I nor our descendants would ever venture there, for its history is such a record of death and disaster and things unexplained that he was convinced that whatever lurks there seeks to harm the Bayless family – and any other who disturbs it, also.'

'I cannot believe that,' Tom interrupted. 'Your father was born there and so was my mother. They spent the whole of their childhood there without apparent trouble and our grandfather lived there from a young man until he died.'

'Yes – and do you know *how* he died?'

Tom stared at his cousin. The pale eyes blazed and there was something in them that he could not quite fathom. It was difficult to drag his gaze away. He shook his head. 'I understood that he had a stroke.'

'He did . . . oh yes, that is quite correct – but his death came about when the crippled sister whom he had cared for all her life, bludgeoned him to death with a brass candle-stick . . .'

Tom stared at him, frozen. 'Who was that sister?'

'Amy Bayless.'

'But . . .'

Charles dropped his eyes. He seemed suddenly uncomfortable. 'Look, Cousin. There are many things from the past that are better left unsaid. It is more than fifty years since all those tragic things occurred and, except for your mother, the participants are no longer with us. Things happened then which we cannot explain and as we have none of the answers to the many questions that must spring to our lips – and they have to mine just as they will to yours – it is better that we do not ask them. Lavenham is a most evil House, so evil that it resisted exorcism when your mother and father attempted to have it done – and caused the deaths, by some means not known to us, of the three unfortunate clerics who tried to perform the ceremony. May we speak of other things, if you please? I hate even to say the name of that place.' His pale face looked pinched and gaunt and more sepulchral than ever.

Tom sat silently chewing his lip for a moment. He *had* to know about Lavenham. The name, with such a delightful lilt to it, had always conjured up pictures of a charming sprawling mansion, dignified and huge with turrets . . . even battlements, for that was how, as children, they imagined great English houses to be. From his earliest years it had called to him, that name. Somewhere at the very back of his mind there had always been a need to be there – almost a yearning for something loved and lost.

Charles watched his face. Then he stood up and there was kindness and regret and something else in the washed-out eyes as he held out his hand to Tom.

'I think I had better take my departure now, Cousin. Think of what I have said of that place and let us not talk of it again. All the other aspects of our relationship, by all means – though there are enough regrettable areas better left in the dark there also.' He laughed, a short grunt. 'Our gypsy forbears seemed to ride roughshod over every principle laid down by Church and polite society – but then, they were not Christian in their hearts and nor did they appear to care a fig for polite society.'

He took Tom's hand and shook it warmly. The grip was firm and warm. 'I shall not acknowledge you before your companions,' he said quietly, 'for reasons clear to both of us. But be sure that there will be ways and means of speaking together now and then. Mistress Furze is a kindly soul and thinks much of you.'

Tom nodded and watched Charles as he buttoned his coat and made for the door.

'If you are in need at any time, Mistress Furze will always be able to get a message to me.'

'I need only one thing, Cousin, and that is my freedom.'

Charles bowed. 'The one thing that I can do nothing about. It is my great regret, I assure you, sir.'

Then he was gone as quietly as he had come, closing the cabin door behind him with scarcely a click. Tom slowly picked up his dish and the empty tankard and returned it to the little pantry that housed the officers' tableware.

Lavenham. The name attracted him but repelled him also now. Why did Mother not tell them more of it? With an ocean as vast as the Atlantic between them, how could it harm them from that distance?

Amy Bayless. He had known that she had been Mama's mother but that she was Grandfather Jess' *sister* and not his wife had not once been even hinted at. She had died, they were all told, as a cripple and in her last years had been confined to her bed. It seemed unlikely that she would be able to commit such a crime upon one to whom she was so devoted if she was unable to walk. So many questions – and out of each one, another and another now sprang.

He buried himself in thought, curled up in a corner of the main-deck behind the galley, oblivious to the warmth of the sun on his head, to the flies which hung about the ship, settling on eyes and mouth. Food for serious thought was rare in such confinement and today he had been given a veritable feast.

The letter which arrived from Tom in England had taken four months to reach the house at New Midhurst, four miles south of Boston. It lay in Violet Heritage's lap and she sat in her chair with her eyes closed, pale-veined hands folded across the single, tightly-written page. The questions that he asked had been asked by the children since they had stood at her knee and yet they still created this hard knot of fear, of loathing which churned in her stomach when the subject was mentioned.

He had met Charles Bayless; described him, related the conversations they had shared. Charles – he was nothing to her, this child of Lawrence. It was enough that she had helped to finance his upbringing and education, that she had acknowledged his gratitude graciously enough, that he had not wasted her generosity but was well thought of in Chichester and now was obviously doing his best to see that the sufferings of the prisoners in the hulks under his jurisdiction were eased in any way he could. But he was Lawrence's son and within him surely dwelt an echo of that weakness and cruel greed which had turned her from the father.

Time, in many ways had indeed been the great healer.

She no longer thought of Lawrence with all the pent-up hatred of her youth. He had caused the death of Giles Croucher soon after their betrothal had been announced but he was long gone from Lavenham by the time she had met Desmond Heritage and her life with him had been filled with a happiness and contentment that she had never known in youth.

All gone now – all gone.

The late summer had taken him gently from her and now the fall was blanketing his grave with a carpet of yellow leaves.

How was she going to write this next letter to Tom with such news . . . that Papa was gone and now Catherine also, in childbirth. Dear child, dear sweet Catherine with her father's fine bone structure and her mother's headstrong will. We had thought that she would always be our youngest one – but then, five years after her birth, Caleb had been born and a year later, Tom. Sons at last to a man who had hungered for them while loving his three daughters with such gentle passion.

Lavenham. The years in Boston and then Midhurst had taken up all her attention so that she thought only very occasionally of the place, and even then it was only when she

woke in fear from some unremembered dream – and knew
that her memory was reliving those last terrifying days and
nights at Lavenham. Now here was Tom, within a few miles
of Apuldram and filled with an innocent curiosity that
Charles' very fear of the place had only fanned into what
seemed to be becoming a dangerous obsession.

Uncle John Freeland had mentioned in one of his letters
that Charles appeared to recall nothing of the occasion when,
as a small boy, he had strayed into the Lavenham grounds
and then into the House itself. Whatever had happened to
him there was now lost deep down in the furthest recesses of
his mind for he could recall nothing of that visit, save to cry
out against the terrible bees in his nightmares.

The Lavenham bees.

How well she remembered the bees.

The sight of her mother's body lying in the leafy orchard,
rich with summer splendour – under the plum trees with the
two skeps across which she had fallen tipped over on their
sides and the honey running from them like thin blood from
the combs. There had not been one glimpse of her mother
beneath that dreadful droning cocoon of vengeful bees. Her
body had seemed to undulate with the movement of their
wings in a terrible brown wave of death.

She shivered and opened her eyes in an effort to wipe the
picture from her mind.

Tom and Charles.

Her heart cried out against the meeting.

Tom was the only one of her children to bear his mother's
great grey eyes but he seemed to have no sign of the terrible
Gift that accompanied their strange colour in the case of her
father, Jess Bayless, and of Lawrence and herself.

She had watched Tom closely as a child, in fear and dread
of the possible consequences to them all if he showed signs
of possessing that Gift of Death – but he had grown normally,
an attractive and mischievous small boy out of which emerged
a tough young patriot with all of his father's devotion to his
country's struggle. He developed into a strong personality
with a fine disregard for either the business, which Caleb
managed, or for the daughters of their neighbours. She had
thought at one time that he would settle for Hettie Timberlake

46

but, when news of his capture by the British reached them, Hettie gave her favours to another young man and now lived over in Cambridge with one small son and another baby due.

My Dear Son . . .

How am I to tell him that in the space of but half a year he has lost his father and the sister who was closest in his affections. . . ?

How am I to tell him that the answers to his questions are still too painful to put on to paper or even into words?

Your Grandfather and Grandmother were brother and sister. The House you yearn to know about was not a proud home but a place of fear and shot through with hate and lust and unspeakable nightmares.

You come from a kind of Hell, Son. That is how your mother was begat and from whence she came. Think only of your father who was all that was good and had nothing in his background of which he was ashamed.

Bayless. To see the name written down in your hand brings sudden terror to me, my son. I thought that in this great world of ours, I had put a large enough ocean and sufficient miles between us all and that dreadful place and those who remained close to it, that the two might never meet until all trace of those memories had died . . .

News of his father's and his sister's deaths reached Tom shortly before Christmas. The letter came with the first great bag of correspondence for the prisoners to be brought by the American Agent, Joe Trotter, for close on four months. Trotter lived in London and appeared to trouble himself infrequently about the welfare of the Portsmouth and Langstone American prisoners. Letters were sent to him with every passing week by the men, asking for their mail, for emergency clothing, for any amount of small needs which it was his duty to try and provide. When he finally made an appearance, the winter weather had once more set in and he hesitated three days before even persuading himself to be rowed out to 'Fortunée'.

*. . . and so, my dearest Tom, I must seal this sad letter and
send it on its way to you. Forgive me for being the giver of
such pain but you know how deeply it is shared by your
brother and sisters – and by me also. Your father and I had
the happiest of years in each other's company. I was not a
'letter' bride but one whom he had met on her own home
ground and whom he had chosen freely. He gave me a joy
for life that I had not possessed in youth for there was a
different kind of weight upon my shoulders then and the
filial love I had for my parents was so deeply tinged with
other emotions also. I cannot bring myself to write of them
to you but may only hope that I am still here when this
dreadful struggle is over and you come home to us again.
Then we will talk – I promise you. In the meantime, I can
only tell you that, in spite of the terrible conditions under
which you are existing, I am GLAD that you are there –
and not lying dead at the bottom of the sea. At least you
are very much alive. You are overly precious to me, my
son . . .*

*Give Charles Bayless my kind regards. Be wary of him,
though, Tom. How unjust it is to speak of him thus . . .
but he is his father's son and there is something of the
parents in every child. I can say no more than that . . .*

He stared, dry-eyed across the shining deck where wind and
recent rain had scoured it of the litter of its overcrowded
cargo. The landscape had lost its colour and was etched in
shades of black and white, the marsh robed in thin mist. He
saw nothing, felt only the shock of initial loss, that he would
never again see his father – never again share his woes and
joys with the ever-sympathetic Catherine, loving companion
of his childhood.

Charles' sympathy and concern at the news of Desmond
Heritage's death was as surprising as it was genuine. 'It may
sound fanciful to you, who had brother and sisters aplenty,'
he said to Tom on hearing the tidings, 'but I was a solitary
boy and my absent family was almost more real to me than
were the ones with whom I grew up. I created my own image
of my Uncle Desmond and Aunt Violet and he always seemed
such a colourful and romantic character, arriving at Dell

Quay off a Bayless vessel and sweeping Aunt Violet off her feet and carrying her away from all the troubles she had here.'

He laid an arm across Tom's shoulders. 'In many ways, I can well appreciate what you are suffering, quite apart from the physical deprivations. I was such a lonely boy for most of my childhood, never close to the Freelands even though they had children of my own age. Mother and I were foreigners to them, I suppose. I'd have liked to have known old Manfri and Polly Bayless and their family a lot more intimately than I did. They lived for a time at Newbarn, quite close to our cottage – but they didn't heed me much, either. I wasn't a Romani – and I was my father's son. So I grew up with you American cousins as my private familiars and absorbed every small crumb of knowledge about you all that I could glean from Great Uncle John Freeland before he died. When he went, I almost wrote to your mother, Tom. Then I found that Great Aunt had already done it. I wish now that I had had the courage to establish a correspondence with Aunt Violet, for she did so much to give my mother and me a stable and comfortable life.'

He hesitated. There was an almost anguished earnestness in his expression. 'What think you if I were to write to her now? Would she think me presumptuous? I did write once but there was no reply. Would she get comfort from news of you and your well-being?'

Tom, still filled with the grief of his loss, was scarcely aware of the significance of this sudden confidence. He heard the pleading in Charles' voice and thought only that he was being offered words of comfort.

'Please do,' he said with gratitude. 'And you should know,' he added later '. . . that you are to me, now, very much the same lifeline as we must have been to you. It's a chastening thought, but you are all the family I have in this hemisphere – and I hardly know you. We meet so rarely in private. We know little of each other's natures. And yet we share so much.'

They shook hands and parted, both moved by the warmth of their separate needs.

He said nothing immediately of his loss to Moses who, seeing that Tom's mail had brought him sober tidings, forbore to question him.

'I heard something today,' he said mysteriously.

Tom looked round at him, mind miles away. 'Oh?'

Moses tried again. 'I heard me a little gem this morning, while we was loadin' at Cut Mill. There was three, four men from the Mill sittin' on the jetty wall while we was loadin' the flour. Talking about three prisoners on parole in Havant. They said there were many such men, French . . . American . . . the like, though mostly officers. They were saying that the South Coast towns are full of paroled prisoners these days for there just isn't room for them all in the prisons and the hulks. What say we investigate this one? You at least might have a chance of being paroled, bein' an officer.'

Tom shook his head. 'We could look into this one, sure. But I'll not leave anyone from the "Free States" aboard while I swan it in lodgings. No, sir. The only way I shall leave here until a Peace Treaty is signed is by making a run for it – with as many of the lads as will join me.'

Moses grunted. 'We all say that, Master – but no one from this hulk has yet found the chance. Ole Toady looks after us too well . . .'

There had been few break-outs from 'Fortunée' and only two prisoners had succeeded in getting away for good. The others had been recaptured and two had died in the gaseous slime of the marshes.

'Reckon there might be one way we could get out,' Moses said, staring across the distant smudge of bullrushes to the tree-line marking the shore. 'Remember last week we was down in the cargo hold, swabbing decks afore a fresh load of supplies was loaded on? I sat me down for a quick crap an' made an interesting discovery. 'Tis where we all crap in that hold. I leaned against the bulkhead, an' oh man . . . there's a piece of wood maybe three feet in length and eighteen inches in height which is soft as a sponge and I poked my finger right into it, right through it, by the Lord, for I felt the outer timberwork an' I swear that that's just as soft. Didn't think much of it at the time, except to wonder how soon we'll sink.'

Tom was now all attention. He folded his mother's letter carefully and tucked it into his shirt. 'Let's go see,' he said shortly.

Too many hare-brained ideas had been fashioned for

possible escapes during the two years of their imprisonment, marvellously intricate plans which had all come to nought. Now with the approach of 1803, despite the pardons, the exchanges, the paroles that were the main topic of conversation these days, the men aboard 'Fortunée' seemed to have been forgotten, for not one of them had been thus blessed. It was bound to be Joe Trotter, the American Agent who was at fault again, but whoever was responsible for their segregation, the atmosphere among the prisoners was becoming frustrated and resentful and the increasing attempts to escape from shore parties had made the marine guards – and Captain Furze – ever more vigilant.

Escape from the hulks, especially during the winter months, was not considered a serious likelihood. The waters of Langstone Harbour were full of treacherous currents and the mudbanks were quicksand that had engulfed several victims over the years. All the same, the very state of the old ship's timbers was so bad that she would, long ago, have been broken up, had it not been for the critical shortage of accommodation for the thousands of prisoners taken in Britain's wars with the newly created American Republic, with France, Egypt and Holland. Already five of the hulks had been withdrawn from the Transport Office's list of prison ships because of their state of dilapidation. 'Fortunée' had been a French vessel, already elderly, her timbers rotting when she was captured. Extensive repairs had been carried out while she was being converted to her present use. Maybe the planking had been overlooked where Moses had found it – maybe it was simply the continued use of that spot for latrines that had saturated the timbers. The men were required to dispose of their own faeces over the side but there were many who ignored this rule and the whole lower-deck area – all three levels – stank so strongly that the parties of visitors had given up coming out to the ships in high summer.

Tom followed Moses down one ladder after another, through decks tightly packed with men in every stage of health and occupation, into the very bowels of the old vessel. The place reeked of excrement, mould, the rotting of her timbers and human death. They bowed their heads beneath cross beams only four foot nine inches high and crouched their way through storage compartments to a space directly over the ship's Black Hole.

There was no light and their eyes, even accustomed to the gloom of scarcely lit lower-decks, were no match for the solid blackness that surrounded them. They felt their way along the stacked barrels of grain and dried fish, with the scratch and scamper of rats magnified in their ears.

'Sounds like a herd of buffalo down here,' Moses muttered, invisible ahead of Tom. He stopped and Tom cannoned into him. 'Wait. I'm countin' the bulkhead stays from the hold section.'

'Well, keep talking and I'll follow your voice.'

Moses hummed under his breath, now and then muttering a curse as his foot slipped on the sticky decking.

Tom, fingers spread out along the dank timber wall, inched his way forward until Moses' muttering stopped in a quick hiss. 'Here . . . and here . . . Yes, I'm sure as sure I'm not wrong, Mas' Tom. Feel that — yes and here too. It's as rotten as soaked bread.'

Tom was beside him and he reached out and guided his hand along the edge of a slightly recessed length of timber. 'Press.' His voice floated away in the black limbo all about them.

Tom pressed the tips of his fingers into the section under his hand. It gave under the pressure like pressing into a piece of uncooked liver. Moisture seeped under his fingernails.

'My God, how much more is there like this?' he said, aghast.

Moses chuckled. 'Ya, I know what you're thinkin'. The bottom's goin' to fall out of this ole wreck one day – an' we don't want to be aboard when it happens. I went all the way along this side as far as the next bulkhead an' the other timbers are sound. Can't speak for what's in the storage hold, behind all them crates and barrels. All I know is, if there are more timbers like this on the starboard side, then Lordy me, I's a gettin' off . . .'

It was as Moses said. Just the one area of rotten planking which they worked at patiently for the next four days whenever any of them used it as a latrine. The saturated wood fibres looked very much like the faeces they were required to bring up and dispose of and all nine of the 'Free States' crew were brought into the plot to help with the work. The possibility of escape was discussed at length and all the men encouraged to break out with Tom and Moses. After much whispered argument and head-shaking only two of them were prepared to brave the icy harbour waters in winter. The others were, however, more than willing to double up for them each muster until the gap in the outer timbers was discovered and a closer scrutiny was taken of the roll calls.

The four men were all emaciated with little but their own despair to combat the freezing sea but all four gradually became fired with enthusiasm and the others, ripe for adventure of any kind to break the boredom, built up their anticipation with their own excitement.

'For God's sake, stop looking so pleased with yourselves,' Tom said to his crew, concerned that their absorbed, almost happy faces might be noticed by the guards. 'The plank is now cleared and we won't, *daren't* start on the outer timber until we are ready to go.'

'When's that to be then, Master?'

Tom smiled at the face of his carpenter, Stace Harbottle. Stace was as fit as any of them and more so than some for he was only just past his twentieth year and, uncomplicated and trustful by nature, tended to take every day as it came with commendable patience. It was unusual to see frustration on his face.

'Wind's been blowing hard all day,' Tom said softly. The men crouched closer, the better to hear his quiet voice. There were others far too nearby for they had been battened down for the night and the sleeping hammocks were hung so close together that there was only an eighteen-inch allowance for the width of each man. Tom crouched on the deck beneath two hammocks in which his men lay on their stomachs, the better to catch his words. The others crowded in on either side, backs to a group of *Rafales* who were so furiously and noisily engrossed in a game of *Plafond* that nothing existed outside their circle. The only illumination at their end of the deck came from the *Rafales'* tiny fat lamp.

'That means that it will either blow up again tomorrow

and set into an all-out gale or else, by nightfall, it could have blown itself out. I suggest we try for it tomorrow night. There's no point in waiting . . . The sooner we're out the better our chances. All right with you, Moses . . . Stace . . . Lunt?'

There was so much to go over. It would take the four of them an hour or so to hole the outer timber work and even then the hole must be too small for Moses to get through or its chances of detection before nightfall would be almost certain. There was a twice-nightly boat patrol which circled the vessel, so the hole must not be started until the dusk patrol had completed its round and they must be gone before the midnight patrol was due. Worktime was narrowed even further for the prisoners were battened down at sunset. They would have to miss the head count and hide in the storage hold, being careful to keep out of the way of the sentries and the fellow who inspected the Black Hole.

'What happens to us if we survive the swim?' Abel Lunt was the oldest of the four escapees. He was a hard man, hating all Britishers since General William Howe's soldiers had killed his parents and ransacked his home during the war. He wanted nothing but to carve his way out of England, cutting down in the name of his dead family all who crossed his path.

Tom turned his head towards the disembodied voice. 'Each man for himself,' he said shortly. 'We know nothing of the countryside, nor the people. We know that there is some sympathy for the American Cause here in England – but without names, one man's face is much like another's. There is just one aim for us all now, to take passage across the Channel with all speed. None of us has any hope of staying free for long while we are on English soil.'

Their location was discussed. Langstone Harbour was to the East of the Southern shore, facing the Isle of Wight. They were in the vulnerable underbelly of England where her coasts were most closely guarded against the threat of Napoleon's invading forces. Portsmouth with its busy marine traffic was a possibility but dangerous. Emsworth or Bosham were more likely places to pick up a boat but exactly how far they were along the marshy shore was not at all clear. They would just have to trust to luck – and the possible goodwill of some isolated farmsteader.

'I know where I'm going,' Tom said to Moses when the little meeting had broken up.

'Yeah, Master, so do I . . . you'll be off looking for that place where yo Mammy come from. Not far, you've been saying all this time – but how far is "not far" when you're a stranger an' cain't ask the way an' have no clothes to keep that pokey old wind off your jennies?'

'Not far is nearer than across the Channel,' Tom said, suddenly filled with longing by the thought of what lay ahead. To see Lavenham . . . to be there under the very roof that his grandfather had built. To roam the place to his heart's content until he was familiar enough with every inch of it, and satisfied about the truth of its legends, to be able to leave and make his way back across the Atlantic.

'What do you plan to do?' he asked, suddenly aware that Moses had said nothing about his own ideas.

'Hows about making room in that empty mansion of yours for a free black American? Cain't say as I'm overly hopeful of gettin' across that li'l old Channel being the colour I am. Jus' as likely to end up back in the slave pens unless I come with you.'

'You can travel at night. Long as you keep your eyes and your mouth shut, there's no one can spy a black man at night.'

'Reckon it'd be harder to stop my tongue from awaggin' and my eyes from arollin' than t'will be to bust out of this ole wreck,' Moses said, the laughter in his voice making even deeper the rich oily tones. His good humour was in no way rattled by the possibility of recapture or, worse, that other option of losing his precious freedom at a slave auction.

'I'd be glad of your company, Moss,' Tom said to him. Indeed, he discovered that this was the truth. Moses had strength and dignity as well as that infectious humour. He was also an excellent discourser with a hunger for learning that Tom found exhilarating. It would be good to share Lavenham with this best of men – and later they would return to Boston and Moses, now writing and reading under Tom's guidance, would be the perfect partner in setting up a chandlery business with the money that Papa had left in trust for him. To hell with the disapproval that such a partnership would create among the doyens of Boston. He and Moses understood each other.

Moses clasped his hand and shook it hard. 'Thank you, Suh.'

There was no more to say after that for each knew the strength of the other and was glad of it. They settled into their hammocks and tried to rest their bodies for the coming travail.

Chapter Four

Morning brought a freshening of the December winds which whipped across the harbour from Hayling Island, churning up the water into muddy peaks and smashing it in curling white spume against the stands of rushes and spongy moss along the shore. The old hulk rode sluggishly at her cables, dipping and rolling, her timbers groaning as she strained against the power of the current. Weed trailed thick green fronds from her hull at water level. The roofs of the ramshackle shanties aloft were scoured and limed with the droppings of the scavenging gulls.

There was no shore party that day but Charles Bayless and his two clerks arrived during the forenoon with the weekly soap allocation. With the vessel heaving and shuddering under their feet, the prisoners gathered on the main-deck, heads bent against the salt-rimed gusts. They stood shoulder to shoulder, waiting to join the queue, stamping their feet and blowing on their hands to keep the circulation going in the bone-chilling air.

The contractor's desk was set up, as usual, in a corner of the deck with its back to the galley. His two assistants busied themselves, one with his ledgers and the other with sacks of block soap. Each greyish block must be cut and weighed into two-ounce tablets, the weekly allowance agreed for prisoners of war. Slowly, the men began to form a queue and the laborious business began.

'Abbeville . . . Ansell . . . Amhurst . . .'

They filed slowly past the desk, silent but for the shuffle of their feet, the wind barging through the untidy clutter of improvised sheds which housed the galley and sickbay, and the hoarse commands of the 'Snake's' general clerk. A man collapsed as he came to the head of the queue and the ship's doctor came across to examine him.

'Hmm. The fourth this morning,' he said briefly to Charles. 'His ulcers have a phagaedenic appearance and are destroying the tissue right down to the bone. Sergeant Kemp, get a couple of men to take him to the sickbay.'

Charles sat quietly, unaffected by the men's mortality. He leant an elbow on his desk, quill in hand, ticking off each man's name as he received his ration. There were not many contractors doing this irksome task themselves, but it was the only way to ensure that the prisoners were not short-shifted by a light-fingered clerk. He saw little gratitude in the men's eyes, but then he expected none. Their wellbeing was of little consequence to him. His good reputation was, on the other hand, of prime importance.

'Haines . . . Herbert . . . Heritage . . .'

Their eyes met for a moment as Tom took the dirty grey tablet from the weighing scales. They would not be speaking together this day for Mistress Furze had taken the boys over to Portsmouth for the week to stay with one of her sisters.

Tom bowed over his soap. 'Thank you, sir.'

Charles raised his head, straightened his back and smiled broadly. Surprised, Tom turned away thinking that he must be getting used to Charles' sepulchral looks for he seemed almost handsome this day. The wind was having little effect upon his impeccable turnout, as usual, but there was a jauntiness about him that spoke of some private inner joy. His wife was in better health? Something to do with his young sons, maybe? Or could it simply be that his business was doing particularly well at present. Whatever it was, some hidden flame was burning strongly in Charles Bayless, giving animation to the sculptured features.

He was not the only one to notice the phenomenon.

'Snake was lookin' pretty pleased with himself this morning,' Stace Harbottle said later.

'Sure was,' Moses agreed. 'He even asked me if I was

58

keepin' my muscles in trim for another contest next spring. Never heard tell of him engagin' the prisoners in polite conversation before.'

'Doubt if he will again, either,' Lunt grunted. He was whittling away at a shinbone with his knife. The beginning of a tobacco pipe bowl was emerging. 'After tomorrow, he won't feel like no polite conversation 'cos there'll be four ungrateful Yankees ranging the countryside, preferring to do without his company. Arrogant bastard.'

The crewmen from the 'Free States' were gathered together round the four who were to leave that night. It was difficult to keep the excitement out of their faces and inevitably some of their companions had guessed that something was being plotted.

'We must take our rest during the daylight hours,' Tom had said. The whole group had clubbed together and bought jackets from the latest batch of prisoners to arrive aboard. Solly Abrams was this minute putting in patches on the largest jacket so that it would accommodate Moses' broad shoulders. There was nothing else to give, but each of the four had sewn his personal papers into his clothing in the hope that the salt water would not completely destroy those few letters and documents that were precious to him . . .

They did their best to sleep, stretched out in their hammocks, heads buried in their rolled-up jackets. It was never wise to sleep with any loose clothing across the hammock for it would almost certainly have been taken by the time the owner awoke. They dozed and fidgeted, with the exception of Moses who had a talent for being able to sleep at any time, in any position. Now he lay in a deep sleep with his knees bent in his usual uncomfortable position for his hammock was a good two feet short for his great length and he had had to learn to curl up to suit its inadequate dimensions.

Tom lay with his eyes closed. Sleep eluded him. He tried to curb the racing throughts which slid through his mind but someone was singing the same little song over and over again nearby, and the irritation of the offkey, nasal sounds cut through any attempt to drift off. In the main hold, somewhere below him, two of the men were, this minute, loosening the spongy fibres of the rotten outer plank while the others were either keeping guard or else hovering near to the resting foursome, making sure that they were neither disturbed nor robbed.

These early winter days were more than usually long and painful when the absence of shore duties or even daily ship's fatigues stretched the hours into unendurable length. Think of home ... Mama at the tea table, mistress of the pastry plate, the steaming silver kettle on its little trivet ... the sprawling, clapboard house at Midhurst would be looking bare now as fall gave way to winter. The beautiful beech trees would be shorn of their russet capes and the long stands of pine and cedar would be coming into their own, dark green sentinels against the frost and snow, the resinous fragrance of their bark a well-remembered sweetness. He still found it possible to dream up the smells of winter, for the air was so much cleaner there than on any part of this over-populated island he had so far encountered. Even Lavenham had a distinct smell, Mama had said once, for there were saltpans right beside the property and the odour of rotting seaweed and drying salt was so unpleasant in the summer months that in New England at least, the salterns were always to be found well-separated from residential areas.

Charles Bayless ... The change in him had been astonishing this morning. He had looked like a boy with his first love ... as though his body could hardly contain the vastness of some secret joy. Whatever it was, it had even brought a suggestion of colour into those sallow cheeks of his and a warmth to the wintry eyes. Funny how he regarded Charles' eyes as cold for his were the same colour, grey as the back of a turtle dove and he had never thought of them as being cold. Mama's were the same and they were still beautiful, in spite of her age for, although her hair was now quite white, her lashes were the same long black ones that had so delighted Papa when she was young. She must be all of seventy-four now. That was old indeed. The thought brought him out of his doze with a jerk. *Pray God that she stays in health until I get back to her.* She said nothing in her letters about her own well-being. She was always so strong and full of life that everyone tended to take her robustness for granted. Caleb would care for her . . . and so would the girls. Catherine had been the most attentive as the parents grew older – but she was gone . . .

He must have slept, for someone was shaking his arm and a voice said in his ear, 'It's time.'

He was awake instantly. Darkness enveloped the orlop-deck, darkness shot through with the sounds of men struggling with the nightmares that dogged their overburdened dreams. Nearby, someone was weeping in muffled gasps. Someone told him to be quiet with a snarl. Snores and the small cries of uneasy sleep were all that broke the reeking night.

'Wrap up well. The wind has died but now it's raining and the sea is choppy and running fast.'

He rolled out of his hammock, grabbing jacket and blanket. 'That you, Bo'sn?'

'That's me, Master Tom, Sur . . . Moses be down in the hold already. Stace an' Abel and yourself got plenty of time for it's two hours to midnight by the sandglass. We reckon you should be away within the hour.'

His eyes became accustomed to the darkness slowly. At the other end of the orlop-deck a light glimmered feebly through the tightly-packed hammocks. Somewhere nearby was a suggestion of movement. The *Rafales* were insatiable and thought nothing of paying their debts in all manner of Godless ways. He rolled up his blanket and pressed it under the bo'sn's arm.

'Here, Burton, take it. If I return, you can let me have it back . . .'

They crawled beneath the hammocks, avoiding floor sleepers where they remembered them. Now and then, draughts from the barred but open ports slid icy fingers across their faces. Tom shivered. In a corner directly beneath one of the unshuttered ports a rough trapdoor had been cut in the deck planking. Each deck had at least one of these 'private' hatches to the deck below so that it was possible for the men to move freely and undetected between decks. Inspections were almost unheard of, for the pent-up feelings of seven hundred men might well have found expression against their captors had they ventured below. It was enough to give the prisoners light and fresh air each day by opening the hatches

61

and ordering them out onto the main-deck and into the Pen. What went on below was best ignored.

The two men prized up the boards gingerly. Below was the main hold which was patrolled by sentries several times during the night hours. It was vital that the loose boards remained undiscovered, for others would need the freedom of the vessel to assist their own escapes.

Below them, a whispered greeting floated up. 'C'mon there! Thought you'd decided not to try for it, after all, you bin so long a'comin'. Patrol went by ten minutes ago, by my counting.'

Tom lowered himself through the gap and swung for a moment, then let himself fall. Hands steadied him and the Bo'sn's whisper came after him. 'Good luck to ye, Master Heritage. God go with ye.'

He heard the planks being replaced. They would be opened again for the other two.

He stood against his guide in the heavy stillness of the hold, listening. The silence rang in his ears. There was less movement from the vessel down here where they were close to water level but the old timbers complained loudly with creaks and groans from every joint in her mouldering super-structure. The rats were ever active here also, not as bold as those who rooted among the prisoners but busy, watchful – scurrying among the sacks and barrels.

'Take a grip on my jacket,' the man with him ordered. The sound of his low voice seemed magnified in the silent darkness. For a moment the sounds of the little scurrying creatures stopped as if they too were waiting for danger, breaths held.

Tom felt for the man's coat and took a firm hold of the back flap of the jacket. They set off, moving cautiously along the gangway towards the little forward compartment. They had not gone more than twenty paces when it happened.

'*Gotcha* . . .' a voice snarled beside him and hands closed on Tom's arm with a vicelike grip. He spun round, heart thumping at the unexpectedness of the attack. One of the guards must have been lurking without his lantern and heard his descent from the orlop-deck. What he was doing down in the hold at that time, without his companion, was a question that there was no time to answer. They were so close to freedom – too close to let themselves be taken now by one man. He twisted in the man's grip and felt the rage pour through him as it had done the last time he had been surprised from behind. He felt his companion tear away and then his hands were on the sentry's throat and he was squeezing, feeling the Adam's apple trembling against his thumbs while the man struggled and tore at him with frenzied fingers.

He was stronger than Tom. His knee came up, aimed at Tom's crotch but the force was deflected into his hip where much of the impact was lost. It was enough to loosen his grip about the man's throat, however, and Tom felt his fingers loosening and sliding. He dug his nails into hard flesh and felt the man's eye sockets under his fingers. He dug and gouged with all his strength and felt the squirming body jerk. A vast excitement in the movements welled up into his chest. The sentry began to scream and Tom pressed down on him so that the gasping shouts were muffled against his shirt front.

The tearing, scrabbling hands pulled at his hair, his ears, his threadbare shirt. The red rage filled him and he pressed the man's eyeballs harder, feeling the oval softness of them bursting like fat plums beneath his jagged nails.

The man went limp suddenly. They sprawled together against a bale of cloth and slid to the deck. Tom lay for a moment panting across the still body of his unseen assailant. He was still alive, for his breath came in shallow pants. Cautiously he shifted his weight. The body remained limp.

'Are you still there, Pinder?' he rasped up into the darkness.

'What 'chew done, for God's sake? You killed him?'

His guide's frightened voice sliced the heavy silence from a few yards away.

'No. Just put him out, I hope. I can feel him breathing but he won't be seeing us go. Come on, we must hurry before he is discovered.'

Feeling their way, they dragged the unconscious sentry behind some barrels of pig fat, out of the way of the next patrol's lanterns. Then they made for the forward compartment. Tom could hear the man counting under his breath. With their hands stretched out in front of them, they slowly paced the hold until they collided with a bulkhead and paused. This had to be not six paces from the hull breech.

'You there, Moss?'

63

'If you cin see ma teeth, man, then I must be here . . .'

A small chuckle in the blackness and a shifting of bodies. The air was very cold here and spots of water sprayed Tom's face. A faint grey glimmer. They had successfully breeched the ship's side.

'Best hurry and go,' Harry Pinder said. 'They'll be missing that sentry any time.' The tension in his voice made the words snap like a whiplash.

'Take it easy,' Tom said quietly. 'It's all gone well so far so don't get jumpy at this stage or there'll be more risk for the other two.' He gripped the man's arm in the darkness and felt the tension ease in rigid muscles.

'We were jumped by a sentry back there,' he went on. 'I had to attend to him. Don't worry, I didn't kill him. Just made sure that he'll not see what we're up to.'

'You're sure he's not dead, for Chrissake?' the Bo'sn asked anxiously. If a sentry had been killed the whole ship would be in trouble. There would undoubtedly be heavy reprisals amongst those who remained and there would be twice the reward on the escapees' heads.

'No,' Tom said quickly. 'I think I may have blinded him but he was breathing, though passed-out when we left him.'

'Thank Christ for that. Be off with ye now – and don't come back . . .'

'Hey, possum . . . Thought you was a friend,' Moses said, his voice rich with hurt. 'We'll be gone soon enough. Let Mister Heritage button on his waterwings and put a comb through his hair first. This is li'l old England we be about to invade in the name of the Federated States of America so we gotta be properly prepared . . .'

There was a nervous snigger in the darkness. They were all on edge now – even Moses, though he was making a better show of being relaxed than were his companions. The attack on the sentry was bound to have repercussions, however slight his injuries.

'Give me your word that you will lay the blame for the sentry's injuries on me,' Tom said to the Bo'sn. 'Tell 'em what a nasty temper I have, eh?'

The invisible group huddled about the open wound in the ship's side, sniffing the cold sharp saltiness of freedom. Water sprayed in every few seconds as unseen waves troughed and flung themselves along the slimy timbers. There was a strong odour of salt mixed with tar in their nostrils.

'Right,' Tom said, gripping what he knew must be Moses' arm from the hardness of its sinews. 'There's no point in waiting for the others as each minute we stand here brings us closer to discovery of that sentry and the next boat patrol. Moss and I will go now. Is Fred standing by for the signal?'

Above their heads a crewman waited for the knock on the wood at his feet. It would signal the moment for a diversion and he would swing his lantern round his head so that the man on the far side of the deck could see the sign and start banging on the bars of the port on the starboard side. With luck, the unexpected sound would bring the sentries over to investigate the rumpus, as far from the escape hole as possible.

'Follow me closely, if you will, Moss,' he said. 'Water has never been my favourite element and I don't rejoice in it as you do.'

Hands fumbled at his waist, looping a rope round him and testing the slip-knot. They had all taken turns in making the ropes, from tatters of clothing, from a cannibalized hammock – from a short length of hempen cord that Tom had picked up in the schoolroom. Now the two of them were joined by the rope so that one might help the other in case of difficulty.

Hands gripped him in the darkness. They had all been together for a long time and there were no words for such farewells.

He straddled the long open gash, lay along the rotten planking for a moment as he felt the old hulk dip into a trough and then lift against a roller. He waited until she had begun to sink into the next and then thrust his body outwards and away from the ship's side. He fell, whipped by spray and a vast roaring in his ears. He seemed to be hurtling through the air for an age – and then a sudden shock as the next wave received him, forcing the air from his lungs. He dropped like a stone, turning over slowly, holding his breath until his head began to sing and his heart threatened to burst in his chest. He had thought that he was still sinking when his head broke the surface and he was tossed forwards – and thrust under again. He caught his leg in the rope which seemed to be snagged on something for it was taut and cutting into his crotch. He struggled to right himself, gasping each time his head broke surface. The blood thundered in his ears and he could no longer feel his body at all.

'Is this drowning?' he wondered, for the pain in his chest was excruciating and all about him the water movement was rushing and roaring. Then the rope slackened and he found himself treading water in total blackness, his body moving forward within the momentum of a wave. He moved his arms and legs, spreading his arms outward. Somehow it seemed to unbalance him for the current took him again, turning him over and over.

He had not been happy about the fact that he could not swim but Moses had waved aside his doubts. 'I'll be right behind you, man,' he had promised. But where was he now?

The cold took possession of him. He did his best to keep moving but his limbs were like lead weights and he could not be sure if he was really moving them or not. 'Let yourself be washed ashore,' Moses had said. 'Don't fight the current for it is stronger than you and you'll simply waste precious energy. Just try to tread water with your arms out and head back.'

It was an incoming flood tide and there was every chance that they would be brought to land – if they didn't drown first. *Don't forget . . . just keep your head above water long enough to take in air and tread the current . . . don't fight it. Moses, where are you?* Somewhere in this freezing morass, for the rope was still taut and that surely meant a body on the other end.

Time seemed to freeze with his limbs. Once he thought he saw a light in the distance. Another time something struck him a hard blow on the right leg.

'*Moses.*' He tried to call but there was only saltwater in his mouth and he choked, drawing it into his lungs. Coughing and retching he spun and rolled out of control, the limp plaything of relentless unseen waves. Something burst inside and he slid away in an explosion of fiery stars.

His cheek was pressed into something soft.

The waves had ceased their tortuous buffeting and cradled

him gently as a mother with her babe. His chest hurt. He was very cold. It dawned on him that the gentle rocking motion was within himself and that he was lying face down on firm ground. He drew a deep breath of clean dry air into lungs that agonized at the movement. He groaned, creasing into a foetal curl with the sharp pain.

'Shh, man. Stay silent.'

A hand gripped his shoulder and held him pinned against the ground. He opened his eyes. Daylight: grey overcast and the soft pearling of chill misty air. He was lying on spongy moss with his shoulders against a tree trunk whose bare branches dropped rattling and shivering round him. A curtain of rustling rush and long grasses penned him in. He turned his head and the grip on his shoulder tightened.

'Don't move a muscle.' Moses' voice was scarcely more than a breath in the air between them. Tom's eyes focused onto his face, ebony skin gleaming only inches away from his own, haggard and drawn in the grey light. There was a look of fierce tension in the bloodshot eyes.

They lay like stone figures, breathing shallowly. Sounds filtered through the curtain of marsh reeds; a rush and hiss of the waves, in the distance the ever-familiar screech of greedy gulls wheeling and swooping above the hulk's galley roof. Closer to the shore the clunk and dip of oars.

'Patrol's searching the shore. They're only a hundred yards out from us. There's geese feeding on a stretch of ground just beyond us. Make one move an' they'll be up into the air and give us away for sure.'

Tom closed his eyes. When he opened them again the light was stronger and the mist thinner. His chest still hurt. Some other part of him hurt also. He examined himself, letting his mind slide from head to neck to chest. It was his knee. He remembered something striking it hard while he was in the water.

'Moss,' he said, his voice a croaking whisper. 'For God's sake, let me move.'

Moses was crouching close to him, head turning slowly from one side to the other. He bent over Tom and pushed the hair back from his face.

'Do it slow, then. Those darned geese are still there an' any sudden movement'll send them up like a big finger pointin' down on us an' saying: "Here they are – all tucked up in the bullrushes, Masters – just a'waiting for you to collect them . . ." '

'How're you feeling?' he asked later.

They were curled up close round the stunted bowl of the oak as much for warmth as for cover. 'Chest hurts when I breathe,' Tom said.

'That's from the saltwater in your lungs. Man, you were so waterlogged, it took me half a lifetime squeezin' you out. Why didn't you do like I said? Mouth shut in the water . . . open in the air.'

'I thought I did. Thought I was doing quite well at first but then the current was so strong, it just seemed to set me spinning till I didn't know what I was doing. I never saw you at all.'

'Took me a time to haul on the rope and get close to you. The undertow was real wicked, man. We must have been in the water for the best part of half an hour before we fetched up in these reeds. Pulled you through them to this bit of dry ground. My word but that bog is hungry. Did its best to suck us in, but I didn't get this far to finish in a bog!'

'Any sign of the others?'

Moses shook his head. 'Good thing, too. If'n I'd seen them, so would the patrol boats. There are four of them out there now snooping about along the shore. They've been going up and down since daylight. Too much fog about to tell the time of day but I guess it must be not far off noon by now.'

There was no question of them moving in daylight. Moses watched the browsing geese sadly. 'What wouldn't I give for a taste of baked fowl,' he said, eyeing them with longing. 'No good trying to trap one of these, though. Too close to the water. Guess there might be more of 'em wintering along the coast that we can give chase to another time.'

They lay close together, their mouths inches from each other's ears.

'I remember my Mama telling me how *her* mother baked,' Tom mused, trying to keep his mind off the throbbing in his chest and leg. 'They were Romanies, you know. Folks in England call them gypsies. Coloured people from another place the other side of the world. The English are pretty suspicious about strangers, I'm told. But then these gypsies are travelling folks with no homes apart from their tents and what they carry by the cartload.'

'Ain't none of them in Massachusetts,' Moses said. 'Nor in Virginia, where I was born.'

'They are olive-skinned, not as dark as you. More like the inhabitants of the Indies. Dark colouring and black hair and with a language of their own. My Mama was from these people on both sides but her folks had left the tribe and Grandfather Jess had built himself a house. That place I told you about. Lavenham. Became real wealthy too, from running contraband goods out of these waters.'

He grinned at Moses. 'Shall I tell you something that'll surprise you? My mother's name was Bayless . . . and she was sister to Master Bayless' father!'

Moses puffed his cheeks out and blew hard into the sharp air. His breath bunched into a cloud and drifted away from them. 'The Snake? But he's white as a lily, man. Cain't be no mixed blood in him.'

'Well, there is, for he and I both stem from a line of pure Romani gypsies from Grandfather Bayless back. Charles Bayless is my first cousin.'

'My . . . my . . .' Moses said in wonder. He shook his head and lapsed into silence. Far away in the distance they heard a ship's bell. 'Noon,' he said. 'I weren't far wrong.'

They remained crouched in their cover, limbs stiffening, for the whole of that day. The searching boats passed and re-passed and they pressed into the dank ground as the voices of the patrol floated across the marshy foreshore. The sea fog stayed with them all day so that they were only just able to see the vague shape of the old hulk on her moorings. The other prison vessels, 'Captivity' and 'Portland' were blanketed in mist, the ghostly clanging of their bells the only clue to their whereabouts.

Tom and Moses pressed themselves close to each other as the dank air and their wet clothing slowly chilled them to the bone. They dozed and woke with a jerk when a brace of plover rose screeching above their heads.

'We'm gonna live like kings once we get away from here,'

Moses muttered, eyeing the speckled white underbellies of the retreating birds. He leaned across and pushed up the breeches on Tom's right leg.

Tom winced. 'Leave it for now. There's nothing can be done for it here. We can look at it later, when we've found some safer cover.'

Dusk came swiftly and the restless geese settled close together along the mud flats. There was no wind to clear the air and the sea mist hung close. As darkness fell their eyes accustomed themselves to the gloom and by the time the last light had gone they were on the move. Movement presented an immediate problem for Tom. He had increasing difficulty with his right knee which burned with a deep pain and would scarcely support him. Their progress away from the marsh and the flocks of geese was tortuous and before they found a resting place at the end of the day, Moses was eventually obliged to carry him. The knee had swollen up inside his breeches so that the rough cloth was stretched tightly across it. At first, Tom limped painfully doing his best to ignore the throbbing ache which welled up more painfully with every step into his groin.

They left the marsh behind and found themselves in dense thicket. Moving from bush to bush in undergrowth that had seen little of the passage of man meant progress by inches at a time when stealth was of greater importance than speed. They knew nothing of the area and might well be close to one of the sentry posts which had been erected round the harbour to net escaping prisoners. A fresh breeze sprang up and whined in the trees above their heads. When the first glimmers of a red dawn heralded a new day, they found that they were still in sight of the water, though the hulks were nowhere to be seen now. They came across an overgrown path and followed it, ready to sink back into the undergrowth at the first sound of life. There was none and the little path led them into open woodland which bordered a spread of rolling common. Sheep grazed here and twice they came upon the small wild pigs which roamed the southern oakwoods. Moses tried to catch one but the little creature was swifter afoot than he and it fled from him, crashing through the brambles, screaming shrilly.

Hunger gnawed at their insides. They had been hungry for more than two years but some kind of sustenance had been available each day. Now they had been without food of any kind for a day and a night. The cobs were still unripe in the hazels and they rooted for bulbs to chew to stop the cramps in their stomachs. They found a fern-filled hollow, screened by thickets and laid themselves down to rest. It was as though they were the only living creatures in this land which dictated the rules to countries so much larger than itself. Except for the hunting soldiers, they had neither seen nor heard a single human being in the thirty hours of their freedom.

'Maybe this is all marshland like so many of the great bays and estuaries at home,' Moses said as they burrowed into the ferns and dead leaves which lined their hiding place.

Tom screwed up his face in the dim light. He did his best to think of other things than the sharp throb in his knee and the nagging hunger in his stomach. 'I don't think so. When I was a child we were always poring over maps of this area. I can't for the life of me remember clearly but it seems to me that this main harbour was broken up into smaller ones by the intrusion of two or three little capes and islands close to the shore. Somewhere not far away is Emsworth, I know, and as Hayling Island was on the "Fortunée's" starboard side and Thorney Island was on its port, it seems to me that beyond Thorney was water again and then more land with water and land after that. Oh God, why did we not try and learn more of the coast before we left?'

'You still waterlogged or somethin'?' Moses grunted, putting a hand like a slab of meat to Tom's brow. 'If we hadn't gone when we did, someone else was going to lean against that mouldy li'l old wall and come to the same conclusion as we did. Don't you fuss so, Master Tom. Look at it this way. We may be hungry enough to eat a horse but oh, Lordy Lord . . . we's two free men at this moment. Just feel that freedom, can't you? Here we are in this wood – why? Because we chose to come here, that's why. We chose to leave that li'l old hulk of our own free will. Oh man, we've not had that choice for over two years. We're alive, we've two for company and as soon as we've had ourselves a rest, we'll make some more progress towards this mansion of yours.'

'Hey, Master Tom . . .' Moses suddenly said a little later. 'Where does the Snake . . . begging your pardon, where does your cousin, Master Bayless, live? Would he not help us now that we are away from the ship and out of his territory, as it were?'

Tom had already been thinking about Charles and was undecided about him. There were many sympathizers for the American Cause in England, he knew that and he had gained the impression that Charles might even be a little sympathetic to his American cousin. Whether this sympathy might be born purely out of gratitude to his Aunt he could not decide.

'Well, we won't be able to find the answer to that until we can make contact with him,' he said. 'And we can't make contact with him until we can find some sort of human life in this land. Let us first discover someone to risk speaking to – then we can toss the coin about Charles.'

They dozed as the red morning sky turned the branches over their heads into fine black lace. It was not a good sign and when they woke again it was to chill gusts and a steady drizzle. They left their warm lair and plodded eastwards, keeping within the line of trees that fringed the gorsey common.

Within the hour they saw a shepherd. His back was to them and he was already some distance off on a slight rise and moving his sheep away over the crest of the mound from them. He was gone soon after they spotted him. Still, he was their first sight of humanity and their growing weakness and low spirits lifted a little. They found themselves in sight of water once more and then Moses stopped and pushed his hand back against Tom's chest.

Houses.

No, a mill with three cots nestling close to its landward side, smoke trails rising invitingly from their chimneys.

They crouched amongst a tangle of hazel and bramble, trying to decide how best to approach this place.

'Stay you here while I go and take a closer look,' Moses said. 'If they are not friendly, there is no way that you will be able to run from them, with that leg of yours. I'll go and spy out the land and see who is living there.'

It seemed reasonable but for one thing. Moses was black

72

and there would be few black freemen roaming the English countryside. Freemen there certainly were, for it was here that the growing movement to free all the blacks had been born, but at the same time, Negroes in England were still either to be found living on the estates of the great houses or in London, where their sponsors were many.

It was finally agreed that Moses would go and take a look at the buildings and return to give his report to Tom. If things looked hopeful, Tom would then ask for food and also enquire about Lavenham. It was best not to bring in Charles' name at this point for it must be known to most that he was the Langstone contractor and if it had been spread abroad that there had been an escape from one of the hulks, enquiries after Master Bayless might lead the Authorities straight to them.

Moses settled Tom down in thick undergrowth and loped away. He left the shelter of the trees and cut across the Common, struck a lane and followed it round two fields to where it dipped down to the Mill and its broad jetty. From their vantage point among the trees, a small rise had hidden the other houses. He discovered that he was approaching a large village. Moses stopped and hesitated. From where he was he could see the spire of a church and further along the shore the lumpish silhouettes of warehouses. He was surely looking at Emsworth.

The Mill was working. He could hear the clash of the water-wheel and the rumble of the grinding stones before he even approached the first building. It was a pair of very small cottages, their windows almost obscured by the weight of their reed-thatched roof, which overhung them almost to ground level in places. The door of the end cot closest to him was open and steam was pouring out. He poked his head through the opening, eyes smarting as smoke billowed round him. There was only one room. A woman was standing over the fire, poking feverishly at something in the embers. Now and then she stamped her foot and finally she flung aside the ladle that she had been dipping into the fire.

'Temper, temper,' Moses said reprovingly.

She jumped. 'Mercy, who be you?'

The steam billowed round them as Moses came through

73

the open door, the light behind him. He picked up the ladle and deftly removed the remains of six charred pigeons from the embers.

'I'm sure that's how me mam used to do 'em.'

She was very young, with the white pinched face of sustained hunger so familiar to him. Moses squatted down and patted the last sparks from the burnt carcasses. His stomach rumbled at the tempting odour of the charred meat.

'Well, ma'am,' he said, turning one after the other over on the stone hearth. 'That's three . . . no four . . . past redemption. I reckon we'll be able to save these two, though. You put them into the embers too soon, you know. All this wood is still too filled with flame, it should be glowing down to hot embers before you start to cook – and where I come from, ma'am – we pack a flour and water dough round the meat to protect it or if flour is scarce we use mud.'

The girl seemed to have heard nothing of his words. She clenched and unclenched her fists, her eyes darting about the room as though searching for a hiding place. 'Oooh, sweet land. I've my husband's dinner burnt there – and his Da's an' all.'

She could not have been more than fourteen years old.

'Did your Mammy not teach you to cook?' Moses asked gently.

Her little white face was streaked with smoke tears and now fresh ones joined them. She shook her head miserably. 'He bought me from the poorhouse last week. I bin there so long, I dur'st know much of cooken' proper food an' meat. OOOH.' She had suddenly noticed him through the thinning smoke.

'It's all right, ma'am . . . no need to be feared by me. I've just come to lodge in Chichester with Master Charles Bayless, no less. I'm the official agent for American blacks and we've business to discuss. Came over from France yesterday but he was not at the quay to meet me so I reckoned on walking to Chichester.' He grinned at her and rubbed a hand over his face. 'I guess Chichester is further than I thought. Would you be good enough to direct me?'

She had been staring at his shining face as though she was in the presence of the Devil himself. She backed away and put

74

the kitchen table between them. He watched her hand grope behind her and close on the handle of a heavy fletching knife.

She opened her mouth without taking her frightened eyes from his. He tensed, ready to turn and run if she should start to shout. 'It's . . . it's away to the east.'

He did his best to look relaxed, interested and made no move.

'Out of here and back up the lane and onto the highway,' she said in a small, breathless voice. 'You pass through the Bournes and then Bosham. New Fishbourne be after that and Chichester two miles on from there. About eight miles in all.'

He bowed. 'That is very good of you, ma'am. I am eternally in your debt.'

They eyed each other. She became a little bolder. 'Why you dressed in them rags, if you be an important person?' Suspicion suddenly gave her face a waspish look.

'Ah, ma'am, when you are my colour in a foreign land, you travel as inconspicuously as possible for fear of ruffians.' He rolled his eyes at her and assumed a look of deep grievance. 'As it is, I was robbed on the vessel between France and Portsmouth – for while I slept, some villain relieved me of my money pouch. I am endeavouring to reach Master Bayless as quickly as possible for I'm hungry enough to eat a buffalo . . .' His eyes had wandered longingly to the loaf standing on the table between them.

She hesitated and then leaned forward and tore off a fat wedge. 'Thanks for rescuing the pigeons,' she said hurriedly, wanting to be rid of him. She held out the bread and he took it, trying not to snatch in his eagerness and touching his brow with a forefinger.

'Very good of you, ma'am. Thank you for the directions . . . and good day to you.'

He backed away and fled, ducking round the side of the cottage with his eyes fixed on the safety of the trees. Behind him someone shouted and he turned without thinking.

A man was hastening along the path towards the cottages. 'Hey – you! What chew doen' in there?'

His voice was a rough growl with something familiar in the tones. He started, seeing Moses' dark face, even though he turned away and began to lope up the path, recognizing with a sick lurch the face of one of the Hayling Warehouse clerks.

The recognition was mutual.

'Hey, you're the nigger off'n "Fortunée". You come back here! Stop! *Stop* . . .'

Moses fled with huge bounding strides, fed by his fright. The man's shouts and pounding footsteps faded into the distance as he leapt into a field and ran along the hedge, hunched and nimble, in the opposite direction to Tom's lair in the woods. It was not difficult to double back, once he was sure that the hue and cry had streamed off towards the highway and the purple downs.

Tom greeted him with relief. 'Thought you'd been discovered, for sure,' he said. 'Either that or you'd found a lonely goodwife to tarry with.'

Moses grinned. 'Reckon the night-time's best for that. They cain't see the colour of my skin then and I'd keep 'em just too darn occupied to light the lamp . . .'

They shared the bread, tearing ravenously at it with groans of relief.

'Home bake,' Moses murmured appreciatively as the last mouthful disappeared. 'That's the best, the richest meal I've had since I left Boston.'

They drank rainwater from the leaf curls around them and submerged the continuing pleas of their stomachs.

Emsworth.

The highway was, according to the young girl, little more than over the next rise. It would be madness to use it by day but at night all things were possible and the flat road would greatly increase their progress. They slept and waited for dusk.

It was not difficult to locate the highway. In the gathering dusk they left the trees, found the little lane and headed inland, melting into the hedge when footsteps or a bobbing light heralded the approach of other travellers. They stopped within sight of the Emsworth tollgate and cut across a field which had been partly ploughed. It was a simple matter to creep along the hedge in the darkness and when they emerged onto the highway, it was as though a new world had opened up out of the dusk. Pools of light pinpointed a scatter of cottages along the broad ribbon of road and the traffic was still quite steady, for dusk was only lately deepened into darkness.

'By Jehovah and all His witnesses,' Tom muttered, hobbling for the umpteenth time into the ditch as a group of horsemen approached. 'How long is this bedlam going on for? The road is as busy as the middle of town. I thought we were on a rural roadway.'

The traffic gradually thinned down to a trickle of empty farm carts and lone riders and they were able to move on, leaving Emsworth and the harbour water behind their right shoulders. They stole through the villages of Prinsted and South Bourne, pausing only to drink from the horse troughs in the tavern yards.

As the first cracks of silver dawn broke to the east, they found themselves close once more to habitation. Another tightly-packed community with church and harbour. It had to be Bosham.

Chapter Five

Bosham was busy. December might have been thought to be a slack time of year in the routine of a small coastal harbour but Tom, limping painfully along the path which led to the long jetty found his progress slowed by farm carts, loaded and empty, carriers, pedestrians and children. He nursed his swollen knee and eventually settled himself in a corner of the sea wall and held his hands out to passers-by with a touching beggar's supplication.

It had been agreed that Tom was the best bet to appear in a place of this size, being less conspicuous than Li'l Moses. Moses settled himself comfortably enough into the hayloft of a large barn and prepared himself for a long wait. Tom was to go into the village and beg, borrow or steal some food for them and do his best to discover how close they were to Apuldram and Lavenham. Hunger was now making them even more weary than had their long slow progress through the night hours. He burrowed deep into the hay and went instantly to sleep.

Tom gradually relaxed and began to enjoy his begging role. He was out of the wind in his little corner of the sea wall with his back against the front of a small general store. The slipway into the creek was to his right and it was fascinating to sit quietly and watch these men, women and children going freely about their lives without the least concern for the hundreds of wretched men who were at this moment mouldering in the hulks out in the middle of their own estuary. He studied their faces and found them much the same as the faces of his own countrymen, speaking the same language, farming and marketing and fishing as Americans did. There was kindness too, for his outstretched hands were rewarded with several coins before the morning was over.

The damaged leg throbbed remorselessly. They had discovered, on close examination, that the blow to the knee had been so severe that it had displaced the cap which was now floating in the inside of the joint and, within the great swelling, seemed even to be detached. The whole of the knee area was badly bruised and three small abrasions were beginning to suppurate. He sat with the leg straight out in front of him for it was fractionally less painful when it was not bent.

As the morning progressed, he discovered just how enjoyable it was to sit and watch the everyday functions of others after his long detention. It was most pleasant to watch the steady stream of activity both on and off the water. He watched a large barge nose in to the creek and one of the busy little bumboats go out to it. There were eight rowers in the barge and it was surprising to see a young girl hopping over the side and into the bobbing shell. There was something vigorous and colourful about her even at that distance – for she wore a green kerchief round her neck and a thick waterfall of crinkly black hair cascaded unchecked over the shawl about her shoulders. His eyes idly followed the boat's progress across the stretch of choppy water and then she was over the side with a swirl of skirts and bare ankles, onto the mud and running up the incline, hopping over puddles, skirts hitched into her belt. There was a basket on her arm. She reached the slipway and clambered up onto it and came swinging past his resting place, eyes searching ahead, mind clearly on other things. Her foot caught his outstretched leg and, as he cried out with the pain of the sudden wrench, she tripped and staggered against the wall beside him. In a moment she had regained her balance and whirled on him to slate him in words that had no meaning for him. Seeing the screwed-up agony on his face, her eyes dropped to the offending leg and the bloodstained bulging limb.

'Oh, sorry . . . I didn't see! Sorry, Bor.' Her quick irritation melted into abject apology. She squatted down beside him and put a hand very lightly on the damaged knee.

'There is poison here, Bor. You must attend to it if you don't want to lose your leg.'

Tom opened his eyes. The pain still coursed through his whole side and up into his body. 'I would if I had the means . . . but I have nothing.'

She was nearly as bedraggled as he, her hair blown into black tangles by the sea breeze. He could see little of her face through the dishevelled curls but her voice was gentle, deep, as she stood up. 'I must be away for the provisions or Nat'll be gettin' the fidgets in a moment. I'm really sorry for hurtin' ye.'

She was gone and there was nothing of her in the memory save for the sincerity in her voice. It was the first time in more than two years, he thought ruefully, that he had spoken with a young woman. Even such a ragged scallywag as that one was still . . . a woman. He would be able to tease Moss when he got back with his takings. Pennies meant food, but speech with a young woman was the stuff that dreams are made of . . . He began to feel a little light-headed and sat with the piece of stick which he had used for a crutch, extended over his leg to warn other passers-by to watch out for it.

He dozed, opening his eyes once when an old man threw a farthing into his lap. He smiled up as the man turned away. 'Thank you kindly, sir,' he called after him and wondered vaguely why his voice was so thin and scarcely more than a hoarse whisper. He sank back into his drowsing state and then there were hands on him, shaking his shoulder gently.

'Wake up . . . I've brought you stale bread and onions to soak in water. You must make a poultice with it and wrap it round your knee. D'ye hear me, now?'

He looked up but somehow his eyes would not focus and he saw only a dark blur from whence came that voice – he had heard it before somewhere.

She was leaning over him, muttering something foreign under her breath.

'Ma'am,' he said with an attempt at some kind of dignity, 'I should welcome bread but I would not put it round my leg. It would go straight into my mouth for my stomach is in even poorer shape than my knee . . .'

The waves of dizziness lapped round him and he closed his

eyes against the confusing blurs of light and shade that danced before him. He was aware of movement, of pain, of cold and then heat about his leg.

The next time he opened his eyes he felt better. The sun was shining thinly over his head and a baa'ing flock of sheep streamed past him into one of the flat-bottomed barges that plied to and fro between the east and west harbours during daylight hours. His hands were folded neatly in his lap and beneath them he found a large loaf of new bread. His breeches were slit at the right knee and a poultice had been laid over the swelling and wrapped round with a green kerchief.

He sat staring at his leg for some time, trying to recall his benefactor. All that came to him was a gentle chiding voice, muttering to him in a mixture of words which were mostly gibberish to him. He lifted the loaf and pressed it to his face, the delicious scent of warm, fresh bread making his mouth water so that he tore at the crust and sat munching savagely until guilt forced him to stop. Half the loaf was for Moses, who must, with his great frame, be even hungrier than he was.

Two small boys hovered near him, staring . . . whispering together. They looked, he thought, as though they had been there for some time. He watched them carefully, for the little ruffians might well be planning to rob him of the coins in his lap.

'What's your name?' he said at last to the smaller of the two. He was regarded suspiciously by a pair of frowning brown eyes in a dirty, freckled face.

'C'mon. Cat got your tongue, has it?'

The children regarded him stonily. 'What you done to that?' The elder boy pointed to Tom's leg.

'Fell under a horse and got kicked for my trouble,' Tom said shortly.

'We see'd that gypsy binden' it. You was hollerin' somethen' terrible. People was looken' . . .'

It seemed important that people had been looking. More so than the suffering of the unfortunate beggar. Tom was inclined to agree with them – for being the centre of attention was the last thing he wanted.

'Who was looking?'

The boys shrugged and the small one moved closer to Tom. 'Missus Broadbridge, she said as how beggars shouldn't be allowed to mess up the walkway. She said as how you should be taken to the poorhouse or into cells.'

Tom looked at them with alarm. 'Whoa, bless my soul. We can't have that. No, sir. Sounds as though I'd best be on my way, afore any other goodwife gets ideas like that. Would you two boys just give me a hand getting up?'

He stuffed the half-loaf into his jacket pocket, hearing the four pennies of his morning's begging clink comfortingly. Pressing his back hard against the wall he tried to lever himself upward with his good leg and the stick. He was too weak and did little more than pant and strain to no avail.

He looked at the boys. 'Please give me a hand, lads. I've little but my thanks to give you but you can see how I'm placed with this leg of mine.'

They stared at him doubtfully and then the small one came forward and put his forearm under Tom's armpit. The other boy followed suit and between them they heaved him upward until he was standing with the wall at his back. The leg thumped and jagged pain shot up into his groin. He gritted his teeth as he slowly put some weight on it.

'I thank you most kindly, lads,' he said when the agony had subsided into a dull throb. He offered them a farthing each but, after a momentary hesitation the larger boy shook his head. Tom put out a grimy hand and ruffled the unruly curls in thanks.

A thought occurred to him. 'How far be Apuldram from here, would you say?'

'That where you live, is it?' the elder boy asked quickly.

Tom nodded. 'Working on the roads there,' he said. 'Came over here a'courting and got half-kicked to death instead . . .'

'How come you don't know yer way back, then?'

He's sharp, this one . . . Take care now.

'Hitched a ride in a boat, see. I only been here a short time. Came all the way from London Town before that. Hoped I could find a boat to take me back but I seem to have come to the wrong part of the shore . . .'

The small boy nodded. There was still suspicion in the elder boy's eyes and he said nothing.

82

'You need the Hoe, not the town quay,' the small boy said. 'Better still, there's always a ferry boat at Park Farm slip for it's right opposite to Dell Quay. Follow the path round the creek here and cut across the fields to the Hoe Lane, where it joins the Fishbourne Lane. There's a pathway to Park Farm and the slip a few paces from there.'

'I'll do that. Thank ye kindly, boys,' Tom said gratefully. 'I shall just go and rest this leg for half an hour and then be on my way.' He hobbled off up the street.

'Hey – not that way! The creek path is over there,' the taller boy called after him.

He stopped for a moment to catch his breath for the pain was suddenly excruciating. 'I know. Just going to try and get a word with my little maid . . .' He limped away from them, gritting his teeth and concentrating on just keeping moving. Up the inclining lane away from the water and the clash of carts and pedestrians.

The children stood and watched him go.

'Funny, I never seen him afore,' the big boy said.

Moses woke and lay comfortably in his nest, drinking in the warmth of his lair and the sweetness of the scent of clean hay. It was a never-ending source of pleasure to him, this sweet purity in the air. Noses and lungs had been blunted by the pungent stench of the hulks for so long that this wondrous freshness everywhere was almost more therapeutic than food.

FOOD . . . No, nothing was needed more than the quenching of his hunger and thirst at the moment. 'Come on, Master . . . don't forget your old black friend here.'

He listened to the scuffle of the creatures who shared the barn with him and chewed on a straw, wondering whether he should risk spying out the land in the vicinity, now that daylight was well-advanced. Maybe there was a house nearby where he could lay hands on a crust. A raucous clucking just below him brought him up with a jerk until it dawned on him that he was sharing the barn with hens and that what he was hearing sounded like laying noises. Hens and eggs? Either would be wondrously welcome. He peered out from his high lair. Ten feet below he spied three hens scratching in the dust near the barn door. He crouched very still for some time watching them. The hens clucked and crooned among themselves, oblivious to everything but their own contentment. Another hen appeared from directly below him. Had she finished her laying?

He slid very quietly out of his nest, down the side of the rick and well out of sight of his prey. He crouched, muscles tensed, waiting . . .

It seemed an age before one of the hens strayed into view, bent on the tiny particles of grain embedded into the barn's earth floor. She never knew what hit her, for Moses pounced the second she was within his reach. He flung himself across her frantic body, hands round her neck, twisting sharply before she had time to do more than screech once.

There was instant confusion among the other hens. They flew into the air, shrieking and panicking but Moses was already back in his nest, the hen's warm body pressed against his chest.

He waited a long while for the survivors to recover from their fright but then he had plenty of spare time and by noon, he had caught and wrung the necks of three of the five birds and had discovered a little treasure trove of eggs. He broke and ate two and laid the others aside for Tom. By the time his sharp ears picked up sounds of movement outside the barn, he had plucked two of the three birds and was in process of drawing their innards.

The sound that made him pause and listen was so slight that at first he did little more than register it. It was more of a thump than a footfall.

He raised his head and listened. The barn was quiet, save for the slightly agitated clucking of the two surviving hens below him. No sound from outside intruded upon his ears. He frowned. The thump had had a heavy suggestion to it, as though someone had collided with something. No footsteps approached or retreated. Was there someone out there, listening?

A light wind sprang up and whined through a gap in the thatch over his head. Tom?

The continuing silence began to worry him. He laid the hen aside, wiping the blood from his hands on the straw and slid

84

down the back of the rick. The two hens, sensing movement, flew screeching into the air and Moses froze. They perched high above his head on a roof beam, fluttering and cackling in their agitation. When their fears had abated into watchful peace he moved quietly through the dusty shadows towards the door.

Shafts of bright daylight slashed the gloom between the wood planking. He peered out through a crack. The barn stood on a slight incline at the corner of a field. He could just see the edge of another building at right-angles to it. The open space before the barn was empty. A wealth of weeds and dead grass between the cobbles of the forecourt suggested that this place might have been abandoned. As he stared out at the narrow vista his crack allowed, another sound came to him and he froze.

Deep and then shallow breathing. Someone or something was panting close to the barn door.

'Moss . . .' a hoarse whisper. 'Moss, *for God's sake* . . .'

He leapt to the great door and pushed it open a few inches. Tom was lying on the ground, his face grey with pain.

'Thank heavens,' he said as Moses dragged him inside. He lost consciousness and Moses lifted him and carried him round the back of the rick and made him comfortable. Someone had bound up the infected leg. He discovered the bread in Tom's pocket and ate it ravenously, gulping down the mouthfuls as though they were his last. Tom opened his eyes before he had finished.

'Sorry,' he muttered. 'This confounded knee seems to be going bad on me. Had to come back. Caused a bit of a nuisance down in the village. Kept passing out with the pain or something and folks were beginning to look at me suspiciously.'

Moses fed three raw eggs to him and they seemed to relieve him a little. It had, after all, been a fruitful day for they were the richer by four coins and three birds, and they had bread and eggs to stave off the worst of their hunger.

'Now, if we can only get as far as this slipway opposite Dell Quay,' Tom said later, 'we stand a good chance of getting a lift across. The children said that this place Dell Quay is the port for Chichester and lies close to Apuldram.'

Moses looked at Tom's strained face. 'You don't look fit to move one pace, Master Tom . . . so how's you thinkin' of travellin' half a mile or so?'

They regarded each other in the half-light. The beginnings of fever made Tom's grey eyes sparkle oddly.

'We're so near now, Moss. Just get us there . . . somehow.'

They moved off in darkness, leaving the comfort of the barn with some regret. The night was cold again though there was no frost, but neither was there a moon. The village was peaceful except for sounds of enjoyment from the direction of the waterside tavern.

'What would I not give for a tankard of frothing ale and a seat by the fire in there,' Moses mourned as they turned their backs on the sounds of singing and laughter. Christmas was only days away. He wondered where they would be when it was upon them. In the Black Hole in 'Fortunée's' bilges?

They followed the track round Bosham Creek. Progress was very slow for the knee would not now support Tom at all and Moses was obliged to carry him on his back. They paused when the track suddenly branched out in three directions.

'The children said something about turning off from the Fishbourne bridlepath,' Tom muttered. He was having difficulty in separating reality from a dreaming trance into which he was sliding ever more often. He was reasonably comfortable on Moses' back but found his grip on the big man's shoulders kept slipping.

What had those boys said? That there was a path to Park Farm close to the junction of the Bosham, Hoe and Fishbourne lanes . . .

'Look for a farm track. They said there was a path to Park Farm from somewhere round here.'

'I reckon this calls for a one-man hunt,' Moses grunted after starting down one lane and finding that it suddenly curved away towards the west again.

He laid Tom down against the hedge. 'I'll find the path and come back to you, soon as I can.' He realized that Tom was not listening to him for his head was sunk on his chest. 'My word, we got to get some help for you and *quick* . . .'

He squatted beside Tom and made him as comfortable as he could, pulling the wet grasses up round the thin body to give some protection against discovery. He stood up then and snapped off a thick twig from the hedgerow. The clean white end gleamed in the darkness. It was as good a marker of Tom's presence as anything.

He combed the Fishbourne Lane and eventually found a break in the stone wall bordering the road which might well be the path they were seeking. Standing in the middle of the rutted track he hesitated and then started along it counting his paces. The opening had only been thirty-two paces from where he had left Tom. It would be wise to see whether it actually did lead to the Chichester Channel while he was free of the burden of his friend. He moved fast now, almost running until a thought occurred to him. A man running at night was suspect. If the farmer heard him he would be unlikely to offer any assistance. Honest men don't run at night. He forced himself into a walk. The track was deeply rutted by the passage of heavy wheels through the claylike mud. Now and then, stones patched the deeper holes but the going was slow and soon mud splashed his legs up to the knees. The trees lining the track and the path itself were smudged shadows against the grey night.

He was beginning to consider retracing his steps when the ground flattened beneath his feet and he found himself in a yard. He stood still, waiting for his heartbeat to recover and trying to pierce the night with nervous senses.

He became aware of movement. Cattle in their stalls, tails swishing softly. A quiet moo, a rump being rubbed slowly against the side of a stall. Comforting farm sounds.

A hand gripped his arm and he spun round, swivelling his body, arm raised to chop down the unseen assailant.

'Hey, don't 'e hurt me,' a voice gasped. Moses gripped the figure by both shoulders and peered at the pale blur of the face upturned to his.

'I can help you but let go of me . . . you're half crushing my arms to pulp. I bin awaiten' here for you since sundown.'

'What do you want of me? You don't know me.' Moses found he was whispering as the stranger was.

The man turned his head and searched the vague outline of the cattle bier. 'Hush . . . There are six of them across there. Come you into the kitchen where we can talk.'

The unexpected friend ducked out of Moses' relaxing grasp. 'Come on, follow me quickly and make no sound . . .'

Moses crouched and followed the shadowy figure which beckoned him round a scatter of outhouses. They stopped once when a growl in the darkness warned of another watcher.

'Stay, Scamp, it's only me. In here, come quickly. One of them might be scouting round . . .'

A door was opened and then closed without a creak, behind them. Warmth and the scent of woodsmoke and the kitchen stewpot enclosed them. Something pressed itself against Moses' ankles and miaowed, a small crystal sound of welcome.

'Fran, you there?' The voice hissed somewhere across the room. More movement and a footfall descending bare wood stairs. Whispering and a flurry of skirts. Moses stood where he was, certain of nothing but the small purring creature about his legs and savouring the excellence of the fragrant air.

He heard the scrape of the tinderbox and light scoured his eyes, the soft orange translucence of flame held between cupped hands. A lamp was being lit. He stared across a heavy table at the two elderly figures suddenly etched in light against the yawning backdrop of an open doorway.

The woman held up the lamp towards him and her round face registered surprise, a sudden uncertainty at the sight of the size of him. The man smiled and there was relief and pleasure in his eyes. He came round the table towards him.

'Well, we didn't expect you to be such a giant,' he said gently. 'We was told to watch out for a nigger and a white one. You are very welcome in our house, whether you be white-skinned, black-skinned or one o' they red fellows. I'm Ben Chase of Park Farm and this is Frances, my good wife.'

They sat him down beside the kitchen range and Mistress Chase busied herself with kettle and stewpot until a feast was spread before him, the like of which he had only dreamed in

88

the years of his captivity. The old man, bent from a lifetime of hard work, settled down on the other side of the range so that the glow of the fire engraved his bearded face with pink light and plum dark shadows. He talked in a hurried undertone, pausing now and then to cock his head and listen to the wind rattling the shutters on the outside of the windows.

Soldiers and two harbour officials had arrived at the farm just before dusk. They had materialized stealthily from all sides and converged upon the house and outbuildings, going through the place with cold thoroughness and leaving no stone unturned. They had been warned by some children of a beggar – a stranger in Bosham that day, a ragged fellow with a voice that did not suit his poor clothing. His description tallied with that of one of two prisoners still at large out of four who had escaped from one of the prison hulks in the harbour off Langstone a few days before. Of the other, a negro, there had been no sign but the fellow under suspicion was badly lamed and was scarce able to hobble. He had asked the boys how to get to Apuldram – and they, having told him of the little ferry from Park Farm slip, had gone with all haste to the Customs post on the Hoe and reported their suspicions.

'It was their bad fortune – and your good luck, that my brother and two of my sons have made their homes in Charles Town, New England. Our young Georgie . . . he went to war over there for what he believes in, just like you did. We don't know what happened to him.' The old man's eyes glittered across the table.

Moses wolfed down his food and tried, without success, to take in all that was being related to him. The sudden change in their luck was more than he could believe. There had to be some terrible snag in it somewhere.

'I thank you, ma'am,' he said to Frances Chase as she refilled his pot with small ale. He smiled up at her with such gentle gratitude that she paused and put a hand on his shoulder.

'We know that you have had a really terrible time in that dreadful place but do not worry that you will be sent back to slavery, my dear. We have such sympathy with you Americans – and even more with the abolitionists of slavery. We'll do our best for you.'

Moses sat up straight and grinned at her. He bowed from

the waist with lofty grace. 'Mistress Chase, ma'am. You're lookin' at a rare creature for I'm a freeman and mighty proud of it, too. Master Heritage freed all eight of his blacks ten years ago an' I joined the crew of one of his vessels of my own choice. Sort of felt that I could show my gratitude best by keeping a watchful eye out for his sons – an' that's been my privilege ever since. The beggar those scamps reported to-day is Master Tom Heritage, ma'am, First Mate of the "Free States" and second son of Master Desmond. He hurt his leg bad an' I carried him to the crossroads, top of your lane, and left him so's I could spy out the land an' see if I could find this place.'

'Oh, poor soul. Is he badly hurt?' Mistress Chase was all concern and then, without waiting for his answer, 'Ben, we must quickly go and bring him in before he catches his death of cold . . .'

Ben Chase tutted at her. He was clearly accustomed to being chivvied by his wife's kind but impatient heart. 'Yes, dear . . . Yes, yes . . . we'll do all that but there is little point in bringing him in if we are to be discovered. First we must be sure that the militia is not on the prowl. Moses and I will go and bring the poor boy back and you, Fran – maybe you would put your shawl on and go down to the Sergeant by the boat and offer them hot drinks or something to keep them occupied.'

Moses leant back in his chair with a sigh. He felt refreshed and warmed by the unexpected goodness of these old people. The food and drink were making him sleepy and he had to force himself to make a move.

'Sir, I c'n fetch Tom in on my own. He's light as a feather and not far away. Just you keep the soldiers occupied long enough to allow me to get up to the crossroads and back. He's going to need all Mistress Chase's skills for he's mighty weak now from that knee.'

He left them, slipping out of the back door and round the rear of the dairy and drying sheds with Ben Chase's instructions etched in his mind. They would wait for ten minutes and then Ben would go down to where he thought the men were in hiding. He would try to engage the Sergeant in conversation, finally inviting him back to the farm for some warm refreshment on so cold a night. Moses was to bring Tom in by the front parlour door and take him straight up the stairs to where Mistress Chase would be waiting. The presence of the Sergeant would, they hoped, ensure that there would not be another search made upon the house.

The little lane with its cart-ruts filled with the muddy water of night-long drizzle seemed much longer than it had when he had crept down towards the creek. It curved to the left and then twisted back on itself through a strand of dripping trees. Then the gateway loomed out of the darkness ahead of him and, seeing it with relief, he pulled his rain-soaked shirt closer round him and broke into a lope.

Tom was where he had left him. He raised his head and there was a tremor in the welcome in his voice. 'Thought you were gone for good. You were only going to be a few minutes but it seems like hours have passed.'

Moses grinned and gathered him up in his arms like a baby. 'Stopped to give myself to this little golden-haired milkmaid I found,' he said, his voice a whispered rumble deep in his chest. 'Now, just you wait an' see the surprise I've got for you, Master . . .'

Tom grunted. 'Bad habits die hard, you great clod. I'm not your Master, I'm your brother in the sight of the Lord . . . so be kind enough to use the name my mother gave me!'

White teeth flashed in the darkness. 'Yassiree!' Then they were on the move. Tom seemed content just to have Moses back. He asked no questions but lay with his wet head against the negro's broad chest.

'You's not to say a word until I says you can, you see, Ma . . . Tom? I found the farm but those little lads you spoke to alerted the Authorities so there's a nice welcome committee of militia down by the ferry boat, just waitin' for you an' me to stroll down there and give them an extra guinea in their pay packets. You an' me, Brother, the Lord is on our side for He found us some real good friends an' a warm place to hide like you never thought you'd see again . . .'

Frances Chase filled the heavy kettle and set it on the hob. As it heated it sang with a thin pure whistling note. A curl of vapour trailed upwards from its spout. She lifted the lid of the earthenware jar in which the bread was stored. Two loaves still fresh. Enough until she made more in the morning. Her hands shook and she could feel the tremble in her whole body. What they were doing was dangerous enough to get them a transport sentence if they were caught. It was for Georgie, though. All for Georgie.

They knew that he had been fighting over there in the Colony, fighting his own countrymen – but no, that was wrong for America was his country now and they must accept it. There had been just the one letter from Harry to say that word had reached them of Georgie's capture by the King's Navy but there had been no word of him since then. No word in nearly ten years. Harry had quite accepted that his brother was dead. He had not wanted to fight, still remembering the friends of his youth and knowing that he might be faced with one of them on the end of a bayonet. He had pigs to rear and a family to feed. He had not been persuaded to go to war.

Georgie was their last-born. They were proud that he was prepared to offer his life for his ideals. It was what they would have done in the same situation. The long silence was a terrible sadness to them – and yet they could not bring themselves to accept that he might well have been killed. It was less final to hope that he was a prisoner, maybe over there, better still maybe back here. Letters to the Transport Board had brought no sign of him to light, but they knew that many of the prisoners were not accounted for, for the Secretariat was known to be grossly inefficient. They lived on a diminishing possibility . . .

They had helped another prisoner to escape five years before. He had travelled all the way from Chetney Marsh on the River Medway, driven south by packs of chasing soldiers. By the time Ben had picked him up and stowed him in his waggon he was on the outskirts of Crowborough, hiding in the wild land south of the hill. It was the time of Ben's annual visit to his brother at Mayfield. The fellow had never heard of their Georgie, though. He was with them for only three days and nights and they hadn't liked him, for he was filled with fanatical hatred for anything that was English. They had found him a passage to France and were glad to see the back of him.

Maybe these two would tell them where Georgie was. It was hard to lose two sons to a place across the ocean where one might never see them again. It was even harder to lose your youngest boy, to feel that his life had been wiped out by this fat and sickly Hanoverian monarch who sat on the English throne without knowing who he was these days and his Regent was no better – just an empty, pleasure-seeking creature with no morals, judging by his *affaires* with the butterflies of the Court. To have such a good young life taken in the name of such creatures . . . better the Cause of Freedom and Justice for America where the men were at least fighting for red-blooded ideals . . .

Ben Chase went down to the slip with his lantern on a long pole. The ground was slippery here for the mud was thick and viscous, churned up by the hooves of generations of cattle. He knew that the ambush of waiting men would be near to the flat-bottomed boat, for it was expected that the Yankees would attempt to steal it and row across to Dell Quay under cover of darkness. The black man would make them too conspicuous by day, so they had reasoned – and they were right for there were few dark skins in the area.

'Sergeant Cross,' he called, his old voice cracking as he leaned against the gusty wind. There was movement and a hoarse voice growled close to him.

'What you up to, Master Chase? We're tryin' to catch two villains and if you're waven' that thing around all over the place, they'll be able to see it all the way to Fishbourne. Dowse it at once.'

Ben lowered his lantern and opened the shutter to blow out the guttering candle. 'I'm sorry, Sergeant,' he said. 'Never thought of it like that. We was rather nervous, my good wife and me, you see. Not young any more and two prisoners on the loose with murder in their hearts . . . well, we was a little frightened that they might come to the farm and give us trouble – seeing that you say they are on their way to our slip.' His voice was a little querulous as though the soldiers themselves had brought about this danger.

'S'not you they want, gaffer,' the Sergeant said. He was

irritated by the lack of action on such a dirty night as much as by this old fool. Indeed, he and his men had been crouching in the undergrowth for four hours now and there was no sign of anyone on the slip. He stretched and shook the stiffness from his shoulders.

'If you please,' Ben said with great respect in his voice, 'my good wife has just warmed up a pot of excellent broth and she bids me ask whether you would like to take a bowl of it with us? It's right nasty out here and with a good six hours yet before dawn, it'll give you extra warmth. The house is only a stone's throw and one of your men can fetch you if anything happens . . .'

The Sergeant hesitated, surprised by this unexpected gesture. Certainly he was beginning to think that they were on a wild goose chase for the Americans would surely have made an appearance by this hour if they wanted to be clear of Dell Quay by the time the first lighter arrived a good two hours before dawn.

The temptation was too good to refuse.

The scowl on his granite face eased. 'Thank ye kindly, I'm sure, Master Chase. That would be very welcome, just for a few minutes, mind ye. Go you back to the house now while I instruct the men, an' I'll follow ye up.'

Ben trudged back over the mud and up the bank to the yard. 'Sergeant Cross'll be glad of a bowl of broth, m'dear,' he said carefully, his eyebrows signalling their own message.

She shook her head at the unspoken question. 'That's good. Sensible of him,' she said comfortably. 'I think he might even benefit from a little glass of that raspberry liquor I made in Century year.'

With an additive of good strong French brandy to it. She had no need to add the last words for he saw the intention in her face and nodded, the lines at the corner of his eyes crinkling.

The door opened and the Sergeant came in, stamping the mud from his boots and bringing with him the briny smell of the sea.

'Very kind, I'm sure, Missus,' he said to her, touching his forehead with a muddy finger.

'Well, we couldn't sleep,' she said, pressing him down into

94

a chair close to the range where Moses had sat only a short time before, and pouring more water into the already steaming kettle. 'We came down to see that all the shutters were secure and the doors bolted against those men if they should come. Then we thought of you out there in the rain. It didn't seem right to heat this up and not offer you any. Let me make you both comfortable and then I shall return to my bed and leave you in peace.'

The steaming soup-pot filled the kitchen with an aroma of meat and herbs which brought the saliva into the Sergeant's mouth and he gratefully accepted the brimming bowl she held out to him. Nor could he refuse a tankard of strong ale. The warm kitchen and friendliness of the old couple suddenly seemed like very good company. He settled lower into his chair and raised the soup bowl to his lips.

Fine rain, whipped by a strengthening wind, stung their faces as though a thousand wasps filled the night around them. Moses had shifted Tom round onto his back again, as they passed through the farm gate, so that his hands might be free in case of emergency.

'Hold tight round my neck just for this short distance,' he said to Tom without much conviction, for his strength was so depleted now that his arms could do little to hold him on the big man's back. The poisoned leg hung down limply so that he could only grip Moses' hips with his one good leg. Moses steadied Tom with one hand under his rump and the other gripping his hands as they tugged weakly at his jacket collar. By the time he picked out the squat shadow of the outbuildings, both were short of breath and utterly weary. He felt Tom's arms slipping.

'Nearly there, now . . . I can see the house,' he whispered. 'Hang on tight, Brother. This bit is the trickiest.'

Their breathing sounded like a herd of cattle blowing, the harder they tried to keep it shallow. Moses' bare foot caught a sharp stone and it rattled, bouncing away from him. He gritted his teeth against the curse that rose to his lips and pressed into the thick shrubbery on one side of the main entrance. Nothing stirred apart from the wind riffling through the trees that lined the bank of the creek. From inside the house came the faint sound of voices raised in song. Cautiously, he moved forward once more, hitching Tom's body more securely onto his shoulders. Two windows, Mistress Chase had said. Then one small window and then three steps up to the front door. He put out his left hand and counted the sills. Then the steps were under his foot and he felt his way up them and laid a hand on the door. It moved and opened silently.

Stairs on the left. Parlour on the left. Dining room on the right. Passage to kitchen straight ahead.

The kitchen door was closed but light streamed under it and the singers within were now embarking with sleepy enjoyment upon a ditty whose chorus demanded the banging of mugs and stamping of feet. Clever old folk to think of masking the sounds of his entry. Someone laughed as the song continued. It was a harsh, throaty sound. Not Ben Chase.

Feeling the smooth, polished wood of the banister rail with his right hand, Moses went slowly up the stairs, praying that Tom would not suddenly cry out or groan. On the landing he paused again to get his bearings.

Turn right and go into the first bedroom. There was light here also and suddenly he knew that, with Tom's dead weight across his shoulders, he had not the courage to turn the handle and go into that room where trouble might well be waiting. He gritted his teeth and knocked softly.

'Yes, come in.'

Mistress Chase. Her voice sounded high and brittle as though she was as filled with terror as he was. If she and her husband were part of the ambush party, she was going to be a heroine now and her courage in effecting the recapture of two murderous escaped convicts would quickly become folklore in the area. He took a deep breath, lifted the latch of the chamber door and stepped into the dimly lit bedroom, cradling Tom's limp body in his arms.

Chapter Six

The rain turned to snow in the night.

Tom opened his eyes to a white and silent world beyond a strange window. He lay comfortably in a bed with a bright chequered blanket covering him. He was warm and clean. There was a hot brick at his feet. The throbbing in his knee reminded him of who he was.

Moses' head bobbed up from beyond the end of the bed. 'Morning, Brother.' His eyes had lost their bloodshot look. He was refreshed and ready to face the world. 'Slept here on the floor so that I'd not risk bumping your leg in my sleep.' He grinned happily at Tom's astounded examination of their surroundings. 'Now, don't you ever say I'm not the brightest li'l ole Moses on two feet, findin' us the best lodgings and nursing in a strange land . . .'

'Where are we, for God's sake? I remember little but waiting for you in a wet hedge.'

'Park Farm, that's where. Right in full view of that li'l ole ferry and Dell Quay on the opposite bank of the river. Real kindly folk, these two old people. They was even on the lookout for us, can you imagine that? Just 'cos the soldiery told 'em you was making for here. Old Farmer Chase, he was in the barnyard and stopped me from going down to the slip where the soldiers were hiding out. They're gone now. Went just after daylight – and a right sorry-looking bunch they was too, after a night out there in the rain and snow. How're you feeling?'

The fever was still in him and the whole of his leg was on

fire but now at least it was the only immediate problem left to fight. He settled down into his pillows, feeling relaxed and secure in the warm chamber. His hunger was gone and so had the usual stink of his own stale sweat.

'I'm fine,' he said with a sigh. He closed his eyes again. 'I'm just fine.'

Ben Chase came upstairs to see his visitors at noon. 'Ye must stay up here until the leg is healed,' he said to them both. 'Sorry to imprison you again when you have already suffered from too much of it but this is a busy thoroughfare during the day and any sight of strangers here would have the Authorities swarming all over this place once more. There is quite a stir in Bosham, you know, with everyone keepen' their eyes peeled for you.'

'What happened to the other two who escaped with us?' Moses asked.

The old man scratched his head. 'I seem to recall the Sergeant mentioning last night that they caught one an' the other drowned and they hung his body up on the mast as a lesson to your companions.'

'Won't be no lesson, sir,' Moses said. 'It's every man for himself in them hulks. Despair breeds scant respect for obedience . . .'

On the second day at Park Farm, Tom felt a little stronger. He allowed Mistress Chase to prop him up in a nest of feather pillows and put a comb through his hair. He watched her face with its network of lines and pouches under the kind eyes and knew that she was playing a private game of having her sons about her once more. Neither he nor Moses had come across Georgie Chase. Looking at the sad affection in her face he knew that he would try hard to discover the fate of this loved younger son.

'You must stay here with us until you are quite fit,' she said when his head looked tidy enough, the tangles patiently removed.

'Ma'am, I was only fired to come this distance for one reason and that was to stand on the earth that gave life to my forbears. Moss and I are forever in your debt, you know that. There is little enough that we can do to show you the strength of our gratitude for all that you are doing for us – but we'll get some kind of news to you concerning your son, that I promise. First though, I must get back on my feet and cross that water to Apuldram.'

'Is that where you hail from, then?' She looked surprised, even pleased. Was it possible that he might be a connection of hers, for her own folk came from Birdham, not two miles south of Apuldram.

'I don't know too much about them,' he admitted. 'That's why I must go there. Mama has always been very reticent about certain things. Her name was Bayless, though. I am Thomas Bayless Heritage.'

She paused in the act of picking up his washing bowl and the empty water jug. 'Bayless . . .' she frowned. 'That name rings some kind of bell. I'll ask Ben for he was born and raised in this house and his father and granfer before him. There b'aint a family from Dell Quay or Apuldram that'd not be known to him.'

Ben Chase came up to see them later that day. Moses was prowling round the upper floor of the farmhouse like a caged animal. The regular food and rest had already renewed his energies so that he longed now for nothing more than to be able to exercise himself.

'Pity I can't use some of that muscle out in the yard,' Ben said, seeing Moses' ill-concealed frustration.

'Maybe I could do a few jobs for you after dark,' Moses said eagerly. 'I'm as strong as an ox, sur, and getting fitter every day with the feedin' up that Mistress Chase is givin' us.'

Ben smiled. 'It's a great joy to her to have a couple of chicks to fuss over,' he said. 'She's a born mother, my Fran, and it was a grief to us both that we were only blessed with the two boys, for there were no more after young Georgie. She'd have bin in her element with the house filled with little 'uns.'

He sat on the edge of the bed and studied Tom's thin face. 'Looken' better each day, 'ent yer?' he said.

There was something in the back of his eyes that Tom had not seen before. Uncertainty . . . maybe even fear? Had he come to tell them that they must move on? The leg was a little better but he was still not able to put any weight at all on it.

'Is something troubling you?' he asked Ben anxiously.

The old man shook his head. 'No, no . . . the hunt for you

has moved away towards Portsmouth now. Soon you will be forgotten, as long as you don't show your faces to the wrong folks.' He hesitated. 'Fran tells me that you are aimen' on taken' a look at yer Mam's old home.'

Tom nodded. 'I daresay someone else is living there now and I shall have to be mighty careful, but we are so close to it here and I would never forgive myself if I were to sail for France without first having stood where my roots began.'

'There 'ent a soul liven' there, sir. Not for nearly fifty year now.' He narrowed his eyes and Tom watched indecision chase across the old man's granite features. 'You say your mother was a Bayless?'

The feeling was strong now in him that Ben Chase was not happy. Mystified, Tom nodded again. 'Yes, sir. She was Violet Bayless, born and brought up across that water – and so was my grandfather, Jess Bayless.'

Ben stared at Tom, taking in the heavy black hair and high-bridged nose. 'Yes . . . I see her in you now,' he said slowly. 'I was no more than a sprig of fifteen or so when she went away with her American gentleman but I remember her well enough for she was a striking lady an' most of us young 'uns was half in love with her . . .'

Tom smiled at him, delighted and yet – there was still this odd tension in his host. 'Tell me about her,' he pleaded. 'Do try and remember. My parents were always so reticent about Mama's younger days. Father died last year and I have had no word from my mother for several months now so it may even be that she has followed him. She would be all of seventy-four or so by now, you see.'

'I know.' Ben rubbed a hand across his eyes. ' 'Twas a rum do with them Baylesses.' He dropped his eyes and gazed down at the liver spots on the backs of his hands. 'I 'spect that if she didn't tell you about her life, it was because she decided 'twas best you shouldn't know.'

'Ben.' Tom put a hand over the old man's. 'In a few days' time I'm going to be well enough to take my leave of you. I shall go over there to Lavenham and I shall find out for myself all that I need to know about it. I beg of you to tell me if there are things that my family are ashamed of for I would rather hear them from you, my good friend, than from less kindly lips. I have already heard that Grandma Amy was Granfer's sister.'

Ben regarded Tom's white face with the black-lashed eyes like pleading grey pools. So like his mother but with less of the fire and the magnificent pride of her. 'Reckon it's hardly my place to talk about things as intimate as all this,' he said gruffly. 'There be other Baylesses about here still as 'ud be more suited to tell you all you want to know.'

'I know it, sir. I already know my cousin, Master Charles Bayless of Chichester. He is contractor to the Langstone hulks and it was not difficult to discover our connection once I heard his name.'

'Did you also know that Master Bayless has the Chichester coaling contract with Colonel Hamilton over there at Dell Quay?'

Hope began to shape all kinds of possibilities and Tom leant forward eagerly. 'No, I hadn't heard that. He made no mention of his other interests, apart from telling me that he owns three sea-going vessels. We rarely had the opportunity to speak together but when we did, it was mostly of our families.'

Moses had been standing in front of the fire, listening impassively. 'Well, he sure knows by now that his cousin just escaped,' he said, his voice a deep rumble in the quiet room. There was a small silence. The mantel clock ticked the seconds away behind him.

'I suppose he must. I had not given him much thought.'

'Would you like me to make contact with him and test his reaction?' Ben suggested.

'No . . . no. That might prove a very bad thing for us all for I was never very sure of where his sympathies lie,' Tom said quickly.

'Then may I suggest that I bring another of the Bayless clan to see you? I think I know who would be the right one.'

'Ben – please. Why is everything suddenly becoming so complicated? We don't need anyone else knowing we are here. The fewer people involved with us, the better. I just want to visit Lavenham for a short while – and then get us across the Channel and onto a Boston-bound vessel as quickly as we can.'

'Lavenham be a bad place,' Ben said. The two men looked at him without understanding.

'Lavenham be filled with evil spirits,' he said sourly and a dull flush reddened his leathery face. 'Look, sir, I'm not one for fancies, never have bin – but there are things I see'd with me own eyes that defy explanation in that place. I see'd as clear as I'm seeing you now, that House burnen' to the skies one night – flames coming through the roof an' rafters open to the skies – an' yet when mornen' come, there it was across the water with the lawns so trim an' the rose creepers growen' so sweet across its west face – and inside was three dead men . . . Yes, I promise – dead. Three clergymen gone at your mother's plea to exorcise the devils from it, for they had started to get to her as they had to her father, and as they had to young Master Lawrence Bayless' poor mother. Yes, sir, as they had to the very labourers who built the place, so they always said . . . I tell ye, Master – leave well alone. It's ben good and quiet there for almost half a century now. Best leave it that way.'

Tom had been staring at the old man, disbelief chasing astonishment across his face. 'It's certainly true that Mama had, at one time or another, referred to Lavenham as "a bad House" or an "unpleasant place".'

They had all, as children, thought the terms intriguing but had not dared to probe further for the forbidding expressions upon their parents' faces. That they had thus avoided admitting that Lavenham was possessed in some way was, after all, quite a feasible explanation. Curiosity and a tingle of apprehension made him press Ben further but the old man had had enough. He stood up.

'No more, if you please. That place fair gives me the creeps. I 'ent thought of it in many years, even though it sits across the water, right opposite my pig wood.' He made for the door and paused as he went out. 'I'll bring you someone better able to tell you all there is to know but don't ask me no more for I feel the wickedness of it creepen' through me bones just to mention the name of it . . .' He shut the door behind him firmly.

Moses blew out his cheeks with a loud wheeze. His eyes had begun to pop as he listened to Ben's words. Now there was a greyness about his dark face which had not been there before. 'Phew, Brother, that sure put the wind up him! What you goin' to do now? Cain't go crawlin' round a place full of ghosties — leastways, not with you you cain't. I feel those ghosties a mile away, makin' ma skin creep and crawl and pluckin' the very soul from ma body. No siree . . . I'm not goin' near a place soundin' like that.'

He held up his hands in front of Tom and looked at the tremor in them. 'See that? See how it is with me? My Pappy and my Mam, they took up with this Christian religion to get away from things like that. Nothin' to be feared of if you're a good Christian, they wus told — but Lordy Lordy . . . the wickedness they knew from their old African beliefs with the medicine man rattlin' his bones and takin' the life out of a man with one look . . . Eee, no. That's not for me.'

Just watching Moses revelling in his superstitious fears steadied Tom's own shock at Ben Chase's words and he lay back against his pillows, watching the big man's shoulders shaking like a young girl's. He stifled the laughter that welled up inside for the man's fear was quite genuine.

He said placatingly, 'For God's sake calm down, Moss. I shan't be going anywhere until this leg is better — so just take yourself off the boil. All I want to do, anyway, is to see the damned place once, so that I can leave here for good and not have it nagging at me as it has done since I was a child. When I'm fit enough, I shall go over on my own for an hour. You don't have to come. I'll be back before you notice I've gone and then we shall avail ourselves of Master Chase's kind offer of a passage to Cherbourg. Will that suit you?'

Moses stared at him and nodded. The fear was still at the back of his eyes.

The swelling in the knee persisted. Although Tom's fever was now under control and he was feeling stronger each day, the heavy throb through his leg still restricted his movements, though he tried each day to rise and move about the bed-chamber. The pain was still so great that he was always defeated after a few steps. Frustration began to chip at his temper and he did his best to control it by pulling from his memory the now pleasingly familiar picture of that blithe and entrancing figure of the wild-haired girl who had tended him. Moses, on the other hand, was quite content to rest during the daylight hours for he was now allowed to work long and hard at night and had already chopped more young trees for the wood pile than the Chases had had for many a year. His activities in this direction came to a swift halt when someone commented on the sudden growth of the log pile. Now he was having to be content with the rebuilding of the inside of one of the cattle sheds. His physique, which had been impressive before, was becoming monolithic. His rich burnished skin shone with his return to health, and the tight black curls on his round head gleamed with the animal fat he daily rubbed into it. His natural good humour made him excellent company and he was most warmly regarded by their hosts.

Tom, idle and weak with pain, gritted his teeth on the injury and flirted in tantalizing detail with the girl in his thoughts.

Two days after the conversation with Ben, Mistress Chase brought them a visitor. Moses was sleeping on his back, stretched out on a feather mattress on the floor at the end of the bed. His mouth was open and comfortable snores punctuated the peace of the room. Tom, drowsing as he listened to Moss' heavy breathing, started at the light tap on the door.

'Come in,' he called. It would take more than his voice to wake Moss now. Once he was asleep he would stay that way through thunder and lightning.

Mistress Chase put her head round the door. 'Are you respectable?' she said.

'As respectable as I shall ever be, ma'am,' Tom smiled, wondering why she should ask such a question when she usually walked straight into the chamber with scant warning.

'I have brought someone to look at your leg.' She stood aside and ushered in her guest. 'Don't worry about Moses there,' she said airily. 'He will sleep for hours yet. Master Tom, this is Dudie Smith. She has a wondrous way with bones and infections and if she can't get you on your feet, no one will.'

The girl came across to the bed smiling broadly.

Tom gaped at her in astonishment and she nodded her head at him, putting her basket on the covers by his elbow. 'Yes, Bor, it was I who bound your leg that day in Bosham. I felt badly about tripping over it as I did. Mistress Chase here has let it be known that she has an ailing relative in her best bedchamber. How are you now? You look a better colour.'

He was unable to say a word but just lay among his pillows, staring at her like any idiot youth. It was certainly his nameless angel of mercy, but today she was wearing a clean blue gown, there were boots on her feet and the wild mop of springy black curls was tied demurely away from her face with a bright green ribbon.

She was perfect; tiny, slim as a willow and with an elfin air of amusement in her heart-shaped face. She waited patiently for his reply, suffering his open-mouthed stare with a sparkle in her bright blue eyes which threatened any moment to burst into open laughter.

'Ma'am,' he finally mumbled, embarrassed at his lack of manners. 'I'm mighty glad to make your acquaintance. I didn't thank you that day for your kindly act . . . and I have your kerchief still –' *and would keep it*, added the look on his face.

She examined the leg, clucking under her breath over the swelling, and the swift and tender way in which she removed the dressings said all that was needed to be said about her skill. He watched as she took his knee in both her small cool hands. She closed her eyes and her fingers explored the puffy skin, fingertips and thumbs, testing every dent and bulge.

'The kneecap is definitely misplaced,' she said, opening her eyes. 'It would be best for me to manipulate it right away, if you can bear it, for the longer it is out of its cradle the harder it will be to get it back, especially as there is tissue infection there in any case.'

He nodded. She had a most provocative cleft in her chin and one dimple on the left side of her full mouth.

Moses snored on.

The two women bent over the knee, absorbed in its treatment. Tom lay back and watched Dudie Smith. She looked very foreign with all those dark curls and straight black eyebrows. Her skin was unusually clear and unblemished for a labouring woman, olive-tinted and healthy. She looked as though there was a strong splash of Spanish in her blood. Despite her gown and the well-brushed hair, she was still the lovely wild girl in a hurry who had haunted his thoughts since she had spoken to him. Fever and his pain had almost blotted her out – but now here was this different, clean and comely version of that memory and it was infinitely more fascinating.

The two women turned towards him.

'Would you mind if I try to shift the cap back into place now?' Dudie asked. He bowed his head in agreement. How could such a small girl have such an air of authority – and such enormous eyes. They seemed to dominate her whole face. Delphinium blue, two bright jewels framed in thickly curling black lashes. He sank into the warmth of their regard. She could do whatever she pleased with him and he would thank her for it.

He didn't thank her a moment later.

She placed her hands firmly on either side of the swollen knee, adjusted her weight, then with a sudden jerk she twisted the whole joint and he reared up with a yell that sprang Moses from his slumbers.

'I told you it would be painful,' she said with a grin.

'You didn't say how much, though,' he groaned, rocking back and forth on the bed, the blood roaring in his ears.

'Hey, what's goin' on here?' Moses complained. His eyes alighted on Dudie's broad grin and they smiled at each other. 'Hey, Brother! Why should *you* have all the nursing? Have you told this li'l lady 'bout the ache in ma shoulder?'

'Make your own introductions,' Tom groaned. 'That li'l lady has just about killed me . . .'

'Well, we'll just have to wait and see about the truth of that. Patience is nearly as good a healer as Dudie is,' Mistress Chase said soothingly. She too, had been startled by the sudden strength and speed of Dudie's attack on the knee joint. Poor Master Tom was now in great pain again, but the next twenty-four hours would show whether the girl had been successful in putting the kneecap back into place.

Dudie stood up and let Fran Chase usher her towards the door. Tom's head was still hunched over his leg.

'I'll be back to see how you are in a day or two,' she said lightly, bowing her head to Moses.

'What a little doll,' he sighed after she had gone.

Tom grunted. 'Your little doll half-murdered me,' he groaned, sliding back under the covers. It was some time before he would admit that she had done him any good at all. By that time he was, to his amazement, on his feet and hobbling round the chamber in considerably less pain.

Chapter Seven

Dudie came again to inspect the knee but not immediately. It was, Tom thought peevishly, as though she was deliberately staying away from the farm. The hours dragged through one day and then another and he wondered what had become of her. Pride forbade him to enquire. Moses talked dreamily of the small wild girl until Tom turned his face to the wall and the big man looked over at the humped figure in the bed thoughtfully. He had never known Tom Heritage to be ill-humoured before, not even in their worst moments. He guessed that the leg was only part of it and stilled his tongue.

Then, without warning, she was back again, whirling into the chamber like a breath of fresh air. She was clearly in a hurry this time and was wearing the same ragged skirt and shawl that Tom had first seen her in. She greeted them both with airy friendliness but there were two bright spots on her cheeks and her eyes were dancing, despite her casual attitude. Tom became visibly more cheerful.

She was pleased with the leg's progress though severe about her patient's new mobility. He took his scolding stoically. Moses was not slow to notice how, surprisingly, Tom's good spirits had returned as soon as she opened the chamber door.

'The tissue holding the kneecap in place is all torn and inflamed,' she said to him, tutting over the joint. 'If you try to use it before it is strong enough to support you, it will never heal. Stay in your chair by the fire – and if you are obliged to move, then hop . . .'

'Yes, ma'am. Whatever you say, ma'am.'

She was so small and fierce. She stood over him, jaw set in a determined jut and the bright blue eyes pinned him into his chair as though daring him at his peril to defy her. He fought a sudden desire to stroke the unruly tumble of her hair, untethered this day and falling about her shoulders in a cascade of dark waves. She and her brother Nat would be off to Portsmouth by the noon tide, taking pig iron across the harbour and returning with coal.

'I can't stay for long this time. Nat's goen' to be fretten' as it is.'

She was glad to be persuaded into accepting a cup of mint tea, all the same, before returning across the channel to the waiting barge.

'Dudie is an unusual name,' Tom said as they sat close to the fire's warmth with hands cupping mugs of steaming tea. He felt quite tonguetied now that she was here and could remember none of the things that he had discussed with her in the fantasies of his dreaming thoughts. She looked so small and vigorous sitting between the two men on a footstool, pink-cheeked and smiling. The day was so cold that there were delicate frost flowers engraving the insides of the casements with fronds of silvery fern.

'I was named Boudicca after a great warrior queen who fought the Romans here in Britain long ago.'

It was unexpected to discover an element of learning in this untutored girl. Tom was intrigued. 'What was the great attraction for her?'

She laughed at him. How transparent these gorgios were sometimes. 'How can I say, sir? The choice was my Puri Daia's, Saiforella Bayless. She had the book learnen' among us . . .'

Bayless.

He sat forward with a jerk that made him wince. 'Bayless? Are you another Bayless then?'

The smile was there again, sparkling with the pure enjoyment of this secret that she had been holding from him. 'My name is Boudicca Smith,' she said. 'The Romani people marry mostly amongst their own folk unless they wed a gorgio. The Baylesses are nearly pure Romani, save for Joshua Bayless who married Mother Hator. My Puri Daia was the sister of

your own granfer, Jess Bayless. We share our great grandparents, Jasper and Grace Bayless.'

She watched a flood of emotions chase through his still pale
face. The hair hung limply round his ears and there was no
sheen to it. It would be many weeks before his constitution
returned to full health.

'Do you know of Master Charles Bayless?'

Her eyes became watchful and the smile left her face. She
looked down into her cup of mint tea and gently swilled the
contents round. 'Yes . . . I know Master Bayless.'

For a moment she was very still as though the name had
turned her to stone. Then her head came up and there were
two bright spots in either cheek. She looked at once defiant
and vulnerable – and very young. The urge to touch her went
through him again.

'Why are ye so set upon haven' me tell you of these things?'
she asked him. 'Master Chase says you've bin quizzen' him
somethen' terrible about Lavenham. You were born to money,
Bor – and all the comforts you could wish for and never had
to struggle for your bread until you went to war. Why are
you prying through the Clan in this way? Why do you need
to know about us? You and your kind would not be proud,
sir, of admitten' to haven' gypsies for your kith and kin lest
it be to mock them.'

'That's where you are so wrong, Miss,' he said sharply.
'That may well be Master Bayless' reaction but it is not mine.
I have three sisters and a brother and we were, indeed, brought
up in an atmosphere of comfort and Godliness. But there has
always been a gap in our knowledge of our forbears on my
mother's side which caused a great curiosity in all of us, for
our parents were not inclined to be drawn on the subject.
Now, after all this time, coincidence or the fortunes of war,
what you will . . . brings me here, within sight of Apuldram
and my mother's beginnings – surely you cannot blame me
for a very natural interest. We are, after all, talking about my
flesh and blood.'

She looked at him solemnly over the rim of her cup. The
steam from the hot liquid curled up round her small nose and
vanished into her hair.

'What is it that had to be withheld from us all this time?' He hesitated and then went on, 'I am aware that my grandparents were brother and sister. Charles told me that. It was a shock at the time but I have heard of such things before, ungodly as they are. It has made me all the more concerned to know the rest.'

'It is the Gift, I suppose, that your mother felt she had to hide.'

He frowned at her, mystified.

She contemplated him thoughtfully for a moment and then seemed to make up her mind. 'All right, Bor, I shall tell you what I know. Have you ever felt the presence of the Gift? No, I see that it means nothing to you. Well, this is going to sound like a foolish, nay wicked, tissue of untruths but it is, I vow to you, no less than the absolute truth. Your granfer Jess was the seventh child of Jasper and Grace Bayless. They had nine children in all, every one a girl but for Jess. My Puri Daia was Saiforella, the eldest of them. Your Puri Daia was the youngest, Amy. They and Jasper's brothers and their families, worked the saltpans across the creek through the spring and summer of every year and then every October they took to the roads as all the travellen' folk do. This was the pattern of things for three generations

'When Jess was just a nipper, no more than five years old, he was in the woods over there, when something strange happened to him. There has never been an explanation of what took possession of him but he became another person from that day. He had the Sight of things to come, and was possessed of a wisdom not usual in little children – and above all, he had the Killing Glance.'

'What was that, for mercy's sake?'

She gave him a look of such sorrow at the touch of banter in his tone that he was instantly ashamed of his flippancy.

'He was able to kill by fixing his eyes on anything . . . animal or man, it made no difference. To have a gift like that is to bear a terrible burden.'

He looked at her and the intense expression on her face forbade ridicule. 'Go on,' he said gently. At the moment nothing made sense. It was more like a child's fairy tale.

'I know what is in your heart. I know how difficult it is for you to take such a statement seriously. I can only tell you that it is the truth and that there remains in the memories of too many people in these parts, the evidence of what I am telling you. Jess was the only member of the Clan to have grey eyes, it seems. The others were mostly brown except for Jasper and his brother Vasher who were blue-eyed. Those grey eyes seem to have had something to do with Jess' Gift, for he had two children by two blue-eyed women – and those children had his eyes . . . huge and grey and arresting with a most unusual beauty – but filled with that terrible Power. The interesting thing seems to be, so it was said in the family, that the Power gradually faded by the time they had grown to young adults. Certainly Jess was said to have lost it by the time he married Lavinia Freeland. He was a very good man, you know, and having become accustomed to his Sight, used it only for hunting or for night running, which was how he amassed his fortune. Now there are two separate things to tell you. First, the House he built . . . Lavenham. He built it, so he told the Clan, in the place where the thing occurred that altered him so. He raised it there to protect some old stones which he said were from some ancient shrine. Those stones lie within the foundations of the House today . . . and it would seem quite likely that it is they who have made of that House the place where no man will go.'

Tom nodded. 'At least I know the truth of that for Ben Chase was very positive in his loathing and fear of the House when I mentioned it to him.'

'Everyone in these parts feels the same,' she agreed. She put a hand lightly on his arm. 'Sir, I am not making up tales to amuse you. The curse that seems to be upon Lavenham and those raised there is all too real. Take Charles Bayless' father and your own mother. Violet Bayless was not actually born in the House as Lawrence was – but they were both conceived there – and they both had their father's strange eyes and the Power that went with it. It is fortunate for you that your mother was so close in character to her father, for she also learned to live with her Gift and if she used it as a child, no one knew of it for she was always a levelheaded and fine person, so tradition has it. Lawrence, on the other hand, was weak and spoilt and grew up into an evil man who had to flee this country to avoid the hangman's rope. Charles Bayless was the only son of his union with Donna Dolores. He was born in Portugal. His eyes are the same shade as yours, Master Tom ... not like mine, not like the blues and hazels and browns of the rest of the Clan. Yours and Charles' eyes are like those that carry the Power ... though neither of you shows signs of actually possessing it.'

Tom shivered. It all seemed too far-fetched for truth – and yet he was the only member of his own family to have his mother's eyes, it was true. 'Is there more?' he asked.

She shook her head. 'No. Isn't that enough? It is why, though, Charles was never permitted to go anywhere near Lavenham – and it is why we all beg and implore you to observe the same advice. You were not conceived on Lavenham soil which is probably why you are not infected by the wickedness there. But if you were to become involved with Lavenham, who knows what might happen.'

'And Charles. He has really never gone there, in spite of being brought up within sight of the place?'

She nodded. 'That is the truth. He is very unwilling ever to touch on the subject but he did say once – after he had discovered you aboard "Fortunée" – that his memory was completely blank and that he can recall nothing at all of the one time he tried to enter the place, as a small boy, save clinging to iron gates.'

'Dudie.' His attention had been diverted as she was speaking. 'Do you know Charles well?'

That still look came down over her face again. 'Well enough,' she said shortly. 'Ned an' I be worken' one of his coalen' barges. Why should we not know him?'

'Does he recognize you as kin?'

'Why should he not? We are.'

She would not be drawn further. It seemed to him that she had no great love for their cousin.

Tome and Moses had been in hiding at Park Farm for seven weeks before Tom was able to walk properly without a stick. His knee still ached if he put his weight on it for long, but by the time February came he was taking short evening walks in the deserted oakwoods which lined the shore.

It was nearly time for them to move on. They were strangers now to the emaciated bags of bones of a few short weeks before. Their bodies had filled out, their skin was losing the crops of boils which had formerly festered in every fold. Their hair had stopped falling out in tufts and grew with a new shine, proof that Mistress Chase's shampoo of ammonia, salts of tartar and tincture of bergamot was indeed the fine medication she vowed it to be.

Each evening in that dusky period which preceded nightfall, Tom exercised his leg, always using the same route along the banks of the Channel and each time forcing himself to go a little further. There were a few bright days when the wind was less boisterous and the late sun shone in slats of mellow golden light through the bare branches over his head and birds swooped as they settled, their fluting warbles echoing through the empty woodland. He walked with his eyes fixed on the bank on the east side of the Channel, always waiting for the House to reveal itself to him.

It was on a fine evening of almost springlike warmth that he found himself, through the tangle of brambles fringing the banks, almost level with a building on the opposite side. He stopped, pulses quickening, and stared across the fast-flowing water but, from where he stood, the roof appeared to be too low for it to be Lavenham. He moved along the bank, pushing through the dead leaves of last autumn's fall, until he was close to the edge of the water. He could see more clearly now, for the wild growth of elder and bare young oaks was patchy on the far bank. Over his head the woodland birds murmured and sang. The wood was warmly peaceful.

The building that he could now see more clearly across the stretch of silver water was one of several barns, squat and sturdily built. There was one large central barn around which the others were grouped. In summer they would be invisible from this shore, but now with the trees and bushes little more than bare skeletons, the outline of the once-thatched buildings was quite easy to distinguish. He thrust his way through the undergrowth to get a better view. A gaggle of old fruit trees now, gnarled and unkempt like ancient gossiping women round a fairground booth, bunched amongst a wilderness of saplings and dead creepers. He moved on, treading carefully amongst the thorny brambles – and suddenly it was there.

The old orchard seemed to draw back and with it the dying sun broke through light cloud and shone behind his head, filling his whole body with a warm radiance.

Even in such wild disarray the House was breathtakingly beautiful. It lay at the top of a wide incline which had obviously once been sloping lawns; an L-shaped House built of warm, yellow-grey stone with old-style casements and one huge gallery window which rose up almost to the roof eaves. The sun's orange light glinted like reflected fire upon its leaded panes, across which great ropes of bare creeper twisted and spread.

Lavenham.

A great excitement rose up in him. He stood and stared, his imagination stripping the unkempt overgrowth away from its walls and terraced front, clothing it once more in all the graciousness that had once been its right. 'Come over and look closer,' it seemed to beckon. 'The true heart of me is not the way that others see me. I was built to be lived in . . . cared about . . .'

The sun sank below the trees and blue shadows mantled the wood. The spell broken, his leg began to throb. He tore his eyes away from the House and retraced his steps, head bowed in thought.

'You've seen it, haven't you?' Moses said later.

They were in the kitchen having their evening meal with the Chases.

Tom nodded. 'I'm going over there,' he said.

Ben Chase put his hand over his wife's as she drew in her breath, eyes full of sudden alarm. 'Tell you what, then. Bain't no good tryen' to stop you when yer mind's clear made up . . . but go ye round the property only. Do not go inside the House.'

'I won't tarry there long,' Tom said, feeling the old people's fear. 'I just have to satisfy myself about one or two things and then I shall be ready to take that passage for France which you have so kindly fixed with Master Timms. Would you be good enough to row me across?'

'Now look ye here,' the old man began to bluster, anger cutting through his apprehension. 'If'n I row ye over in broad daylight it'll have to be to Dell Quay. No one goes within half a mile of that land. Even the old Hempsteddle field where Master Hamilton's built the dryen' barn 'ud be too conspicuous to land you. An' don't try and suggest us goen' over at dusk because I wouldn't even look at that place from this side of the creek once the sun's down.'

'Moses could row me in,' Tom said mildly.

Moses rolled his eyes and his chin began to quiver. 'Told you, Brother, I ain't agoing near that devils' place, neither. Not now nor any time – even fer you. I know when things are best left alone and this is surely one o' those times. Don't you go there.'

'I have to. I'm sorry but I just have to see Lavenham once to lay all the ghosts that are right here in my own heart.'

'Then go without me, Brother . . .'

Dudie came later that day.

She had ceased to be interested in Tom's knee for time and his own healing powers were the best medicine now. She came once or twice each week, they concluded, just to give the two of them some company, which they greatly appreciated, though Moses watched Tom's swiftly changing moods and had come to further conclusions also. He excused himself after a brief and friendly exchange and left them alone.

She sat herself in the windowseat and stared out at the cold grey afternoon. She was quiet this day. He noticed the shadows under her eyes as though she had not slept.

'I have seen the House,' he said and waited for the surprise to animate her face. She turned from the window and there was nothing but sadness in her.

'It is calling to you, Bor,' she said and her voice was almost a whisper. 'It is a great black spider in the centre of a beautiful web hung with drops of dew like stars. Such a wondrous thing, that web . . . one of nature's most precious treasures. All the same, it is nothing better than a death trap for the flies that are lured there. That is how Lavenham is. Do not be enticed there by a beauty as dangerous as that.'

He was suddenly exasperated. They were all of them one more doleful than the other where that place was concerned.

'For pity's sake, why can't any of you understand!' he said impatiently. 'I have no desire to go and live there – *ever*. My home is in New England. My only wish is simply to go there for maybe half an hour and look over the old place before I leave. I will disturb nothing. I will take nothing. I wish only to *see*! What possible harm can there be in that?'

She might not have heard him. She had turned her head away and was once more staring out of the window. 'How sad nature is at this time of the year,' she murmured, watching droplets of rain casting shining trails down the casement. 'The earth is bare and barren. There is no colour anywhere but shades of grey and the air is full of rain and gales. Nothen' agrowen' yet. Nothen' to eat from the woods.'

'You do sound sad, Dudie. What ails you?' He came over to her from the fireplace and gently stroked the unruly tumble of her hair. She leaned back against him and there was a droop to her that he had not seen before.

'What is wrong? I don't like to see you look so. I'm sorry if I shouted at you. I've had that place on my mind for so long that I have shut out anyone else's thoughts and problems. It's not like you to be low in spirits. You always brighten up our days, Moss' and mine, whenever you come and see us.'

She straightened her back then and smiled up at him. She took both his hands in hers and turned them over, tracing the lines in his palms. 'You have a great deal of luck in your life,' she said, searching his right hand.

He grinned at her. 'I've heard about people who think they see another's lifespan in the handlines. Never thought *you* were that way, though.'

She looked up at him. Her face was serious. 'Don't scoff at things you don't understand, Bor. My Dadrus and my Puri Daia could read the hand. I have been able to do it for as long as I can remember. Treat it how you will.'

She turned back to his hand lying warm in hers. 'Here you see, here is your life line. It is a good line, though thin at this point. It says that during the third decade of your life you will be in poor health. Is it not true, Simensa, for you have been a prisoner and your body has been deprived of its health? And,' she smiled, 'you are in your third decade right now.'

He was impressed.

'Here is your health line . . . and here the heart line. You will not have many *affaires* of the heart, I see – but whoever you give yourself to, there will be truth and sincerity in the relationship. How different . . .' She stopped and turned away from him.

'Dudie . . . dearest Cousin,' he said very gently. 'Something really bad is troubling you, I can see it. Please tell me. I would like to help you if I can in any way, for you have been such a good friend and have brought me back to full health with such skill. What is the matter? Unburden yourself, please . . .'

She turned to him then and the blue eyes were bright stars of unshed tears. She drew away from him slightly and sat very straight in the windowseat. 'It is the thing that all women who are subject to harsh masters dread the most,' she said simply. 'I am with child.'

Warm winds for two days and the sporadic appearance of the sun were beginning, at last, to bring the first green shoots up out of the cold earth. Night was a shining darkness with no moon or stars but a strange clarity in the great vault of the velvet sky.

Moses rowed strongly, eyes down with deep concentration. A woollen scarf was wrapped round his head and nothing of his face but the whites of his eyes was visible. The tight hunch of his shoulders voiced his unwillingness to be there at all.

They crossed the Channel, butting through the choppy water until they were in the lea of the east bank. They rowed into the incoming current then, keeping close to the overlap of foliage that trailed into the water at high-tide. At the point where the reeds and bushes thinned, Moses raised his head and worked his right oar so that the boat nosed round through the rushes and its keel ground into the mud.

'Farmer says this's Hempsteddle field. I'm sure as sure not going further than this, Brother,' he said grimly. 'You insist on this tomfoolery, so go ahead an' I'll wait for you here. But just you remember, you not returned here in two hours an' I'm going back to the Farm, see?'

He watched as Tom clambered out over the bow, splashed

through two paces of shallows and scrambled up the bank.

'*Moss.*' His whispered voice sounded rough in the silence. There was only a slight movement of the air to rustle through the reeds. 'Moss . . . Thanks, friend. I won't be long.'

Moses strained his eyes as Tom's crouching figure moved along the bank.

Then he was gone.

The night was very quiet. Somewhere in the heart of the woods something squealed once. Moses shivered and hugged himself, trying to control the trembling in his limbs which had little to do with the cold.

There was a curious clarity to the night as though moonlight lit the way, but there was no moon. Tom moved slowly down the long field, keeping close to the hedge as he saw the lights of a cottage beyond the far boundary. The dark mass ahead had to be the Lavenham woods for there was nothing south of Hempsteddle but the Lavenham grounds and buildings and beyond them, the oakwoods that screened the House and grounds from Ayles' saltpans. He moved carefully, for his leg was still weak and he must not fall and damage himself now. Lavenham today – and then away to France . . . and home.

The ground was suddenly more springy under his feet. He bent down and felt shorter grass. He was on ground which had been differently husbanded. His foot snagged in something hidden under the dead undergrowth – the remains of a fence post which had broken off close to the ground. He felt the rotten wood and crumbled it between finger and thumb. A rectangular shape loomed out of the night to his left and he turned towards it, pushing his way through thicket which tore at his hair and cloak. Round his neck hung the little lantern that Mistress Chase had insisted he carry. The tinder-box lay snugly in his belt pouch. There must be no light until he was well inside the grounds. Then it would either not be seen at all – or put down to Lavenham demons . . .

He stood still, feeling the hardness of cobble through grass under his feet. The sighing of the night air in the trees had faded away into total silence. The blood sang strongly in his ears. He felt, rather than saw, the buildings on three sides of him. There was none of the expected menace in the night around him, no feeling of skin-prickling warning. He lit the little lantern and raised it up over his head.

He was in a weed-choked barnyard. Ahead of him loomed a massive Dutch barn, its great doors barred with rusted iron staves. To the right of it jutted a two-storied wing, to the left an archway joining it with another building forming three sides of a square. The stable yard where the legendary Lavenham horses had been bred for racing? He swung his lantern back to the archway and moved across the thistle-choked yard towards it.

A slight gust of wind played round his cloak as he emerged into what must have been the main driveway. The black silhouette of the House loomed before him. He swished through tall grass and dead thistle, while trailing fronds of bramble clawed at his legs. His boot tripped on an unseen step. There were three, wide and shallow and he climbed them carefully and found himself on a stone terrace with graceful urn-shaped balusters skirting it.

He stood at the top of the steps and raised his lantern high. The House towered over him, the arms of its L-shape enclosing him. The mellow Bembridge stone was crisscrossed with great swathes of unruly creepers, stretching the length of the building, covering the windows, drooping almost to ground level over the massive oak door at the entrance.

He tested his senses. Nothing warned him of unseen dangers. The night was quiet, holding its breath, for now there was no sound of wind sighing in the trees beyond. The House waited.

He limped across to the door, tearing at the tangle of leafless creeper and tried the iron handle.

It moved. Time had rusted the catch and hinges but, unbelievably, it was not locked. He put his shoulder to the wood panelling and flung his weight against it. It resisted and then moved slowly as though it were held from within. The grating of the rusted hinges protested hollowly inside as he staggered forward, clutching his lantern, the weak leg wobbling beneath him.

*

The Watcher groaned, feeling the familiar sliding beginning all over again. The pain in his hands faded and he was standing at the top of the stairs.

He was here after all. Another piece of the jigsaw from which he was fashioned. There was nothing in this one that spelled out that recipe for disaster to which the House would cling. No extremes of emotions on which it could feed. Yet there WAS something gathering about them both. He probed the deepest recesses of the House and his heart sank. Recognition came to him suddenly and the blood turned cold in him for there was nothing that he could do to help this one since he presented no case for death.

Tom stood in the hall, swinging the lantern above his head. It was a large, galleried place with the sweep of a broad staircase ascending over the entrance door. There was a capacious hearth and three doors to left and right. Dust and dried leaves had been driven by gusty draughts into swirling drifts about the paved floor. Countless tiny creatures had passed and repassed, leaving the faint print of their passage in trails in the carpet of dust.

Someone had destroyed a long dining table in the centre of the room, smashing it into two splintered halves which lay on their sides.

He sniffed the air, aware of great silence without menace or fear. There was only the faintest odour of mould and damp but it was overlaid by another stronger scent, of sweet basil . . . lavender . . . something soft and essentially womanly.

The House waited quietly, presenting each of its secret beauties as the soft light of the lantern picked out finely-carved dining chairs, a serving table on which was a clutter of blackened platters and cutlery and a great bowl in its centre. Tom picked up a plate and rubbed the middle of it thoughtfully with a damp finger. A dull gleam of silver was his reward. He stared at it for a moment and then gently replaced it exactly as he had found it.

In one corner stood a clock, its delicate filigree hands stopped at ten minutes past nine. He held the lantern up close to its ornate face, marvelling at the quality of the inlaid marquetry in its walnut case and the finely-painted swathe of flowers interwoven round each of the numerals.

Ten past nine. In the morning or the evening? Had it stopped when the people had been driven out or had it just died when the mechanism ran down?

He explored every room, losing track of time as he discovered a treasure trove of beautiful furniture whose woods still glowed as he rubbed the dust from their surfaces. Nothing had been disturbed and they were as they had been left by his mother all those long years ago. It made him feel suddenly close to her.

'Don't go away yet, Mama,' he said to her. 'Be there at home when I get back. I shall at last be able to talk to you about all this. I shall be able to tell you that whatever was here is gone now.' For it had. Of that he was certain, for every breath he took he could feel the welcome gathering in the darkness beyond the glow of the lamplight.

Up the wide stairs the landing opened into another spacious galleried hall. There were pictures along the passage to the bedchambers, but his excitement led him past them with scarcely a glance. He could examine them more closely later. The rooms were like some forgotten fairy tale, for the beds were made up, their linen and blankets dusty but still good. There was one room which warmed him in particular with wondrously intricate carvings of fruit and flowers on the inside of its door. The bedhangings were heavily embroidered, the once brilliant colours now faded into gentle age. The panelling on the walls was pale linen fold stripped oak. A cushion in the wing chair beside the empty hearth had a finely worked 'V' in its centre. He knew with absolute certainty that this had been his mother's chamber.

He sat down carefully in the chair, for his leg had begun to throb. He rested his arms on its comfortable padded sides and closed his eyes. The room enfolded him. Even up here was that faint scent of lavender in the musty air and something touched him lightly on the forehead. He opened his eyes but the room was empty, save for the furniture dear to a young girl's heart and the almost audible beating of his own. It must have been a cobweb. He settled back to rest for a little while, loath to leave this peaceful haven which could so easily protect him if he should wish it.

He dozed and dreamed of loving hands stroking his face. Lavenham. Here at last and only loving ghosts after all, to make him welcome. It was such a perfect refuge and he just couldn't leave it right away. There was so much here to examine, so many treasures lying rotting. They might be able to transport one or two back to Boston. No one would come hunting for them at Lavenham with its legends still remembered. Moses must be persuaded to join him – just for a short while. Then he would go back to Boston content.

A fresh wind blew in from the sea about midnight. Moses felt it and knew that a storm was gathering somewhere out in the ocean wastes. Tom had been gone for too long. What was he about? Where was he? Had something happened to him? The questions chasing through his head went unanswered. Only one thing was certain.

He should have gone to that Godless place with him.

If there was no sign of him by dawn he would have to row back to the Farm and get help. He tried to control the tremble in his body at the thought of entering any part of that wicked place. Maybe Dudie could be found and persuaded to help. Maybe the Snake would have to be brought into it, after all. Even imprisonment in the Black Hole aboard 'Fortunée' was better than being torn asunder by some dreadful Force as it had destroyed those clerics.

Trying to keep his mind from the possible consequences of Tom's curiosity, Moses did his best to plan his next move if he did not appear before the fast-approaching dawn.

PART TWO

Dudie and Charles

Chapter One

He woke with the sound of his own cry echoing in his ears. He lay on his back and felt the sweat clinging to the warm flannel of his nightshirt. His heart was still pounding hard against his ribs and he made himself breathe slowly and deeply through his nose to try and bring it back to a normal pace.

The odour of his terror was sour in his nostrils.

It was the third time he had had the nightmare in the last month. He wiped the moisture from his face with a corner of the padded coverlet. It was not just the perspiration of his fear but tears also . . . the tears of a small, terrified boy and as always, his mind was even now closing upon the reasons for that fear, blocking all memory of the experience within moments of waking.

He had lived with this same, doggedly repetitious nightmare for as long as he could remember. When he was a small boy his mother, not understanding what lay behind them, had been distressed by his recurring terrors and, ever-protective of her only child, had taken him after each disturbance into her chamber and into her own bed for the remainder of the night. He had always been reassured by her warm and loving presence, but as he grew older she had begun to find his nocturnal daemons irritating and did her best to scold him out of them with little success. They still happened with the same ferocity. He was obliged, after his thirteenth birthday, to battle with his terrors alone.

They were always the same, these fantasies. A yawning cave of a place, cold and dark and filled with stealthy movement beyond his vision. Without warning, every one of his senses was suddenly assaulted with appalling horror, for in the air about him, emanating from harsh slashes of light, was the deep-throated drone of bees . . . small, vicious flying things which gradually formed themselves into a single deadly weapon of death.

Stench of an indescribable filth assailed his nostrils, making him retch and above his head, descending a shadowy staircase, was a figure that floated like woodsmoke. There was no firm shape to this central entity save for the impression of hatred in the angular blur of its face. Such loathing exploded in an uncontrolled babbling . . . a jumble of shrieking words which drilled themselves into him and shrivelled his very soul.

'*GET OUT OF THIS HOUSE, LAWRENCE . . . WHITE SPAWN OF A GOAT'S EXCREMENT . . . FILTH OF A DEAD COW'S WOMB . . . DRABANEY SAPA, SHAV . . . SHAVA NE KENNER . . .*'

There was no meaning to some of the words but they were always the same, always spat at him with such utter detestation that, by the time he came to manhood, they were engraved, without comprehension, upon the subconscious areas of his soul. In the wake of those words, the droning burst upon him and the bees were all about him, crawling on his body, his arms and legs, face and eyelids and the terrible agonising sword thrusts of their stings were a million burning daggers pumped into his flesh.

He screamed – and screaming, could not stop and his hands stretched out to ward them off and he took hold of iron bars and shook them with all his might . . .

And woke, shivering and terrified for the instant before consciousness drove out the memory of what it was that brought him to such a state . . . It was all the stranger that the whole thing was gone from him soon after he woke and it was never possible for him to remember the details of the dream in the morning – only that he was a child alone in that place and utterly, stupefyingly terrified.

He smiled bitterly, remembering the blessed relief and comfort of snuggling close to his mother's warm body and feeling her strength slowly wearing away the terror.

It was the memory of that warmth that had moved him to

wed Leonie Farndell. The choice had not been a good one. Oh, she had done her best, there was no doubt of that. She had given him two sons and regarded him with lofty respect – but she was too weak, both spiritually and physically, to retain his interest. A delicate chest in youth had quickly turned her into an invalid, becoming more so with every winter that passed.

She also appeared to be increasingly nervous in his presence. There was no offer of comfort from her now, no refuge from the terrors which still assailed him. She had always been frightened by the ferocity of his anguish and removed herself from his bed quite early in the marriage, after the birth of John, the second son.

It was the private shame of a lifetime that Charles Freeland Bayless was still, in middle life, so afraid of the dark that it was a nightly act of bravery to climb into his single bed. Weeks would pass and his sleep would be so deep and dreamless that the tension eased and he was able to go about his business with vigour and enthusiasm. Then it would be upon him again and with the shock of his waking, the fear would gnaw at him for days and nights afterwards. He had never, though, had a recurrence of them so close upon the last – as was happening to him now. Coming as they did, so soon after the other recent shock in his life, he began to wonder whether they were actually generated by it in some way.

It was soon after he had accepted the contract for supplying victuals to the three prison hulks in Langstone Harbour that the incident occurred which he would later think of as a milestone in his life. At the time, the position had seemed an excellent project, for he had contacts aplenty from his own Import Company with warehouses at Emsworth and Bosham. He was involved in various businesses, the most productive being the coaling transport with its yard at Dell Quay. It was common knowledge that the contractors for the Transport Office were generally a thieving breed of opportunists who made their fortunes from short-shifting the ration allowances and pocketing the difference. With this in mind, Charles Bayless set about creating for himself a shining reputation for fair dealing. It was, admittedly, a calculated move rather than one generated by honesty, for it would do more to enhance his reputation in other spheres than could any other single act.

The second time he visited 'Fortunée' with the Burgoo rations, the Master, Herbert Furze, said casually to him, 'One of our inmates shares your name, Master Bayless. I made so bold as to question him about it. His mother was called Bayless and came from this area. Any of your folk emigrate to New England in the past?'

Charles hid his surprise. 'No, Master Furze. I think not,' he replied coldly.

'The fellow doesn't bear much resemblance to you, I'll say that – so it must just be a coincidence.' He sounded disappointed, cheated out of a fine topic of conversation which might well have proved embarrassing for this cool and pallid gentleman.

It was no concern of Herbert Furze, whose gossipy tongue would have made much of such a situation, Charles thought with distaste, but it was common knowledge in the family that Aunt Violet Bayless had married Master Desmond Heritage of Boston and had fled from Lavenham after the tragedy there. It was, of course, quite possible that this prisoner had something to do with that family.

It was when he was going through the roll call for the next soap ration that he discovered the prisoner's actual identity.

Thomas Bayless Heritage. Aged thirty-two years, of Midhurst, out of Boston, Massachusetts. Son of Desmond Heritage of that city. Captured on 2 November 1799 from the rebel vessel 'Free States' in which he was First Mate.

He gazed at the inky scrawl with a queer sensation in his stomach. His had been a calm and regular upbringing from the moment that Mama had arrived in England from her native Portugal, following his father's death at sea. She had come straight to Great Uncle John Freeland at Apuldram, as Papa had instructed – and had met with abiding kindness and a lifetime of financial protection both from him, and from Papa's only sister – the distant Aunt Violet across the ocean.

The Colonial aunt, Papa's half-sister, had paid for his

education and he had not disappointed her trust in him. There was, so the elders told him, something of his grandfather Jess in him for he worked hard as a young man. There was no talk of Lawrence Bayless, though – for who would wish to call Father a man wanted for treason and murder on the high seas?

Charles observed Tom Heritage thereafter at his leisure. Quite apart from the man's general state of debilitation, they could not have been less alike, but then Lawrence and Violet had been that way also. The comparison made him feel strangely close to this unknown cousin.

He had long been aware that his own unusually pallid features were repellent to some, although women often appeared drawn to him. Tom, wasted though he was, a dried pea rattling in the husk of his shrivelled frame, was dark-haired and olive-skinned and there were still the remnants of dash and swagger about him that told of a confidence in himself which had not been eroded by his present situation.

Strange that the one feature they shared should look so different on each of them, for his own grey eyes simply added to the impression of an almost fishlike colourlessness, whereas in Tom they were an arresting and attractive attribute which he used, with his ready smile, to great advantage.

The younger man had all the natural assets which were lacking, Charles knew, in himself – and yet, without knowing anything more about him, he was drawn to Tom Heritage. There was something most likeable and charming about this unsuspecting Colonial cousin.

When Tom was brought into the Furze household to tutor the Master's dull children, he was made aware of their family ties by that boor, Furze. No word was spoken but the recognition was there at the back of Tom's eyes on the few occasions when their paths crossed. Because of his situation as a prisoner, Tom waited for Charles to make the first acknowledgement, and Charles, ever devious but increasingly eager to talk with his newly-found relative, made contact in covert manner through Mistress Furze. She was a good and sensible woman, not given to chattering unwisely as was her husband.

His curiosity about the Boston family – and Aunt Violet in particular, filled Charles' thoughts more and more. Sooner or later he would have to see Tom Heritage and identify himself.

It was while Charles and Leonie were dining at Sibford one night that the idea of a wager was discussed. The Tankervilles were an energetic, modish couple who lived every day on the crest of some adventure of their own making. One day it was ballooning over the South Downs, another it was racing a fleet of private yachts round the Isle of Wight. On the evening in question it was decided that Sholto Harris, the mighty wrestler who was also a Sibford herdsman, should fight a contestant from one of the Langstone hulks. The idea caused quite a stir amongst the guests for the hulks and their ill-assorted cargo were a constant source of romantic curiosity to all who saw them lurking like monstrous black hunchbacks in the remoter corners of the Southern estuaries. A visit aboard for a closer look at the prisoners would be a fascinating diversion.

Arranging the contest proved to be more difficult than had first been imagined. 'No one could be found to volunteer aboard 'Ceres', 'Captivity' or 'Portland' – for none of the men were fit enough to fight anyone other than each other . . . until Master Furze finally offered a mighty negro wrestler from 'Fortunée' – and the wager was on.

Charles was thinking about the doubtful justice of such a contest as he went about his rounds of the coaling barges. He had recently taken on six new bargees and was surprised this day to see that one of them appeared to be a woman. He stood on the edge of the wooden jetty at Dell Quay, watching the baskets of coal being filled from the tar-black barge moored alongside, hauled up to the quay on heavy sisal ropes the width of a man's arm, and stowed into the line of waiting carts. As each cart received its load it moved away, pulled by four huge Suffolk Punches and another took its place.

He saw again that the slight figure at the tiller of the barge below him had a definite female shape.

'Hey, you . . . what are you doing there?' he called down into the boat. Six faces looked up at him; faces blackened by coaldust so that the features were blurred and only the eyes retained their sparkle. She pointed to herself and he nodded.

'Your clerk took me on with me brother Nat, yer Honour.

132

I'm a good navigator an' he said that he could get another sack of coal from the weight saved in the boat.'

She grinned up at him, a smutty, ragged creature, entirely lacking in the deference expected of her, an air of cheeky independence in every line of her small body. She put her head on one side and regarded him intently as though she was perfectly confident of winning any battle of words they might have.

He shrugged and turned away. If the clerk had hired her, she must be of some use to him.

He saw the girl again the following day as he rode out from Chichester to Dell Quay. She was walking ahead of him along the road from Chichester with a man at her side, a large basket of groceries on her head. The coaldust had been wiped from both their faces and he was struck by the similarity in their straight backs and features. He must be the brother of whom she had spoken. He had a brief impression of black hair and two pairs of piercing blue eyes raised to his before he was past the two well-laden figures. He lifted his crop in greeting and was rewarded by that flashing smile again. It stayed with him for the rest of the day.

He had the nightmare that night and, waking, found himself yearning for the comfort of a warm and loving refuge. Sparkling blue eyes and those long, strong arms about him . . . He took her image and held it, burying his face in the memory of that riot of blue-black hair.

They were gypsies, Nat and Boudicca Smith. They had been travelling in the southern forests and now were camped on the Common beside the River Lavant. They had presented themselves to the Dell Quay Office when Nat had heard that boatmen were being recruited for Master Bayless' new barges.

Gypsies had always intrigued him secretly for there was gypsy blood in him which was never referred to by the Freelands – nor by his mother, who knew of the story but, being from Portugal, had no clear conception of what a gypsy was.

Grandpapa Bayless had been a gypsy – albeit a wealthy one – or else he would not have been permitted to wed Lavinia Freeland. His blood still rankled in the family, though, so that

Charles had been reared to conceal that relationship, to feel ashamed of it. He had, nevertheless, always nursed a deep curiosity concerning his Bayless relations and because they were considered undesirable they assumed an exciting importance in his mind.

'Who were they? Where did they live these days? What was their situation? These questions had never been answered. Now, as casually as he was able, he rode up onto Apuldram Common in search of the Smiths' encampment.

Summer softened the barren lines of the common. The few trees, huddling close to the river banks, had been fashioned into strange shapes by winters of fierce gales off the sea and grew at a slant, their tops scythed and leafless. Closer to the ground new grass was a thick verdant green and the hawthorn bright with pink and white blossom. He came upon the little camp in the shelter of a stand of young birches, the lace of their upper branches heavy with 'witches knots'. A covered waggon was tucked into a flat strip of chalky ground where the curving bank of the stream sloped down to the water's edge. Two shaggy ponies looked up at him briefly as he slid off his well-groomed chestnut and knotted the reins round the silvery bowl of a tree.

Beneath the waggon a long-nosed lurcher dog growled at him, crouched behind one of the wheels. The fellies and spokes were painted in bright slashes of yellow and red.

The girl was there. She was squatting over a fire, behind the waggon, stirring something in a large iron pot. She looked up as he appeared and rose to her feet at the sight of him. She waited for him to approach her, standing quietly beside the bricked-in hearth with all the dignity of a small duchess in her own withdrawing room.

He raised his hat. 'Good morrow. I was crossing to Fishbourne and saw your waggon there,' he said, suddenly feeling less certain of his excuses than he would have liked.

She smiled then and her face was suddenly alight with impishness. There was no indication of archness or servility. 'Sar shan,' she said.

Her voice was deep for one so small. There was a softness, a huskiness there that he found delightfully pleasing.

'My clerk tells me that you and your brother are gypsies,'

he said, standing across the fire from her. A trail of thin blue smoke curled up between them. Something in the cooking pot smelt of bruised herbs.

She inclined her head and then pointed at the grass slope. 'Sit you down, sir. Will you take some refreshment at our hearth?' She glanced toward the waggon and back at him, making assessments. 'Nat, he be over to the Quay. Should be back soon if it were him you was seeken'.'

He unclipped his cloak, shrugged it off his shoulders and settled himself down in the springy grass. 'I'd love some,' he said, sniffing the aroma appreciatively. 'No, it's not Nat especially that I came to see. Maybe you could solve the puzzle as well as he.'

Her hair fell over her face in a heavy drape of unchecked waves and soft curls. She brushed it back over her shoulders and hurried across to the waggon. In a moment she was back, two large mugs in her hands. She dipped a ladle into the steaming liquid, poured it neatly into a mug and held it out to Charles.

He sat, cupping it in both hands. 'What is your name?'

She smiled at him. 'Boudicca Smith, sir.'

'I've not seen you or your brother in these parts until recently. Have you come far?'

She was squatting beside the hearth again, poking at the glowing embers with a short iron prong. Her hands were small and brown but very narrow, long-fingered – strong. 'Well, Bor, we always travels in a circle, see. We keep on the move except when we've work to do in any place and then we stays until we have enough saved up and can move on to the next place.' She grinned at him, quirking finely-drawn black eyebrows at him. 'Never outstay our welcome, Simensa, if you see what I mean.'

It was very pleasant sitting in the shade of silver-dappled birch trees, sipping a strange and delicious concoction and listening to the soft husky tones of this small ragged, fascinating girl.

'You have a strange language,' he said. 'What does "Simensa" mean.'

She grinned at him again and her eyes danced. She had a deep cleft in her chin and she rubbed it. 'Cousin,' she said.

Her face became serious, the clown's grin hidden away for the moment. 'Simensa means cousin of our people.'

'Do you call all visitors to your hearth "cousin" then? A very friendly term. I like it well.'

She shook her head, bouncing the sunlight off the shining waves of her hair. Laughter returned to her eyes. 'Not *anyone*, Bor. Just you.'

They sat on either side of the fire, searching each other's faces through the thin ribbon of woodsmoke.

'I'm sorry,' he said at last. 'I don't understand you.'

'Think then, Cousin. Did no one ever tell you that you get your name from Romani folk?' She smoothed the front of her brown woollen skirt with careful fingers. 'Put it this way, if you will. Your Granfer Jess Bayless an' my Great Granmer were brother and sister. He was seventh child in a family of nine, the only boy. My Great Granmer was Saiforella Bayless, the oldest daughter of Jasper and Grace Bayless.'

She sat back on her heels, calmly watching the impact her words were having upon this coolly elegant gorgio. 'Under all your nice clothes an' learnen' – you're still a Bayless, Bor. Just like Nat an' me.'

He sat like a figure of stone, shock, outrage and fascination chasing each other across his face.

'I know,' she said calmly. ' 'Tis a great shame to claim you for cousin when you see me with the coal dirt of your barges under my nails. Nat an' me, we're no great cop, are we?' She watched the shock slowly fade from his face. 'We've not come here to shame you, sir. We only stayed by chance when Nat heard that there was work offered. No one will know from either of us of the blood we share.'

She put out her hand and placed it squarely over his. For a second he would have snatched it away from her but she regarded him steadily with neither insolence nor familiarity. The warmth from her small palm steadied him and he took the hand and held it in both of his and from it there seemed to flow a strength which softened his rejection, permitting him to relax. Her eyes lifted and looked beyond him. She took her hand away to push the hair from her eyes again.

'Here's Nat, come back at last,' she said and there was a

faint regret in the way she said it that remained as a tantalising echo in his mind after he had left them.

He threw his mount's reins to the stable lad and strode into the house from the yard door, his steps echoing down the passage as he went.

'Ah, there you are, Charles. We wondered what was keeping you.' There was a suggestion of petulance in his wife's voice as she looked up from her chair as he put his head round the withdrawing room door. She was entertaining four other ladies and a portly elderly gentleman wearing a most unfashionable periwig and frockcoat. Charles, hovering in the doorway, bowed to the ladies.

'Good afternoon to you, Mistress Wood, Miss Audrey, Miss Cecily, Mistress Pescod . . . How are you, Parson?'

'Will you not join us then, my dear?'

He shook his head at his wife, his eyes cold. 'Forgive me if you will, but I must change and take the carriage over to Goodwood. I have business with His Lordship at six o'clock. I shall have a word with Freeland and John before I leave. Excuse me, if you please.'

He bowed again and closed the door on the chorus of disappointment. Damned old maids' tea parties were not for him. He took the stairs two at a time. Really, he was feeling remarkably happy. What an extraordinary meeting that had been, out there on the Common. What a fetching little thing his gypsy cousin was . . . and how pleasant her brother Nat also. A silent, watchful man but there had been no animosity in him. If anything, the animosity had come from Charles himself at first. Rough and untutored peasants, that is what the Smiths were and yet it was astounding to discover, as they told him of their blood ties, such simple pride that he had left them with the distinct impression that they truly thought it was he who should feel honoured to claim relationship with the Hator Tribe.

There were portraits in ornate gilded frames on the stair wall, mostly of Leonie's Farndell relatives, and a couple of Freelands. A huge chandelier hung from the roof in the curve of the stair. Its crystal droplets and flower petals glittered in a million reflected diamonds from its candle sconces. He had been proud of that purchase for it was similar to a fine pair in the ballroom at Sibford. Now, suddenly, it looked a little ostentatious. He thought of the brother and sister at rest beside their camp fire with the gentle pink light of the embers tinting their olive skins. What a contrast. What a yawning chasm existed between his kind of life and that of the Smiths. Looking round the door of his sons' schoolroom at the two boys lounging in leather chairs with a table of cards between them, he wondered whether they might not have been much happier if they had been toasting chestnuts with Nat and Dudie.

It was not difficult to check on the Smiths and their movements, after that. A quick glance at the manifest books in the Office at Dell Quay gave him all the information he needed to know. Dudie only went over to Portsmouth with the barge when the cargo was on the maximum load line. There were many days when Nat worked on his own with the other men. Charles soon discovered that on these days he would often be gone all night, for he caroused with his companions in the taverns, and if there was a woman to be had, would stay with her.

He returned to the camp often after that first day, drawn by the warmth of his welcome from both Dudie and Nat, and telling himself that it was just to hear the talk of his forbears and the fascination of this life of theirs which was so different, so unfettered compared with his own. At the back of his mind the other reason hid behind his fear of it. It grew a little every time he was with her.

He discovered that he learned something new with every visit. He was always given the same cup and plate when he ate with them. 'A man and a woman must never use the same dishes,' Nat explained. 'If I ate from Dudie's plate or you drank from her mug it would be Mokada. It is Mokada if a woman steps across the plate of food you may leave on the ground. Then both the food and the plate must be destroyed. It is Mokada to eat the flesh of a fox, a cat, a rat. These creatures are unclean, for they are meat-eaters.'

138

The Romanies, he discovered, lived off the land and ate mostly fruit, nuts and fish with the occasional bird or hedgehog when the season was fruitful. Anything with bristles was clean and therefore acceptable to eat; the wild boar, pig and hedgehog – but even then the meat had to be cured with salt and saltpetre for several hours.

The rules were absolute.

They were never disobeyed.

It was one of the main strengths of the Tribe.

The Smiths considered gorgios like himself – and all his cultured contemporaries, to be unclean in their habits and their hearts. To live in a house was to live in your own filth. Romanies moved all the time, rested on fresh grass and harboured no germs about them. They bathed in spring and summer and kept their bodies clean, as the Romans used to do. They suffered from fewer illnesses and lived longer than the gorgios. Their teeth were less inclined to decay and fall out. Their breath was sweeter. They considered themselves to be leading better lives than the gorgios and harboured no envy in their hearts.

Charles, astounded by this new angle upon his life, was inclined, upon reflection, to agree with them.

In the weeks that followed he talked at length to Dudie about his life – about the father of whom he had been brought up to be more ashamed than of his Romani blood: 'I know that the events of his life brand him for his wickedness but I still can't help feeling that something must have goaded him. Aunt Mary Freeland is old but there is nothing the matter with either her memory or her senses and she always recalls him with great affection.'

It was, Dudie saw, desperately important for Charles to discover the good in his father. The uncanny likeness between them, judging by the only portrait he had of Lawrence as a boy, made him constantly doubt his own motives in the most trivial instances. He wanted, she saw, to be a good man – and for it to be seen that he was so.

'Our Daia always thought that Lawrence Bayless was driven to distraction by his Aunt, Amy,' she said, feeding the eagerness with which he received her words. 'Remember what currents must have been present in that Kenner, for there were two women each with a child, both loved by the man under whose roof they lived together. Amy was crippled and had suffered from an attack by a gorgio in her youth. She had more pressures upon her than had Lavinia . . . in fact, Amy herself was Lavinia's only problem until the House began to destroy her. Would you not think it likely that Amy would lose no opportunity to hurt Lavinia through Lawrence?'

Then there was Amy's daughter, the ever-absent Aunt Violet. 'Did the Clan know much of her?'

His curiosity was unquenchable for she had done so much to fashion, through his education, the person he was now.

'Violet was always a Romani at heart,' Dudie said. 'Much is known of her for she was very much the daughter of Jess Bayless – and Jess has long been one of the strongest figures – after Mother Hator – in the lore of our Clan story. Violet might still be alive, over there in Americky. She was so strong, that one . . . so clear in her ways. She was good to all the family and sent money when our Puri Daia died. In that letter she spoke of her happiness with the gorgio she was wed to – and of the daughters she had given him – and the two sons in later life. That letter is in the family coffer with other treasures for our descendants,' she said to him. 'Do you hear from her?'

He shook his head. It was several years since he had last written to her. She had not replied. There seemed little point in mentioning the presence of one of those sons, locked away this very moment aboard 'Fortunee'. It was certain that she would do her best to persuade him to get Tom out of there. Since that might prejudice his contractorship, he had no intention of lifting a finger to get Tom released. Not at this point, anyway.

The evening before the contest between Li'l Moses and Sholto the Great, he was late finishing the books at Dell Quay and it was past sunset by the time he swung up into the saddle and turned his horse towards Chichester. He took the new lane past Rymans and St Mary's Church and cut out across the Common towards the twist in the river where the Smiths were camped.

He saw the glow from their hearth through the trees and drove his heels into his horse's flanks. He was utterly weary.

The night before had been shredded with yet another of the terrors that were slowly draining away his health. He just must see Dudie. Maybe she could help him.

Her name drove his heart up into his throat. He thought of little else these days than the warmth and fierce tenderness of her, soothing the canker of fear and tiredness from him.

She was alone in the camp. Nat was off to Portsmouth and would be back on the morning tide. Leonie had taken to her bed with another of her indispositions. *One day she'll have one too many.* The thought of being without her made him groan with longing. *Oh, Dudie.*

She seemed almost to have been expecting him for she came down from the covered waggon as he leapt from his horse. She was dressed in a bright red skirt that glowed like a great poppy, and a scarlet bodice that showed the froth of a white blouse beneath it. It was as though the sun in setting had left its reflection upon her. Round her shoulders was a shawl, knitted in a clash of brilliant colours. She had been combing her hair and now it fell about her shoulders in a shining cape.

'Sar shan, Simensa,' she said calmly.

He picked her up from the bottom rung of the waggon ladder and swung her round in an arc. She was so light, like a doll, and she smelt of woodsmoke and mint. She steadied herself, gripping his upper arms. He bent his head and kissed her for a long time.

She did nothing to escape his embrace but put her arms round his neck and settled to the exploration of his mouth, the contours of his face, the vast longing which she found in him.

He thought that she had dressed herself for him. There was no point in telling him that this was Poorano Rarti, when the joy of the Romani survival through centuries of hardship was celebrated with song and dance and every man, woman and child dressed in their finest togs and gave their spirits joyfully to the occasion. It was sad that Nat was away on this festival night and that she could not go and spend it with other Romani families. She had decided to prepare herself as though there would be others beside her hearth – and then dance and sing and break Panum on her own. At the back of her mind she had known that her evening would not be solitary.

He was such a deeply unhappy man, this Charles Bayless. Just how troubled he was, he obviously did not realise himself. He was badly scarred with the bruises of a past which were not of his making but the wounds went deep and from them he would simply wither and decay if no joy were ever to enter his life. She sorrowed for his situation and the sorrow brought with it a kind of love.

'Come!' she said to Charles, sliding out of his embrace and taking him by the hand. 'Today is a special day for all Romanies. It is the time for thanking God for our survival and asking for the continuance of the Romani Tribes.'

He did not want to think of gypsies and their quaint customs. He had just discovered that there was, after all, a capacity in him to burn . . . to want . . . to love, to feel for a woman the way he had never been able to feel. There had been such a feeling in him only once, some years before – but it had been generated by a young Arab youth whose beauty and tenderness to him had created an *affaire* which had lasted for seven passionate months. The boy had then turned his lovely melancholy eyes upon an elderly but extremely wealthy Duke and had died the following year of a mysterious and agonising illness.

Now, suddenly, here it was again. That glorious liquid burning of the body and soul when his heart thundered in his chest and threatened to leap from his throat. He wanted just to take this small and vibrant creature and lose himself in her. He put an arm round her waist but she turned to him, gently extricating herself and a warning was in her eyes.

'Help me to celebrate, Bor. Nat is away with the boat or we would be making very merry this evening. Drink and eat and dance with me. Please?'

He did as she wished. Indeed, having settled among sheepskins beside the fire, he found that he was more than comfortable and it was exquisite titillation to watch her as she brought him food which she must have been preparing all day.

For the first time in his life he ate hedgehog, cooked in the Romani way. The little bodies were wrapped in wild mint, packed round with clay and then baked slowly in the embers of the fire. When the clay finally began to crack and flake away they were scooped out of the ashes. As the clay was removed, the prickles and skin came away with it and the tender pink meat of the little creature was moist and succulent – and quite as fine a delicacy as veal or baby sucking pig.

She brought him cakes made from hazelnut and dried plum, and plied him with a strong sweet liquid made, she told him, from elderflower three years before. It was a fine rich liqueur and he could feel it blurring the edges of his vision.

She sang for him in a low, sweet voice. She sat across the fire and crooned strangely haunting songs in a language he did not recognise. She clapped her hands in time to the rhythm and then leapt to her feet and began to dance. Night came down and drowned the world and there was emptiness every-where save for the one globe of leaping firelight in which they dwelt in breathless isolation.

She came to him in the end, dropping down beside him, her breast heaving with the exertions of her dance. Her hair had lost its sleek orderliness and was once more a mop of rioting black curls stuck about her damp forehead. He drew her close to him and wiped the dark tendrils back from her shining face.

She let his hands discover the neat small breasts within the white blouse. Later she sat on the waggon step and let him unlace her bodice front.

When she was naked to the waist she took him into the waggon.

Chapter Two

'Would you care to accompany me aboard "Fortunée", Freeland – to see the wrestling match between Lord Tankerville's
man and the big negro?' Charles asked his elder son. The
carriage jolted them over a rut in the ill-tended highway and
the boy winced and steadied himself by bracing his feet against
the plush-covered seating opposite him.

'I don't really think so, Father. I'm not very interested in
common ruffians grappling with each other.'

Charles smiled thinly. 'The object of the exercise is not so
much to watch the men "grappling" as you call it but to
weigh up their chances and lay a wager on who you think
will be the victor.'

The boy looked at him with world-weary patience. 'I know
that, Father. But I have no interest either in pugilists of any
kind or in betting. Having already been aboard one of those
dreadful floating prisons once, I see little point in ever going
again. They stink to high heaven and it's pretty hateful being
obliged to look at those poor wretches who are fast becoming
little better than human beasts. Please excuse me.'

'Very well. I thought only to offer you a little amusement.'
Charles watched as the boy turned his face away and gazed
out of the carriage window. What could be in the boy's mind?
He was always so remote from his father. It seemed that they
had little in common apart from their physical resemblance.

Freeland was fast approaching his fourteenth birthday.
Already he was nearly as tall as Charles but slim, narrow-
hipped and fine-boned as a dancer. He bore the distinctive

Freeland features and pale gold colouring but there all further resemblance ended. He had his mother's languid indifference, which was difficult to penetrate. Indeed, Charles found it almost impossible these days to have a reasonable conversation with the boy. He was not much inclined towards any effort with his education, either. He had been at Winchester School for two terms now and his masters were beginning to make disappointed reports on his progress. Neither was he interested in physical sports. Had he been prepared to shine in the field, his boredom with learning might have been overlooked but the boy seemed destined for a life of idleness – for poetry and his mother's company appeared to be all he required from life.

Young John now, that was another matter altogether. John was eleven years old but already had a finer command of the written word and of mathematics than had his elder brother. He was the antithesis of Freeland in every way, from the stockiness of his young body to the darkness of his colouring. The family had always chosen to say that he took after his Portuguese grandmother's family. Lately Charles had decided that there was a strong dash of Bayless in his younger son.

The two boys were, surprisingly, very close companions. They rarely disagreed and right from their earliest years it had always been the tough little John who had danced attendance on his elder brother, fetching and carrying for him, fighting his battles as they grew older and taking the blame for any indiscretions of which Freeland might be guilty. He was still too young to accompany his father but he would one day. Of that Charles was certain.

He had a deep affection for his second child. John obviously enjoyed his father's company and sought it regularly – as he sought his mother's also. Indeed, he was a friendly boy and was well-liked by the household staff and all the relatives. He was already showing a keen interest in the Bayless businesses and lately father and son had taken to discussing all sorts of mythical but exciting possibilities for improving the area in the future. Looking at his elder son with real regret, Charles knew that there was little that he would ever share with this remote and slightly contemptuous son.

Dudie . . .

Her name kept flooding his mind like a great warm wave. He would never have sired a child as indifferent as this one on a woman of Dudie's strength and sweetness.

He shifted in his seat and closed his eyes so that the sheer glorious sense of well-being in him should not attract his son's attention. She had taken him into her with such touching tenderness and then such ferocious passion. There was so much she had to give him.

His body tingled afresh even as he tried to veer away from the memory of her but felt his genitals hardening like a guileless boy's . . . as the boy sitting opposite him should soon be discovering for himself . . .

He had remained with her until dawn had sent him sleepily home to change his clothing and appear at the breakfast table in some sort of order. He had not wanted to go, even then, but she had climbed over his weary body in the waggon bunk and he had watched as she fetched water from the river and then washed herself from head to toe. Leonie had never stirred herself to do such a thing after the brief coupling which had brought them sons rather than satisfaction. She had suffered him to enter her, suffered him through to orgasm but there had been no movement, no response in her own body, no interested exploration of his.

But Dudie had taken her time – and made him take his with her. She had used her body, her fingers, her mouth and had created in him a sustained and perpetual excitement which had lasted through the long night hours, turning them into minutes. His continuing arousal at the slightest thought of her only heightened his satisfaction. He had given her immense pleasure – but she had done something infinitely more amazing. She had, he decided, ennobled a manhood long made suspect.

The secret dreams of his mother's warm body which had brought him to his first climax were washed away now, in his forty-third year, by a girl young enough to be his daughter, who had given him a taste of gratification as he had never known it.

'No, you must not come this evening,' she had said firmly. 'Nat will be back then.' Her eyes had softened at the lost urgency in his face and she had put her arms round his neck and nibbled the lobe of his ear very tenderly. 'There will be other times . . . if that is how you wish it, Simensa.'

There will be other times.

Other times . . .

The thought buoyed his spirits throughout the rest of the drive back to Chichester and after, when he went about his business aboard the hulks. Everything seemed cleaner, brighter this day. He bowed to Tom over the heads of the other prisoners in the exercise Pen on the main-deck. He even exchanged a few kindly words with the shambling giant who was to fight Tankerville's man the following day. He felt physically exhausted and yet his body clamoured, begged for Dudie . . .

The day of the wager was perfect for entertainment aboard 'Fortunée'. The sun cast a gentle balm on the air but light sea breezes kept the worst of the hulk stench at bay. Charles came aboard with the Tankerville party, giving his undivided attention to Lady Dangerfield, an elderly coquette who flirted with him with the enthusiasm of a young girl throughout the afternoon. He played up to her attentions for it was not difficult to keep the woman happy without having to engage his full attention. She had once been a fine-looking woman, he knew, but Court life and the infections that were passed from lover to lover had taken their toll. She still had an echo of that beauty, for her eyes were fine, but she was now well-wrinkled, her neck was as scrawny as a turkey's and the almost bare breasts of the day's fashion, which clever corsetry had squeezed and thrust upwards out of a transparent lace fichu, were little more than limp dugs.

The Sibford party was in gay mood. The ladies all wore the exotic head dressings which were presently the rage at Court. The painting of lips and cheeks and brows accentuated the sensuality of both men and women and made a mockery of the over-emphasized stately manners with which they addressed each other. Seeing the look in the eyes of several of the guests, Charles applied his attentions most solicitously to the comfort and pleasure of the elderly and gregarious Sophia, Lady Dangerfield.

The Tankerville wrestler arrived as the party drank wine and chatted in the stateroom. Word that the contestants were limbering up brought some of them out onto the half-deck, glass in hand, to stand at the deck rail and stare at the bowed and emaciated gnomes scratching at the lice that bred in the body hairs and creases of their scrofulous frames down below them, in the barred Pen.

Sholto the Great was standing beside the boarding ladder like a granite carving, flexing an unbelievable set of over-developed arm and leg muscles, ringed by a group of his supporters. The sight of him obviously caused a certain consternation among the prisoners who began to mutter angrily at the view of his rippling body. As the visitors wandered out into the warm afternoon sunshine and paraded their exotic brocades and bejewelled feathers, indifferent to the astounded stares of the half-human creatures herded tightly together below them, Lady Dangerfield spotted the other contestant.

'Denise, Charles darling . . . Frederick, come quickly! I can see that perfectly splendid Negro who is to fight Sholto. Just look at him, darlings. Isn't he just the most divine thing you ever saw? Imagine the height of him, Denise . . . It makes me feel quite faint to imagine the rest . . .'

Behind the laughter and delicious perusals of the contestants' various attributes, Charles found himself looking down at Tom Heritage who was making way for Li'l Moses to reach the arena. It was all there, the Bayless look. Shrivelled and weakened by recurrent fevers, to be sure — but the sharp features, the dark foreign mystery which made the old portrait of Violet Bayless the finest in the Freeland collection was strong also in this unknown cousin. Was Amy in him also? He stood watching the two men surrounded by the little group that he knew were the crew of the 'Free States'. The Bo'sn was having a last attempt at getting the maximum bloodflow through the mighty Negro's body, flicking at each portion of the man's gleaming torso with a small string swatch. He was more like a gargoyle than a man, his toothless face lopsided as though it had been squeezed by an iron fist, leaving little but a corrugated husk of dried skin and bone.

Tom stood quietly beside them. Now and then he said something to Moses. Charles watched him absent-mindedly cracking the lice from his shirtcuffs under his thumbnail.

The decks were abuzz with anticipation now and the Tankerville guests, after looking the two contestants over began the serious business of laying bets. The huge Negro was a fine-looking fellow, that was beyond a doubt, but in his present state of debilitation there was no suggestion that he would win the day. The wagers were against the time it would take Sholto to put him to the floor.

'Get me another glass of that delicious wine, darling.' Lady Dangerfield held out her glass to Charles and made a little *moue* at him, pursing her painted lips into a cupid's bow. There were dark hairs growing on her upper lip. The scarlet lip paint was beginning to run at one corner of her wrinkled mouth.

He smiled at her and the very grotesqueness of her lizard's face made her a sad and ridiculous old clown beside his image of Dudie. She saw the inner light shining from his pale eyes, warming the grey of a winter sea into cold flame.

She arched and pressed herself against him. 'What strange fires you hide behind that coolness of yours, Master Bayless,' she murmured huskily behind her fan.

He bowed, withdrawing hastily the hand she clasped to her chest to replenish her glass. 'Fuelled by your charm, dear lady,' he said lightly and slipped from her side before the conversation could be carried further.

The contestants were ready. Tankerville went down onto the main-deck where the ring had been roped off to keep the prisoners from interfering and announced the conditions of the contest. The ladies stood at the rail, eyes flicking over the crowd of starved skeletons who, nevertheless, still showed signs of the youth or good looks with which nature had previously endowed their abused bodies.

The Negro walked through the tightly-packed crowd of prisoners and stood before His Lordship, quietly listening to the little speech. He seemed relaxed and unworried by the presence of such a daunting opponent. He glanced up at the waving, gossiping gentry and smiled at the colourful throng.

'Mon Dieu, but isn't he handsome?' Lady Dangerfield muttered to her friend. He was indeed looking very fine, despite the obvious wasting in his great frame. He had oiled and polished his skin until it shone like waxed wood. His round curly head, high cheekbones and long neck were a perfect contrast to the vast girth and bulging muscles of his opponent.

'How *too too* sad that Sholto will make mincemeat of all those lovely features,' Lady Dangerfield mourned, taking her filled glass from Charles and drinking thankfully. 'Failure is always such a depressing thing to witness, don't you think? When it is applied to such fine horsemeat, at any rate.'

Charles lifted pale eyebrows coldly. 'Sometimes there can be a certain dignity in failure,' he said. 'For in some, it denotes the desire for achievement and must therefore be worthy of our respect.'

'Take your stance.'

There was a general press forward towards the deck rail. Charles made way for two small ladies who rewarded him with mascaraed fervour, and he moved backwards through the jostling crowd of bodies and, when he was able, took a position against the stern rail from whence he could listen to the contest, rather than watch it. Without young John beside him much of the enjoyment of such entertainment was lost, for wrestling had never held the same excitement for him that he experienced in the cockpit.

There was a sudden gale of laughter from the quarter-deck guests. Lord Tankerville's drawling voice floated upward, telling the American Negro how to commence with a handshake. His voice was heavy with controlled exasperation. The Sibford guests were vastly entertained. Charles raised his glass and drank deeply, watching the posturing and gesticulations with dislike. There was none of that in Dudie. She was artless without seeming gauche, direct without ignorance. She would hate these empty poseurs but would not be the one to lose face in their company.

There was a note of tension in the crowd now. A heavy silence enveloped the vessel. Even the gulls screeching overhead seemed to settle into the rotten rigging to watch the two men facing each other in the ring.

'My God, they've started with an arm wrestle,' someone whispered.

Charles moved forward and stood behind Lady

Dangerfield, craning now to see what was happening through the waving scarlet plumage of her ostrich-feathered head-dress. His eyes searched the tense throng of men below him and there was Tom, standing beside the ring rope, eyes narrowed as he watched the muscles in Sholto's neck begin to bulge. There was an unexpected look of quiet satisfaction on his face.

'Look at that nigger,' someone muttered. 'He hasn't moved a muscle. Just look what he's doing to Sholto.'

Unaccountably, the Sibford herdsman was actually weakening. His whole body trembled and even as they watched they could hear him gasp through clenched teeth.

Suddenly, he seemed to collapse. His head went back and he slid forward against Moses' chest. 'Let go, damn you . . . I concede, concede . . .'

The ladies let out little shrieks of amazement. Their consorts looked glum. Several fat purses had been wagered on the time it would take for Sholto to crack Moses. Few had bothered to do the reverse.

Moses stood his ground. He did not loosen his grip upon Sholto's fist. A thin trail of blood streamed down the cowherd's quivering arm. In the same instant Sholto's knees folded and he collapsed and Moses, still holding on, knelt over the dazed man.

Lady Dangerfield clutched the lace at her bosom with a moan. 'Oh, it's just too marvellous. Look at his sincerity, Denise, the control of him. It is almost as though he has learning. Is he not the most marvellous treasure?'

The spell was broken. Cheers broke over the black man and his companions surged round him like dirty surf about a rock. He seemed to stand in his own quiet pool of thought in the midst of turmoil. Then he raised his eyes and grinned up at the visitors. With another little moan, Lady Dangerfield pulled a diamond and agate clip from her head-dress and threw it down to him.

'I would give much to have that creature as part of my household,' she said, clearly deeply affected by his performance.

'Tush, Sophia, we all know what part of his services you'd be after!'

Charles was still watching Tom. He could not shake off a feeling of extraordinary attachment for the emaciated man who was blood of his blood – just as Dudie was to both of them. Tom Heritage would understand about this all-consuming sensation that Dudie had lit in him for, as a man he must be capable of the same sensations. Maybe he had already tasted this heady intoxication of the senses.

Tom turned from Moses for a second and something made him raise his eyes. They locked into Charles' and something was passed between them. The acknowledgement was mutual and welcome to them both. With light heart and a wide smile Charles lifted his hat and openly doffed it with a courtly sweep.

Chapter Three

'What has come over you lately, Charles? You seem almost drunk all the time!'

Leonie was most concerned. She stared anxiously down the length of the breakfast table at her husband's flushed face as he tucked into an immoderately large helping of devilled kidneys.

'Are you quite well, my dear? You are surely running some sort of fever for I have never seen the colour so high in your face before.'

Charles laughed. He wiped his platter clean with a crust and then leaned forward and helped himself to more bread and damson preserve. 'I am in the pink of condition, my love, have no fear,' he said with complete satisfaction.

Indeed, he was. He had never felt so vigorous, so truly alive in his entire life. Everything seemed to be happening at once and the last few days had seen great things occurring which made him certain that Fate was suddenly smiling with extraordinary benevolence upon him.

He had found the moment, kindly created for him by Mistress Furze, to talk, at last, with Tom Heritage. It had been a delightful exchange, lacking in any of the patriotic animosity that might have been expected, and would lead to more such meetings, he was certain. Added to that, a sudden and unexpected step had been taken in the direction of the private dream he was sharing with his young son, John.

Lord Egremont of Alfold had set the wheels in motion to float a company intent on building a canal system whose aim would be to join the River Wey with the River Arun, thus creating a commercial waterway between London and the South Coast. Feeling as he did about the need for such a system between Portsmouth, Chichester and Arundel, Charles was now in a fever to see Egremont and, if possible, to join the Wey and Arun Navigation Trust, once it came into being.

As if that was not excitement enough, he had been with Dudie again the previous night when Nat had stayed in Chichester. It would fade after a few weeks, he kept telling himself. This feeling of light-headedness would settle down into its correct perspective and the visits to Dudie would become the natural expression of occasional release that a man should get from such warm womanly attentions.

The heady feeling of intoxication remained. Reason told him that it was certainly the result of his general optimism at the moment but he knew in his heart that all of it was Dudie.

She was a witch, that small beautiful girl. She was like no other woman he had ever come across. Her skin was young and warm and smelt and tasted of fresh flowers. She had washed her hair in the river at least three times since he had been visiting her, and afterwards rubbed into it some fragrant herbal juice which not only enhanced its luxuriant shine but gave it a curious scent of something which made his mouth water. Leonie was not a dirty person, that was certain – but her maid only washed her mistress' head two or three times in a whole year. There was some theory that the natural oils would otherwise be lost. Dudie's black hair shone with health. There was no question of dryness or head lice.

She was so young and yet she had the most surprising attitude towards him for she was not in awe of his age or his position. Rather the reverse, for she attended his mind and later his body with the same intense concentration upon exposing every smallest sensation which might bring him even greater pleasure. And aside from such devotion she regarded him with a strange mixture of motherliness and compassion.

It was not love with her.

Maybe it was something more permanent. There seemed no words to describe what was now, for him, a madness of the heart. He was more than content to wallow in it and let the whole experience follow its own course.

'There are various things afoot at the moment which are particularly attendant upon the business,' he said to Leonie to quieten her fears for him. 'Some of them are working out very satisfactorily towards the quality of our life at the present time. Much of it is concerned with the future of the boys. Though Freeland never ceases to concern me, he is a comfort rather than a worry to you, I know. John is going to be the supportive son of our old age though, I feel it strongly – and yesterday I was informed of the possibility of being involved in a venture which has long been a talking point between the boy and myself.'

He drained his coffee cup and reached for the pot to replenish it. Leonie seemed to shrivel before the bounding good humour of him. She coughed into her kerchief. He stared down the damask-covered table at her, seeing the livid red patches on either cheek.

'Really, Leonie, why must you insist on taking breakfast with me at this hour when you would be wiser not to leave your bed before mid-morning!'

She cleared her throat, biting back the pain in her chest. 'I am your wife,' she said simply. 'Other women may lie abed all morning but this is the best part of the day and I like to try to have it with you during the summer months at least.'

For the past three winters she had travelled abroad on the recommendation of Dr Sharples, following the sun of milder climates than England's, in search of warmth for her thin body as her own circulation now forbore to give. The change of air and pleasant warmth had helped in the beginning but now even that attraction was becoming too much for her failing health.

Suddenly, he longed to tell her about Tom. She knew his family history though it was seldom mentioned, for the Farndells were wealthy millers and there were branches of the family in many of the villages south of Chichester including Henry Farndell of Apuldram, Uncle to Leonie. Baylesses had made too deep an imprint upon the life of that village for the details of its dramas to be lost upon its neighbours.

She knew of his father – and the string of crimes attributed to him. She knew also of Aunt Violet Heritage and the strong memories that had been left of her in Apuldram along with the oval portrait in Great Aunt Mary's hall at Crouchers.

No, he could not mention Tom, for the one thing that already overlaid their new relationship was Tom's fascination with Lavenham. Funny, he had not thought of that place for years, not uttered the name even in his subconscious. Yet now it was with him again, returning to chip away at his peace of mind – and all because he knew that in some way, by fair means or foul, Tom Heritage would find a way to set foot there at some time in the future.

The nightmare enveloped him once more that night.

In the morning, still sweating from the experience, it came to Charles that Dudie might be the saviour of his sanity as she had been in so many other ways.

She was away with the barge and the Manifest Book recorded that she would not be back before noon of the following day. He felt unreasonably bereft, as though he was denied the thing most precious to him – which indeed he was.

He visited the Bayless camp on his way home that evening and sat on the steps of the waggon, out of reach of the long-haired lurcher, who still skulked on the end of her chain between the brightly-painted waggon wheels.

The hearth was a dampened scar of ash beneath the iron tripod. The cooking pot was stowed away and there was little save the waggon and the empty ashpit to remind him of her presence. She was tidy even in absence. There was only the rejection of the closed doors at his back, rich with their designs of painted flowers, to give him the feel of her. He traced the brush-strokes of leaf swags with his finger. She had painted all the decoration on the waggon, Nat had told him with considerable pride.

It came to him, as though Dudie had suggested it, that he should go to Lavenham before Tom. He could hear her voice, hear the calm reasoning in it.

'Go and take a look for yourself, Bor. Those dreams, they be the memories of your childhood woven into fantasies of imagination. Go there and see for yourself what it was that frightened you as a small boy. The worst that can occur is that the same thing will happen again . . . and now you are a fully-grown man. Now you have the gift of reason to protect you . . .'

Go now?

He simply could not endure the terror which instantly gripped him. Ask Dudie to go with him? She almost certainly would, for the gypsy Baylesses still thought of the property as being their private province and there had been several sightings over the years of Romani caravans encamped on the overgrown west lawn.

The idea soothed the panic in his chest and he stood up, decisions made. As he swung up onto his horse once more and left the camp, a fine rain began to fall across the Common.

Dudie inclined her head, as always the sage, his uncomplaining mentor.

He had a very pleasant voice, even when he was relating something as frightening to himself as his recurrent nightmares obviously were. She watched the frustration in his face as he struggled to recall any smallest detail but it was all buried too deeply. There was nothing to relate, saving that trapped feeling and the grasping of iron railings.

He buried his face against her hair and she held him tightly, feeling the tremor in him.

'There is one thing you can do, you know,' she said. 'Keep a pen and paper beside your bed – and when you have the dream, write it down while it is still clear in your mind. Then, at least, you will be able to share it.'

Such simple advice and so practical. Why he had not thought of doing this years before, he could not imagine. Within days of her words it happened again – and this time he was ready and wrote every terrible detail on two sheets of paper whilst the reality of it was still in him. Afterwards he lay back and fell into a deep and dreamless sleep, as though the conveyance of his experience onto paper had halved its capacity to afflict him.

The essay, for that is how it read back to him, brought with it a great flood of memory – and with it, a strange peace. For the words were those of a small boy, long gone. With a deep sense of gratitude he took it to Dudie and she sat on the top step of the waggon with the lurcher curled quietly round her feet and read the whole piece slowly, silently mouthing the words to herself.

. . . They said I was not to look at the big house but the garden is so pretty. There are plums in the orchard and I can just reach a low branch. The sun is warm and the air hums. It feels so pleasant and safe here . . . Who will ever know if I just look in these windows? There is a perfect rose growing on the creeper here. It is almost white on the outside but the middle petals are a lovely deep pink. It smells like Mama's perfume in the blue bottle on her dressing table. I will pick it and give it to her.

There is so much dust on the windows, I cannot see very much of the inside. There is a big hearth across the other side of the room and the carved staircase window beside me shows long sunbeams across one end of the room. If I try the door, I shall only push it open, so that I can stand in the opening and look in without moving off the step. It is not even locked . . . the sound of the rusty hinges makes me jump.

It is a very large Hall. Everywhere is dust and dried leaves which move on their own with the wind from outside. If I go inside – just a little – I can see the whole staircase. I wonder what is up . . .

There is a funny humming sound all round me in this place. Suddenly the room is not so warm and pleasant any more and I am frightened when the door slams shut behind me with a sudden CRASH . . . It is dark. The sun has gone from the long window. I wish I had not come here. There is something I cannot understand. Mama . . . Mama . . . I want to go home. The great humming sound is in my ears – all round me. The air is getting thicker now that the door is shut and there is a terrible smell everywhere . . . terrible . . . I feel sick . . . Mama, help me.

Oh, the staircase! Something is up there – a misty cloud, coming down into the darkness and yet I can see it . . . there is a face and a voice and yet there is nothing. I am so frightened. Oh Mama, I want you!

Tears and fear . . . trembling as the droning in the air

158

*picks up a dreadful gobbling voice. It hates me. It is coming
to destroy me. I cannot understand what it is saying:
'OUT WITH YOU, LAWRENCE. OUT OF THIS PLACE.'
Please, I'm sorry. I did not mean to come in. I am Charles.
I am, I am ... not Lawrence ... Something on my face,
and then more and more. Things are crawling all over me
and suddenly they are stabbing me, burning my face and
arms and digging for my eyes.*

    *I am running ... and the terrible screaming hate is mixed
up with the drone of the burning bees all over my body.
'DRABANEY SAPA, SHAV ... SHAVA NE KENNER
...' The words mean nothing but I know they are vile
and cursing and full of a dreadful violence. I run and, crying,
cannot hear my own sobs, only the voice and the roaring
drone of those furious, deadly bees. I run into something
but my eyes are too swollen to be able to see. My hands
grip iron bars and I shake them in my terror for I can hear
my Mama calling and I cannot get to her. Oh Mama ...*

Dudie looked up from the page in her hand. 'Do you remember
writing this?' she asked.

Charles shook his head. 'It's extraordinary. I remember
nothing but going to sleep – having the dream and waking,
feeling oddly refreshed in the morning. I knew that I had had
the dream but then I saw that I must have written it down
for there were the sheets, covered in my own handwriting, on
the night table beside the bed. There was no fear or shaking.
Just a sense of relief.'

She scanned the page and turned it over, then took up the
second sheet. 'Here,' she said, pointing. 'Do you know what
these words are?'

'No. They mean nothing at all to me. Maybe my imagination made them up the way that children invent things
sometimes.'

Her smile was a swift flicker and was gone. 'No, Charles,
you did not invent them. They are Romani words ...'

He stared at her, his sandy eyebrows bunched low over his
eyes.

'I will tell you their meaning. They are a curse, you see. They are words only uttered under the greatest possible provocation: '*A curse upon you, snake spawn of a snake's rut. Begone before death in all generations. Death to you in my house . . .*'

They sat close together, gripping hands, silent.

It was there, then, the reality of all the old tales. Strangely, he felt as though a great weight had been lifted from him as his eyes wandered over the pages of scrawled writing.

'I think,' he said, 'that it is Granfer Jess' sister Amy. She was a cripple and insane in later life. The Freelands have always maintained that she really hated Grandmama, and Papa too. My mother used to say that Papa had had a very unhappy childhood. Maybe SHE made it so for him . . .'

They went to the gates of Lavenham together.

They walked from the Common down the new lane, past St Mary's Church and Rymans with its single, solid-looking watchtower and the tall solar windows; past the empty shell of two workers' cottages and south to where the lane met the toll-road to Dell Quay. A right turn and then left onto the track which led to Newbarn Cottage. Charles paused and stared at the untidy muddle of buildings.

'I remember these so well when I was small,' he said. 'There were Baylesses living there at that time. I used to play with the children but Mama thought little of them – Granfer's cousins who used to run the breeding stables with Aunt Violet. In those days it was quite an honour to own a Lavenham horse. They were some of the finest horse flesh in England, so Uncle John used to say.'

'He was right,' Dudie agreed. 'They are still around, you know. Less pure and not as swift and powerful as they were in Jess' day – but still with the distinctive honey colour with white mane and tail.'

He was surprised. He had thought that the Lavenham Stud had ceased to exist with a generation when the Baylesses left Apuldram.

'Manfri Bayless and his cousin Rueb lived here for some years,' Dudie told him. 'It was Manfri's grandchildren that you probably remember. They are back on the road now, you know. Manfri and Rueb are dead and Polly, who was married to Manfri, she only died two or three years ago. She was a gorgio, of course. Polly Ayles . . .'

Charles put his arm round her shoulders. 'You are a walking fount of knowledge,' he said, giving her a little squeeze.

She smiled up at him. 'It is the way we are reared. We all have our lineage firmly fixed in our heads from a very early age.'

They moved on down the rutted track once more.

'It's just as well, for it seems that I must spell out your own family tree for you as well as my own!'

The track curved suddenly to the left and on the right side a pair of tall gates stood, choked in a straggle of twisted undergrowth. Charles stood still and stared at them.

'This is the entrance,' he said, feeling his throat tighten. The gates were of iron, wrought into a design of oak leaves in a central medallion with straight bars on either side. Creepers had long taken charge and imprisoned them in a blanket of convolvulus so that little of the elegance was now visible. He tore at the clinging greenery and pulled it away roughly. Beneath the stringy tendrils the delicate metal leaves with their tiny acorns had rusted through the peeling black paint. The stone gate pillars stood firm, each topped by a single orb of Ventnor stone.

Dudie said nothing but stood on the grassy track and watched Charles tearing at the wild creepers on the gate. He worked silently as though time were running away with him. Then he stood back, rubbing the palms of his sap-stained hands down the sides of his breeches.

'Iron bars . . .' he said. He gripped them with both hands and shook the gates with all his strength. Rust flaked and fell, showering his coat with red dust. 'These were the iron bars of my dream . . . I recognize them.'

'Except that it was no dream, Bor, but a child's clear memory,' Dudie said softly behind him. He turned and stared at her.

She tucked her arm into his and held him close. 'Don't you see? What you've dreamed about all these years is the memory of what actually happened to you. You were very small, only five or six . . . and had no explanation for what befell you in that empty Hall and so you pushed it right down into the back of your mind, denying its existence – even though you KNEW that it had happened.'

The right-hand gate suddenly swung away out of his grip and fell with a crash into the waist-high brambles of the overgrown drive. Charles, startled by the involuntary movement, leapt backwards with an oath, his face blazing white. Dudie held onto his arm and felt his whole frame trembling with shock.

'Come away now, Simensa,' she said gently. 'I will come back with you another day and we will take it a step further. There is plenty of time.'

The dream deserted him. His nights were untroubled, save for the depth of his desire to spend them with Dudie. Sometimes he took the pages of his writing out of his night table drawer and re-read them but somehow, to see the events written down in clear pen strokes, to be able to go over each word again and again, seemed to remove the horror and his fear receded. With summer in full flood he knew that he could bear to venture closer to the House hidden so securely behind the marching oakwoods.

Dudie was pleased when he approached her on the subject. 'I was wondering how long it would take you to gather your strength,' she said. 'It has to be done, you see. You have to go there as an adult and see whether there is still a presence to be experienced. I shall be there . . . another Bayless with Jess and Amy's blood in my veins. Maybe Lavenham is now just an old and empty ruin like any other house which has not been lived in for half a century. If there is something still there we can face it together, Bor.'

Nat Smith was most concerned when she told him of the plan to visit the old House. 'Don' 'e go, Dudie. Let 'im go alone if 'e has to . . . but don' go too. That place is Mokada. We all know it. Why defy what IS?'

'I must go with him,' she said simply. 'He relies on my strength. You know that.'

'What I know, Pen, is that you're letten' him get away with

too many liberties,' Nat growled. 'Oh yes, I know you can look after yourself, an' allus have done. But this is different. He wants too much from you. I'm not blind, Bor. I c'n use my eyes when I have to. You'll be too clever by half, one day . . . just you see. You'll end up with that gorgio's Chav and then you'll never see 'im again. Let 'im work out 'is own salvation.'

She turned away from him. There was no point in trying to explain her feelings for he knew well that she felt no love for Charles Bayless – only a kind of compassion which had its reward in the obvious joy he felt in her. She would help him to lay the ghosts of his family past – for they were not his ghosts and yet he had been paying for their sins all his life. She would give him all her support until he had cleared his mind and was able to cope more naturally with normal relationships. Then they could move on. In the meantime she would continue to sluice her genitals with the ointment made from ground ivy and to drink before each of his visits the concoction brewed from Blue Cohosh root which prevented conception. It had served her well up to now but recently she had begun to worry for she had not been Mokada for six weeks.

'Walk with me down to Lavenham and let us go Mushgaying, Bor. Let us get the whole thing over – now, this very minute,' Dudie said to Charles one afternoon.

He lifted his head from the pillow and leant over her on one elbow, searching her face, feeling an urgency there which was out of character with her. She lay on her back looking up at him, the question in the lift of her eyebrows. Her mouth was moist, upturned at the corners. She felt the peace and compliance in him after the purging of his passion.

It was high summer. Birds sang above the waggon in the highest branches of the leaning trees. Out in the harbour the gulls screeched and swooped over the dark hulls of the prison ships.

'Very well,' he said. 'If I think about it for long, I can always find an excuse for putting it off. If we go together, on a perfect day as this is, after such an afternoon with you as we have just enjoyed – I don't see how the experience could be anything other than pale in comparison with the feelings you stir up in me, Dudie . . .'

She put a finger over his mouth. 'No more words,' she said softly.

They dressed after splashing in the curve of the little stream as Dudie had taught him. Cleansing himself after being with her was now part of the ritual of loving Dudie and he knew that he would follow this pattern always. Dressed, they wandered slowly over the Common and down the network of high-hedged lanes, impervious to the sharp glances of passers-by. He was whole in her presence only – and she, feeling the depth of his well-being, turned on a sparkling animation to cover the unhappiness slowly growing in her.

It was almost time for Nat to make the decision to go, almost time to withdraw from this complex and passionate man whose untapped and certainly unconscious violence within had begun to worry her of late. How would he react if she were to admit to him that she was almost certain that she was carrying his child? It was quite within his capability for him to kill her. His affection for his sons must never be threatened, she knew. There was more of his father in him than he realised. Still, if he was able to exorcise the fears of that House, he would gain the strength necessary to support himself after she had gone.

They paused at the entrance and then picked their way through the brambles, over the fallen gate. Charles leaned down and hauled it up and leaned it against its stone pillar before following Dudie through the waist-high sweep of grass and fern which choked what had been the drive. They walked slowly, thrashing the overgrowth and staring about them. Trees had marched unchecked across an old paddock and the wall of the kitchen garden to their right was almost invisible now. The House emerged slowly, firstly the roof with a nest of small chimneys and what had once been two stacks of tall, Jacobean chimney twists, broken now and long since tumbled invisible into the long grass. Charles gripped Dudie's hand and went forward, his face almost grey in the sharp sunlight. They skirted a fallen tree and came out into clear ground with the House displayed before them. He sucked in his breath and Dudie watched him closely. There was no need to look at the House for she and Nat had been here several times – as had most of the Bayless Clan since the day that Violet Bayless had fled from it.

There had never been the slightest sensation of horror for any of them. The bengs that were here were within the balance of Charles' own mind.

They walked very slowly round the side of the House and onto a terrace whose flagstones were uneven, lifting under the growth of weeds beneath. To their right a wild expanse of high grass was all that showed of the fine lawns which had once rolled in emerald perfection down to the banks of the Chichester Channel below Dell Quay. Here and there a sudden splash of bright colour drowned in undergrowth suggested the flower gardens of former years. As they picked their way along the terrace a flock of noisy crows rose up in a frightened black swathe from the roof of the House and swung screaming out over the water.

Charles stood still. His hand gripping Dudie's was damp and the strength of his fingers almost made her cry out.

'It is here.' His voice was hoarse, almost a whisper. 'I can feel it. Hatred . . . withdrawal . . . warning . . . Can you not feel it too? Right here in the sunshine. Even on the outside of the place?'

She did feel something, it was true. There seemed to be a brooding watchfulness about its dust-blinded windows, as though it was drawing a cloak about itself and denying them the right to explore further.

'I only feel what you are telling me – because you are telling me,' she said gently. 'I have been here in the past with Nat and there was no atmosphere then . . . just a fine old Kenner with a lot of valuable stuff inside that no one has ever felt inclined to take.' She laughed. 'That's the part that I have always found so strange. Not the tales of mullos and evil happenings but the fact that it is fully furnished with paintings and fine furniture and even silver in there . . . and no one has taken a single spoon.'

They sat on the wall, looking up at the House. Let it get used to them. Let them absorb some of the atmosphere and get the pulse back to a normal rate.

'If you and Nat have been here,' Charles said, trying to keep the surprise out of his voice for she had never mentioned this before, 'why did you not take a souvenir or two? I'm told that most gypsies have few qualms about seconding property that is left unprotected.'

'You do not take from your own Clan.' She made no attempt to keep the disapproval out of her voice. 'In any case, we did look round and Nat picked up a metal bowl in the Hall to see if it was made of silver. He breathed on it and made to rub it with his sleeve . . . and an adder ran between his feet, so he put it down again. An adder between the feet is a very bad sign, Bor . . . you don't argue with the signs if you know them . . .'

She stood up. There was a slight singing in her ears and she realized that the suggestion of nausea which she had begun to feel as they walked through the lanes was now quite liable to erupt suddenly. If she were to be sick in front of Charles it was possible that he might guess the reason – and that was something that she had no intention of admitting to him.

'Come on,' she said shortly, holding out her hand to him. 'Let us go inside and see how it feels in the Hall. There is plenty of light and we need not stay long. Just the Hall today – and the rest of the House later.'

Rising, he took her hand and she felt the ice in him. He stood at the edge of the terrace, looking up at the soft pink brickwork. He was still very white and there was an almost blue tinge to his lips. A pulse beat strongly in his right cheek. She drew him towards the oak front door.

It was not locked, but it needed all her strength, as she pressed her shoulder to the wood, to get it open. When it did, it was as though something which had been holding it closed suddenly let go and the door swung back on creaking hinges, almost unbalancing her.

The smell rushed out at them and Charles recoiled. 'No,' he said thickly. 'I can't go in there. The stench is still there . . . that same awful reek.' He flung her hand away and ran over to the side of the terrace and bent, retching over the balustrade. The odour of decayed stomach acids and excreta was an almost tangible cloud billowing out of the open doorway. For a moment Dudie could have sworn that she could see a creamy mass billow out past her and envelop Charles but her own threatened sickness rose up then and she bent and let her stomach void itself into the brambles. When she was more in control again she raised her head.

Charles was lying on the terrace, rolled up in a foetal curl. The stench had gone and the afternoon was bright and blue and a little hazy. She bent over Charles and found that he had lost consciousness.

'Come on, Simensa,' she said, crouching beside him and stroking his forehead. 'It's all gone now. There's nothing here. We'll go home . . . wake up, Charles.'

He stirred and small animal sounds of fear came from him and she kissed his cheeks and patted his hands, repeating her comforting words of reassurance until he opened his eyes and looked wildly beyond her head. Then he seemed to grasp his position and where they were and struggled to his feet.

'I can't go in there – not now,' he said, pushing her in front of him as he made for the end of the terrace.

They retraced their steps in silence. No word was exchanged until they had passed through the gates and were on their way back up the old carriage track to the Dell Quay Road.

'You felt it too, I know you did,' he said, head down and eyes averted. He seemed to have no control over the depth of his fear, so that even a firm determination to override his feelings was no match for his instincts.

'I smelt a nasty old musty smell, yes,' she agreed, trying to play down that indescribable blanket of evil gases.

'It must have been just as appalling to you as it was to me, for I saw you vomit just as I did, Miss, so do not try to dismiss it!'

She looked at his pinched face. It was a death mask, cheekbones protruding through the colourless flesh. His mouth was a cruel lipless slit drawn back from the teeth in a half-snarl. She could not tell him that her own sickness came from quite another source. Observing this new and strange Charles, she wondered whether his father, Lawrence, had looked this way when he flamed things with that terrible power of Death in his eyes.

She put her head down. 'Nat will be back at the vardo by sunset. I must hurry to get his hobben into the pot.'

There were no words between them when they parted, almost like strangers. His thoughts were far away from her and he scarcely noted her withdrawal.

The following morning he heard that Tom, with Li'l Moses and two others, had made their escape from 'Fortunée'.

The whole ship was seething as he came aboard. Expressions of a varying nature were imprinted into the face of every soul aboard: anger, trepidation, exhilaration and just plain fear concerning the consequences. Furze was pacing his office when Charles looked in. His rage was so intense that he appeared to be puffed up in danger of an apoplectic fit. His resemblance to a great purple toad was quite startling.

'Can you imagine the wickedness!' Furze had to keep his voice low for it was striving to burst from his lungs in roar after mighty roar and that would only bring on his gout again. 'That double-crossing son-of-a-sea-cow, after all the privileges we have given him here in these quarters . . .'

Charles flipped his coat-tails deftly over the back of a stool and sat himself down calmly. 'Now, just stop all this ranting and raving and try and tell me what has happened,' he said in his most soothing voice. 'I gather from Sergeant Milburn that you've had an escape.'

The little Captain winced and lifted his weight off the painful foot. He sucked in his breath and hobbled round the desk to slump back in his chair, the breath wheezing like a pair of ancient fire bellows in his chest.

'You could say that, sir, and you would be right. Four of the dirty lummocks, there were – literally dug their way out of the side of the ship, too. That's bad enough but when I tell you that one of them is the fellow who has been teaching my own boys – Thomas Heritage, no less – you will see why I scarce know where to put myself. Heritage, that great mountain of nigger flesh, Moses Abelson and two others.' He banged his pudgy fists on the desk in front of him, lost in the instant for words.

Mention of Tom had been a profound shock to Charles. He had been well aware of Tom's determination to see his mother's birthplace before returning to New England but it had been in the minds of both of them that he would be one of the first to be paroled when the lists came through for Langstone. That Tom would take the law into his own hands and desert his shipmates had not once crossed Charles' mind. He scarcely heard the words that Furze was uttering, hardly took heed of the trembling in the man's body.

Tom would go straight to Lavenham.

Once there, who knew what would develop, for the House had had no one on which to feed for a very long time. Suppose it took possession of Tom? It certainly seemed to have rooted itself in his grandmother, Amy Bayless . . . With an effort he closed his mind to all the hideous possibilities which might now be forming to destroy Aunt Violet's younger son.

'We caught one of 'em skulking in the mud on North Binness Island,' Furze was saying. 'Put him in the Black Hole forever, as far as I'm concerned – till 'es cracked, at any rate. That'll make the varmints think. Fished another of them out of the water. Dead as mutton. Had half the harbour in his guts. Strung 'im up in the bows as a pretty figurehead, just to remind the other sullen buggers what'll happen if any of 'em try that one again.'

'Have the other two been sighted?'

Furze snorted. 'You'd have thought a black monster the size of that buck might be difficult to conceal but, stap me, Master Bayless, there's not been a breath of wind about him – or Heritage either, since they went two nights back. They're probably gone to ground with some Yankee sympathizer – or even taken ship across the Channel by now.'

He fell to muttering about the dilapidated shape of the old vessel, grumbling over the difficulties of keeping it secure when its very timbers were soft as sponge.

'One of these days,' he said gloomily, helping himself and Charles to a glass of fine claret, 'we shall all wake up at the bottom of this confounded harbour. I'm surprised that none of the damned hulks have foundered yet.'

Charles drank his claret in thoughtful mood and excused himself at the earliest moment. He felt the restless mood of the men as they filed past him for their ration. Anger and dejection overshadowed those who celebrated the continued freedom of Tom and Li'l Moses. It was not surprising that a break had been made. The men had been imprisoned for the most part of nearly two years, some for even more. Their bodies were crying out for fresh fruit and vegetables – for good red meat – for water in which to bathe the sores upon their desiccated skins. He averted his eyes from the boy who crouched almost double before him at that moment. He could not have been more than twenty but the hands that were held out to take his ration were dried-up claws and his face was a nightmare of rotten tooth stumps, bleeding guns that protruded, spongy and swollen so far out of his mouth as to give the poor creature an oozing, bulbous sneer, only contradicted by the utter grief in his eyes.

Scurvy . . . What horrors it made of men.

'Have you been to the sick bay?' he asked the boy, sickened by the terrible stench of putrefaction that emanated from him. There was no understanding the gobbled reply that came from that dreadful mouth.

Charles turned to one of his clerks. 'Get his name and see that he is treated before he drops dead,' he said.

' 'Twould be better if he did,' someone said under his breath.

Charles put his head down and ignored the aside. He could do little else but agree with it.

Chapter Four

It was a day for making trap nets. Dudie sat as she had done since one of the first tasks of her childhood had been taught her, cross-legged on a flat piece of ground, with three pieces of newly-made hempen netting piled up beside her. The day was fine after the night rain and the moisture in the mild air was just right for tightening the fibres.

She spread one piece out on the ground, smoothing it flat with her hands. It was about five feet square, made of a fine half-inch mesh which she had completed the night before and left upon the ground to absorb the dew. Over this net she laid a coarser one of the same size, then rolled the two up together and folded them over so that the wide meshing was underneath and the fine net on top. Finally she laid the third net, the same four-inch gauge as the first, on top of the other two, producing a netting sandwich which she sewed together with large stitches of hempen thread round the outer edges.

It was the perfect time of year for netting songbirds, mostly bullfinches, which were then mated with canaries, a very popular domestic pet, before being returned to the hedgerows. Dudie had three caged canaries, the largest a gift from Charles who had also presented her with a Java Sparrow, a lovely little creature with soft grey plumage and a pinkish red breast. Sadly, before there had been time to mate it with an English finch, it had died. The canaries were thriving, however, and had already hatched one family each which she had sold in the Chichester Tuesday market at a handsome profit.

The Romani method of trapping fascinated Charles for

there was no damage to the bird and the little creatures seemed almost unconcerned by the experience.

Dudie lifted her net and folded it over her arm and shoulder. She set out across the Common to where a wild patch of scrubland divided the parishes of Fishbourne and Apuldram. Here there were birds aplenty and it was only a matter of minutes before she had marked a fine young finch. She spread her net in a gap in the hedgerow, over a ditch close to where the birds were feeding. After a few minutes the little creatures began to flutter back to the spot and Dudie, having stood well back from the hedge, now began the business of moving very slowly towards it, driving the bird of her choice, step by step, towards her net snare. The colour of the hemp blended perfectly with the hedge twigs, so that it was not visible until it was too late. The bird gave a hop and a quick flutter as Dudie took a step forward. The movement drove it right into the net, through the first wide mesh into the fine second mesh. The impact of its small, frenzied body created a little pocket between the meshes and so it was held, secure yet with no restriction upon its body and wing feathers. Dudie gathered it up, removed it deftly from its open prison and thrust it into the safety of her stocking box. She caught three more birds in this way and then returned to the camp.

Nat was back from Dell Quay by the time she had finished. 'Emsworth's all abuzz today,' he said as she brought him food and tore a hunk of bread from the loaf he had bought. 'Ben' a breakout from one o' them convict ships off Langstone . . . four prisoners cut right through the ship's side, cheeky saps. One of them drowned, they say, and one was caught by the tide in the marsh and was hauled out like a mudworm. But the other two are still free. Good luck to 'em, I say. I'd not want to be battened down in them floaten' coffins. Prefer to chance me luck with the Authorities, any time.' He sipped noisily at a large ladle of soup and swilled it round his mouth. 'Good luck to 'em, I says.'

She thought about the escaped men a lot that day. The following dawn would see her off to Portsmouth with Nat and the other bargees and the camp would be unguarded until their return. She locked everything as securely as usual but left the bolt loose on the waggon door. Inside she put food which would normally have been buried in the cool box. If the poor creatures came looking for refuge, they would certainly find a bit of a welcome here.

The night was misty again. Summer storms had swept through, leaving a period of still air and oppressive heat. They narrowly missed ramming a gentleman's yacht as they rowed out of the Channel round Bosham Hoe and made for the Thorney Cut. The barge was low in the water, weighed down by tonnes of large, rough-hewn coal from the Kent colliery. By the time Dudie had steered them skilfully through the Thorney and Hayling Cuts and they were approaching the Hilsea Stream, the day was brightening, a yellow lozenge of sun burning away the steamy dawn mist. They nosed their way along the narrow waterway which made an island of Portsea, and into the mud-silted reaches of Portsmouth Harbour and then they were rowing strongly again, making good headway past Whale Island and on towards the busy dockland of the greatest sea port in the south of England. Away on the starboard bow, a sinister line of prison ships rode at anchor off Portchester Castle, like a rope of murky beads strung together by great rusting hawsers and attended, as always, by clouds of screeching gulls.

Dudie listened to the oarsmen's laboured breath and the occasional curse or joke tossed like small gifts between the striving of each mighty thrust. In . . . out . . . in . . . out. She leaned on the rudder and the boat veered a little to skirt a Naval bumboat crossing their bows.

She hated Portsmouth, with its narrow streets and rank air, foul with smoke from the forest of chimneys inside the city wall. Her lungs seemed to clog up with the coke fumes when there was no wind to blow them out across the ocean. It was said that the dirty yellow haze over Portsmouth could be seen for miles out to sea.

She sighted the entrance to the coaling jetties and turned the barge in towards the shore.

Nat and the others would have to forgo much of their carousing this night for they were due back in Dell Quay before midday, which meant leaving at dawn. She was content to go and visit with their sister Sarah who was married to a Red Marine. He was seldom at home and, childless, Sarah was always glad of her company. She would make sure that Dudie was back aboard before dawn, in good time to check that the barge had been sluiced down and the coaldust cleared. There was the Chichester cargo to be checked to save Nat the job and then she could tuck herself up in the stern with the rudder pressed into her armpit and let her attention wander over the other vessels in the coaling basin already about their business under the uncertain light of hanging lanterns.

It rained in the night, scouring away the last of the sea mists so that the return trip was uneventful and visibility opalescent clarity. The men were in cheerful mood and Nat's fine singing voice echoed through the Thorney Cut, as they made good progress with their light return load. Coal to Portsmouth, baskets of fish back to Chichester. There would be a fine meal for them all that evening.

She remembered the escaped prisoners as they skirted the three hulks off the Langstone marshes. Suppose they had been to the vardo and eaten all their victuals? Nat would not be happy.

'Drop me into Bosham,' she called down the boat to him over the heads of the three rowers in front of him. 'I need to get supplies from Mistress Priday.'

'No time,' Nat said shortly. He hated any deviation from routine for delay could spell reprimand and they needed the work for a few more weeks yet. 'We'm due in before midday and we'll need to keep goen'.'

'Hey, Bor,' Dudie laughed. 'Look at the sky. Sun's up, riden' Birdham Church tower. We've three hours in hand. 'Twont take me but half an hour to fill my pannier and leave a message for Master Chase that his baskets are ready for him to collect with the cart.'

He nodded, defeated as he usually was before her reasoning, and she leaned on the long arm of the rudder and watched the water cream in their wake as they joined the traffic entering Bosham Creek.

The tide was running away and a tiny boat like half a chestnut shell came out to bring her in. She clambered over the side and sat high in its miniature prow as the fat ferryman poled her in towards the shore.

'I won't be long. Wait for me, if you please, Dan.'

She hitched up her skirts, hopped over the side onto a mud bank, and waded through the ankle-deep water and up onto the gravelled slipway amongst the straggle of village houses. She swung her empty basket and hummed under her breath, her mind on those days, far ahead, when she and Nat would once more be jalling the drom. It was then that she fell over Tom's outstretched and reeking leg.

'Oi, dik ai, Chav . . . dik ai . . .'

The dirty bundle of ragged humanity had raised its head – and that fine unbeggarly face had found an instant niche in her mind.

'Oh, sorry, Bor . . . I didn't see you there.'

His voice, when he spoke, had a refinement that belied his clothing. There was a warm burr in his pronunciation that suggested the Western counties. In spite of his obvious pain he was polite as a king would be to his courtier. How strange it was to discover charm in such rags and decay.

She bought wire for her clothes pegs and fat for cooking and tobacco for Nat and sal volatile for her medicine box. Then she left her message for Farmer Chase, bought fresh bread from the baker, and onions as an afterthought. On her way back to the little ferry boat she squatted down beside the drowsing beggar and gently shook his arm.

He opened eyes that suddenly cleared and looked at her as though she were an old friend, soft grey orbs ringed with long black lashes, penetrating eyes that gazed right down into the most private recesses of her soul and smiled at what they saw there.

'Wake up . . . I've brought you stale bread and onions to soak in water. You must make a poultice with it and wrap it round your knee. D'ye hear me, now?'

He seemed to gather himself together with a great effort. The smile he gave her had such wry sweetness in it that she longed to put her arms round him to give him comfort.

'Ma'am,' he said in that deep blurry voice. 'I should welcome bread but I would not put it round my leg. It would go straight into my mouth for my stomach is in even poorer shape than my knee . . .' The long lashes closed over the bright feverish eyes again and his head went down onto his chest.

She soaked the bread and pulled the onion apart, layer by layer and packed the knee firmly with them. Then she took a green kerchief holding the mane of springy black hair off her face and bound it round the poultice.

'Hey Dudie . . . Hurry up there!'

Nat's voice brought her to her feet and she ran down the muddy shore to the waiting boat.

He was not a beggar. Of that she was certain. It was more likely that he was a gentleman fallen upon hard times – or even one of the escaped American prisoners. What disturbed her, whenever she thought of the small incident after that, was that though he was a complete stranger to her there was something profoundly familiar about him all the same.

It was nearly a week after the incident at Bosham that a note was left at the Dell Quay Office for Dudie. She picked it up as she collected her pay and stood against the wall outside the Crown and Anchor, next door to the Office to read it.

She was not a very fluent reader but the scrawl was large and clear and she recognised Mistress Chase's hand.

Thank you for the baskets. They are real good ones, so strong and tight woven. Ben and I do have a favour to ask of you. We have a visitor real sick and I don't seem to be having much success with curing the malady. We'd be much obliged if you could bring your balms and pots of salve over to Park Farm at the earliest moment.

She was due to go to Portsmouth the following noon. It would be no trouble to pop across to the Farm first, for it lay directly opposite the Quay, a hundred yards or so across the Channel on the Bosham shore.

She had somehow sensed who her patient might be in Mistress Chase's guest chamber even before she saw the agitation and twin spots of pink excitement in the old woman's cheeks.

Fran Chase was at once exhilarated and frightened at the risk that she and Ben were running but even as she gave Dudie a brief account of their rescue mission, it was clear that she was delighted with her visitors, both of them. *Both*?

'Oh yes, my dear. One of them is as black as the coal you deliver – and such a splendid person – enormously large, just like a giant but such a gentle soul, courteous in the extreme – and so amusing . . .' It was clear that this member of the duo had already found his way into her affections.

'And the other?'

Mistress Chase was already hurrying her up the stairs and she turned and glanced over her shoulder at Dudie. 'A very special young man, my dear . . . You'll soon discover why. Do your best for him in any way he asks, I beg of you, for he has real need of your help, quite apart from the health problem . . .'

It was as she had guessed.

The Bosham beggar was lying in a high bed, propped up by as many of Mistress Chase's pillows and cushions as she had been able to find. His matted hair had been washed and combed and the dark stubble on his chin shaved away.

Dudie grinned broadly as his mouth opened in astonishment at the sight of her. Premonition had given her just a moment's advantage.

'Good day to you, sir. Yes, it was I who fell over you in Bosham last week. How are you now? You are certainly cleaner and brighter than you were.'

He appeared to be struck dumb and lay back in his pillows, gazing at her with such concentration that she wasted no more time on polite conversation but set about examining his leg right away.

Stretched out, fast asleep on the floor at the bottom of the bed was the largest and blackest man she had ever seen. The hunch of his great shoulders almost rose to the level of the mattress. Even though he was curled on his side, he seemed to fill the floor between the bed and the window-seat.

Mistress Chase put her finger to her lips. 'Shhh. That is Moses. We had no other place to put him, so he sleeps there rather than share the bed with Master Heritage, here, and risk hurting his poor leg.'

Tom said, 'Don't you worry about waking him, ma'am.

Once he's asleep it'd take a stampede of wild horses to wake him.'

The resonance in his voice smote her, as it had done the first time she had heard him speak, quickening her pulses.

With Mistress Chase to help her, Dudie unwrapped Tom's leg and her small fingers crept over the puffy knee, probing so lightly that her patient seemed oblivious of discomfort and was content to watch her absorbed face.

He had, he told her, kept the green kerchief with which she had bound his knee. Mistress Chase had washed and ironed it. He seemed inclined to wish to keep it.

The knee was not only infected, it had been dislocated and must be put back into its socket before he put any weight upon it. Whilst he was in the strangely benign mood she saw in his expression, she wasted no time in manipulating the joint back into place. It was something that she had always had a talent for but the yell he gave as she jerked the lower leg round, woke his companion and an astonished ebony face, eyes apop, appeared at the bottom of the bed.

'What's going on here?' Moses asked, still bleary with sleep. Dudie introduced herself and, seeing how she was ministering to Tom, he was instantly appreciative.

She liked Moses at first glance, and he obviously returned the compliment, relishing her youth and clearly approving of what he saw in her. There was no time, that day, for friendly conversation and, while Tom still hugged himself and moaned with the pain she had inflicted upon him, she bade them farewell and left them without more ado. The barge was due across in Portsmouth before nightfall and time was running short.

'I will come and take a look at him in a few days,' she said to Fran Chase. She turned away and the old woman put a hand on her arm.

'There is something that you should know, Dudie.' She seemed hesitant and then drew in a deep breath. 'That young man, Tom Heritage, is here with a purpose.' She gazed intently into the gypsy girl's olive face. 'His mother is Violet Bayless, born over there at Lavenham. He has come to look at his birthright.'

She had sensed the bond of their blood, even as he lay on

the ground at Bosham. The Bayless eyes, not the piercing blue version that she and Nat possessed, bright stars generated by the first gorgio crossed with a Hator six generations ago. No, these were the other eyes. The grey ones which came and went without apparent connection, in this part of the family and then again, for no apparent reason, in another part. It was said that Violet Bayless had possessed them. So too, did Charles Bayless. It had been the only inheritance from his father, Lawrence.

Would the child within her have those eyes? There was no sign in either Charles or Tom of the terrible Gift that sometimes accompanied those deceptive grey pools.

Word would have to be sent to Janatha and Prentice Bayless, the current heads of the family, over in the dense oakwoods outside Wickham. It was possible that a dangerous situation was beginning to gather here for both cousins, it seemed, were obsessed with the House that had brought such evil upon both their families.

'Sarah will have to go over to Wickham and tell them,' Nat said when she broke the news to him. 'You cannot leave here in case you are needed across the water.'

He was sitting beside the fire, whittling a hazel twig with his paring knife. He raised the long twig and tapped her lightly on the arm with it. 'Best tell of your own involvement too, Pen. I don't like it. He's too keen, Master Charles. That kind of feelen' c'n end badly if'n you handle it wrong . . .'

She cupped her chin in her hands and stared into the hot embers of the dying fire. 'It has no roots, Bor. From the first I offered him my support, not my love – for his soul was ailen', poor man. Bruised and witheren', it was.'

So you say but he's had enough now and just be usen' ye . . . he won't let go easily for it's mighty convenient to have yer fine rawni on the one hand and yer poor girl to tumble when ye will on the other. He'll give ye trouble, see if he don't an' when that happens I'd not stand by and watch. You know my temper. An' now, darn it to hell, there's this other one.'

She smiled and a little dimple came and went beside her mouth. He frowned for there was suddenly a dreamy softening in Dudie's face. The vigorous strength in her became muted with uncharacteristic gentleness.

179

'Don't you go getten' involved there, for Scran's sake,' he said sharply, even more alarmed by this sudden change.

'I'm not, Pral.' Her voice was mild. 'I'm just nursing him. He's got a knee there that could lose him his leg if I don't make him respect its critical state. He'll sail away to France as soon as he is fit – Ben Chase will see to that – and anyway, we shall be gone from here by then.'

He was not convinced. Dudie was a fine-looking girl who had turned down the attentions of Matthew Boswell and one or two others around their own Tribe fire. When their mother had died and Sarah had married, Dudie had persuaded him to take her with him in search of work, away from the Tribe for most of the year. She was a good companion and not given to flightiness. He had never had cause to worry about her until now.

Now – he did not at all like the look that was back in her face as she watched the fire pictures glowing between the half-burned logs.

'Why are you so silent?' Charles asked her.

He picked her up and brought her into his lap and sat with his arms round her, feeling the warmth of her body against his chest.

'I do not mean to be.'

She sat obediently against him but once again this day was quiet, unresponsive – as she had been for the last four. There were no small signs of her affection, no curling of a lock of his hair around her finger. No nuzzling against his cheek like a kitten seeking attention. Her compliance was as negative a response to him as Leonie's limp subjection had always been.

'What is ailing the girl?' he thought in irritation. Since their last visit to Lavenham there had been a subtle change in their relationship, not – he was convinced – of his making for his need of Dudie was as great as ever. Maybe she was beginning to feel that she could use her attractions to her own advantage. To tease him into a state where he would promise her anything she wished for. Women were designing creatures and her coolness certainly had the effect of angering him.

'Are you sick?' he asked. She looked well enough and had suffered his eager coupling without complaint. He had even been able to bring her to climax which always titillated him in the extreme for it still, after all these months, gave him the most powerful gratification. He turned her round and pressed his mouth against her breast. The nipple rose enticingly against his tongue and he buried his nose between the tight, full little mounds.

She drew back from him with a gasp. 'You're hurting me,' she said sharply and there was a stiffness now about her that he had never felt before. The very withdrawal of her was a new sweetness. He lifted her so that she straddled his lap and held her tightly against him, entering her hard.

She fought him.

She beat at him with her fists.

'God, you're fierce,' he said hoarsely against her hair, holding her down into his lap. Suddenly she was like a wild thing, tearing at his hair, sinking her teeth into his shoulders, clawing at his face. It was exquisitely primeval.

Afterwards, he said to her, 'Why did you fight me like that? It was an exhilarating experience – but look, you are still angry with me. What have I done?'

But she shook her head, avoiding his eyes.

Later, to change the subject he said, 'Those two escaped prisoners from the Langstone hulk – have you heard anything about them?'

She stared blankly at him. 'Why should I? They never came here.'

She was still angry. He said gently, 'I need to know. One of them is related to me – to you too, for that matter, for his mother is Violet Bayless.'

He had her attention now. She was combing her hair, wet from the river. She stopped for a second and then continued with slow combing sweeps, eyes fixed on his face with an empty waiting look.

'We know the history of Violet Bayless,' she said. 'If you knew he was in that stinking hole, why did you not move mountains to get him paroled?'

Here it was – the very thing that he had tried to avoid. 'I would probably have lost my contractor's licence if it came to light that one of the prisoners was my own cousin,' he said shortly.

'Is your business so much more important than your family, then? Certainly the Romani strain has been bred right out of you, which must be a relief.'

'Look, Dudie.' He changed his tone, doing his best to smooth away this uncharacteristic criticism in her. 'Of course I care about my flesh and blood. Maybe not as passionately as you people do –'

'We gypsies. We riff-raff. Why do you not come right out and say it for that's what you mean, isn't it?'

'No, that's not what I mean. I think that the closeness of the Romani tribes is a most commendable and astonishing phenomenon and there are times when I try to feel that way too, but I just cannot see the sense in jeopardising a line of business that I have taken great pains to build into a very special concern, simply to give unlawful protection to one man who was a complete stranger to me until recently.'

She threw down the comb. It fell to the floor with a clatter and slid beneath the narrow bunk. He had bought it for her in London; a pretty thing made of bone with a silver inlaid handle.

'How quickly you forget when it suits you.' Her words were hard little lashes. 'Did his mother never do the same for you? . . . a child she had never seen . . . Did she weigh that against your needs?'

He stared at her in astonishment. She was clenching and unclenching her fists, eyes blazing.

'For God's sake, Dudie. What IS wrong with you? We are speaking of help for one stranger from another, not making accusations. The man is at large. It may be that I can now help him. I couldn't before.' He took her chin and turned her face towards him. 'Well – I could not, could I?' His voice was soft, persuasive. The grey eyes pleaded. His thumbnail pressed the flesh of her cheek, insisting.

Dudie turned away from him in disgust. 'Look, Master,' she said coldly, 'I have things to do before the morning. Be good enough to leave me now to get on with them.'

This was a new Dudie, an imperious and beautiful woman with complete assurance. God, what he would not do to get a submission from such a prize. He started to speak, to cajole her but saw the look in her eyes and stopped, suddenly mortified. Damn and curse her. The vixen had dismissed him like any pot boy.

He stood up and went down the waggon steps without a word. Before he had time to turn and bid her farewell she had closed the painted doors behind him with a sharp slam. He heard the bolt being drawn across.

She had sent him packing in a more summary fashion than many a titled lady might have done. Dudie Smith, a grubby little gypsy – in his own employ. He raised his riding crop to hammer on the door and saw Nat Smith standing beside the hearth, silently watching, his dark face glowering.

'That sister of yours needs to curb her temper and keep a civil tongue in her head,' he said. Nat said nothing but stood like a stone. The stick in his hand had a heavy knob on the end. It usually lived in his belt.

Charles withdrew and rode back to Chichester with the anger in him slowly rising to fury. Bloody little vixen. What right had she to question his actions? It was only later that night, when sleep eluded him and he thought back to the furious excitement of that beautiful, angry, struggling, hurting body and the extra eroticism of mounting it that it occurred to him that Dudie might be tiring of him.

Chapter Five

Tom was out of bed by the time Dudie next went over to dress his knee. He had even, he admitted with a certain sheepishness, done a little exercising, pacing the room with a painful rolling hobble that had quickly been too much for him.

'How can you be so foolish?' she scolded, to cover her pleasure at the warmth of his welcome. He was propped up in a comfortable chair with his leg on a footstool. He was looking well-cared for, even happy, his face shining with soap and his dark hair queued neatly with a bone clip. From where he sat he could look across to the busy jetty and untidy sprawl of warehouses and buildings that was Dell Quay and on down the Chichester Channel until it curved out of sight beyond Birdham. His eyes were bright and the deep hollows and bony ridges of his starvation were beginning to soften out in his face, returning his youth.

'Well, one good thing is happening,' she said, fixing him with a fiercely critical frown. 'At least Mistress Chase's excellent food is having its effect for you have surely gained weight in the past few days.'

'Yeah, ma'am,' Moses drawled from his seat in the window. 'That fella eat so much, I reckon's he'll never get out of his chair again . . . ever – 'cos his por li'l ole pins is not goin' to be able to support his stomach.' He rolled his eyes complacently and stroked his own hard midriff with well-calloused hands. 'Now me, Mistress – Moses eats whatever is put on his platter and thanks the Almighty an' Mistress

Chase for their generosity but all the night long I works and sweats an' in the morning I'm flat in the belly and ready fer more. This old man here, I swear he's in the darndest all-gone crazy mood, he just sits and dreams and eats these pore folks clean. T'aint good for him, ma'am, so get him onto his feet soon, won't you? Even so's he can ease what's eatin' at his l'il old heartstrings and chase you round the furniture.' His soulful eyes danced at the two of them.

'Take no notice of Moss,' Tom said, aiming a friendly blow at the big man's barrel chest. 'He's just jealous. At heart, he's the idlest nigger on earth, just you deny it, Mosey. Cain't bear to see others resting while he's aworking, that's all.'

They grinned at each other, both knowing the raw restlessness which burned in both their hearts under the banter. However comfortable their lodgings, however beguiling the company, they wanted only to be gone now.

'Well, however fat he's getting, he'll have to stay that way for a while yet,' Dudie said after examining the knee. It was certainly improving but should have been less inflamed by now. The weight upon it as he tried to use it had re-opened delicate new tissue around the cap.

She accepted a mug of mint tea after she had re-dressed the knee and sat between the two men, content to listen to their good-humoured bickering. When Moses uncoiled his great frame from the windowseat and left them, they sat silently, content in the knowledge that polite conversation was not necessary between them.

When they began to talk, it was not of Tom and the distant family across the vast expanse of ocean, as she would have wished. He dominated the conversation, questioning her closely about herself, about the life of the Romanies living in the southern forests. She told him the story of Boudicca, the great Queen of the Iceni, and was amused at his surprise at her unexpected learning. Without intending to be patronizing he showed his astonishment that the Romanies, who for the most part neither read nor wrote, could still embellish their own folklore with the highlights of gorgio history.

'Romanies love a good story,' she smiled. 'Give us the simplest incident and we'll dress it up until it becomes the most exciting of sagas. There be times when we're afeasten' that the stories go on being told all through the night – an' not a soul thinks to sleep for he might miss the best of it.'

He shook his head in wonderment. When she sparkled at him in that fashion it was hard to get his breath.

She was not prepared for the next question.

'Do you know Master Charles Bayless then?'

Somehow, she had thought that he would ply her with questions concerning their own relationship and the great family of Jasper and Grace who had sired both their grandparents. Mention of Charles reminded her of less pleasant things and the smile left her face.

'Yes. I know him,' she said shortly and lowered her head to sip at her cup of tea.

Tom sensed the withdrawal in her and forbore to ask more.

He watched the struggle in her and then she said suddenly, 'Master Chase, he told me how you was asken' so many questions about the Baylesses and that old place across there . . . Lavenham. What do you want to know so much fer? You've got your family and all the comforts that money can buy, back in that Americky place. What you want to pry into the Clan fer? You cain't want to be one o' us, not with all your book learnen' and fine ways . . .'

She had touched a tender spot, she saw at once. He straightened his back and jutted his chin, in such a similar fashion to Charles when crossed that she almost cried out.

'That is where you are wrong, Miss.' His voice was almost curt. 'That may well be the way that Master Charles sees you but I only ask about my mother's family out of affection and interest. We have been kept very much in the dark about Lavenham and the Baylesses by both our parents and the curiosity of my brother and sisters and myself is quite natural, I assure you.'

He hesitated, not knowing the extent of her knowledge. 'I know about the relationship between my grandfather and his sister, Amy. Charles told me. But there is so much more that puzzles all of us back home – so much that I would like to discover while I am right here, on the threshold of that past life.'

She took a deep breath and then placed her hand over his,

as though to offer comfort for what she was about to say. He covered it with his own hand.

She told him how the Killing Glance had come into the family, falling as she spoke into the comfortable vernacular of Romani tale-telling – with its colourful descriptions and subtle gildings of the events.

'. . . I know there is doubt in your heart and that you cannot believe what I tell you but it is true in every detail. I swear the truth of it upon our grandparents' memories. There are so many folk still living who would tell you how it was, and that your own mother was possessed of the Killing Glance – as Charles' father also was. Your mother never felt the need to use it, so they say, but Lawrence Bayless . . . he let it become his God – and the wickedness it wrought in him eventually destroyed him.'

Tom sat close to her, his expression a mixture of puzzlement and ridicule.

'The villagers say that the evil lives on in Lavenham. It is a place where no man from these parts, excepten' the Clan, will go. There was too much Death there, you see.'

He nodded. 'I know the truth of that, for Ben Chase said much the same thing and told me of what he saw there with his own eyes.'

She squeezed the hand that held hers so securely. 'Sir, I am not making up fanciful tales just to discourage you from going to Lavenham. I have been there and it is a place of great beauty. It presented no threat to me, nor to Nat – ever.'

Memory swept through an image of Charles, his pale face tinged with a small boy's terror that was all the more frightening to behold in the face of a grown man. She had made him go with her to Lavenham and face up to his boyhood fantasy – only to find that the evil was still there in the House and all too clearly no fantasy after all. She had put him through that nightmare out of her own ignorance. It must not be allowed to happen a second time.

'If the dangers are for those who bear the grey eyes,' she said slowly, picking her words with care, 'then it is wisest that you do keep away for its rage is truly terrible – or so it has been said by many many folks who have SEEN the result. If the Place seeks another kind of person upon whom to vent itself, then I don't know how to identify them. Charles is still suffering now from that one experience in his youth. Don't you think that its hatred might be even greater against you . . . an adult?'

Her face, unguarded and anxious, was turned to him, only inches from his own. It needed sudden strength not to shift very slightly in his chair and kiss the worry lines from her smooth young forehead.

She went on, 'You – and Charles also – have the grey eyes that carry the Power . . . though neither of you shows signs of actually possessing it. But then, you have not set foot in that House, have you? So you don't know how it might affect your own personality if you were unwise enough to challenge it?'

In spite of his scepticism, a shiver ran down Tom's back.

'Dudie,' he said to her to change the subject since it was leading them nowhere and there was something that he suddenly needed to discover: 'How well do you know Charles Bayless?'

Her hand clenched in his and she withdrew it to smooth away invisible wrinkles from her skirt. 'Well enough,' was all she would say. 'Nat an' I be worken' one of his coalen' barges. Why should we not know him?'

She would permit herself to be drawn no further and rose to take her leave, knowing that she was leaving Tom – and Moses – with some very strange food for thought and discussion. She could only hope with all her heart that he would not be quite so eager, though, to investigate Lavenham on his own.

The knee mended slowly. Moses saw to it that Tom did nothing of which Dudie might not approve and gradually the ligaments knitted and strengthened so that he was able to walk with the aid of a stick. She went over to Park Farm once or twice each week and with every visit was tempted to make the journey more often. Nat was never far away from her these days however, watchful and fiercely protective and not understanding at all how she felt about her visits to this other cousin.

'We have problems enough with Charles Bayless,' he muttered, concerned and angry with her. 'What do you want to go involving yourself with the other for? If Charles gets wind of Tom Heritage's whereabouts, he'll probably send in the Militia – 'e's so anxious to keep 'is name shinen' – and then you'd be taken off as an accessory. You know what that'd mean . . . Ten years transportation or even the gibbet.'

He was right, of course, she knew that. Charles had become so demanding of her now that things would come to a head before long and he, Nat, would swing for it before he would let that bastard hurt her.

'Hush, Pral, hush.' She tried to soothe the anger from him. 'Only a few weeks or even days now and then we can go from here. Until then, we'll be wise to stay out of his way.'

But they had little opportunity of keeping a low profile for the evening of the following day Charles appeared once more at their hearth . . .

He had been in private torment since the day that Dudie had sent him away from her. At the time, hurt pride at so curt a dismissal had thrown him into a black mood which seemed impossible to shake off. He swung like a metronome between despair, contrition and sullen rage which vented itself upon his employees and family alike. Since he was not usually given to such churlish ill-humour, for his temper was cold rather than vicious, his behaviour was viewed with concern, and Leonie, bowing her head before his degrading contempt, was afraid that he might, through overwork, be on the threshold of a brain-storm. He was, however, in the grip of a despair so great that the very magnitude of it shocked him. His feeling for Dudie, who was after all only an uneducated peasant, logic protested, was now so intense that should he return to her good graces he was going to have to clarify his position.

Would she permit him to set her up in her own little home where he could visit her and they might share some recognizable relationship together? It was possible that she might be tempted for he could certainly ensure that she had every comfort her heart desired, a servant of her own and a groom for her carriage. Then, when Leonie's declining health had finally broken and he had gone through the correct period of mourning . . . was it so unthinkable to consider wedding Dudie? Grandmama Freeland had wed a gypsy, after all, and they had been accepted for the most part by the community.

He hung onto these fantasies for days after his dismissal and finally, buoyed up by the hope they gave him, went to the Common to make his apologies.

The visit was a grave mistake for he only managed to create an even greater rift between them. He had felt close to breaking point for he seemed to have no control over his feelings at all, however hard he tried to hold himself in check. When he saw the look on Dudie's face at the sight of him, a stranger seemed to take hold of him.

'I came to apologize for my rudeness,' he started to say and then the words stuck in his throat for she was standing beside the waggon step with one hand on the top rung, her slim body half-turned as though to ignore him. There was no warm greeting in her face, no forgiveness. The lovely fine features, with that proud way she carried her head with its great mane of hair, were those of an Empress dismissing a lesser mortal.

She said nothing at all but hesitated with one foot on the bottom step. He felt like a tonguetied boy and at the same time mortified to know that her coldness would have been more than justified in a young woman of his own breeding.

'Dudie, please don't shut me out. I was entirely in the wrong to have forced myself upon you and I apologize. I simply cannot live this life of mine without your affection. I feel very deeply for you, you must have realized that. You probably knew it before I did. Forgive me . . . I beg you.'

He took a step towards her and held out a hand.

'Don't you come any nearer.' Her voice was low and harsh. She moved slightly, shifting her weight from one foot to the other and he saw the gleam of a flensing knife in her hand.

'Oh Dudie, I'm not going to hurt you. How could you think that I would?' The pain in his voice was so sharp that she hesitated and then laid the knife on the top step.

He made one movement and had his arms round her before she had time to turn.

'It is so foolish to be afraid of me, dearest Dudie,' he said and the ragged breath was almost a sob against her hair. 'See, I shan't even kiss you if you don't wish. I just need to hold you and know that you are not angry with me any more.'

She stood woodenly against him, saying nothing and he held her back from him, looking anxiously into her closed face.

'Dudie, come and live with me. Let me find us a little cottage somewhere that is your very own. I can visit you and we shall be together in so much more natural circumstances than this furtive relationship we have now.'

She said – and her voice was flat, featureless – 'We have no relationship any more, sir, other than the accident of our births and your control of Nat's and my employment. This is all the home I want, now or ever. It's what we be born to and Nat would not allow it to be any different . . .'

'You and Nat. Is that all you think of?' He was horrified at the sudden fury in his voice and the words that came out with it were uttered by a stranger. 'You and Nat. Is it common practice, after all, for gypsies to love their brothers more than other men?'

Oh God, why had he said that! It had never been in his thoughts for a moment.

She jerked out of his grasp and dealt him a blow across the mouth with her clenched fist that split his lip. The warm salt taste of blood came off his tongue. His hands went up, gripping her shoulders hard, digging his fingers into the coarse oiled wool of her shawl, feeling the rounded flesh beneath. He shook her – and in the movement his anger blossomed, shot through with the awful need of her. She saw the look in his face and brought her knee up into his crotch and he cried out and released her, curling up and rolling away in agony. She ran up the steps and flung herself through the waggon entrance. He was in too much pain to hear the bolts being shot on the inside of the door.

He rode home in pain, the bruised crotch the lesser of two ills. Pride and wretched humility tore at him. He excused himself from Leonie's company that evening and attended a cock-fight in Nyetimber.

The time for silence was over. Dudie sat outside the firelight with the flensing knife in her lap and bowed her head at her brother's fury as she told him of her condition.

'But why did you not tell me this before, you dinelo gurnii? I'd have thrashed the smug smile off the bastard's face . . .'

'That's why I said nothing, Bor. What is the point of risking your own life for something that has already happened? It's too late – and in any case, I haven't told him. It would give him more hold over me in his eyes.'

Nat picked up a stone and flung it with all his strength into the dusk. A long way away it fell with a splash into the river. 'My God, Dudie. Do you realize what will happen now?'

She nodded, head still down. 'The family will have to know. I've thought of that. But they need not know who the father is.'

'Oh, that is simple then, isn't it? Just refuse to name the man – and it will look for all the world as though you've been sellen' yourself with my blessen'.' The sarcasm was underlaid with hurt and she scrambled up and went to him and hugged him tightly.

'Dearest Nat, the reason why I was allowed to come with you on the road was simply because of the family's trust in you as my brother. They know you – and they know me, too. I would no more fall into those ways than you would permit it if I tried. I shall tell them who was responsible – and how it happened. It is my punishment for permitting the situation to exist.'

Nat sat by the fire, building it up again and again into the early hours of the new day.

Charles tried to see Dudie to apologize twice after the last furious meeting but somehow she never seemed to be at the camp when he rode over there. Worried and becoming daily more distracted by his increasing obsession, he made a wrong decision with one of his investment ventures and suddenly discovered that his abstraction was costing him dear.

It was time to sit down and try to put his house and his heart in order. Certainly he was going to have to try other ways of regaining Dudie's approval for he knew now absolutely that he could not exist without her.

He had brought Nat into his office as soon as the barge had completed de-coaling. There was no good purpose to be served in approaching the subject carefully and he came straight to the point.

'Look Nat, I know that I've gravely offended Dudie and I'm paying the price with every day that I don't see her.'

Nat stood silently before the desk, blank-faced. His hands, engrained with coaldust, curled and uncurled at his side. He was neither cold nor friendly and stood beside Charles' desk with studied indifference. Charles tried to keep the agitation he was feeling from his voice.

'What am I to do, Nat? Give me some guidance for I only wish to do the honourable thing by Dudie. She is all the real happiness that I have ever known, you see . . . It is not easy for me to talk to you this way, please appreciate that, but how am I to get her to forgive me and bid me welcome at your hearth again?'

Nat shifted from one foot to the other. His voice was a deep rumble somewhere down in his chest. A muscle twitched in his jaw.

'Happen she's had enough, Bor,' he said, his eyes scouring the floor. 'Happen she's found she don't want ter dandle with another woman's husband. She be a fine Chavi, see. Make a good strong wife for one of our own kind but not you, Master. She'd be no good in your Kenner. You be gentry – even if there's Clan blood in yer – and already wed to one of yer own who's born you sons and don't deserve to be cuckolded. There be no future for you with Dudie, Master Charles. Best leave 'er be.'

'But I cannot. *I cannot*.' The words were groaned across the desk, the very pain in them a lash which flayed both men.

Nat looked up at him then and there was no pity for Charles in his stare, no understanding of one man for another's torture. Utter contempt was a scourge in his eyes, his rejection carved in the grim jut of his hard jaw.

'You'm goen' to have to, then. She's not fer you, Bor. She gave herself to you from pity, not love. Not love as you wish it. Just pity, that's what it was. Pity for a man with all the gifts of an easy life and none of the simple pleasure of contentment – an' now that's gone – so she feels nothen' for yer. Nothen'. By pressen' her for attention, you only make it worse, only make the nothen' into actual hate. Best keep away from 'er, I tell ye . . . for scorn in Dudie is painful punishment an' you're on the way to earnen' it, the way you're goen' . . .'

It was the final indignity.

'We'll see about that,' Charles said and there was that in his voice which made Nat's brows shoot up into his curly hair.

He left the Quay Office then without another word. The reckoning of this day would shortly be upon them.

It was the day Dudie told Tom of her condition.

It was late afternoon and Dudie was sitting quietly in the windowseat at the Farm, letting the mellow rays of the sinking sun warm her. Moses was fast asleep in the feather bed, an occasional soft long snore betraying the depth of his slumbers.

She had been reading Tom's hand and making a fair impression on him, despite his overlying scepticism. Her mood was pensive, not tinged with the laughter and quick wit with which they usually wrestled.

'Is something troubling you today?' Tom asked for the second time. He withdrew his hand from her lap and put his arm round her shoulders, drawing her towards him. She shook her head, safe within the circle, and was content to stay there. He made no closer move and just held her lightly as he might have comforted one of his sisters. Conversation became patchy for both felt the presence of something unsaid between them and when he asked a third time she had no strength left to deny him.

'I am with child,' she said in a low voice and raised her eyes to scourge herself with the disapproval she must see in his face.

There was shock there. It was something that had never occurred to him, that she might have a life and a lover outside the weekly visits to the Farm. Yet here she was now, accepting the intimacy of that comforting arm about her shoulders and obviously as warmed by it as he was. She watched the blood drain from his face, leaving it pinched and grey and two lines appeared on either side of the grim set of his mouth. Then the hard lines all relaxed and he let go the breath that had been stopped in his chest and hugged her.

'Oh Dudie, why did you not say so before? We could have cheered you up, Moss and I – even if we are powerless to give you any proper assistance. Are you happy to have a child of your own? Do you intend to marry? . . .'

He stopped the questions which flooded out, drowning a growing sensation of utter anguish which was slowly threatening to engulf him.

Her face was an open book of misery struggling with compassion which told its own private tale.

He stroked the curve of her cheek for she said nothing but turned her face from him.

'If this is an accident,' he said slowly, 'is there not a cure for the condition? Romanies have the cure for most things, do they not? Have you not the answer in that medicine box of yours?'

She shook her head. 'We do not believe in killing unborn babies,' she said. 'My worry is not in the child, for there is plenty of room for it beside the fire. My concern, my curse is in the father – and of what the child will therefore turn out to be.'

She felt Tom's iron control reasserting itself, his striving to comfort through some secret anguish of his own. She felt the sudden dawning of his feeling for her, unspoken – but there in growing strength – and was warmed by it, knowing it to be right.

The rest had to be in the open between them.

'The child is Charles Bayless'.'

Nat had little to say to anyone on the trip over to Portsmouth that day. The others, seeing the black look on his face and knowing the ferocity of his temper on the few occasions that they had seen him lose it, exchanged warning looks with each other and left him to himself.

He needed the time to think.

Thinking always cost him for he was a man who worked with his hands and his will. Thinking took up too much 'doing' time. Now though, his future suddenly looked rocky. He and Dudie were in a very dangerous position and he had to devise a way of getting them out of it without trouble.

Charles Bayless had not sacked him there and then. He had walked out before more words could be exchanged. They could simply strike camp and move on. That would be the easiest and wisest thing to do. But Dudie seemed obsessed with this other one and he knew that she would not hear of it. He had tried ordering her to pack the kettle irons and go. She had refused, wearing that particular look of baleful obstinacy which warned that she was the equal of him – and if he went, he would go alone.

There was no question of that.

One day he would wed, but not before Dudie. He had to see her safely cared for by a good Rom of her choice and his approval. He had thought for one short but worrying period that the man might have been Charles Bayless but she had explained her feelings there and of the depth of her pity for the void that dwelt deep within the gorgio. It was only her open-hearted compassion that had permitted the intimacy with him. Neither of them had expected him to become so deeply involved, for they both assumed that he would simply take advantage of Dudie's kindliness and make the most of a pleasure which had been denied him so far in life.

The child, if he were to know of its existence, would only make it more difficult for them to extricate themselves. It was fortunate indeed that she had said nothing to him about her condition but he would not long be in ignorance for within a short time it would begin to show.

And now, to complicate their situation even more, Dudie was suddenly reacting in a very different way to Tom Heritage.

'He has not made any advance towards me,' she had assured an exasperated Nat when he had accused her of playing Charles and Tom against each other. 'Indeed, he treats me with great politeness and respect. But I am very drawn to him, Nat. I feel our kinship and cannot help the warmth of those feelings for there is something so alive and vital about him . . .'

She could not, or would not, be questioned further but he saw it in her expression, the response, the wanting – even the beginnings of withdrawal from him.

At the end of the shuttle he shook his head at joining his companions in the Crown Tavern on the Quay and, seeing the mood in him they wisely let him go. He walked the mile back to the camp and his thoughts had come to no conclusion.

Dudie was waiting for him and it was soon evident that her thoughts had also been busy. 'I have told Tom Heritage,' she said to Nat as she prepared the waggon for sleep. 'He thinks that we should go from here with all speed —'

'— and I agree with him there.' Nat scowled, cursing the whole situation. 'Charles is like a snake with 'is victim, keepen' et tremblen' and waiten' fer to be struck. He was in the Quay Office, for his horse was tethered in the yard an' he'd have known I was bo'sn in the barge but 'e didn't send fer me. I says we get out of here an' soon. Why should we wait while 'e plots some kind of trouble fer us at 'is own convenience?'

'Yes, but Tom says that he escaped from "Fortunée" in order to visit Lavenham and he is going to do that almost immediately, though I think that that is another kind of madness. He thinks that we should go there also, for it is one place that Charles will avoid at all costs. I took him there and tried to get him to lay his fears that time, remember? His ghosts were strong in him still, though . . . and Lavenham would surely be the last place in the world that he'd ever go searchen' now — even for me . . .'

'Look, Dudie . . . it's time we went right away from here. We both agree that, yes? Well, that doesn't mean just striking camp and setten' up a mile away. It means we strike camp here and jall the drom. We can go east to Goudhurst or west to the Family at Wickham. We can go wherever we want. The last thing I'm doen' is hangen' around here for one moment after we harness old Sukie, see?'

'I know, Pral — and we shall do that, I promise. But not before Tom has been to Lavenham. Not before I've seen him safely off to France. I cannot explain why, but I HAVE to be there when he is in that House. If something bad were to befall him on his own, no one would ever know the truth of it. I must — no, WE must, for the blood that ties us, be there to see him through it.'

Nat lay on his pallet in the waggon and listened to her voice in the darkness. There was a slight breathlessness in it. She wanted to obey the man. She would obey him.

'I am your Pral,' he said harshly. 'I tell you what you must do. There has been enough of this consorting with gorgios, blood brothers or not. They bring nothing but trouble and danger. Let us be away on the drom right now, before dawn. We should not wait for the whims of others. Our own necks might well be in danger if Bayless feels like repaying your rejection with some trumped-up charge of thievery or worse. Once gone from here, you will soon forget about Tom Heritage and having the child will give you all the outlet you'll need until one of our own people claims you.'

'No, Nat. That isn't going to happen.' Her voice was soft, floating disembodied in the night air between them. 'Tom Heritage has more need of me than he knows for I saw things in his hand . . . and I saw my own presence there also.'

'Are you saying that you really want this American? That he is the one you would jump the broomstick with?'

There was anger in the muffled reply, masking her uncertainty. 'How am I to know? Why do you ask such a foolish thing when the very state I am in must surely make anything of a permanent nature impossible. He's a prisoner of war, escaped and therefore with the price of a bullet on his head. How can there ever be talk of him being for me when I shall be seen' the last of him in a matter of days, maybe hours even . . . Oh, let me be. Maybe the mornen' will make things clearer.'

He stretched out his hand in the dark and patted her arm. 'I'll see to it that no harm comes to ye,' he said gruffly.

And in the morning, Ben Chase came with the first streaks of a red dawn. 'Tom Heritage went over to Lavenham in the night,' he told them in great agitation.' Moses rowed him across but wouldn't go all the way with him. Said that he'd wait two hours for him. He waited until first glimmer of day an' then came back on his own. Very frightened, he is too. Said that Tom had no intention of staying in that place alone and he's mortal feared that something's befallen him. Go to Lavenham, I beg you. See if he's there. Find him and bring him back for I've arranged passage to France for the two of them in three days' time. It's asken' too much of good fortune for them to stay around here, for Mistress Chase says that Master Bayless has been seen, sniffen' around Bosham yesterday an' talken' with those boys who reported Tom and Moses to the Militia.'

Two red spots flowered in Dudie's cheeks. 'That's the answer, then,' she said to Nat and there was a steady flame in her eyes which meant that there was little he could do to refuse her.

'We'll go over there soon as we've harnessed the horse,' he said to Ben Chase. 'We're leaven' here in any case today, so we'll camp down below Hempsteddle, in the Lavenham paddock where Master Bayless won't think to venture. Rest easy, Master . . . we'll find yer wanderin' John Cheese an' get 'im back to you, safe and sound.'

They stood together watching the old man, muttering to himself in his agitation, hobbling away across the Common in the eerie blood red dawn.

The decision had been made for them, as Dudie said. Without speaking they began to gather up the cooking pots and paraphernalia of their long stay and stowed them on the shelf beneath the waggon. Nat stamped the last of the fire's embers into the ground and they washed in the stream and girt themselves for travel.

Before the dawn had split the night sky into the bright blue of early morning, they had saddled their waggon pony and were on the move.

'I see that Nat Smith has taken the coal to Portsmouth,' Charles said casually to his clerk later in the afternoon.

'No, sir.' The man looked up from his ledger and a twitch of annoyance brought his white eyebrows together. 'He should have taken her but he's not turned up today. I had to put another man in his place. There'll have to be a very good reason why he never showed. Not even a message to say he was indisposed. I've a mind to sack him for such carelessness, except that he is usually most reliable and not given to dropping out – and he's a fine boatswain. The best we've got.'

Charles said nothing. He hurried over the Common to the camp as soon as time allowed, praying that he might find Dudie on her own – and found the place deserted but for the remains of the overnight fire. He stood where the waggon wheels had dug deep runnels into the soil and cursed himself, for she would not have turned her back on him like this if he had kept a tighter control of himself.

But they were gone and he knew that he would never find them in this place again.

It was certainly he who had driven them away.

The realization of it stabbed at him, twisting the heart in his chest, making him close his eyes upon the pain of the familiar scene with the little River Lavant running a silver frame round the slight dip in the Common that had given the camp all the shelter it needed. She was gone from him now, gone for good. He was as sure of that one hard fact just as he was certain, without anything other than his instincts to back him, that Tom Heritage was hiding at Lavenham.

The Watcher stood back in deep night shadow, watching the man limping slowly up the stairs, brushing aside long swathes of cobwebs as he went. A full moon outside the gallery casements lit his way with stark white clarity and etched the traces of an old suffering on his intent face.

There was a strange peace in the House. Lavenham held its breath, watching this seedling of its creator, and beginning even now to probe his mind and the objective behind his presence. There was no sense of menace with this one but he was not aware of the rules. The House would beguile him, smooth his way so that it would seem natural for him to linger there a little longer . . . and a little longer. The forces of its strength would be at work already, bending wills, creating a situation from which it would finally feed – and in feeding grow in its carnality.

SHE would watch over him. The Watcher could feel her already, almost see her luxuriating in this young man's innocence, the limping gait a parody of her own. She would smother him with the protective passion that she had felt for Jess but even with all the fierce strength of that love there was little real power in her to protect him from the Place.

It was so eternally mystifying, the Watcher thought, that he had the power of death at the moment of life only. There was nothing that he could do to help this one. Who was he?

Only the name would give him the period. The fellow's clothing meant little – for breeches, shirt and jacket were all plain in the extreme. Maybe this was the nineteenth century at last.

Another realization came to him at that moment.

Strange that while he was in this suspension his burnt hands felt no pain at all. He stretched and flexed them, grateful for the short respite from their tortured throbbing.

PART THREE

Lavenham

Chapter One

A persistent jingle woke Tom and he sat up with a jerk that made him wince. There was a brief moment of sharp fear before he recognized his surroundings, expecting the comfortable security of the farmhouse bedchamber and finding instead that he was curled up in a capacious armchair in a chill and dusty room, steeped in swathes of enormous cobwebs, its heavy furnishings faded almost to a uniform mouldering grey and the heavy silence accentuated by the scratchings of small scurrying things behind the woodwork. He stared about him in confusion until memory flooded back and in the same instant he heard again that distant penetration of silvery horse bells which had woken him.

He levered himself out of the chair and went stiffly over to the broad leaded casement, rubbing his aching leg. Husks of long-dead cockroaches hung in cobweb cradles at the corners of the window frames. Dust coated the panes, obscuring his view and he rubbed one with the sleeve of his jacket and peered out.

Dawn was just breaking in purple bands of light across the night sky, shot through with growing slashes of a livid red. The fiery bars cast a sullen bronze light over the oakwoods and waters of the Channel, turning the outbuildings on one side of the house into monstrous black sentinels.

Just disappearing through the archway leading into the main stableyard was the back of a covered waggon . . .

He stood leaning against the folded shutters, momentarily shaken by the unexpected sight of movement, of life. He had become cocooned in the silent contemplation of himself and the House, closing his mind to everything beyond the boundaries of this legendary dream which was suddenly reality. Now, feeling a rude jolt at the intrusion, it was almost as though he felt the disquiet of the House itself.

No one ever came to Lavenham, so it was said. Ben had been adamant about this and Charles and Dudie too, though Dudie had qualified the bald statement a little more adding that the exception was the Bayless family itself — for the gypsy Clan considered it family property and camped in the south paddock occasionally.

Dudie? Could it be that she had convinced Nat, after all, that they should come over to Lavenham? His musing spirit lifted at the thought.

He had only meant to wander through the House and return quickly to Moses but there was something here which beckoned him, made him feel unaccountably at home and then there was something else which held him. Everything around him seemed strangely familiar and his feeling of well-being spread into a warm euphoria. He had felt this same way before, no doubt especially after drinking too many pots of French wine. Light-headed . . . happy. Feeling a ridiculous urge to sing aloud through the quiet, abandoned rooms.

Intrusion by others would destroy the spell.

He peered out through the single pane of clear glass but no further movement caught his eye and he turned away, the waggon and its occupants put aside for the moment. They would probably, if it was Dudie and Nat, come banging on the door in a few minutes. If it was someone else, they would not know of his presence and he could inspect them, unobserved, in his own time.

The House called to him NOW. Taking a deep breath of the musty air he gave himself up to it and wandered across the room making scuffs in the dust as he went. A small thread of reason persisted at the back of his mind.

He really must hurry and return to Moses. A pity because he wanted more than anything he could ever remember to stay on here for a while and account for all that the House contained. Mother would wish that of him for the contents were of considerable value, as the daylight quickly showed him, and she would be comforted to know that her father's treasures were still waiting safely for her here.

He opened the chamber door and stepped into the gallery, pausing to study the portraits at length, the waggon forgotten. There was no doubt who the subjects were, for they were such an integral part of the whole Lavenham story, as easy to identify, each one, as though he had known them all his life. They stared down from their gilded frames with bright, youthful faces, his own features stamped on two of them and those of Charles Bayless smiling down at him from the others.

Charles.

Something erupted in him without warning. A rage which had boiled away deep inside him since Dudie had told him of her condition. He had always been careful to control his behaviour, having inherited his father's strong sense of right and wrong. In this House, though, all thought of Charles Bayless brought blinding hate suddenly into focus and he snarled aloud at the welling up of it through every nerve in his body.

'Whoa there . . . nothing is worthy of that kind of feeling!' he told himself, startled by this uncharacteristic venom. Charles had always quietly done his best for the prisoners and it would not have been in their interests for him to have admitted having a relative amongst them. That he had brought trouble to Dudie was a tragic situation, made all the more so by her lack of real affection for a man who was obviously devoted to her. She had been quite honest, sparing nothing. Charles had even offered her a home – and was not yet aware that she was pregnant. In his eyes, Tom thought, it gave Charles the benefit of the doubt over the sincerity of his intentions, even though he had a wife – however sickly. Nor was it, in all honesty, either his or Charles' fault that they were both smitten by the same woman.

Tom resolutely closed his mind on the anger which continued to push to the surface when the thought of Charles Bayless strove to distract his attention from the pictures of his mother and her family. He turned away from the portraits with their almost-living faces. There seemed to be something very odd about this place for it was affecting him in a way that was most disturbing. He limped along the gallery, concentrating on raising as little dust as possible on the staircase and made his way down to where he could get a better view of the waggon in the yard.

There was a stone passage leading off the Hall, passing the kitchens to an outside door. The hinges on the yard door had completely rusted and the noise he made trying to drag it open must have been heard all the way to Newbarn Cottage. It was hardly surprising when his concentration was shaken by a sudden sharp hammering on the oak panels.

'Tom . . . *is that you?*'

Dudie's voice sounded faraway, disembodied . . . but the anxiety in it was unmistakable.

'Yes,' he said. 'It's me, right enough, as you'll see if only I can get this thing open. Push, if you will. The hinges are rusted solid.'

He heard a murmur of voices. So there was someone else out there with her under the entrance arch. He could hear a muttered discussion and stood still, straining to catch their words. Had she brought Charles with her, after all?

'Who's there with you?' he called.

'It's only Nat, Bor . . . don't worry. I'd not bring anyone else.'

The door suddenly gave and crashed back against the passage wall, catapulting two figures across the threshold.

'Phew!' she said, grinning up at him in her imp's way from where she sprawled at his feet. 'Sar shan, Simensa. Welcome to Lavenham.' She clambered to her feet and pulled her brother forward.

'This is Nat,' she said. 'We've left our camp on the Common for he and Charles had a few unfriendly words yesterday and, in his present way of thinken' it's likely he'd give us some trouble there. He won't come here, though. Master Chase come over not an hour ago, and warned us that you'd come here so . . . we thought we'd keep you company until it's time for you and Moses to go.'

The bulky shape of Nat Smith appeared at Dudie's back. Tom knew who the rangy figure must be for here was the kind of gypsy that Mistress Chase had described to him. Foreign-looking with his long, pale face, black curls and brooding, distrustful eyes. The high cheekbones and sallow skin were there in Dudie also, but they looked very different on her – giving her dark beauty a sharp sensuality.

'I'm pleased to see you. Thought you might have Moses with you when I heard voices.' The disappointment in his voice was overlaid by something else and she narrowed her eyes at him in the dim passage, trying to read his face.

He looked tired but there was an excitement in him, a breathlessness as though he had made a great discovery and was hugging it to himself, loth to share it.

'Come on in.' He turned and limped away from them down the passage, back towards the Hall. They followed, looking about them cautiously. The red dawn had strengthened and paled into a pinkly overcast morning. There would be no sun this day to burn through the heavy rain clouds which stood off the land on the horizon like great purple cliffs.

The Hall in daylight was impressive. Its ceiling was lofty, like the nave of a church with the stairs and gallery giving it unexpected elegance. The destruction of the table at its centre added a sense of ancient drama and the three of them stood uncertainly bunched together, eyes roving slowly over the smashed refectory table lying in two halves, its legs mouldering like broken bones amongst the dust eddies.

'I can scarcely believe the story of what was meant to have happened here,' Tom said, resisting the urge to whisper.

Nat moved away from the table. 'There be bengs here, all right,' he growled, the deep voice echoing back at them. 'Best to leave 'em alone, I say. They've done no harm these many years an' I'm all for leaven' it that way. You come back here and stir 'em all up again – an' who can guess at what might happen.'

He crossed to the parlour door which was hanging back on one hinge. He stepped out of their sight and they listened to him moving about in the room.

Dudie slipped her hand into Tom's and he drew her against his side. They examined the shattered table and Dudie shivered.

'What a tremendous impact something must have had,' she said, tracing a splintered shaft of oak with a finger. He didn't answer and she looked round and found him staring up at the gallery, frowning. 'What is the matter?'

209

He shook his head and for a moment continued to search the shadows above them. 'I'm not sure,' he said at last, dragging his eyes back to her. 'I could have sworn that I saw someone up there looking down at us.' He laughed. 'It's surprising what fancies you can dream up if suggestion is planted in the mind first.'

His voice was light but she could see that he was still not convinced that there were only shadows up in the gallery.

'Shall we go up there and see?' she said, matching her tone to his. 'Nat, we're taking a look at the chambers,' she called. 'Come up with us. We haven't looked round the upper floors before.'

Nat appeared in the open doorway with a large ledger in his hands. 'I will in a minute,' he said. 'Just having a dikker through these books. Very interesten' . . . Have you seen them, Bor?'

Tom shook his head and started up the stairs with Dudie. 'There's so much to examine, I'd have liked very much to stay a while longer and go over everything thoroughly.'

They wandered through all the rooms, picking up a garment here, stroking the fine wood veneer of a chest there, each lost in their own thoughts as Jess Bayless and his descendants began to take on real meaning at last.

The upper floor consisted of five chambers and a linen room. From the servants' quarters a spiral staircase descended into the kitchen regions and rose upwards into the attics. The main staircase curved gracefully down from the picture gallery which was splendidly illuminated by one huge oriel window. The rooms held their own fascination, for each was very different and clearly reflected its last occupant.

At the head of the stairs, double doors opened into the master bedchamber. This was a large and airy room, despite the closed shutters and crimson brocade curtains drawn across them. The room was tidy and so had obviously not been in use when the catastrophe had happened. There was a magnificently carved four-poster bed dominating the room like a scarlet catafalque, its rich draperies long since faded, choked with dust and cobwebs. The coverlet had been stitched in an intricate and beautiful design of trailing roses by loving hands. The room was empty of atmosphere, the imprint of its occupants long gone.

They tried the door of the next room and were shocked by the contrast they found.

No colour here.

Nothing.

Bars at the windows. No curtains to keep out the cold. No carpet on the planked floor, a single iron-framed bed the only item in the room. It was very cold and a smell of mould and decay pervaded the air. There were deep gouges and slash marks down the inside of the door as though some desperate animal had been caged there.

They turned away quickly, glad to close the door behind them.

'I didn't much like it in there,' Dudie said. 'Maybe it was where they kept poor crazy Amy.'

Tom made no comment but knew that he would not go in there again. He had had the distinct feeling that something hovered over him in that place, that something crooned to him, stroked his head. The sounds had been within himself, he knew but the feeling sent prickles down his spine.

'Look! Look at the pictures.' Dudie started forward, pulling him after her. 'How easy it is to tell who they are . . . Just to see how beautiful the Rawni in that one is. She must be Lavinia Freeland, beside Jess here.'

They strained upward, the better to pick out every detail of the four portraits in their ornate gilded frames.

'How strongly Charles resembles his father.'

Tom looked at her quickly, catching the sadness in her voice but there was no regret reflected in her face, only spellbound absorption. He clenched his teeth against the rage which gripped him again. Why did even the thought of Charles Bayless have such an effect on him in this place? He stared down at Dudie, watching the rapt attention in her face.

'You,' she said a moment later. 'You are not exactly like your mother, are you? . . . but enough for me to know that this is she.'

There was no need to add that the likeness stemmed from the one thing that stared back at them from three of the pictures. The calm grey eyes, deepset within their frame of long lashes.

He stood back and examined his mother's portrait once more. There was another one of her at Midhurst, quite similar to the face which stared down serenely at him now. This one though, was younger and there was a tension, a watchfulness in her perfect features which were not present in the Midhurst picture.

He put up a hand and touched the canvas, feeling the brush strokes that had created the curve of his mother's cheek. What a beautiful girl she had been.

Something cool touched the back of his upraised hand, holding it against the picture for a moment, and was gone. He lowered his hand and looked at it.

'Mama is still beautiful,' he heard his voice say fiercely and yet knew that it was not he who had uttered the words.

Dudie was still staring up at the picture of Lawrence Bayless. She smiled round at him. 'That is because you love her. Age doesn't exist where there is love.'

He shook his head in confusion. 'Dudie . . .'

How do you protest that you have not said something which both of you have just heard you say?

The picture of Violet Bayless stared down at him with just a trace of amusement in the lovely eyes. 'Mama is old now and is not ashamed of it,' he said, more to the portrait than to Dudie. 'Her beauty is in her character rather than her face these days . . . and yet, looking at this picture, everything that was in her features in youth is still there – or was when last I saw it.'

Something rushed between them and they started apart.

'What was that?' Dudie recoiled and Tom pulled her arm through his and held it tightly.

'There *are* things here, I can feel them.' He spoke slowly as though searching for the right words. 'And yet they do not frighten me as I would have expected. I have the strangest feeling of being at home. That's why I stayed last night, though I only closed my eyes to have a nap and then suddenly it was daylight.'

The remembrance brought back the subject of Moses.

'My God, I must get a message to Moss. He'll be imagining

that all the ghosts have gathered to banish me to the fires of Hell by now.'

They heard Nat stamping up the stairs behind them, his heavy footfall echoing round the Hall and gallery. He appeared in a cloud of dust, disapproval written all over his face.

'You'll go and get Moses later this morning, won't you, Pral?' Dudie said. 'Though I shall be very surprised if that great black dinelo will find the courage to cross the threshold of this place.'

They left Nat staring up at the pictures and Tom said, drawing Dudie into the chamber where he had slept, 'What do you make of this room, then? I slept in that very comfortable chair next to the mantle and would give much to take it back to Midhurst with me.'

She wandered round the room, stroking the walnut bedposts as she passed. The single pane of clean glass cast a square of moving rainbow lights onto the floor, picking out the glimmer of pattern on the faded carpet in its prismatic colours.

'Your mother's room, maybe? It has the feel of youth about it and look – it was being lived in when the tragedy happened!' She went over to a table containing a handsome gilt-framed mirror with an ornate girandole beside it. The surface was littered with the paraphernalia of a woman's toiletry. He had not noticed it before and was touched by the sudden feeling of closeness it gave him to that long-gone girl.

It was a curiously private clutter of female accoutrement. A silver and tortoiseshell tableset of brush, comb, hand mirror and *poudre* case had been pushed to one side as though she had risen from the dressing stool hurriedly. A silver pot had fallen, spilling its contents of long and short hairpins across the table.

There was a soft, blue silk reticule containing a fine lace handkerchief, a tiny hussif in an embroidered case. A spyglass enframed in fine chased silver and initials on the back – V.B. He picked up the comb and examined it. Entwined in its teeth was one long black hair.

There were bottles which had once held colognes and fragrant lotions. The contents had evaporated long since but each bottle still held a faint suggestion of their scents.

There would be time to look more closely later on. He turned away, feeling that he had intruded upon a womanly privacy. 'We haven't finished yet,' he said to Dudie. 'Come on, let's get on with the tour. Then maybe you could find me something to eat in your waggon. I've just realised that I'm famished. Haven't eaten since noon yesterday.'

They found another chamber which was, they decided, a guest room for there was nothing there that suggested habitation. There was only one room left to see after that. It was opposite the finely-carved panels of Violet's chamber door.

'Have you noticed that these doors are all different?' Dudie asked as she lifted the latch and peered into the room. The shutters were open and daylight streamed in, giving every piece of furniture a sharp clarity. This place was smaller than the others and its window, the bay filled with a well-upholstered windowseat, looked out over the east side of the House to the paddock and Salterns Woods and just visible, the roof of a house beyond the driveway and entrance gates. The single bed had a plain green coverlet. One small rug, a corner eaten away, was all the floor covering there was. On the dressing chest stood a fine model of a brigantine, its sails stowed neatly and the name in faded gilt just discernible. 'Grace'.

They stood inside the doorway, both overcome by a puzzling sense of intrusion upon a place to which they were not welcome.

'How odd,' Tom said, almost to himself. 'I'm getting the strangest feeling that we shouldn't be in this room. Not the way we felt in the empty room but as though I am intruding upon some special privacy. I don't have that feeling anywhere else in the House.'

'I feel it too.' Dudie took a step forward and recoiled, falling against Tom, as though she had been hit.

'What in heaven's name's the matter?' Tom held her tightly against him.

'I don't know.' Her voice was muffled against his shirt. He felt the warmth of her breath through the cloth and resisted holding her closer. She drew away from him, looking confused – and turned back into the room.

'Something dealt me a blow across my head, I swear it . . . and I thought I saw a face, I think . . . I'm not sure at all, though.' She made as though to walk across the room towards the green damask-covered bed – and then thought better of it. 'I think something does not want us in here,' she said, turning back towards Tom.

He stared at her. 'My God, what is wrong with your face?'

She put a hand up to her cheek, feeling a burning on her skin. Her fingers found long weals from eye to chin. They backed out of the room and slammed the door behind them.

He took her into Violet's chamber where Nat was staring out of the window through the single clean pane.

Dudie went across to the table mirror and stared at the reflection of herself in astonishment. A white-faced stranger gazed back, one side of her face scored with great swollen weals, as though some large angry creature had drawn its talons down her cheek.

Moses sat at the kitchen table. A neat row of butchery knives lay in front of him and he spat on the whetstone in his hand and began sharpening the first knife with neat short strokes. The whole of his body trembled a long way down inside as he listened to the old man. Whatever Reason might say to him, however logically it argued, the trembling continued.

He was frightened right through to the very marrow of his bones.

'C'mon now. You an' Tom have ben together for a long time,' Ben Chase pleaded, elbows spread across the table from him. He was leaning forward on his arms, the anxiety of his own fear recognizing the depth of the primeval fear in Moses.

'Dudie an' Nat've gone over so you won't be alone, but if they can't get Tom away then you have a much better chance than most others of taken' him. You're nothen' to do with that family – an' you're a fairish bit stronger than most. If need be, you can pick the bugger up and carry 'im away from there like a sack of potatoes.'

'I'm not setting foot in that place unless I have to,' Moses countered, face like thunder. A sudden tremor in his jaw set his teeth chattering in his head. They both knew that he would give in eventually for there was too deep a feeling for Tom for him to do anything else, however deep his fear of the unknown.

'Dudie an' Nat are sure to bring him over shortly. Now that they're there, I cain't see what's bothering you so.'

'Unless he hurt his knee again, like you thought last night – an' then they'll have to come all the way round in their waggon. That's near on five mile through the lanes. Take even more time.'

Someone hammered on the front door and the two men froze, eyes locked. In one movement Moses was up and across the kitchen like liquid lightning. He slipped into the coldroom and closed the door without a sound. Ben pulled himself up and went round the table to the chair that Moses had just vacated. He sat down as he heard Fran creaking down the stairs to open the door.

'Oh, good day to you, sir.' He heard the surprise in her voice. It was just a little louder than usual, the bright welcome a little too sharp. She was warning them of someone.

'Good morrow, Mistress Chase. Is your husband at home? I'd be glad of a few words with you both.'

Charles Bayless.

He picked up the whetstone and began sharpening the knife with slow, practised strokes.

'Come you into the parlour, sir, please. Ben be in the kitchen, I think – if'n he's not in the barn.'

'Good, I'll just go through then. Don't worry about the parlour . . .'

'But you'll take a little refreshment, won't you, sir . . .' She was doing her best to delay him. To his keen ear, anxiety rang like a discordant bell in her voice.

'Do not trouble yourself, thank you, Mistress Chase.' Charles' voice was smooth as silk. He could probably see the confusion in her honest face. 'I'll go through, if I may, as I'm short of time and come with me, if you will, for what I have to ask concerns you both.'

The door opened and he stood on the threshold, immaculate in blue velveteen jacket and a clean froth of white ruffled shirt. In the first instant his glance slid past Ben without a word and he held the door back against the wall, looking about him with his pale snake's eyes flicking from corner to corner.

Ben stood up, wheezing his welcome and looking as pleasantly surprised as possible. 'This is a pleasure, sir,' he said, moving slowly round the table. 'Won't you come to the parlour and take a glass of claret with me? 'Tis more comfortable in there.'

Charles smiled at him grimly and shook his head. The grey eyes looked the old man over, as though they slid down into his very soul, missing nothing. 'I have no time for more than a few words with you. Pray, let us sit right here.'

Ben pulled the harvest bench forward from the wall and ushered Charles into the chair he had just left. Frances busied herself at the range where a pot of barley broth was always brewing. With her back to them, Ben knew that she was doing her best to regain her composure after the shock of Master Bayless' sudden appearance.

Charles permitted Ben to settle him down and then perch himself on the bench.

'What can we do for ye, then, sir?'

'You can tell me where the two escaped prisoners are.'

Ben stared at Charles blankly. A frown creased his weathered forehead. He scratched the thin hair on the top of his mottled head with fingernails worn short and thick. 'Sorry, Master Bayless, but I'm not understanden' ye. Which prisoners would ye be meanen'?'

Charles put both his hands on the table in front of him, sweeping away the neat row of knives. The skin on the backs of his hands was white and slightly freckled, the fingers long and sensitive. His well-manicured nails had seen little manual labour.

'Now, let us not play games.' And the lightness of his tone did nothing to hide the hardness behind the words. 'Come, come, sir. It is common knowledge that two prisoners of war escaped from one of the Langstone hulks some weeks back. It has just come to my ears that they found sanctuary here. No – don't deny anything until I have finished. This farm was searched and no one was found at the time but there are plenty of eyes around, you know, Master Chase. Plenty of folks who are not slow to add up the sum of recent changes around here. Item one. This place has not been so well-fenced in years as it is now. Done during the past few weeks, am I right? Item two. You have been very busy in your west barn, for it has a fine new floor laid in bricks with a design that I have not seen in these parts. How did you learn that?'

Ben flushed and swore to himself. 'That be the way my son Georgie showed me, sir, when he come avisiten' from New England afore the troubles.'

'But Master Chase . . .' Charles' voice was very soft, almost tender. 'Your son George was only a lad when he went over to New England and he hardly had the chance to visit before the rebels declared war on this country. We both know that he has not been here since.'

Ben opened his mouth to protest but closed it as Charles waved aside his words. 'Item three. It has been noted that Mistress Chase does a great deal more shopping in Bosham and the Chichester markets than would seem necessary for the needs of two elderly people. I think that, because of your loyalty to those American sons of yours, you have been, and possibly still are, harbouring those two men. With your permission I shall examine the rooms upstairs. Please to accompany me, Mistress Chase.' And before either could protest their innocence further he was up on his feet and through the kitchen door with the speed of light.

Ben remained seated at the kitchen table. He picked up the whetstone and a knife and spat on the stone before running the blade across its length. He looked at the slight tremor in his hands. No sound came from beyond the coldroom door. He heard Charles Bayless' firm footfalls going from chamber to chamber, with Mistress Chase following, her voice querulous in its affront. Doors opened and closed, voices became muffled. There was silence for a short time and then he heard them returning, clattering down the oak staircase. Charles came back into the kitchen and his face was set, the pale eyes slitted. If he was disappointed he showed no sign but returned immediately to the attack without apology. He strode across the kitchen and opened the coldroom door. He stood for a second, eyeing the long slab of well-burdened slate shelf and the half-carcass of lamb hanging from one of the beam hooks.

Then he closed the door with a small click that sounded more like a pistol shot to the two old people.

'The fact that the rooms are empty means little, sir,' Charles said to Ben coldly. 'Pray answer me another conundrum, if you will. Dudie Smith has been coming over here to tend a sick person. This is known amongst your neighbours and she has told me so herself. You and Mistress Chase look very fit to me. Tell me, pray, who your ailing visitor was – and where Dudie is now.'

Ben had had enough. He lumbered to his feet, feeling the ache of age in his hips and went across and put his arm round Fran. 'Master Bayless, I am not a discourteous man but you have greatly offended my wife, as you can see, and you have violated the privacy of my home by coming here, full of accusations that I am in no mind to answer. We have no visitors. Some weeks back my own sister came to stay and had a bad fall from which she is now recovered and has returned to her home in London. Dudie Smith is well known to us, she is a regular visitor here, my wife being overly fond of her. She is highly skilled in medicines far beyond my good wife's capabilities and so she was pleased to minister to my sister's afflictions. That is all I can tell you. We have no prisoners here, Master Bayless. No prisoners, nor any other mysteries . . . and now I will have no more questions from you unless you be accompanied by the proper Authorities. Be good enough to leave my house, sir. I bid you good day.'

They stood close together as Charles wavered. Then he turned and left them, banging the front door after him. A piece of plaster fell from the wall and rattled onto the kitchen flags.

Ben gave Fran a squeeze. 'It's all right, my dear,' he said. 'You did very well indeed. I'm proud of you. Georgie would be proud of you, too.'

That name brought the smile back to her worried puffy face. 'I nearly died when he went upstairs,' she said, clenching and unclenching her fists. 'I hardly dared to open the spare room door for fear of some clothing left out or the bed rumpled from Moses lying on it. It was all right, though. Your idea of always tidying up when they leave the chamber was a good one. Except that it was warmer than our room, it looked unoccupied.'

They remembered Moses then, still curled up behind the vegetable sacks in the coldroom. He was fast asleep, doubled up in a surprisingly small ball behind piled sacks of potatoes and flour in the little nest they had made for just such an occasion weeks before.

'I'm glad he heard nothing of that man's accusations and tone of voice,' Ben said, looking down at the serenity in Moses' dreaming face. 'He would have been out of that place like a jack rabbit and given him a good drubben' if'n he had . . . deserved one, at that.'

'You can bet yer sweet life on 'et,' Ben Chase said later to Moses. 'That Master Bayless will be coming back – and bringing the Law with him. I think the time has come for you to join Dudie and Nat – even if you won't set foot in the House.'

There was little point in Moses protesting any longer for he was forced to agree with Ben. Charles had made several fairly accurate assumptions and the Magistrates might well issue the Chases with a Summons. Ben and Frances would be safe enough as long as there was no positive evidence to link them with the escaped prisoners. But if he was found at the Farm, or signs were discovered that he had been with them, Ben and Fran would become proven law-breakers and the courts would not be slow to punish them. These days, harbouring the enemy meant transportation, for sure. It was unthinkable to put them at risk, whatever his fears.

He put his hand over both of Fran's. 'Mistress, you have both bin the best friends a freeman ever had,' he said, and the rough tenderness in his voice brought easy tears to her eyes. 'I'll take myself off after dark this evening if Master Chase will row me across to Hempsteddle. I'll hide in the woods till then, in case he comes back right away. Oh, that Tom, Mistress. You wait till I see him – I'll paddle his head till he don't know the time of day . . .'

Chapter Two

Moses raised his hand in farewell to Ben who was already sculling out into the darkening river, oars dipping into silver flurries. He watched until the old man in his tiny bobbing shell was well out into midstream before turning towards the woods behind him which stood against the opalescent dusk sky like bunched spectators before a fight, silent, speculative – forbidding. He moved along the edge of the field, crouching against the hazel bushes which grew thickly above the water. When he reached the bottom hedge which marked the boundary with Lavenham's overgrown north paddock he pushed himself into the thicket and squatted down to think how best to deal with what was before him.

The evening was warm, the air filled with the bland scent of ripening grain. Black winged rooks wheeled overhead and then swooped away towards their nests in the distant trees. A bee, late wanderer after sunset, droned lazily past his nose and settled on a leaf nearby. The field, pale golden with tall hempen grasses in the dying light, breathed gently, washed this way and that by the lightest of evening breezes.

'How small these English fields are,' he thought, to deflect his fear at the approach of darkness and forcing himself to remember the long patchwork of husbanded land that had been home since his grandfather had been brought from Africa. Two generations of bonded life. It was their good fortune that they had been part of the Heritage Estate during much of that time, for those whites were good Christian people and made sure that their overseer, Anton Pace, had been a man of conscience also. The young Moses Abelson had scarcely known the cruelty and torment of the African people in bondage to the white man. He had spent his childhood hunting the Mighty Hoodah through the woods and haybarns in company with Caleb and Tom Heritage and when he was of an age to earn his keep, had naturally taken his place in the Heritage's grain warehouse on Boston's East Quay. He had done well there, and better than his contemporaries for he had shared some of Tom's schooling and had quickly picked up both reading and writing. Within two years he was directly under the foreman, acquiring a good knowledge of ledger work whenever the chance arose.

When Tom went to sea, it was not long before Moses joined him, even though there would be no chance of advancement for him in the clipper service. Although he enjoyed learning and had no difficulty with it, personal ambition was not one of Moses' attributes. He wished to learn for he was naturally curious about so much of what he saw around him, but there was no zealous fire burning in his belly as there was with many of the partially-educated black folks. At Tom's side, he would be in the best possible company and where better to learn the ways of the world?

He and Tom had been seamen for six years when Desmond Heritage, viewing the increasing disquiet over the slavery question between the ranks of his countrymen, a separate issue entirely from the conflict with England, and feeling his advancing years, gathered his slaves together and gave them all their freedom. It was an unprecedented move and one which made him as many enemies among his neighbours as it made friends among the blacks. He was unmoved by the sentiments of those around him. He had made up his mind and acted as his conscience bade him.

Few of Desmond Heritage's bonded men left his employ. Moses, proud of his freedom amongst the weight of slavery in the American colony, doggedly followed Tom into war when the Revolutionary Council declared the birth of the Federation and severed their allegiance to the English Crown.

By the time the 'Free States' was captured and its crew imprisoned, Moses had found a wife, made her a home at Midhurst and had given her two babies. She worked in the

222

main house as maid to the ageing Mistress Violet, assisting Joelly Parsons who had cared for her mistress since she had come to Boston as Desmond Heritage's new bride. Luella was young and easily given to tears as well as to laughter but she was a fine strong girl with skin as richly shining and unblemished as a ripe plum. Mistress Violet always said it did her heart good to listen to Luella's chatter till she was scolded out of the room by Joelly. It did Moses' heart good just to think of her at all.

He sat in the thicket and drove his mind away from that lingering hunger for Luella to examine that thing which was the most important issue of the moment: to get Tom out of that bad place steeped in the sins of his ancestors and onto the barque bound for Normandy in just three days' time. Then it would be short weeks before they were back in the heart of their flesh and blood families – which was what Tom Heritage ought to be filling his mind with and Moses could make more babies with Luella, the way it should be.

Dusk deepened, etching the horizon of distant trees and Rymans tower in an iridescent moment of purple brilliance before the last of the dying day was drawn into night shadow. The first star in that opalescent sky was joined by another and then another. Squatting in the spiky thicket he watched the changing canopy of the sky and felt the sheer glory of freedom, caught by the momentary perfection of it. Even as he watched all light melted into dusk and Moses crawled out of the hedge and made his way on hands and knees along the ditch towards the river bank and a strip of muddy sand that stretched for twenty or so yards along the Lavenham shore.

Behind him, unseen, a horseman rode down the cart track to Newbarn, the cluster of its farm buildings little more than a wash of darkness beyond the sighing hemp.

It was too early for the moon and there was still just enough light for the keen eye, for the sky was a great roof of bright new darkness, like strong sunshine seen through the thickness of a deep blue curtain. Moses moved slowly, eyes swivelling from left to right as he went, as though to gather up every smallest movement amongst the nocturnal creatures who were only now beginning to emerge.

*

Charles rode his horse fast down the wide track to Newbarn. He forbore to raise his eyes for he had no wish to rest them upon the one broken Lavenham chimney pot which could be seen from this part of the lane.

He had been kept overlong in the Dell Quay Office this evening and now was late, both for the visit to Will Slaughter at Newbarn Cottage and for his meeting with Dr Priestley at Leonie's bedside. The cough had finally become stronger than her will to remain at his side and she was now rasping and bubbling in her bed, all strength spent and her will to live gone. The boys hovered anxiously in the corridor near her chamber door and the whole household was creeping about as though she had already given up the struggle. Exasperated with convention, longing for Dudie, he wished that she had.

A lone star shone in the deepening cobalt dusk over his head. He saw only the ruts in the track, made by the passage of the hemp waggons. Nothing penetrated the intensity of his thoughts but arrangements for the plan he was about to bring into action. He saw nothing of the distant, crouching figure that scuttled from shadow to shadow as he thundered by and melted into the thicket on the other side of the field.

The cottage, dwarfed by the high barn at its back, came into view. 'Good evening to you, Mistress Slaughter,' he said most charmingly to the girl who opened the door to his knock. He took off his hat the better to be recognized and she bobbed quickly, mumbling a greeting in pleasure and embarrassment as she pushed the greasy hair back from her face.

'Is Will home yet?' he asked, his sharp ears catching the sound of movement within.

'Yas, sor . . . he's but newly back, just moments ago.' She suddenly realized that he was standing expectantly on the doorstep and stood aside for him to pass her. 'Go right into the kitchen, if you will, Sor . . . and please excuse the state we'm in. 'Es thatchen' out the back, see.'

Will Slaughter rose from his seat by the open hearth as Charles entered the dark cave of the little kitchen, head bent, for the ceiling was low. Years of cooking had yellowed and then blackened the lime-washed walls so that they were now of a uniform dinginess, the colour of dung. A film of grease seemed to cover everything. An odour of stale beer, burnt pig fat and body gases made him long to reach for his kerchief and hold it to his nose.

He went forward resolutely. 'Evening, Will. May we spend a few moments discussing our proposed main cock fight here?'

The man's heavily stolid face lit up. 'Oh yes, yer Honour. I was awonderen' why you was visiten'. The fight between my French Spangle and Tosser Jelliff's Shropshire Red's bin agreed. I've bin down to the mill and seen 'em and he says he's right willen' . . . real keen by the look of 'un. Drummed up five other pair too, sor. Have you any others in mind? We'll need a few more ter make a good gatheren' on et.'

Charles' pale eyes burned. 'Good, good,' he said, seating himself gingerly on a stool. 'I've been promised challengers from Sir Edwin Griffiths and Master Tertius Page. I shall be entering a couple of birds. I've just acquired a very fine Pile. Beautiful bird. Light feathers and a heel action that'll rip the throat out of anything. Just coming up to two years old now and ready for training. The other's a bit of an unknown quantity. He's a Dun — a Foulsham Downrump. I've not handled one of them before, nor even seen them in action but my Lord of Lennox made me a present of it.' He grinned across at Will Slaughter, seeing the man's attention, knowing that in his coop at the back of the cottage there were five Duns. 'Let us get down to the details, then, for I can promise you a good crowd of spectators and men with money in their pockets at that . . .'

The man's deepset eyes gleamed, a 'cocker' to his last drop of blood and he rubbed his hands together. ' 'Twill take mor'n a week to train em up, sor. Ten days, more like — so what would ye be thinken' of maken' the date — around Tuesday week?'

Ten days. A whole lifetime might have passed by before Tuesday week, Charles thought. 'I'm afraid that won't be possible,' he said. 'I've to be in London then and, in fact am summonsed to my Lord Devonshire's banquet nine days from today.' He appeared to think for a moment. 'Eight days' time, Will. It'll have to be then as I shall be committed too fully later — and I know that Sir Edwin is to be in Paris before the end of the month.'

He rose to leave and Will stood respectfully, only the gleam

225

in his pale eyes betraying his pleasure in the coming contest. Charles turned and appeared to hesitate, remembering something. 'That gypsy – Nat Smith,' he said slowly. 'He's always at local mains. I've seen him at most of the ones I've attended in the last four or five seasons.'

Will scratched his head. 'The one camped out on the Common, would that be, sor?'

Charles nodded. 'I noted with some interest that he has one particular bird that has won at two mains that I have attended. He has moved from the Common and is now camped in the north paddock at Lavenham, so I believe. Maybe you would like to let him know the date of this main for I'd be interested in contesting that fowl of his with my Pile.'

It was quite dark by the time he left Newbarn Cottage. Not a light glimmered anywhere. Even the Dell Quay warehouse was closed. From a long way away the discordant sounds of singing men filtered across the fields from the little Dell Quay tavern. He looked about him approvingly. Newbarn was secluded and remote from passers-by and would be ideal for the cock fight. Ideal also to draw Nat Smith and maybe Dudie as well out into the open. Nat's fascination for cocking had been the main subject of conversation between them when he had been a welcome guest at the Smiths' fireside. It was quite possible to argue for hours on end about the pros and cons of this bird or that. Nat had a coop under his waggon and the birds he raised so lovingly were beginning to earn him a few gold coins.

Bait the trap – and then wait and see how many mice came sniffing at the cheese. It was quite possible that if Tom Heritage was still in the area he might also be persuaded to show himself but it was primarily Dudie who had to be brought out. It was most unlikely that she would appear at the main, for women were rarely in attendance, but if Nat was camping at Lavenham, Dudie would be there too.

The thought of her set his pulses racing.

He turned his face towards Chichester and so absorbed was he in making his plans that it was not until he was riding past the Donnington turning that he remembered Leonie's condition.

*

'Tomorrow I shall leave here, I promise.'

Tom lay back comfortably in a padded chair in the with-drawing room, his feet propped up on a square footstool. Dudie had lit the many-branched candelabra that stood with its matching pair on an oval table close to the west window. She had closed the shutters and drawn the curtains, stirring up a great cloud of dust and a scurrying of spiders that had set them both coughing. Now the room looked almost cosy. The warmth of the evening made light of the slight mustiness in the air.

'Nat will be back soon,' she said, leaning over to hand him a wedge of bread upon which she had just spread a thick layer of pickled cauliflower and peach. 'If we are in luck, he will have Moses with him and then we can plan the best way to get you both aboard the ship for France. Maybe we could "borrow" one of the bumboats from the Quay ... Master Chase's little cotty won't be no good for it'd have to be abandoned an' t'would implicate him if we was discovered.'

He didn't want to think of anything as final as their depar-ture. There were too many imponderables tied up in it. He was filled with a delicious lassitude, comfortable in this place – drawing a bitter-sweet pleasure from the sheer independence of this small and mightily determined girl who was prepared to risk her own safety for his. For the moment he was supremely happy right where he was.

'Why should we not stay right here at Lavenham – the four of us?' He watched her lazily, only uttering the words – which were impossible from any angle – simply to light the explosive animation in her mobile, candlelit face.

'Oh, Tom.' The exasperation in her voice hid her own thoughts well, but he still felt them with the same kind of clarity with which she must see things in men's hands. 'Sometimes I think that you don't even see what a dangerous position you are in. If they catch you, you'll not only be sent back to the hulks but they might even string you up for your trouble.'

She stopped, seeing the sleepy grin on his face. 'Oh, mercy, Bor. Will you stop being a tease for just a moment?'

'Assuredly, ma'am. Would you think I was teasing if I told

you that I don't want to leave here unless I can take you with me?'

She considered. 'Yes, I would think you were teasing, and cruelly too. You forget the child I am carrying. You forget that Kenners are not good places for me and I shall not live in one – ever. You are just playing romantic dreams because you are bored with skulking in an empty house –'

'But I'm not, you see, Dudie.' He had not moved. His body was relaxed and his face almost drowsy. He might have been talking in his sleep. 'I'm not bored with all this inactivity, far from it. This place is a fascinating treasure house from Mama's past and, but for the one room upstairs, I feel nothing but warmth and welcome in it. It would be all too easy to dwell right here quietly until Peace returns to our two countries and then open the place up properly and see whether I could not begin trading between Boston and Chichester.'

His half-closed eyes swivelled round to her. 'And I am not forgetting your situation either, Dudie. What better place could you have for the birth of your child but here? Baylesses have been born here before and no doubt they will be in the future. Would you not consider giving your child a proper foundation for its future? With me . . .?'

The Watcher was angry.

What was the ridiculous fellow thinking of? Had he taken no notice of the warnings of three generations of tragedy in this Godless place? Was it possible that he actually did not realize what happened to children born under this roof?

He pressed forward, forcing . . . forcing . . . battering his warning into the minds of the two figures. In the flickering candlelight, Dudie looked up at him calmly. There was no comprehension in her eyes but for a moment he was not at all sure that he was not vaguely visible to her.

'No child of mine will ever be born within these walls, Bor.' Her voice was soft and a slight huskiness made him look at her more closely.

'This House is more Mokada for birth than for anything

228

else. Your own mother was born out of it, remember. She was born in the Vardo, as all Romanies should be. My child will be born in ours – and I shall not need to be subservient to any man for the sake of it.'

They watched each other covertly, he seeing the longing that was in her to go to him, she grieving at the light casualness of his mood. There was no kneeling on one knee here as Charles had done, to plead for her affection. Not that that was what she wanted. Let the gorgios cavort with their studied poses. The empty courtesies of such manners were not for gypsies. How good it would have been, all the same, had he uttered his proposal from the heart, rather than this casually thrown out suggestion from a feeling of pity, of responsibility for her.

He smiled at her, quite unoffended by the sharpness of her rebuff, assumed a clown's face of tragic regret and heaved himself up in his chair with a sigh.

'Before we continue this conversation I must ask you to excuse me, Mistress Smith,' he said with heavy formality. 'Nature is suddenly even more pressing than courtship. Don't move for there are many things that must be said and I feel that this is as right a moment as we will find. I shall not be long.'

He looked back at her as he left the room. Huge shadows cast by the candles loomed over her small figure, doing a slow weaving dance as the disturbed air of his passing set them wavering.

He stepped out of the front door onto the terrace and stood for a moment, arrested by the tranquillity. The night was brilliant, the quarter-moon attended by a million blazing pinpoints. The air was fragrant with the scent of roses, of honeysuckle mixed with the sea. The wind must be coming off the land for within its heavy sweetness was a faint odour of stable. Tom went slowly down the weed-choked terrace steps and wandered through the archway into the stableyard where Dudie's waggon stood, hidden by the foursquare barns from prying eyes. It took a few minutes to get accustomed to the darkness in the buildings' shadow but the slither of moon was brilliant above now and lit his way.

He relieved himself against the barn wall and was buttoning

229

up his breeches when a movement on the far side of the yard caught his eye. Something substantial had moved between a broken water-butt and the corner of the building.

He stood still, flattening himself against the barn wall, eyes straining into the black infinity of the yard. Another small sound; a furtive swish of movement through the wild growth of weeds choking the cobbles. A pebble clattered against another. The lurcher growled from under the waggon, a long deep sound in the back of her throat. Tom held his breath for it seemed to him suddenly that the noise sounded like a giant bellows in the quiet night.

He could just see the outline of the waggon. 'Nat . . . is that you?'

Tom's voice grated in the heavy silence. The bitch growled again and the sudden rattle of its chain echoed hollowly round the invisible walls. He stood motionless, probing the night beyond the waggon with its tensile guardian. Whatever lurked there waited also, blended with the night.

'Tom . . . are you all right?' Dudie's voice cut through the infinite moment, the anxiety in it making him turn his head.

'Tom . . .?' She was coming to look for him. He moved stealthily along the wall with his arms outspread, working his silent way back towards the arch.

'*Where are you, Tom* . . .?' She came through the archway and jumped as he put out a hand and gripped her arm.

'Shhh,' he said with his mouth against her ear. 'I saw something over by the other gateway. I thought it was Nat but nothing happened when I called out.'

They stood close together, listening to the threatening rumbles from the dog. She growled again, dragging at her chain and making frantic outward dashes from under the waggon.

Something reared up from a clump of bushes only a few yards from where they stood. 'Reckon yor li'l old ears must be full of cobwebs,' a voice said. A set of teeth flashed whitely in the dimness and Moses stepped forward and gave Tom a soft cuff with a huge balled fist. 'I'm mighty glad it was you, Master.' He was breathing fast, as though he had been running. 'I've spent the last two hours creeping along the banks of that murky old river on my belly, getting myself covered in mud and birdshit and waking up all the moorhens and things that nest in them reeds. When I see the roof of this barnyard against the stars, I reckon I'm almost there. Then I hear a creepin' and a crawlin' like there was some mighty large serpent on the loose – an' then that hound of yours starts agrowlin' and carrying on. Next thing I hears someone call out and after that Miss Dudie, ma'am. Reckon your sweet tones done save me wetten' my breeches like I was a pickaninny. Specially when I hears someone waterin' the wall there.'

They grasped the big man's arms in their relief, still shaken by the tension of that creeping, unknown moment.

'Come into the House and let me try and clean you up a bit,' Dudie said, for even in the darkness the moon showed the mud glistening over most of Moses' shirtfront and knee-breeches. He let her pull him through the arch, but rolled his eyes fearfully at the dark mass of the silent House towering over them.

'I'm not going in there. Not in the middle of the night with all them ghoulies and ghosties hangin' about waiting to send me to the pit . . .'

'Come on, old friend,' Tom laughed behind him. 'I slept here last night and had the best sleep since I was rocked in my mother's womb. It's as safe as can be and there's nothing to be afraid of.'

He pushed the unwilling Moses before him as he spoke.

'Huh, you sure must've slept like a babe,' the big man grumbled, allowing himself to be hauled up the terrace steps and in through the wide door. The air was heavy in the spacious place, charged with the faint fragrance of dried leaves and old wood. He looked about him briefly and then turned back to Tom.

'The rest of your buddies've been worried stupid about you. That's the only reason I'm here, I tell you . . .' He stopped so suddenly that Tom cannoned into him from behind. 'Oh Lawdie, Lawdie . . . it's the truth then!'

In the soft shaft of candlelight streaming through the open parlour door, the jagged teeth of the shattered dining table were suddenly alien, shocking.

'Don't worry about it. We just haven't had time to tidy it

all up yet,' Tom said. 'That happened a very long time ago and whatever was responsible for doing it is not here any longer. Come on in and see for yourself.' And he passed Moses into the parlour and began dragging a chair across into the pool of light.

Moses stood and sniffed the air of the Hall. 'He says there b'aint nothing here but I says there is,' he whispered to Dudie. She squeezed his hand tightly.

'There may be, Bor,' she said, matching his low voice, 'but now that you are here, I think we can look after him between us, don't you?'

He shivered. 'I'd go into the jaws of Hell for him if I have to,' he said grimly. 'An' I reckon that's just where we are right now.'

The Watcher turned away and closed his eyes.

They were gathering, slowly drawn together by the cloying tendrils of the Place. Lawrence's son was out there too – not daring to do battle with the forces within these walls, but drawn all the same by its magnetism, reflected so strongly through the girl.

He wept then. It was the first time that tears had seemed at all possible for although they were but an empty expression of his frustration, they were at least a human reaction.

He felt her hand on his shoulder and turned over in the bed and lay on his back, looking up at her.

'I'm losing it,' he said. 'I seem to be sliding further and further backwards and becoming less and less able to control things. How much longer will this nightmare go on, Frances, for God's sake?'

The look she gave him was filled with compassion. 'Until you have resolved what it is that you are seeking,' she said gently.

Nat was asleep in the waggon when Dudie went across at first light to fetch bread and meat. He looked hot and dishevelled and started up with an oath as Dudie patted his shoulder.

'Why'd you not come into the Kenner with the rest of us?'

she asked. 'Moses, he found his way here after Charles Bayless started threatenen' the Chases. He's turned real sour now, that sap.' She put her hand lightly on her stomach where the child stirred with a faint flutter.

Nat grunted. 'You jus' don't know what you've got yourself tied up in with these folks,' he said, turning his face to the wall and closing his eyes against the sharp daylight. 'We'd best be gone from here and let them fend fer themselves, the lot of 'em. Trouble, that's what they are . . . trouble fer me, Pen – and worse trouble fer you.'

He had not been pleased to discover from the Chases that Moses had already left for Lavenham, even though his reasons for doing so were to protect the old couple. It was not to his, Nat's, advantage to be scouring the countryside in search of a man he had never met, only to discover that he need not have exerted himself after all. He had never involved himself with gorgios before, except to earn a living from them when needs must. There was little that he could trust in them – but Master Bayless was not like the others. He had the blood of Mother Hator in his veins just as surely as did he and Dudie. Her association with Charles Bayless had therefore to be endured, for it was what Dudie had wanted at the time and he had known that love had not been part of her gift.

But life had been spawned out of that compassion, in spite of her care. Now the damage was done.

And now, much too late, she could stand back and see Charles Bayless in the same cold clear light as he saw him, without the distortion of her earlier pity. 'Snake' was a fitting title for him, for he would strike now at them, smarting under her rejection.

He turned over in his bunk and watched Dudie gathering the cooking utensils and food into her apron. She looked very small. Her face was serious but there was a serenity about it that was new to her. She was such a headstrong, wayward creature at times, he thought with exasperated affection. But she was still the strongest of them all, despite her slight frame. He knew that he would kill Charles Bayless before he let a hair on her head be hurt.

Nat appeared later in the morning and sat, munching at

the bread that remained uneaten from breakfast, unwilling to join the others as they wandered over the House, trailing through the rooms as they discovered one treasure after another.

There was something about the place that had not been there before. It was as though it was slowly coming alive after a long, long sleep.

Moses sensed the change also and was afraid. He sat outside in the sunshine and prayed for their deliverance and averted his eyes from the shining faces of Tom and Dudie, busy and happy as they made a rough inventory of the House's contents. There was no attempt at intimacy between them, he saw, but there was a softness to Tom's voice, an intensity in his glance which betrayed him at every turn. And Dudie hovered close to him, the bossiness wiped from her regard, her perfect oval face with its faint cleft in the chin alight with shining concentration. They seemed to move on another plane, quite alone with each other. The House enfolded them, inserting itself invisibly between them and their companions.

Looking up at the sightless, dusty casements, blind sockets behind the wilderness of creeper, Moses had the strongest conviction that they were somehow being drawn away from him and Nat, the self-appointed guardians of these two beloved people; like figures seen at the end of a dark tunnel, floating away ... diminishing before his eyes. He rose and thrust his way through the tall grasses of the overgrown lawn, down to the bank of the Channel and stood with his back to the House, staring out resolutely across the water to Old Park Woods. He was filled with terror for the night that must follow this day. He gripped the little bone Cross that he wore suspended from a leather thong round his neck. He had made it from a piece of sheep's knuckle and was quietly proud of the fine quality of the carving, the little fronds of grapevine leaves and fruit that he had taken laborious weeks to fashion with his knife.

'Save us all,' he prayed, gripping the bone Cross, warm from his body. 'Save us all and bring us back to sanity – away from this Godless place.'

The House glimmered at him, reflected in the bright water at his feet. By some odd quirk of the light it seemed suddenly

234

to be all afire, huge shafts of white-hot flame, licking upwards from every window.

He spun round in fright – and found it reposing peacefully beside the oakwood, gently washed in the warm golden reflection of the setting sun.

Chapter Three

There was no sign of the Smiths' waggon in Lavenham's north paddock. Will Slaughter, his terrier at heel walked Hempsteddle, north paddock, Lost Labour and even Boorscroft and found no sign of the gypsies. He traversed the muddy slopes of the salterns past Master Ayels' noxious pans, but the old Bayless camping ground was empty, the scars of their hearths erased from the ground long since. He stopped and stared out over the new tidal wall that kept the winter sea from eroding the pans once emptied, and held in the crystallizing brine during the active summer months. The smell of rotting seaweed and calcifying salt caught unpleasantly at the back of his throat. He scratched his head, perplexed.

'If Master Bayless be positive that the gypsies are here somewheres, then here is where they must be.'

There was no doubt in his mind, for Master Bayless had been quite sure. He stared through the dense undergrowth into the wilderness of gnarled oak trees and thicket which separated the empty House and grounds from the salterns. Could be that they were camped on the west front . . . or by the stables. He had only been inside the Lavenham gates once as a boy, and had been frightened into retreat by a swarm of bees.

Bees would not be swarming now in late summer.

He hesitated, knowing that he should take a look through the yards and gardens so that he could report with truth to Master Bayless. Old wives' tales or not, Master Bayless was a good customer of his and often generous with his prize money at mains. His patronage was valuable and must be cultivated, even if it meant scouring devilish houses for him. Setting his jaw in a hard line, he pushed through the wood towards the old House.

He found Nat sitting on the top step of his waggon in the centre of the overgrown stableyard, probing his back teeth with a twig. The gypsy stared at him stonily without moving as he appeared through the archway and came across the yard, the little brindle and white terrier inches from his heels.

'Hey, good day to ye, Nat Smith. Ben looken' for you over all these blamed acres fer the past couple of hours.' Will Slaughter was hot and he stopped at the bottom of the waggon steps to mop his damp face and neck with his shirt end. The two dogs bristled threateningly at each other but the terrier stayed close to Will's leg.

Nat took the twig out of his mouth and ejected a large gobbet of spittle. It fell with a neat *ptt* close to the little terrier's front paw. From below the waggon the lurcher growled quietly in the back of her throat. She ignored the young terrier, having exchanged hostilities with him. Instead, her bright eyes watched the stranger's gaitered legs intently. One word from Nat and her teeth would be sunk firmly into the back of the man's inside thigh.

'What chew want with me?'

Will eyed the birdcages hanging from the waggon's tail-board. He jerked his head at them. 'Seen you at the main by Kingsmeet tavern t'other Friday. Thought you'd want to come over ter Newbarn main Thursday next week, see'en as it's sorta close ter here. Master Bayless, 'e said as you was campen' at Lavenham. 'E aims ter put up two good cocks. One of 'em, the Dun, 'ud give that Smokey of yours a good run, I reckon.'

Nat put the twig back in his mouth and dug at a wisdom tooth, wincing. 'I'll think on et, Bor.' He watched the man's uneasy hesitation, eyes flicking round the crumbling buildings.

'Big place, ain't et,' he said, peering back through the archway. 'A fine House, though, at one time, ye can see that. I allus wondered what 'twas like en 'ere, but tales was too fearsome when I was a lad. Ghosties – an' other things, so they say . . .'

His voice trailed away as Nat still said nothing but just sat looking at him, chewing on his twig. He shrugged and turned away and began to retrace his steps. Gypsies made few friends outside their own people. Nat Smith had never been a talker though he had a good enough singing voice when the beer was in him.

He had come out of the woods into the tall grass that had once been the west front and found himself close to the lovely old House with its warm brick walls, clothed in the pink and yellow tresses of wild rose creepers. It was much larger than he had imagined – and not especially forbidding. Folks would always be wary of it, though, for all its attractions. Its reputation had gone too deep – and Master Bayless, who could have spoken to Nat Smith himself concerning the main had he been so inclined, was apparently no different from the others in holding it at arm's length.

Will Slaughter whistled to his dog and found it already pressing itself against his foot. It whined up at him, showing the whites of its eyes and shivering, one paw raised. Seems it didn't like the place any more than other folks.

Will sniffed the air and found nothing in it to alarm him, other than the strong odour of mouldering horse manure. All the time, Nat Smith's eyes watched him like cold black pebbles. He lounged motionless on the top step of the waggon waiting for the stranger to be gone.

There was no more to say. Will had delivered the message for Master Bayless and he was obviously not going to get even the time of day out of this fellow. He turned and left the yard the way he had come.

When Will had gone, Nat left his perch and took the Smokey Dun from its cage. The smaller cock in the other cage was not yet old enough for fighting but the Smokey, at two years, had been in six mains and had won each of its fights without serious injury. He sat back on the step with the bird in his lap, held firmly by the legs in the crook of his arm. He was a fine creature of high bearing, the soft grey of his stubby wing feathers outlined by faint black tips and accentuated by the almost wiglike tresses of his long creamy neck feathers. His red eyes were bright and regarded Nat with eager expectation, the twisting jerks of his short combed head, set atop a regal neck, compact and alert. His beak, a pale almost pearly pink deepening to yellow at the hook, was a vicious weapon.

Nat spread one wing and then the other across his knee, fanning out the feathers and minutely examining every tendon of the delicate fan. The Smokey, accustomed to Nat's handling, sat quiet but tense within the firm gentle grip. Satisfied, Nat turned to the legs, feeling for swelling, for tendon weakness. His fingers probed gently, leaving no part of the bird unexplored, and the Smokey, soothed by this daily massage gradually relaxed and lay quietly under its master's hand, drowsy from the stroking fingers. Finally, almost satisfied, Nat dressed the bird's head and eyes in the way that his father and grandfather had done before him, licking the fine head feathers and round the blinking eyes, the sensitive tip of his tongue cleaning with the purity of his own sterile spittle.

'Scourings for you next feed, my Kushti Bor,' he said softly to the bird, stroking the proud head below the hard red stub where the comb had been severed. Only part of his attention was with the bird under his hands. The rest of him was turning over the information that Will Slaughter had brought him.

So Master Charles Bayless was interested in pitting his bird against Nat Smith's fowl . . . How very unlikely it was that a gentleman of his standing would go to the length of sending a messenger such as Will, chasing all over Apuldram to look for just one gypsy with a good bird. There were other contestants who could give him as good a run for his money. No, what was much more likely, seeing that it was Charles, was that the contest was bait – not for him but to draw Dudie out of hiding. It had been him after all, as Will admitted, who had made the first suggestion that Newbarn would make a good place for a fight.

'Master Bayless wants ter see you in action, does he? He wants too much, that gorgio. Too much. First Dudie an' now you. Well, we'll give 'im a little surprise, won't we, Chiriklo? A Duckwing agin ye, eh?'

He grunted with dry amusement, holding the bird up so that they stared into each other's eyes. 'A grey man's Grey Dun. Small game agin' a devil's bird, eh, Bor?' The Smokey cocked its head to one side, its glassy, red-rimmed eyes regarding him with a rare intelligence. 'Devil's Birds' lived up to their reputations with extraordinary regularity for they were game cocks that had been placed in and hatched from a magpie's nest and were regarded by many as unconquerable. So far, the Smokey was fulfilling this expectation.

He laid the bird on the ground and, half a mind on the removal of Dudie from Lavenham, watched it peck fastidiously among the weed-choked cobbles. Half an hour later Moses came through the archway and his eyes lit up at the sight of the beautiful creature.

'My Aunt Susie's headpiece,' he said, whistling through his teeth as Nat lifted up the bird and let it spread its clipped bronze and black wings, beating the air between them with powerful strokes. 'Now, that is *some* game cock. What you doin' with him? Goen' to fight him, maybe?'

Nat nodded. 'Slaughter's haven' a main just across the field from here in eight days' time. Thought I'd give old Smokey here a little flutter . . . specially as me Lord Charles Bayless'll be enteren' his new bird. Melali here never lost a fight yet, Bor. Bayless' new Dun won't be no problem.'

Moses looked disappointed. 'I'd've liked to have seen that but we should be over the Channel by that time, God willing.' He grinned at Nat. 'Man, I had a fine bird one time, long ago. 'Twas a scarlet Polecat and the only cock I ever reared on my own. Went down to a bandy-legged bantam with one eye. Never did find another I cared for so well . . . 'cept mebbe a big ole black rat I trained fer fighting aboard "Fortunée".'

It was common knowledge that the prisoners, with little to occupy them from dawn to dusk, raced anything that moved to indulge the *Rafales*' passion for gambling. Rat racing was a regular occupation and those rats' trainers as dedicated as any. There were even cockroach races, a better gamble for the dedicated, for they were easier to control.

Nat liked Moses. He had the gift of silence when silence was required but would also find humour in most situations. He very much doubted whether there was any animosity at all in the man. The only thing he seemed to fear, to hate with a rare ferocity, was the House behind the arch. As a result, he spent more time out in the yard with Nat or roaming through the overgrown grounds than attending Tom and Dudie who seemed completely absorbed in their task of tabulating the contents of the House for Mistress Heritage.

He cocked his head at Moses. 'They still maken' their lists?'

Moses grunted. 'Reckon that's what they say they're doing. Maybe they even believe it themselves, but ma good friend, what those two are doing is fallen' in love – and in that tainted place that's no good for sweet wholesome feelin's as God-damned natural as theirs.'

Nat thumped a clenched fist against the side of the waggon. The Smokey, aroused from a pleasant reverie under its master's arm, squawked in protest and lashed out with its vicious beak.

Nat put the bird down at his feet. 'She's walken' into trouble, the dinelo mort,' he scowled. 'She shouldn't truck with gorgios. We're travellen' folks, see. Different from gorgios – an' always will be. Dallyen' with 'em only brings grief, Bor – and I ent taken' more of it from anyone, be he your Pral or not. Let him keep his distance from her, you tell him that, Bor, see? Or he'll have me to reckon with.'

Moses nodded. 'We'll be gone directly – and he would not lay a finger on her, I can tell you that. Too much respect for her. Can you not see it, yourself?'

Nat grunted and turned away to put the cock back in its cage. He knew the truth of the black man's words but his temper, slow to the boil, was now beginning to rise in him, stirred by uncertainty at the entire situation. 'What's keepen' you here then? Answer me that. Why aren't ye on yer way now to Harris' Wharf? You could hide up a couple of days aboard ship before she sails. Why let him stay on here?'

'Because I cannot seem to get him to hear me, that's why!' Sudden despair sharpened Moses' face. 'He is happy in the strangest manner, man. Kind of dreaming, even as he speaks with you. I say something to him and he is miles away and seems not to hear. And Mistress Dudie, she seems to be part of it too. Haven't you noticed?'

Indeed, Nat had. She had spent the night right here in her waggon bunk, under his stern brotherly eye but there was an abstraction about her also which was like an invisible barrier between them.

'I reckon that House has something to do with it.' Moses picked up a pebble and threw it with all his might at the sagging barn doors. It made a sharp crack on impact like the sound of a pistol shot.

Dudie's voice cut through their thoughts. 'Come and eat, Nat . . . Moses. I've made a good harvest mess on the hob. Quick now, before it spoils.'

'When are we going from here?'

'Well . . .' Tom began but Moses cut through the slow ease of his voice, suddenly angry at the almost sleepy lack of interest his question had provoked.

'Put it this way, Master Tom. I am leaving here tomorrow with you! I am going to Emsworth, to Harris' Wharf, and I shall hide myself aboard the vessel that is taking us to France and await my fate in a place that at least is one step closer to my freedom and home. All this I shall do, young Master, in company with you — even if I have to break both your legs and carry you there myself . . . This hanging about is a danger, not only to ourselves but to Miss Dudie and to Nat who stand to fall foul of the Authorities just for being in our company. Now that the Snake knows where we are, there is no chance of us staying here in any safety, do you not understand that? Do you not understand what danger we are creating for these two good people?'

Tom looked at him in surprise. 'I expect he might think that we are here but he doesn't know for sure, does he?'

'Yes sir, he does!' Moses' voice began to rumble ominously. Anger was a rare element with him but the House raised a strange violence in his heart. 'Some fellow came into the yard this morning, looking for Nat, just to tell him that there is to be a main nearby in a few days' time. He was told of Nat's and Dudie's presence here by none other than *Master Charles Bayless himself*. Do you see what that means, man?'

Tom stared at him blankly for a moment and then his eyes slewed round to Dudie. Without a word he left the table. Something took him and led him from them, guided him up the stairs and into the main bedchamber. There he stood by the window, looking down into the garden, seeing smooth lawns and orderly flowerbeds and a young woman swinging across the terrace with a basket of roses on her arm. A fine black stallion grazed close to the wall amongst the unshorn grasses. It lifted its head to watch her as she passed. The stables would be filled with horses of the Lavenham stud for he could hear the sharp squeal and whinny of a mare in season. The odour of the stables was suddenly strong, so that it was all about him, rank, sour . . .

He turned away from the window. It was only the House, offering him another of the little memory pictures with which it had been teasing him since his arrival. 'I have to leave,' he said to the room. 'I have another home and greater responsibilities than I owe to Lavenham . . .'

There was a stirring all about him, as though a mischievous breeze was tugging at his hair, his clothing.

Dudie . . .

The thought of her suddenly smote him, churning the tenderness in him into sharply violent desire.

Dudie . . .

He groaned, hugging himself, feeling himself invaded by a lust so alien that in its midst he was sickened to the core. He felt the hot bile rise in his throat even as the blood roared and thundered through his body. Something screamed its pleasure as the furious pulse beat in him with vast drum strokes, turning his legs to water, pouring from him in a fount of uncontrolled heat . . .

Dark clouds rolled away from his eyes and he was in the presence of the Fount of all Life, sliding backwards, back . . .

They finished their stew and still Tom had not returned.

'Shall I go and look for him, do you think?' Dudie asked anxiously. 'He's had long enough to think about things, hasn't he?'

'You stay right where you are,' Nat said grimly, rising from the bench. 'I'll find him. He can't just walk away from a discussion like that. He's to leave with Moses, just like he says, see? An' you and I'll be on our way directly. We've done it your way up to this moment, Pen, but Moses 'as had enough – an' so have I.'

He looked into every room on the ground floor but there was no sign of Tom, nor could he see him outside on the terrace. He went up the stairs two at a time. Damned dinelo. Hiding now was not going to work. They'd find him, wherever he hid himself. But Tom was not hiding. He was stretched out on the floor of the main bedchamber as though a great fist had felled him. His face was the colour of putty.

'Hey, Bor,' Nat said, squatting down beside him and shaking his shoulder. 'What's up with 'e? Wake up . . .'

He was breathing. His lungs pumped air slowly through his mouth in a slight snore. His eyes were closed. There was a trace of blue about his mouth. He made no response to Nat's urgings. Nor did he respond by even a flicker to Dudie's urgent pleas. He appeared to have sunk into a deep coma.

Nat and Moses glowered at each other over Tom's body as they lifted him up onto the bed. He could not be taken in this condition and secreted aboard the Channel trader. It was as though the House was determined to keep him from leaving, for he had been in excellent health minutes before.

Between them, Tom stirred. His eyes flew open and a thin, terrible scream, like the squeal of a terrified animal, was forced through his clenched teeth. Dudie pushed between the two men and leant over him, hand on his forehead.

'Tom, wake up . . . wake up. It's only a dream you're haven'. Fight it, Bor. It'll take your sanity if'n you don't fight it . . .' She looked up, over the top of Nat's head at something beyond the bedcurtains. She glowered, her face suddenly not at all the small, sweet face of Dudie Smith but of a woman, ferociously protective.

Moses, staring at her with sudden fear, saw the face of a stranger and crossed himself. 'What you looken' at like that, Miss Dudie?' he whispered. 'There ain't a body in this chamber but us. You looken' in the corners that way gives me the goosepimples like the Devil himself is out there grinnen' at us.'

She rose up from her crouched position beside the bed and stood very straight, her eyes still fixed at a point behind Nat. 'Not the Devil. Not that,' she said slowly. Her voice was sharp, as though she spoke to someone else. 'I see him, though. Yes – I see you, whoever you are. Be gone from us. We have done no wrong here. And take away this blight from a good man who has no evil in his heart, who wishes you no harm, only to leave you in peace.'

Nat and Moses looked about them furtively. There was

nothing to be seen. Was the House going to claim her sanity also? Then she blinked and bit her lip and the colour flooded through her cheeks as she bent down to Tom once more.

'Sorry,' she muttered to them. 'I swear I saw a figure over by the door. He was quite clear for just a moment. Dressed in strange clothing, too. But he had Tom's features, I swear it . . .' She put her head against Tom's chest and began to weep softly.

The Watcher was deeply shaken. He held out his hand to the girl and pleaded his innocence, raked by the anguish in her face.

She had seen him. In the year 1804, he had been seen positively by a young human being in full possession of her senses. He withdrew when it became clear that the sight of him had gone and that no amount of protestations of his innocence would reach her. He walked on the terrace, deaf to the soft drone of bees about their business, blind to the mellow light when sharp colours meld in a gauze of warm sweetness and the earth drowses.

She had actually seen him.

The implications of visual contact between the years 1804 and 1955 were so far-reaching that the impact of it took some time to sink in. When it did, he ceased pacing and sat on the shallow terrace steps with his back against the balustrade.

That first extraordinary registered act of recognizing in 1804 one who lived and breathed a century and a half later must mean that he was not insane after all, but that he must have become, in some violent fashion, caught in the very kaleidoscope of time.

From this moment on, it was historic fact that she would always know that she had seen him. So would the two men who were with her. The prison was not, then, in his mind at all.

He was an embolism in time.

Charles trained his birds himself. He had done this since game fowl mains had begun to appeal to him some ten years before. At first he had been content to buy birds and let Will Slaughter train them but the fascination of the sport had reached down into his subconscious, finding there the Bayless genes and the fiercely competitive spirit of the cock-fighting Romani. He had one of the stables cleared and limewashed in his yard and began to breed and train his own birds. Visiting the roost became a daily pilgrimage of expiation when the stresses of the day were put aside and he could lose himself in the fascination of fowl training and then watch his handiwork flourish at main after main.

Now he had the new Duckwing, as well as half a dozen hand-reared cocks to put through their paces. It was the Foulsham Duckwing, though, that would tempt Nat Smith, and with him Dudie, out of hiding. He took the bird from its cage, hands gentling the alarm out of the creature, his mind faraway on the coming contest.

Seven days from now. Days of a tight schedule for birds and trainer alike. Upstairs in the house, Leonie was slowly fading away, dying without complaint or fuss, attended by her sons and nurses. He felt nothing for her but impatience for the thing to be over. He ignored the unspoken disapproval of the household, the sadness in his wife's dull eyes. He concentrated on his birds, banishing even the image of Dudie from his mind.

Charles made up his own cocking bread with consummate care. He had learned from Will the subtleties of ingredient proportions and by this time had learned useful tips from others also. Into the cocking bread he added half a spoonful of powdered feverfew mixed with a tea made from dried borage. The tea had an aromatic flavour not favoured by game fowl but by the eighth day of training they were so ravenous that they would happily have made short work of almost anything put before them.

On this first day he was content to spend the evening trimming his five birds. He hummed under his breath as he deftly clipped their long tail feathers and filed back the spurs. Word had reached him that morning that the Master of an Emsworth frigate bound for Portugal was to take on two passengers not registered on the ship's manifest. Portugal might well be the final destination but a French port was likely to be their first anchorage.

246

Close watch was being kept on the south coast these days for escaping prisoners as well as political spies. Times were bad and brother watched brother – for who knew where his sympathies lay. There had been strangers at Park Farm, whatever the Chases might protest. An ailing sister? Was she so ailing that no one had ever seen her? And who had given the old people the finest assistance with their fencing and barn flooring that anyone could hope for?

Strangers. Two strangers would have been grateful enough to repay sanctuary in such a way. And now there were two strangers on a vessel bound for the Continent. He had the strongest possible conviction that the two strangers were Tom Heritage and the big Negro Moses Abelson. If they were, they would not get far for he had sent a note to the Captain of Militia at Emsworth, suggesting investigation. Without Tom to nurse, to fuss over, maybe Dudie would gradually forget him, once she knew that he was gone beyond their reach for good. It would take time for him to creep back into her good graces but, with Leonie gone, he would surely be able to tempt her back to his side and away from the old life. Faint though he knew the hope was, it still gave him a feeling of lightheaded purpose.

He stroked the birds' gleaming feathers and put them back, one by one, into their cloth-covered pens.

Then he went into the house to sit silently at his wife's bedside.

Chapter Four

The fever which had consumed Tom so suddenly lasted four days. During that time he went in and out of varying states of consciousness which were more alarming to the three watching over him than were his occasional periods of total coma. Dudie, distraught at the thought of the ship sailing without them, could do little but sit at Tom's side, watching the strange changes of expression flitting across his dreaming face, every instinct in her body all too aware of the subtly changing atmosphere all around them.

For the whole place seemed different now. She felt stealth about her, as though something crept invisibly in her shadow, watching . . . growing in purpose. It gave her a deep feeling of unease, of looking constantly over her shoulder – of almost, but not quite, catching sight of the thing that stalked her. Tom tossed on the great fourposter in the master chamber, fluctuating between spasms of violent restlessness, the animal growl in his throat sometimes rising to a tortured bellow – and lying like a discarded doll, exhausted by some inner conflict which was gradually sapping the last shred of energy in him.

There were times when he knew her. Then she was aware of a terrible urgency in him, though the words that came from his mouth were unintelligible. For the most part, he was lost in some other place deep down in his mind – a place which terrified as well as gripped him.

Feeling time slipping by and the chance of their freedom diminishing with every hour, she tended him doggedly, almost resenting the occasional appearance of Moses and Nat. And the two men, having nearly come to blows in the frustration of their situation, finally agreed that they could not move Tom until he recovered from his unexpected seizure. They swallowed their impatience to be gone and busied themselves with breaking-up the rotting stalls in the barn for firewood.

Tom floated in a world of fleeting faces and sudden invasions of his body which scoured every nerve and sent him screaming soundlessly back into black shadows. There were times when he was aware of Dudie sitting beside him, her little pointed face anxious and foxy. He tried to tell her to go. Deivos had invaded his very soul and his furious resistance was slowly being squeezed out of him. If he once gave in he knew that he would return to consciousness and sanity – but Deivos would be there in his soul, resting and waiting, waiting for him to respond to the tenderness that Dudie provoked in him. Rage at such intrusion fed his weakening resistance but even the rage was not of the same substance as it had been at first. He knew that when he came back into himself he would not be the same again. The Power was in him.

Halfway through the fifth day after he had been struck down, Tom opened eyes that focused and reached out to take Dudie's hand. She was, as usual, sitting beside his bed, drowsily listening to the light, even sound of his breathing. She started back in alarm as the hand took hers firmly and squeezed it.

'Hello,' he said. His fever was quite gone. His face had lost its grey pallor and he seemed little the worse for his experience apart from an understandable weakness. Nothing that nourishment would not soon dispel, she saw with relief. She quickly brought him broth and bread which he ate ravenously and was soon out of bed, testing his legs.

'I don't know what happened to me,' he said as she gathered up his empty dishes and turned to take them out of the room. The hateful faces and fears of his delirium were already receding into the back of his mind, a bad dream best forgotten.

She smiled at him and there was an expression in her eyes that turned his heart. 'The House took you, Bor,' she said. 'There have been stirrings all around your bed as though the room was filled with people, pressing against each other to get a look at you. You must have put up a struggle for you were filled with violence at times when you were delirious. You spoke in a tongue that was not familiar to me. You even looked like another man at times.'

She gave him another sad little lop-sided smile. 'Your fever robbed you and Moses of your place on the ship –'

'Why should that be?' he asked, puzzled. 'I have surely not been laid low for more than a few hours?'

'Days, Tom . . . days and nights, five of them in all. Days and nights doing battle with something that is here in this House and will be the death of you if you do not come away from it.' She said no more then for something closed behind his eyes although his head nodded in agreement with her.

Shaken by the time-lapse he dressed slowly and went down after Dudie to question her further. There was a strange feeling in the middle of his chest, as though, at the smallest suggestion, his mood would flare up into white-hot rage. He clenched his teeth, holding it in. Ill-temper had never been part of his nature – but then, it was the other one in him now.

Soft summer rain had scoured the pathway between the back door and the stableyard. He found Moses and Nat in an area cleared of weeds, in the act of setting two fighting cocks at each other. The calm scene and the men's intense concentration made him pause and lean against the barn wall to watch.

Holding the birds astride they were set together beak to beak and then released and Moss and Nat hovered attentively as the adversaries lunged at each other, wings scything, talons and beaks seeking, darting with deadly aim.

'Watch that left spur,' Nat said to Moses. 'The muff's draggen' on 'is left there . . .'

Something began to unfurl in Tom. Watching the birds feint and parry, the lust for blood in their beady red eyes, he felt it opening in him like a great scarlet flower. He turned away and ran from the yard, clutching at his throat as the thing began to boil upwards from his chest. Panting, he doubled up, leaning against the wall and vomited into the long grass.

'What yo doin' down here, Master? You should be in your bed.' Moses' deep voice was filled with anxiety. Great hands gripped him gently by the shoulders and took his weight. For a moment, Tom could say nothing. The flower sank back, furling its fury. When he could trust himself he lifted his head.

'It's all right, Moss. I'm much better. I feel fine now. It was just a momentary weakness.'

'Well, sir, it's mighty good to see you on your feet again! Thought we was going to be in the benighted place for the rest of our natural lives, I surely did. The brig left three days ago, you know . . .'

Tom straightened up. The shivering was almost gone now. 'Can't think what hit me. I'm sorry for it, Moss, I truly am. I was coming to tell you that you are all quite right and that we shall be leaving this place as soon as arrangements can be made to find us another berth across to France.'

The big man grinned broadly, relief and the lifting of some great inner self-control making him stand taller, sharper. 'What say we go this very minute? Before you get another good reason for staying? Man, I just hate every minute of this place. Cain't help it. It's bad and I'm unclean just breathin' its air. So are you. What say, we go now?'

Nat appeared beside them, looking thoughtful. He had caged the two cocks and put away the fine leather muffs with which he had protected their spurs. 'You've lost one chance – so why not wait for a better one? While half the countryside is busy at the main over there at New Barn tomorrow, 'twill be a good moment for you to slip through without be'en noticed, see'en as how there'll be plenty of strangers millen' about.'

They sat round the long refectory table in the House's great kitchen where staff and yardsmen had sat gossiping over their dinners down the years before them. Tom said little but Moses and Nat, wanting only to be gone, seemed not to notice.

'Move out after dusk falls.' Even Nat seemed happier now, suddenly more animated than Tom had ever seen him and he realized with regret that since his escape from the hulk he had put all three of these people under enormous strain.

'We'll have to dress Moss up so that his skin is not noted,' he said. 'Even at night those rolling eyes of his'd raise a battalion.'

'I could drape him in some curtains,' Dudie offered. 'There are plenty of them in the linen room, even if they'll fall to shreds before he's had them round him for long.'

'What happens when we've cleared the area?'

Three faces looked at him. It doesn't matter – as long as we get you out of here, said their expressions.

'We'll meet up with you both at, say Ashling, north of Chidham and make for Stansted Forest where some of the Clan are camped this month. We'll have no trouble covering you there, while I ask around in Emsworth an' Havant for a couple of discreet berths across the Channel. They're to be had, as the last ones were – as long as your money is good, Bor . . .'

It was – for Nat had sold to Master Griffin of New Fishbourne a fine set of table cutlery from the Lavenham silver chest and no questions asked. No doubt Master Griffin thought them stolen and was at pains to have his crest engraved upon the handles. Tom patted the leather pouch at his belt and grinned at them. His mother would think it well worth the price of their freedom.

The Watcher saw them withdraw and was relieved.

He had stood close to them as they made their arrangements and they had not been aware of him, not even the girl. There was some strength left, after all, in his Power . . . but who was to say whether there would be enough for him to get to the centre of it all?

He stood in the open kitchen doorway watching the four figures moving away from the House through the archway and into the stableyard. All round him the House was gathering itself, manipulating unsuspecting emotions for the horribly physical pleasure of feeding off the tragic results.

'*Don't come in here again*,' he soundlessly begged their retreating backs.

Everyone was astir well ahead of dawn.

They had slept huddled together in the waggon, Nat and Moses lining up on either side of Tim in case he was overcome once more by the lure of the House. They had sat on the stepladder into the long late hours of night, trying to discover from their own varied reactions just what it was that dwelt like a canker in the heart of the House. It had, at last, been acknowledged by the four of them that Lavenham was possessed by something seeking to feast upon human passion, be it love or hate.

Tom, sickened by the thing that was in him, forbore to tell them that he was no longer the Tom whom they thought they knew. Dudie alone recognized his torment and was uneasily aware of change in him. He had caught her observing him with a keen eye more than once.

He breathed lightly, soothing the rearing thing in his bloodstream, already learning to keep his responses shallow. Was this how his mother had been afflicted? How Uncle Lawrence had struggled with his problematical childhood? He longed to reach out to them, to have the reassurance of a father who knew the depth of the problem as their father, Jess Bayless, had known it. But Jess himself had tackled his possession alone – just as he was having to. Behave naturally, he repeated to himself. Avert their attention away from their almost obsessive concern for him.

'How long do English mains run for?' he asked Nat, striving to clear his mind.

The gypsy shrugged bony shoulders, chewing the inside of his cheek. 'Depends, Bor. Sometimes 'tis all over by dusk – ef'n the birds ent top quality fighters. A brace of good birds'll keep it goen' till the small hours, unless there be a time limit to et. I recken as this 'un could be like that. Master Bayless' are fine fowl – an' that friend of his – that Lord from Halnaker, he's got some birds that've won reglar in the past five year. Then there's my Smokey. He'll never give up till 'e drops dead, that 'un. I reckon it'll go all night.'

Tom nodded, satisfied. 'Could Dudie and I take the waggon with Moses in the back and meet up with you in the morning? You could take the boat over to Ben Chase and borrow a mount from him and join us later in that forest you and Dudie have been speaking of. Then Moss and I will be within striking distance of one of the ports and will try and get berths on the first vessel willing to carry us across the Channel.'

He felt Dudie's eyes on him and turned his head from her. He would be certain death for her if he stayed. Nat and the Bayless Clan would take care of her. Maybe one day he could send for her.

'Don't see why not.' Nat fell silent after that, lost in his own thoughts and Moses, for once mute, the laughter absent from his face, sat hunched between them in the wavering light of the one fat lamp.

Dudie perched on the edge of her bunk in the waggon doorway. She listened to Tom's voice as he did his best to revive Moses' good humour. There was something about him that was not right at all. Something discordant that came neither from his manner, his voice nor even from what he had to say. Something else about him, some new aura repelled and yet fascinated her. She shivered and drew back from the candle glow. The child fluttered lightly within and she stroked it gently with the tips of her fingers.

'I will take them past Newbarn around moon up,' she said to Nat. 'By that time, the drink will have been flowen' all day an' folk will be less interested in what's passen' by. The mains an' byes'll be well advanced by then an' all the attention will be on the pit for those sober enough to be betten' . . . Reckon we c'n slip past without be'en seen. Then ye can bring Smokey back in 'is bag over the water, like Tom said, Nat. The Chases will be the first to rejoice at see'en the back of all of us, I reckon.'

Moses jerked his head up. He had slowly been sliding into a light doze, slumped against Nat's gaitered legs. 'Why don' we sleep on it, 'stead of perching on these steps like a cackle of roosters,' he said.

Tom stood up and stretched and jumped down from the waggon to relieve himself. He went across the yard to the barn wall and leant one hand against it as he unbuttoned his breeches. From inside the barn a horse suddenly neighed close to him. He started. The sound had been so unexpected and so loud that he spun round and saw the others staring across the lamplit yard with still, shocked faces. Before he had time to open his mouth it came again, the shrill squeal of aroused stallion and now they could hear the thump and crash of flying hooves against the barn walls.

'You've no other horse in there, have you?' he called across the yard.

Nat came over to him, his face gaunt in the dim light. 'There was nothen' in there afore nightfall save our piles of firewood, Bor.' His eyes darted round the yard, searching for explanation.

It came again and with it the all-too familiar odour that had driven them from the House. The quiet night was suddenly ablaze with red light and fire shot upward in a shower of golden sparks as the barn roof was engulfed in flames.

Tom backed away from the wall, his need forgotten. Even as he reached the waggon old Pally, smelling the pungence of burning wood, whickered anxiously from the paddock. There seemed to be more than one shrieking horse in the barn for the sound of rage and fear gradually grew until it drowned the crackle of flames and crash of collapsing roof timbers.

'Nat, come with me,' he shouted. 'Someone must have put a horse there. There may be a chance of getting it out.'

He ran across to the gaping glow of the open barn doors. Nat stayed where he was, rooted to the spot. There was something about the frenzy in that terrible shrilling which brought the hairs up on the back of his neck.

'There ent no horse in there, leastwise no liven' horse,' he said. He felt Dudie press close to him and put his arm round her shoulders.

Moses pushed past him and followed Tom towards the shimmering barn door. '*Hail Mary, Holy Mary ... Hail Mary, Holy Mary ...*' He muttered the comforting formula under his breath, watching the black silhouette of Tom against the furnace of flames. It seemed to weave and fracture in the increasing heat.

Tom came to a standstill, warding off the singeing heat with a raised arm. 'It's no good,' he shouted as Moses joined him. 'Nothing could live in that inferno. It's all rotten wood in there?'

'Then why is that thing still screaming?' Moses had to bellow into his ear against the roar of the flames and the continuing crash and screams of the burning creatures.

Tom took a step forward uncertainly and then cowered back. Out of the white-hot curtain of heat a horse appeared.

255

It stood in the centre of the collapsing entrance, magnified in the billowing heat into huge proportions. It seemed to tower above them, huge and black and enraged, its glistening body magnificent and terrible. It stared at them, lapped in flame, the pure malevolence in its rolling eyes so baleful that Moses gripped Tom hard by the wrist. In the same instant the creature reared up on its haunches, the wicked silver hooves thrusting at them.

'Run . . . Run . . . It'll trample us down.'

Tom jerked out of Moses' grip and turned towards the creature. The scything forehooves swerved towards Moses and he cried out, covering his head with an arm and sinking to his knees.

Too late to run. Tom felt the heat of the animal searing his cheeks and released the unfurling flower inside his chest. He stood against Moses' crouching shoulders and felt the sweet sensuality of the Power build up and then burst from him.

There was an explosion as though the whole of a powder arsenal had blown up before them. The great black stallion was enveloped in blue searing light. Tom closed his eyes against it and scooped Moses up, half-dragging him across the yard and past the waggon.

'Run . . .!' he shouted at the others crouching against the waggon's offside. Moses found his feet and stumbled away into the darkness ahead of Tom. Nat and Dudie panted close beside him. Out of the yard and into the paddock where Pally snorted and shambled up and down the hedge in alarm, shaking her old head from side to side. They ran the length of the north paddock, unable to discover a way of getting out into Hempsteddle beyond and finally flung themselves down, huddled together against the dense thorn hedge. Shocked and speechless, they waited for the sound of drumming hooves and that terrible squealing rage.

Silence.

Tom lifted his head and turned to where Moses pressed into the hedge, praying under his breath. Nat and Dudie stood against him like rigid posts. The darkness covered their faces.

'I can't hear anything.' He found he was whispering.

Dudie's hand crept into his and he squeezed it tightly. 'I can see no glow from the barn either,' he said. 'Look – no light at all. No sound. There must be. The barn was about to collapse completely a moment ago and the roar of the flames was deafening.'

They stared blindly into total darkness. Not a sound penetrated the velvet night. No orange glare blazed beyond the paddock wall. The odour was gone and nothing stirred any of their senses other than the peace of total darkness in a grassy paddock in the middle of a summer night. A long way away, St Mary's clock struck a single chime. The sound brought them back to reality.

'That wasn't real, was it?' Dudie's voice was low and clear in the silence.

Moses said nothing. He was still busily calling upon the clemency of the Almighty. Nat gripped her shoulder. ''Twas nothen' from this world, I swear . . . that place be full of mullos. I'm not goen' back.'

Tom found that his breath was returning to normal. In the suddenness of shock and fear the alien thing in him had found pleasure. Now he gritted his teeth together, burying it deep inside as far down as he could.

'It seems to have gone, whatever it was,' he said.

'It must've been real,' Moses said in the darkness. 'I've burned my hand real bad.'

They stayed huddled together in the hedge for a long time, drowsing and waking fearfully to stare round them but the night remained quiet and nothing disturbed them. Before dawn they crept back towards the yard, half-expecting the terrible creature to be there still, waiting to trample them with its vicious silver hooves.

The yard was dark but for the faint glimmer of the dying lantern on the waggon which stood as they had left it. By its feeble light the backdrop of the great barn was a dark sentinel sprawling across the far side of the yard. There was no sign of fire, no sharp scent of burning wood in the air. The whole place seemed as peaceful and undisturbed as when they had first seen it.

The only sign that something had actually happened was the state of Moses' right hand and wrist. In the wavery lamplight it looked as though the flesh had actually boiled before it had burst. Dudie drew in her breath sharply at the blackened and glistening claw he held out to her. She hunted amongst her salves and liniments for something to reduce his increasing pain and found that her own hands were shaking so badly that she was scarcely able to take the tops off some of the jars.

They brought Pally in from the paddock, backed her into her traces between the waggon-shafts and moved the waggon out of the yard and into the drive.

Dudie re-kindled the lamp and handed round a flask of Genefa. Moses was, by this time, in such pain that he was scarcely able to sit still. She made him drink a double tot of the fiery liquor mixed with a sleeping draught. They all drank, feeling the sharp bite of the liquor bring strength back to their tired bodies.

Nat brought the Smokey's cage up from its hook beneath the waggon. The bird seemed untroubled and blinked hopefully at him, looking for grain.

'I've to cut 'im out afore we move,' he said to Tom.

'Well, there's no point in changing our arrangements for today unless we are disturbed further by anything else the place might throw at us,' Tom said. They were all in a jumpy state, he as anxious as the others. But the creature had not actually harmed them, apart from Moses. The roasted hand was more like a warning.

'You go off with your bird and we'll follow after dark. If this place erupts again, we'll have to risk it and go before but it would be too much of a risk for us to move along that lane against the tide of incoming cockers unless we are forced to.'

Nat shrugged and began sharpening his knife to prepare the bird for the Pit. He wouldn't stay here for one moment after first light and the others would do well to leave then also, whatever the state of traffic in the lane. He settled down with the Smokey and gave his full attention to cutting the bird out.

Moses slept fitfully, the injured hand held clear of his cloak in the waggon. Dawn stole upon them drowsing, waking to sit and watch Nat's skill with only half their attention.

Wing feathers had to be clipped and rounded, hackle and saddle feathers cut shorter, vent feathers sheered and then the delicate business of cropping the tail plumage, leaving only the fan, its elegant fall reduced by half to a stiff brush.

Contestants were to be 'shown' in the Pit soon after sun-up as there were many preliminaries to be gone through before the mains and byes actually commenced.

Nat took a double scoop of Dudie's now cold but still thick beef broth, chewing with relish the onions, potatoes and slithers of meat that enriched it. He would have lost pounds in weight by the end of this day, reducing himself in company with his bird as he encouraged it during each fight, perspiring as much with the excitement of possible victory as with the cold stone weight of defeat in the pit of his stomach.

'Man, I wish right down to the soles of my feet that I could come with you,' Moses muttered, the spirit of contest rising through the depth of his fear and pain.

Nat grunted. 'Reckon you'd be good value in the crowd, too,' he said, the corners of his eyes crinkling momentarily. 'That is, until they notices that great black moon of a face of yours, Bor. Then they'd be onto ye like a pack to the stag. There's still a greater price on your head than they'll get in the betten' booths on Smokey.'

He put the bird carefully into its cloth cockbag, drew the leather thong tight and stood up. 'I'm off then,' he said quietly. 'Dawn's breaken', see there?'

To the east the long night had at last been stormed by the new day. Pale streaks were just beginning to split the black abyss of the sky.

'Nat.'

He turned, hesitating, impatient to be gone.

Tom limped across and held out his hand. 'Thank you for your help in all this. It is much appreciated, you know. Even though you'd rather we'd never been born.'

Nat flashed him a look that was half-amused, half-irritated. 'You're all right, you an' Moses. Another time I'd have ben glad to know ye, Bor – but we'll not sleep sound, Dudie an' I, till you're gone.'

He turned away, the stark cut of his bony face set hard, and strode away from them up the drive with the bundled Smokey held tenderly under one arm.

'Kushti Bok, Pral,' Dudie called after him. 'But leave a little here for us too,' she added under her breath. A bee wandered

259

lazily past her nose, in the direction of the orchard. It was going to be a hot day once the sun was risen.

'Jesus and all the Angels . . .' Moses hissed behind them. He had woken and was sitting holding his injured hand by the wrist. Seeing Tom's startled face swivel round towards him, he held it up. His teeth had begun to chatter in his head like castanets.

The hand was unblemished, the skin firm and whole.

Dudie took it in hers and turned it over and Moses screamed. 'The pain is still there . . . It feels as though the fire is still eating it away!' Tears of pure agony spilled down his cheeks and she put her arm round his shoulder and cradled his head until he had mastered the shuddering sobs.

'The nerves are still shocked,' she said to him. 'It happened, whatever your hand looks like now. The barn is whole, too. I shall treat the hand as though it is burned, Bor, and the healing qualities of the herbal juices will soothe the nerves in your flesh.'

The House seemed to shimmer lazily among the green upsurge of its overgrown gardens. The untouched roof of the great barn was just visible behind the distant outline of the stone archway.

Tom leaned against the back of the waggon. Nat was gone. There remained only Moses, nursing his injured hand. Dudie had dressed it with one of her cooling balms and had made him drink an infusion of mandrake and cowslip. He seemed more comfortable and drowsed in the waggon.

The urge to touch her was overpowering. So was the other sensation which now accompanied all his thoughts of Dudie Smith. He glowered at the distant House with its graceful archway, the brickwork already soft with rosy beauty from the first rays of the early sun.

'Midhurst,' he said quietly and it was as though the name of that distant home could cleanse them all of the decay which surrounded them at Lavenham.

'Oh God, deliver us safely back to Midhurst.'

There was already quite a crowd of cockers and trainers assembling in the yard at Newbarn by the time Nat strode past the gate, through the clutter of traps and horses and men sitting in the grass, waiting for the first contest to begin.

He nodded as someone hailed him through the throng but pushed on towards the weighing table where he could see the weigher and his brass scales already busy at one end of the open-sided barn. Will Slaughter's leather tricorn moved a good head above his companions, turning this way and that as he watched the weighing-in and argued the betting odds with his customers. He raised his head and saw Nat. A curious expression flicked across his broad face and was quickly replaced by a quick nod of greeting. Nat frowned, seeing the man's eyes slide over the heads of the crowd to the other end of the barn. There were too many folk milling about for him to see who it was that Will had marked so swiftly.

He stood in line, waiting for the weigh-in with the bagged Smokey in the crook of his arm, warding off elbows and pushing bodies around him. He grunted at the greetings of his companions, in no mood for pleasantries at this stage. First get the weigh-in over, and then think about wetting his gullet before settling down to the serious business of matching pairs.

Smokey rustled impatiently in his bag, sensing the air of expectation and the presence of his adversaries all around him. Then they were beside the weighing-table and the fine set of highly-polished brass scales. The clerk looked up at him, quill poised above his registration sheet.

'Nat Smith . . . single Dorset Smokey,' Nat said, opening the bag and scooping his bird out. He placed Smokey into the scale-dish where the beautiful bird stood swaying, blinking the red rims of its sharp round eyes, disorientated by the sudden light.

'Dorset Smokey . . . Birchen Pile, yellow-breasted, clear-cut with high comb, orange legs and two's in head. Grey centre-nails, one eye grey walled . . . weight three pounds, nine ounces. Owner Nat Smith.'

There was a moment when the bird stood with spine fully stretched, balancing in its golden dish with consummate majesty, hooked beak raised, the long snowy neck twisted towards Nat, the black feathers on breast and clipped tail glowing with a bright emerald sheen.

There was a murmur of approval about the weighing-table. Then Nat scooped his bird up and made way for the man behind him. He returned Smokey to his bag and made for the back of the Slaughters' cottage where three barrels were already being spiked by those with the first thirst of the day.

'Ah, Smith . . . We've been wondering whether you would grace the gathering. Word had it that you had already left the district . . .'

Nat turned slowly. He touched his forehead with a grimy forefinger. 'No sir, not me. Dudie, she took to the road yesterday, off to meet with the family over New Forest way. I'll follow after Smokey'n me 'ave wiped the Pit clean here.'

Charles Bayless smiled charmingly. There was no sign of the animosity which had coloured their last meeting. 'Word has indeed been spreading of the fine bird you have been rearing. A magpie hatch too, they say,' he said lightly, eyeing the sack under Nat's arm with interest. 'I trust that my own Duckwing and Spangles will be spared to give him a fair contest.'

Nat stared after the tall, retreating figure, resplendent in grey doeskin jacket and the new stovepipe trousers. There had been something about the look on his face that reminded him of a large grey cat making ready to pounce on its prey.

Something had been building up in Tom since before the sun had reached its zenith. His head ached and the very sound of Dudie's and Moses' voices chatting as they prepared the waggon for its journey, grated like sand upon a raw nerve. He felt utterly listless, unable even to offer Dudie and Moses his help in battening down everything in the waggon so that they might travel with all speed.

He had the most compulsive urge to return to the House. Once there, he would never leave it again. He knew that with a cold certainty.

The Power was restless, strong in its newfound resting place within him. It drowsed, pulsing gently, only to be roused by the slightest surge of interest that he might register in anything.

He curled up in a little ball with nothing to say to either of the others and pretended to sleep. Moses, aware that all was suddenly not right between Tom and Dudie, stretched his great length with a wary eye in the direction of the House and set about discussing the size and design of Lavenham's stud yard in an attempt to wipe the growing misery from her face.

'When this is all over,' he said to her, 'when we are all many miles from this place and can think back on it without the bad taste I have in my mouth at present, I shall go find Mistress Violet and have her tell me all about the building of all this. It sure is well laid out. Why, in Boston we're only just beginning to set aside separate areas for the stud and covering yards – now in 1804. But all this was already being done here forty years ago and more. I sure would've liked to have met this Manfri Bayless you was telling me about.'

Dudie gave him a lop-sided smile. She was very pale, the great eyes sunk deep into their sockets. 'He died last year, Bor, so there's no hope of that now.'

He winced from the pain in his hand and held it up close to his eyes, prodding it gingerly with a forefinger. 'I saw this hand with the skin abubbling and bursting from the flames in that barn,' he said, stroking the tender parts lightly and grimacing. 'Now it looks as healthy as the other hand and yet the pain is still in it, the flesh thumping and stinging as though the nerves will never forget the shock they had. Will it go, do you think, Mistress? Or am I to suffer this pain always? I sure don't need any reminders of this Godless place. My memory of these days will see to that for there's no second that I shall ever forget.'

'You've ben a good friend to him.' Dudie jerked her head towards the sleeping Tom. 'This old Kenner must have ben on his mind for a long time, to make him come to it in the way he did.'

The cowslip tea was still making Moses drowsy and he grunted, already halfway to another doze. She let him sleep. There was nothing for them to do all through this day except to conserve their energies for the wild dash they must make as soon as the dusk was deep enough. Nothing but to keep their distance from the House – for it wished them ill. They were taking Tom away. She climbed into the waggon and paused for a moment beside his bunk. In the light of day he looked white and the strain showed in the heavy purple smudges under his closed eyes.

Even as she stood looking down at him he stirred and turned on his back. His eyes opened. They looked at each other and he turned away, seeing the blood rushing to her face. There had been something there in his face which was quite terrifying, like looking at her own reflection in a mirror and seeing the evil face of a stranger.

The first main was started an hour after Nat's Smokey had been matched. The battle was brief as one of the cocks would not set to. After that, each contest went smoothly enough and Nat was called before the sun had climbed to the midday peak.

He knew his opponent Renard Fulke, having drunk with him and his birds having been matched against him the previous year. On that occasion Fulke had been on a fine winning streak with a pair of silver blackbreasted fowl but one had been maimed at the end of the season and the other had lost an eye and was now a breeder only. The young black-red which now stood against Smokey was a good-looking bird and not lacking in fighting spirit – but it was no match for the magpie-hatched Smokey. Within ten minutes that vicious lightning beak had ripped open the jugular vein. The black-red bled to death before they had removed him from the Pit.

Smokey had been in the Pit twice more before the sun began its downward slide towards the trees. The barrels of ale were replaced and replaced again and men began to sweat and sing and mop their scarlet faces. The atmosphere, coloured by the heights of financial gains and losses on every side, pulsed with the beginnings of ale-flavoured excitement. A couple of boys started a fight out in the paddock, encouraged lustily by their companions. The crush round the pit increased.

'Master Bayless' Grey Spangle versus Patrick Duffy's Hoxton Dun . . .'

The Dun attacked with a vertical display of spurs and the Spangle retreated, unbalanced in the first lunge. It picked up within moments and turned in towards its opponent's right eye. They sparred and gouged at each other for twenty-eight minutes before the Dun refused on a count of forty.

Charles leaned on the pit-rail and watched his feeder gather up the victorious but still furious bird. He had not been so fortunate with his Spangle which had had a leg all but severed in the previous battle. He strolled across to his feeder as he took up the bird, stroking the fury slowly away from its exhausted body.

'Good fight that, I thought, eh Walsh?' he said, laying a hand lightly on the fowl's back. The man grinned at him as the head came round and the murderous beak slashed out, all recognition submerged in the great red urge to kill.

'Plenty of spirit still pumpen' through 'im, sor. Enough for another half-dozen contests. The Blackie's had enough fer today. He's young an' still needs ter feel the mat a bit more afore we'll set 'im at me Lord Derby's Cockalorum. Eff it pleases you, sor, would ye take a count of his contestants? I think there's two of 'em already cut out . . .'

Charles returned to his home for luncheon.

He had been invited to picnic with the Lennox party but Leonie's condition made it necessary for him to display some show of concern. He was disappointed that young John, instead of accompanying him to the main as he usually did, preferred this day to stay at home, close to his mother's closed door. It was very much to be hoped that he was not, after all, going to favour his elder brother's behaviour and hang about her bedside weeping and snivelling like a limp maiden.

He looked into the sickroom and bent over the bed in the dim light of almost closed curtains. His wife lay dozing, the contours of her face sunk back against the bone of her skull. But for the flutter of breath from her half-open mouth, she might already have been dead. He turned away, fighting repugnance at the sight of her. She had once had such liveliness, such droll sophistication. By the look of her even in the shadowed half-light she should have been coffined a month before.

He looked into the Office on East Street, agreed the sale of a parcel of land over towards Charlton, signed a sheaf of documents that awaited his attention and interviewed a prospective bailiff. By the time he returned to the Newbarn main the light was going and the sound of its progress could be heard all the way from the Wittering High Road.

Six birds were emerging as fit contenders for the Goodwood Gamebird Trophy – a fine silver urn which the Earl of March graciously presented to the winner of Chichester's three best-attended mains each season. It looked very much as though Newbarn, though early in the fighting year, would be among the finalists.

One of Charles' cocks had been badly torn by Walter Chinneok's fowl. Two had had enough and been withdrawn. They were young and new to the pits and had yet to grow wily, reserving their best performance for the last mains of the year.

The Duckwing had won four contests without injury. He looked fresh and aggressive and was matched with a Shropshire Furnace from the Goodwood coop.

'Reckon as the Furnace, Nat Smith's Smokey an' Chinneok's Lavant Mealy be the only cocks 'ere now can measure up to 'im, sor,' the feeder said. His eyes were bright and he sweated heartily. Charles watched him closely. No feeder worth his salt touched more than a couple of tankards while his birds were in contest. The infinite care of his charges was the price of his job.

The same rule did not apply to the owners.

Charles sent the man across to the ale booth with his tankard and meanwhile slipped a silver-stoppered flask from his pocket and drank from it thoughtfully. He had been drinking a mixture of ales, wines and spirits since sun-up and was floating pleasantly in a state of gentle intoxication. It was a pleasant state in which to be, if only he could remain at the same level. The other reasons for being present at the main slid through his mind, quickening his pulse, bringing a sudden dampness to his waxen forehead, and he bent quickly over the yellow silk bag in which his Duckwing, still triumphant, crouched, awaiting the next emergence into the Pit. He laid a hand lightly, firmly along the bird's back and the creature, recognizing its master's touch, forbore to aim a vicious stab of its beak through the cloth. It was still but trembled, the anger streaming through its veins towards the unseen foe.

A cheer went up from the Pit and general movement in the

direction of the ale booth meant that another battle was over. Charles' feeder pushed through the steam of sweating men towards Master Bayless and the two lads caring for the Bayless fowls. 'That's another down,' he wheezed with satisfaction. 'Chinneok's Mealy just refused after almost trouncen' the Furnace. Can't understand it. 'E was the better mover for near on twenty minutes, parryen' mighty canny, sor. Even drew blood close to t'other's crop an' caught 'im a nasty gash in the shoulder. Then suddenly, 'e had enough. Backed off an' just defended up close to the Pit edge till Pit Master set the Count on en . . .'

He saw Charles' eyes wander across the busy yard to where a small group clustered round a rangy figure. 'Nat Smith's Smokey be next in, matched to the Goodwood Furnace. That'll mean one'll rid us of the other an' then we'll take the winner.'

The human tide turned again and swept across the yard toward the Pit. Of regulation dimensions, it was twelve feet in diameter, its woodpanelled sides just eighteen inches high. The inner floor was covered with a single circular carpet made of plaited hemp and the press of betting spectators round the Pit went ten or more men deep. Charles watched Nat, his bagged cock in the crook of his arm, approach the Match Master and judges. He gave his tankard to one of his young cockers and motioned him to get it filled up and moved away from the jostling crowd into the shadow of the cottage garden.

Dusk had given way to night and the lanterns all round the yard were already attracting the attention of moths and flying insects. Something nipped his cheek and he brushed it away, listening to the murmur of the spectators.

There was a moment of hush. Out in the lane the distant clop clop of a horse's hooves and the rumble of waggon wheels came to a halt, leaving the air in momentary stillness.

The referee's thin voice drifted across rapt faces, held breaths – and then there was a shout, echoed in a hundred well-oiled throats, as the spurs were drawn and the contest commenced.

Charles blinked his eyes to clear the slight bleariness from them. He must desist from any more liquor until after his Duckwing's battle with Smith's Smokey. He strolled through the garden and leaned against the waist-high wall which bordered the lane. Further along the track, just beyond his vision in the deepening dusk, the outline of a waggon blocked the way, its driver arguing with a youth who had, until a few minutes before, been fast asleep in his cart pulled into the hedgerow.

The waggon was large and covered. For some unaccountable reason, it appeared familiar to him. He sipped the last of his ale and peered through the night at its blurred and lightless shadow.

A roar went up and his heart skipped a beat.

'Aye fer March, Aye March . . .'

'C'm Smokey . . . in there now.'

A huge groan and sudden drop in the noise. A second of almost complete silence . . . and then, 'Give et 'im, Smoke. That's the ticket. Whoa, watch 'is spurs . . .'

His head was feeling quite light, like a child's humming top, spinning gently on his neck.

A figure had climbed down from the smudgy silhouette of the waggon and was in heated altercation with the boy in the cart. He was about to move closer when the Pit roar erupted into applause and there was a sudden outward rush for the ale booth, the hedge, and the settlement of heavily laid bets.

It was over.

The suspicious waggon suddenly forgotten, Charles pushed through the sea of overheated, odorous bodies towards his cockers. The question in the pale raised eyebrows was answered in two directions at once and his pulse began to hammer with a new excitement.

Across the Pit, seen now through the thinning crowd, Nat Smith stared over the bobbing heads at him. There was a thin, hard smile on his lips which had little warmth in it. Whatever bile was in his soul, he had still taken the bait and Dudie would not be far behind.

'The Smokey 'ad 'im.' His trainer's voice was hoarse from shouting at his side. 'That magpie cuckoo of a Smokey, 'es blessed of a charmed life, sor, I swear et. Thought the Furnace had 'is eye out one time for I swear 'e took a slash right through the pupil – but there 'e is still . . . hardly spent, by the looks of 'im. We'll be lucky if'n our fowl comes out clean.

We've speed on our side, I'd say, sor. Speed and 'e's a fresher bird, two of our contests be'en byes, like.'

Charles hardly heard the man's excited stream. It had just occurred to him that the waggon out in the lane was very similar to the Smiths'. Nat had said that Dudie had left Apuldram the previous day, bound for the Hampshire Forests. All the same, that waggon had familiar contours . . .

He put a hand on the man's shoulder. 'Hold a moment, Cutts . . . I've to see someone urgently. I'll be back before long.'

'We're third in line, sor.' The man's voice floated back to him anxiously.

'I'll be back long before that,' he threw over his shoulder.

'Well, sor,' a voice said beside him. 'Your bird ready for Smokey, is he?' There was no light, no laughter in Nat Smith's face, in spite of the casual banter of his words. The granite face with its high cheek-bones and oily black hair dragged back behind the ears was highlit by the poled lantern in his hand. It gave him a look of menace that drove a knife into the pit of Charles' stomach.

He smiled coldly into the man's face. 'He's been waiting over long, Smith,' he said lightly. 'Still, for the pleasure of such a conquest, he would have been happy to wait even longer.'

His eyes slid round Nat's head. 'Is Dudie with you this evening?' He spoke without emphasis, making conversation.

Nat shook his head. 'She don't come to cock fights. Not got the stomach fer it, like most women. She's off to our sister's up in the Forest, where I'll be goen' after this.'

They looked at each other, reading that other inference in the empty words. Charles shrugged and turned away with a faint inclination of the head. Believe that and he would believe anything. They always travelled together. She had often said so in the past.

'Give her my compliments, if you please,' he said over his shoulder. 'If my bird wins, maybe she would accept it as a token of my respect?'

Nat stared after the tall figure as it was engulfed in the seething throng. What did all that mean? He didn't accept that Dudie was gone. But why keep up his attentiveness to her when she would have none of him? It began to look as though the bastard was up to something more than just trying to get Dudie out into the open.

Chapter Five

Tom sat on the shallow single step at the front door, watching the changes of light over the tranquil overgrown garden. He had allowed himself to be drawn back down the drive by the sheer complaisant beauty of the place. Just one more visit to say goodbye.

Dudie saw him go.

'Let me come with you,' she pleaded. But he shook his head.

'I shan't go inside. I'll just see that the doors are closed and the windows sealed. I'll only be a few minutes, don't worry.'

'Moss and I will come looken' for you if you are a moment longer.' The uncertainty in her voice made him smile. She was like a mother hen with a troublesome chick. He said as much and she grinned back at him as she had done so long ago.

'You're more trouble than any chick could be, Master Tom. You and this place . . .'

The sun was beginning to set into the oaks across the water. It cast a soft pink filter of light, hazy as the skin of a peach, through the fretwork of branches, gilding everything it touched with delicate richness. The scene from the terrace, caught in that special silence between late day and early dusk, was the very essence of ageless peace.

Man had been coming and going over this place, he thought, treading this soil since Creation, worshipping here as he was doing now, bowing before the Greater Elements, the Old Ones . . .

By the time the moon rose, he too with Dudie and Moses

271

and Nat would have come and then gone, their lives altered irrevocably by the hidden violence and emotion trapped within the old House. And Lavenham? It would simply retreat once more behind its creepers and cobwebs, to decay quietly, waiting with infinite patience for another intruder to disturb its slumber.

Would it use the same defensive weapons next time? he wondered, aware of the echoes in the dim Hall behind him. Regret flowed over him, an odd grief which was deeper than anything he had yet experienced. To leave Lavenham now, when he was on the threshold of newness with the Killing Power as his banner . . . To leave this ancient place where he could be its defender, the source of its growth and strength.

How could he be contemplating such a move?

How could he allow others to make such a decision for him?

The folded flower stirred in his veins and he felt the charged blood pump languidly through his body.

The Watcher stood close to the man.

He looked down at the hunched shoulders, the mop of uncombed hair – and felt the House pressing down on the poor wretch's resistance. He must be removed, he thought. He was prime material for disaster in which the Place would revel as it drew its power from his unsuspecting emotions and grew in evil. He dug his nails into his balled fists, trying through the very agony from his blistered palms, to reach out to the man.

'*Hear me*,' he begged him. 'Hear me – and go from here quickly, while you have a fragment of free will left.'

Tears blurred his eyes. Tears of frustration and the sheer agony he was inflicting upon the suppurating flesh with his own fingernails.

'*Hear me, Tom Heritage . . . Go now . . .*'

The sun slid away, a golden windfall plum. There was a momentary flash of yellow-green light as the shining rim glowed and was extinguished.

The last light of the day went in the same instant, as though someone had snuffed out a vast candelabra. The evening greyed over, lustreless and humid. A rumble of thunder far below the horizon growled in its sleep.

Tom turned, feeling the eyes that were on him. He saw the figure standing at arm's length from him and the shock it gave him was muted for it seemed that he had seen him before.

Many times?

Or was that just his imagination and this Being simply so much a part of the House that it was his awareness of constant Presence that he was familiar with, not the actual entity.

He studied the face at some length, shifting his body round in the doorway to do so. It was male, the features familiar for they were Bayless features. The regal, high-bridged nose, the finely-cut bone structure, the cleft in the strong chin. The great grey eyes – filled, he saw, with pain – terrible pain. The mouth moved and the lips formed words but there was no sound. His arm came up then, and he flapped his hand stiffly, waving him away with such agonized contortions of the face that such suffering was a small agony to perceive.

'I know,' he said to it. 'I should never have come here. I shall go as everyone wishes. I know the consequences if I stay.'

As he stood up, he saw the open palm of the man's raised hand. The palm glistened whitely. It was raw, like uncooked meat and in places the fine carpal bones showed through. The flesh had blistered and burst so that the blackened surface skin hung from the inner fingers like ragged brown silk. He shuddered, tearing his eyes from the sight.

In the distance Dudie called and the figure fused back into the Hall's dusty shadows.

'Tom!' Dudie's voice sounded anxious. 'Are you there? Where have you got to?' The House seemed to hold its breath, to draw him inwards, away from the owner of that tender voice.

It was suddenly imperative that he should stay outside the door. And that she should also.

'It's all right. I'm on the terrace as I said I would be,' he answered. 'I'm just seeing that everything is secured.'

The figure in the Hall had disappeared.

Tom stood in the wide doorway hunting the shadows, smelling within the sharp odour of stable which filled the air with sudden menace. He recognized it now. It was that same, throat-catching stench that had accompanied the appearance of the stallion in the fiery barn the night before.

It was as though the Place, having failed to afflict these trespassers so far, had decided to discard its gentle mood at last and reveal the canker beneath its lovely face.

He took the ornate key from the inside of the door, grasped the iron handle in the middle of the massive oak door and, holding it with both hands, pulled it towards him. For a moment the door would not move and it was as though something held onto the other side. Then it gave, the rusted hinges groaning and the great door closed with a hollow slam that reverberated through the building.

He stood transfixed by the finality of the great crash.

Voices clamoured inside his brain, pleading . . . commanding. He gritted his teeth and limped down the terrace steps grimly, covering his nose with his hand to stave off the hideous odour that rose up from the very ground around him. He fought the temptation to turn and drink in one last look at the beauty that was Lavenham. For all its fascination, he told himself fiercely, it was still like a beautiful woman – only a decaying skull beneath the soft beguiling lustre of its exterior and it would be a tragic memory to turn and see the hatred and evil of it reaching out for him.

He limped down the terrace steps and hurried through the high grasses that choked the carriage sweep, towards the archway. But for the appearance of that likeness of himself he might not have found it possible, after all, to tear himself from that bittersweet, yearning temptation to remain.

'Thank you,' he said silently to the figure who was no longer there. Maybe, after all, it had simply been his own conscience.

Lightning played softly behind the haze of heat rising off the horizon. Thunder muttered a very long way off. The air was so heavy, so filled with rank odours that the sweat was gathering in a damp film over his body.

The Power was a leaden lump in his chest. He breathed

deeply to control it, in through his nose and out very slowly through his mouth as he hurried through the archway and out along the drive and to the welcome sight of his friends.

Dudie was waxing the heavy cloth cover of the waggon's hazel-framed roof. The great iron door key from the kitchen, which matched the one in his hand, hung from a hook beside the driver's seat. He placed his key with it. They would be given into his mother's keeping where they belonged.

They pulled the canvas across the roof frame and secured it with hempen rope to the eyelets made in the waggon's wood sides for that purpose. Moses, still drowsy from his medicine, nursed his hand and cast occasional looks down the drive.

'There's still a mighty bad feeling about this place,' he said. 'We aren't finished with it yet, I swear.'

'The House is losing its friend,' Dudie said.

Tom said nothing. She understood about the place without need of comment from him.

The stench curled over them, ever stronger as the day wore on, making Dudie retch into her apron.

'Let's be gone, for God's sake,' Moses said for the third time. His face had a grey tinge to it that made an old man of him.

They moved off once darkness had fallen.

Moses stayed in the waggon, draped from head to foot in a length of floral curtain, silent with the pain of his burning hand.

Dudie perched herself beside Tom on the wide top step, a brightly-patterned shawl draped about her shoulders. He took up the reins and gave the old horse a quick flick of the leathers on her haunches. As she moved forward eagerly, casting her head from side to side, he caught the frightened rolling white of her eye. She too wished only to be gone from this place. Crouched beside Dudie, he urged the horse up the weed-choked drive, leaning out into the bobbing lantern light to check that the wheels did not founder in some unseen pitfall. Behind them was utter silence but for the continuing mutter of summer storms far off below the horizon.

The moon had not yet risen but the young night was opalescent with purple afterlight and even as they rounded the curve that would hide the House from them in daylight, it emerged, a yellow lozenge, sliding out from behind the unseen mass of Salterns Wood.

'Yellow Moon, Grauni Moon. Count yer money, Riches soon,' Dudie murmured almost to herself. 'That's what we used to say when we was nippers.' It seemed important to talk, to ease the fear between them. 'Rich man's moon, that. The way we look at et, Nat will be haven' a good main over there.'

Tom grunted at her side. He turned his head constantly from one side to the other, scouring the darkness with his stranger's eyes. 'So'll all the other punters and contestants then, for they are seeing the same moon, aren't they?'

'There has to be Faith, Bor. There is no meanen' if there 'ent Faith first.'

He turned and looked at her then. Her voice was light, but the warning in her words was clear all the same. He had been so cool with her since his illness, speaking with her only when it was necessary, keeping his eyes turned from her so that she should not see what dwelt behind them. Hurt, she grieved, denied the chance of showing him that she understood, that she only wished to give him her support now, when he needed it more maybe than he seemed to realize.

Now, he looked directly at her – and she saw it there in the depth of his eyes, lit silver by the moon's new radiance.

The unfurling flower of Jess Bayless' Killing Glance.

It glowed in the dim blur of his face, close to her own, at once compelling, magnetic. He turned away directly as he had before, as though he was indeed frightened of what he might now be capable and, frowning, peered out between the horse's ears as the closed main entrance brought them to a stop.

Dudie slipped down to wrestle with the gates. They were rusted and choked into rigidity by great ropes of climbing weeds and Moses, hitching his curtain over his shoulders, joined her. Even here the air was rank with the midden stench. Moses, grasping one of the wrought-iron gates with his good hand and giving it a mighty heave, spat with disgust into the grass.

'Smells like something died here, too. Gets right in the back of my throat, 'nough to give a man the vomits.'

The gate moved and he swung on it, giving it another great heave. 'Say, how did Nat move this danged thing to get the waggon in?'

Dudie stood back panting. 'I swear there was no trouble with it. It was I who opened it, not Nat. I pushed it and it swung back, no trouble at all.'

The stench was increasing, the thick odour of rotting ordure making them gag.

'Get back into the waggon,' Tom ordered them suddenly.

They looked up at him, sitting above them on the waggon seat, a dark blur in the purple dusk. The lantern had gone out. There was a harsh urgency in his voice that made Dudie obey him at once. Moses hesitated, peering anxiously past the waggon in the direction of the invisible House.

'I'll give it one more heave,' he said, turning back towards the gates.

They were glowing.

He stared at the massive wrought-iron work, blades of ice in his veins. Moments ago they had been dirty rusted things, inanimate metal that flaked under his grasp. Now they were alight with orange heat, the beauty of their intricate design of twisted oak leaves suddenly highlit from within.

'Get up into the waggon. Do as I say.' Tom's voice cut through his shock and he backed away towards the now lunging Pally, crossing himself and searching with trembling fingers for the little scrimshaw Cross he had made so lovingly aboard 'Fortunée'. He was on the running board in one leap and inside the waggon a second later, holding on for dear life as Tom struggled to control the terrified swerving of the flame-dazzled horse.

'What in God's name is happening this time?' he whimpered, eyes glued to the gates which glowed red to orange and then almost to white heat even as they watched.

'It is the Deity,' Dudie whispered through clenched teeth. She felt frozen, all feeling suspended. 'If whatever is all around us wishes us harm, there is nothing that any of us can do to avoid it now.'

'Yes, there is.' Tom's voice was harsh, the voice of an old man. 'It is here – in me. Hang onto the waggon with all your strength.'

'Tom . . .' she began, turning to him, but he pushed her roughly away from him.

'Don't look at me, damn you, woman!'

The horse was suddenly mute, standing as though mesmerized by the blazing wall in front of her eyes.

'Look away. Do not watch me, for your own sake. *Look away!*'

The gates suddenly exploded and they were in the middle of heat, sparks . . . a tumult of ripping shock waves and Tom was flaying the hindquarters of the old mare with all his strength. They moved, jerking and swaying into the furnace, through it, beyond it. The impetus of the horse's rattling flight took them bowling up the cart track, bouncing drunkenly over ruts and boulders.

The night was dark behind them, the air still.

The blinding ache in their eyes was all that remained of the nightmare moment.

Moses said hoarsely in Dudie's ear, 'Did I just have a fit, Mizz Dudie? Did we all see what I thought we saw?'

She nodded, hugging her shawl tightly round her chin.

He breathed out sharply, not bothering to hide the tremor in his voice. 'We was surely in the presence of the Devil then, no doubt about it. Fire and brimstone round those gates. Oh Lawd above, Tom Heritage . . . what you doen' playing in such company?'

Tom said nothing but grimly flicked Pally's rump with his whip. She plunged ahead, needing little encouragement to distance herself as quickly as possible from whatever it was that had frightened her. They rounded a slight bend and Tom hauled in the reins with an angry mutter. Newbarn was lit by a host of lanterns, both inside the cottage and barn and out in the yard and the lane. Carts, ponies and sedans lined both sides of the track so that there was little room for the waggon to squeeze by. Judging by the roar that went up from a hundred throats, they had arrived just as a great victory was being witnessed. Moses withdrew hastily into the back of the waggon and pulled the stifling folds of his curtain about his head and face.

'Give the reins to me,' Dudie said quietly. Tom shifted in his seat, handed them over without a word and jumped down to lead the old mare through the mess of carts, jutting shafts and prostrate punters.

A few feet past the cottage garden gate a cart stood, its tailboard and rear wheels thrust into the hedge at such a sharp angle that the shafts and left front wheel completely blocked the lane. Lying comfortably under the duckboards was a sleeping youth, his snores a fit contestant for the noisy crowd in the yard behind the hedge.

Tom leant into the waggon and shook the boy's shoulder. 'Come on, fellow. Wake yourself and shift this cart of yours. You're blocking the lane for the rest of us.'

A sudden hush had fallen. Another main about to begin. The boy slept on, the ale fumes in his head wrapping him in a deep dreamless peace.

Tom picked up a staff that lay beside the youth and brought it down sharply across his legs. 'Jump to it, you scurvy lout . . . Get you up out of there and move that damned crap cart of yours or you'll feel the weight of this about your head.'

The boy stirred, groaning. He opened a bleary eye and did his best to focus. Something had hurt him but he could not make out what the face floating over him was saying. Something smote him hard in the ribs, driving the breath out of him and he sat up and folded over with a long gasp. Vomit soured his throat and shot out of him, hot and bitter. It sprayed outwards across the waggon, flecking the stranger's floating face.

Tom jerked away in disgust, wiping the boy's stomach contents from one side of his face.

'*Control . . . control,*' ordered one half of his brain as the evil flower uncurled. '*Don't hurt him. Keep it for protection like Jess did. Like Mama did. Don't hurt the innocent.*'

'Innocent,' he snarled at himself, tearing at tufts of grass and wiping away the sourness from his jaw.

'Do hurry, Tom. You never know who might recognize one of us here.' Behind him Dudie's voice was tight with anxiety.

He began to lift one of the shafts of the obstructing waggon. 'Moss'll have to give me a hand,' he said over his shoulder to her. 'This is too heavy for me to swing round on my own.'

Moses was beside him in a moment, his curtain tucked tightly round his head and huge shoulders. He held his injured hand against his chest and grasped one of the cart's shafts with the other. They lifted both shafts and began to ease the cart further into the hedge. Something blocked it and they discovered a large boulder, larger than a squatting man, embedded in the hedge. Unless they moved at least another five vehicles, there was no way of squeezing through the gap between the boulder, the cart and the hedge on the other side of the lane.

Tom, frustrated beyond words, searched within the now silent depths of the Power. Was Lavenham still trying to hold onto him, even from this distance, for they must now be nearly a quarter of a mile from the House. He felt nothing from the place now. Those whiplash inner scourgings had dropped away in the instant of crossing the threshold, out through the burning gates that had melted before his gaze. The shock of the full effect of the Power was still strong in him for he had had no idea beyond his urge for freedom, of the pure white strength of it.

'*Control* . . .' something chanted again inside his head and he knew that that faint voice of reason must remain stronger than the other if he was to govern the Power surging in him.

They set to once more, doggedly pushing one waggon into another, shifting a cart, backing a drowsing horse against the cottage gate, which it promptly kicked open.

The air was suddenly in tumult again as a deep roar went up from the crowd in Newbarn yard.

'What would I not give to take a look at that l'il old main in there,' Moses said, gasping as he manhandled a light cart a few inches into the grass, up against the stone wall. Dudie took Pally's bridle and drew her another few feet along the lane.

'I think you can scrape past this one in a moment,' Tom gasped, feeling the wheel hubs of their waggon score a deep furrow along the side of a well-polished pony trap that was roped through both wheels round the bowl of a tree.

'Well, well . . .' a voice said quietly beside him. 'Would you like my man to move my trap for you, Master Heritage? I see that you have already left a sizeable imprint upon it.'

*

280

By the time Nat Smith's Smokey and Master Bayless' Duckwing faced each other across the mat, the crowd had thinned and then swelled, filling up with the contents of three nearby taverns, the Crown at Dell Quay, the Black Horse out on the Birdham road, and the Tallyman, a small ale house that had recently opened on the Birdham road and Donnington Lane junction. A few of the spectators of the day's main and byes, needing to stretch their legs and maybe their pockets, had wandered off from Newbarn at a moment when the ale barrels had run dry and Will Slaughter had sent out for replenishments. It was natural to make for the nearest pot-house where they could relate in fine detail, the progress of events among the contestants.

Nat Smith's Smokey had put a lot of money in local pockets. News that he was contesting against such respected cockers as the Earl of March and Master Charles Bayless brought in a new wave of spectators as night fell. By the time the two birds came together the main had been in progress for more than twelve hours.

Charles blinked across the Pit at Nat as his trainer, the Duckwing under his arm, stepped over the barrier onto the mat. He had not taken any ale for half an hour now, but his focus was still a little blurred. Nat was his own trainer. He joined the other on the mat and they presented their birds to the three Main Judges. There was a brief period of waiting while the birds were examined, their spurs tested, the state of their wounds from previous fights contemplated. The crowd was always in a state of restless shifting at this point, just before battle commenced. It was the time when fights broke out amongst the spectators themselves for much drink had, by that time, been consumed and comments about the birds of each man's choice was often of a colourful nature.

Charles nodded at Nat as the Romani, his bird approved, turned away from the Judges' table and took his place in the centre of the mat. He held the Smokey in front of him with both hands. The lantern light glittered on the creature's golden legs and burnished steel spurs. He stared back at Charles, blank-eyed. Then his head went down over his bird and he stood waiting as the Bayless trainer, the Duckwing passed for contest, took up his position facing Nat.

The noise of the crowd sank to a murmur as the referee held up his hand. 'Contest between Master Charles Bayless' Birchen Duckwing, won seven rounds, lost one, and Nat Smith's Shropshire Smokey, unbeaten in six contests this day. Place yer bets, gents . . . if you please. Present yer birds, Pitters.'

Charles' man stepped into the Pit and placed the Duckwing in the centre of the mat, where the bird strutted before the crowd, rising to beat the air with its fine clipped wings. He was a majestic creature, well aware of his superiority. The small club head, the comb braised, topped long white periwig neck feathers sleeked over black breast, wing and tail feathers gilded with a fine emerald sheen. The bright yellow legs were embellished with chased silver spurs. He turned his head arrogantly from side to side, contemptuous of the crowd's admiration. After a minute the trainer scooped him up and hooded him. Nat swung over the Pit wall and placed the Smokey on the mat in his turn.

The bird stood still as a statue for a moment, staring round him, searching the Pit with eager jerks of his long neck. He also sported long white neck feathers but these were tipped with black and glossed down over a soft grey breast and wing feathers. The clipped tail plume would have shown a cascade of grey and marbled red feathers but they had been sheared as close as possible to the cuticle and stood up like a striped black and grey brush. His spurs were not of silver but of finely-traced steel, so highly polished that they shone nearly as brightly as his elegant opponent's. His beady eyes missed nothing. Yellow lids framed the glassy red glare as he raised his beak, getting wind of his adversary. The rumble of the crowd suddenly checked an instant, for it seemed that he would crow – and face disqualification, but he simply extended his supple neck, turning this way and that and stood rigid as a pointer getting wind of its quarry.

Nat smiled grimly. He knew his bird. Smokey always took note of the air vacated by his opponent. He seemed, by this method, to be able to get the gist of him.

'Close the betting, if you please, sirs,' roared the referee over the noise of the crowd. 'No more bets now. Cockers and pitters onto the mat. Let's get on with it, gents. We 'ent got all night . . .'

Charles, in conversation with one of the clerks from the Dell Quay Office on the other side of the Pit, raised his eyes and nodded at his man as the Duckwing was held aloft.

The two pitters placed their birds on the mat, beaks inches apart and whipped off their hoods. The creatures immediately struck out at each other, the first feints being more of a threat than any wish at this point actually to make contact. Still held by their trainers, they quickly worked themselves into a screeching rage until the Duckwing suddenly made a direct lunge and scored the side of the Smokey's head close to one baleful, red-rimmed eye.

The pitters released their birds and fell back against the side of the Pit, eyes glued to their protégés. Nat heard nothing of the yells of encouragement all round him. He knew that the Pit was jammed with more spectators than there had been all day but Smokey and the swiftness of his movements round the wily Duckwing was all that existed for him now. It was not for the money, this particular main, although he had staked ten guineas on his bird – which was near on twelve months' wages – and the return he stood to gain with a win could see Dudie and himself through many a lean year. It was not even the bitter longing to take Charles Bayless off his lofty pedestal, although that also would be some kind of sweet pleasure after the frustration he had had to feel, standing by while the arrogant gorgio despoiled his sister. It was simply that Smokey was an exceptional fowl, both in speed and intelligence, and deserved to win all the trophies that came his way. Nat had trained him well. No one could deny the truth of that. He had fed him with care and knew the way he would approach this adversary, once he had sized him up. The question was, would the Duckwing give him time to do this?

He crouched low, eyes fixed on the cautious dancing thrusts of the two birds. Then swiftly, without further preamble, they rose up, necks twined about each other, beating the air with ferocious wings, the strange primeval screech of their rage cutting through the delighted encouragement of the spectators.

'Cut 'im out, Bayless . . . Get that eye again!'

'In to 'im, Smokey. That's the way of it ... again now!'

The Duckwing was suddenly astride the Smokey's back, gripping with iron talons, the wicked spurs slicing across the bird's right wing. Feathers filled the air, soft white underdown, a few marbled primaries. Smokey twisted as Nat held his breath. He seemed to pause, to let the Duckwing feel a sense of premature triumph, then, snakelike, he flicked round, unseating his preening opponent. Before the Duckwing had time to re-establish its back hold, the Smokey's vicious beak had torn into its neck and it reared back, almost hissing in its fury and pain.

Charles let his breath out slowly. For a moment there, it had looked as though the Smokey would win the day after all.

Nat unclenched his fists as the two birds backed off each other to stand with half-spread wings and weaving necks, stealing a moment's respite to assess the condition of the other. Then they began to circle and parry, taking little stiff-necked runs at each other, only to back off the opponent's scything beak and spurs, taking their time ... reserving their strength and cunning for the right moment.

The crowd began to get restive. These two had been in the Pit for nearly fifteen minutes now.

'C'mon Smokey ... polish 'im off quick. I need the money for the next pint.'

Laughter and boos. More shouts of derision and encouragement. The birds ignored their audience and sneered at each other. They had all the time in the world until one of them lowered his guard for just an instant.

After a further ten minutes of circling and the occasional flurry as the birds met in mid-air with a clash of steel spur against silver it was clear that the action was visibly slowing down and that the Smokey was tiring. He permitted the Duckwing to bowl him over in the next attack and for a moment the beautiful black-breasted creature stood over him again, neck arched to strike. A long smeared thread of dark blood marred the sleek white feathers at his throat. The Smokey lay panting under his left claw, the once shining back feathers ruffled by the Duckwing's vicious talons.

There was sudden tension in the air.

The Duckwing stretched itself with a mighty sense of theatre, ready to deliver the death blow.

Charles dug his fingernails hard into his palms. *Come on, strike now . . . quickly.*

Even as he leaned forward, the blood pumping like a drumroll in his head, there was a sudden knifelike flurry of movement in the Pit. As the Duckwing struck downward with beak and spur, the Smokey suddenly came to life and with a smooth, snakelike movement, which was almost too swift for the onlookers to grasp, he had rolled out from underfoot and was up and round, delivering a series of sledgehammer cuts to the other's neck and breast.

There was a moment of pandemonium as the two birds, locked together in a flailing, feather-flying ball of shrieking fury, rolled round the Pit, into the air and down again, and then the Duckwing went down. It lay on its side, one wing splayed out beneath it, the eyesocket a mess of blood and torn skin.

The Smokey fluttered twice to rearrange its feathers and went straight in for the kill.

As the roar of victory went up all round the Pit, Charles turned away and strode out of the yard towards the road.

Just beyond the gate was the Smiths' waggon. Manhandling a cart out of its way was Tom Heritage.

Bitter disappointment from the Duckwing's defeat gripped him. The sight of that fine, dark face, fitter now than the last time he had seen it aboard 'Fortunée' . . . the sudden certainty that Dudie must also be close by . . . all rushed together with the long day's drinking.

'Well, well . . .' he said thickly, seeing the vast shape of Moses Abelson sliding round the side of the waggon. 'Would you like my man to move my trap for you, Master Heritage? I see that you have already left a sizeable imprint upon it.'

Tom straightened his back slowly and turned round. Charles, his pale face curiously flushed, stood close to his side. He raised his eyes calmly. 'Good evening, Cousin,' he said. The thin smile held little humour.

Charles recoiled as though he had been struck. The eyes in Tom Heritage's face were glowing a deep arterial red. He stared at the masklike face with shrinking fascination. He had never looked like that when he was a prisoner.

'Have you been hiding at Lavenham?' he whispered, needing no reply, for he could see the change in the man, feel the presence of something that had not been there before.

'Go quietly and I shall not have seen you.' He felt the eyes take his will, felt the rage drain out of him, felt as though he were being stripped of his soul. 'Only leave her with me . . . she would only hinder your passage. Leave me just that one comfort. Please?'

The eyes held him, the mouth quirked into a grin. 'Dudie, it is our Cousin Charles, come to bid us farewell to this Island of England. He wants you to stay with him. What say you? Shall you stay?'

She sat very still above them on the plank seat, looking from one to the other. The fair, willow-thin Charles with his elegant suiting and the wild fear in his bloodless face – and Tom, directly below her so that she could see little of him but the grim line of his jaw and the rigid ramrod of his back. She put a hand out and laid it gently on his shoulder.

'Neither of you be for the likes o' me, Cousins. I shall go where Nat goes and you must both resolve your own lives as you will, without me.'

Charles looked up at her then and the pain in his face was so great that she took her hand from Tom's shoulder and slid it under her shawl against the gentle curve of her stomach. The child stirred against her palm.

'Dudie, I shall shortly be a free man. Pray consider my suit, I beg you. I am able to give you all the things your heart desires. My name also, Dudie. You would not be leaving the family of Bayless but establishing yourself in a stronger side of it. Don't go now. I ask you with all humility to stay.'

'Are you a widower already, sir?' Tom's voice was soft, almost a whisper. 'Are you making a proposal of marriage to our cousin which you can honour – or just indulging in pipe dreams to tempt the pity of a soft-hearted young woman?'

Charles hesitated. The fumes in his brain were clouding what it was that he was trying to say. Anger suddenly welled up in him. He raised his arm and aimed the silver knob of his walking cane at Tom's head.

'Impertinent creature, you convict scum,' he roared, fear forgotten in the despair of knowing that she would never come with him, whatever he offered her. Not now that she had met Tom Heritage. He put all his strength into the blow, aiming the knob at Tom's temple. Too late he saw that thing in Tom's eyes flower and explode.

Tom saw the arm begin to rise, the utter fury and frustration in Charles' shadowed face, felt his need to inflict retribution. He let the flower unfurl in him then, let it well up through his body until he tingled with raw nerve ends in every extremity and felt it burst from him in delicious physical release.

Charles collapsed slowly without a sound, folding like a puppet at the waist, the knees. He doubled up and rolled over onto the ground.

'Oh my dear Christ and all the angels,' Moses whispered behind him. 'My hand . . . the pain has gone. It doesn't hurt me at all . . .'

Chapter Six

Victory is sweet and this victory was made all the sweeter in the knowledge that the Bayless Duckwing had been the finest fowl present at the Newbarn main. In the general uproar and movement towards the betting booths after the fight, Nat gently lifted his Smokey from the mat, bagged him with the utmost care for there were several cuts and a torn wing to see to, and could not resist a feeling of quiet jubilation at the way things had gone. Hands patted his back, the Judges applauded the Smokey's amazing courage and subtle timing. Listening to their comments concerning the bird's performance he felt closer to winning the Goodwood Trophy at the end of the season than he had previously thought possible. Excusing himself from the wellwishers crowding round him, he collected his winnings and turned away from the yard, intent now on making for the river and Ben Chase's Farm where he could doctor Smokey's wounds and take a nap before pressing on to Stansted and his meeting with the others. He opened his jacket front and tenderly eased the bagged Smokey inside where the bird could feel the closeness of him and be comforted.

'Oh, you did well, my Kushti Kanni,' he murmured, warding off the lurching approach of an inebriated acquaintance with strong, outflung hands. He sidestepped the man and hurried round the side of the cottage, out of the lantern light and into the moonlit lane. The old fiddler from Birdham struck up a fast jig from one end of the barnyard. There would be dancing among the younger men until the next main was announced.

'Listen to the boshomengro playen' that ol' Spangler's funeral djillia for ye, Smokey . . . We'll soon have ye fixed up and yer cuts and bruises cleaned up so's you'll feel like a new bird again. Won't pledge ye now till the Pagham main. Let 'em all keep guessen', Bor. Let 'em wait, huh?'

Sounds of the main and its revellers followed him all the way up the track and onto the turnpike road. There were still several rounds to be fought but the contestants had no chance of equalling his score. He would hear the result of the day's success from gossip in the Emsworth taverns later. Let 'em wait.

There was no ferry at Dell Quay. He could see the little punt pulled up for the night above the mud on the other side of the river. The darkness was warm, with a hint of ripening fruit in the air, the moon yellow as a farmhouse cheese.

There was an air of waiting all about him, as though the shadows hid a posse of Revenue men. 'Come on then, if you will,' he muttered at the star-rich sky. 'Nothen' to hide but Smokey an' me . . .' He sat on the end of the jetty and leaned against a bollard, content to drowse and wait for the first boatman in the small hours before dawn broke.

He slept and heard nothing of the main which finally concluded some time after two in the morning. Its last devotees were few and they drove and rode and slouched away, back to Chichester, to Birdham, to Selsey. There were no Bosham men waiting for the little ferry when the old boatman poled his punt across by lantern light, his first fare no less than Ben Chase himself with an out-of-season ewe tethered to the end of his staff.

Nat stood up carefully, the Smokey still cradled against his chest. 'Mornen' Master Chase.' He touched his forehead as Ben climbed stiffly up the jetty stairs. The old man greeted him with surprise.

'Didn't expect to see you again this year,' he said gruffly, nudging the fat ewe away from his bad leg.

'Ben' matchen' my Smokey to the best cockers in Sussex at last night's main over ter Newbarn,' Nat said, stroking the bulge in his jacket.

'How fared ye then?' Ben had never been a keen cocker. There were plenty of less bloody ways to make a bet than to watch two creatures tear each other apart. He peered at Nat in the glow of his lantern, anxious to be on his way. A look of pride sped across the Romani's long face and was gone.

'Left before the end,' he said shortly. 'My Smokey won all his contests so I took 'im out as soon as he'd bested Master Bayless' Duckwing.'

Ben's eyebrows went up into his hat. Even he knew of Charles Bayless' interest in cock fighting and the trouble he took with his birds. He grinned at Nat, knowing the satisfaction that he was doing his best to cover.

'There be more ways to skin a rabbit, eh my boy?' He straightened his back and sighed. 'I must be on my way. Mistress Chase be in her kitchen if you'd take a crust at the farm on your way.'

Nat nodded. 'I was goen' to ask if I could dress Smokey's leg and grazes from her medicine chest,' he said gratefully. 'I'm on me way to meet up with Dudie at Cousin Callum's fireside. We'll be back in these parts later in the year.'

'And our two friends?'

The question had been hanging between them since the conversation had begun. The Chases knew only that Tom had missed the passage to France that they had reserved for them. It was dangerous, even on this deserted jetty to discuss the movements of escaped prisoners.

'They've left the House. Gone closer to shippen' and we're on the lookout for a passage for 'em now.'

Ben bowed his head. The old boatman huddled in his seat against his pole, drowsing against one gnarled hand.

'Go see Master Hugh Skillett. He berths in at Cut Mill Wharf every Tuesday when the weather permits, before goen' in to Emsworth to pick up cargo fer Le Havre.'

Nat nodded, his eyes saying their thanks.

'Good day to ye then, Nat.' The old man turned away and plodded up the slight incline, dragging the unwilling ewe behind him.

Nat clattered down the jetty steps, settled himself in the

little punt and thought of other things as he and Smokey were poled across the current, swinging from side to side on the running tide.

He sat in Frances Chase's kitchen and held Smokey down in his lap as he cleaned the torn flesh, dressed the three deep gashes in the bird's neck and leg with a balm made from the crushed root of narcissus bulbs and covered them with hot bread poultices. He fed the hungry bird with grain and watered him well, putting a drop of the juice of nightshade into the draught so that he would sleep undisturbed throughout the long walk ahead of them. He had rested while waiting for the ferry and felt fresh enough to be on his way.

'Give Dudie my fond wishes,' Fran said wistfully as he prepared to leave her.

He smiled at her, a rare thing and all the finer to see now, she thought.

'I shall tell her that I find you well and anxious for her company,' he said. 'The others also.'

They had not discussed Tom and Moses. It was better so. The less she knew, the less there would be to relate to others under possible pressure.

She smoothed her apron with lined hands. 'They are going to send us news of our Georgie as soon as they are home,' she said. She gave him one of Ben's broad-brimmed straw hats to protect him from the hot sun. 'T'will give the bird some shade as well as you.'

He left her then and turned into the long lane with a firm step accustomed to walking distances. If nothing delayed him, he should be eating at his Cousin's hearth by nightfall. The day was going to be a hot one. Even before a dusty dawn heralded another airless day he could feel the dryness in the air, the ill-humours of night odours in his lungs.

He crossed the main highway just out of sight of New Fishbourne toll, cut across common land and grazing towards the Ashlings and Funtington. The sun rose like a boiling lemon and beat down upon his straw hat. He drank from a stream and found three others dried up. The heavy pouch containing his winnings hung inside his baggy trousers but he forbore to cash a coin and quench his thirst in either the Ashling or the Funtington taverns. Plenty of time for that later. Speed was the only thing that mattered this day. Speed to reach Dudie and her escorts. Speed with which to send them on their way, out of the lives of those they had put so badly at risk.

The going was rough now, for he was already in the folds of the South Downs, where beech and oakwood cloaked the rolling sweep of the land's contortions. The road wound and undulated over hills, round chalk cliffs, skirting their edges and then plunging downward once more into shadowed valleys. He avoided Racton where he remembered the presence of a particularly sour Squire whose aversion to gypsies was well known. It was almost evening by the time he came out of Racton Woods and moved quietly across the sweep of open land that was Stansted Park. There were fine breeds of foreign deer reared here, and they were guarded by sharp-eyed keepers. He had netted a young gazelle in the park one spring, years before. He still had the fine jerkin his mother had made from the creature's soft pelt.

It was nearly dark by the time he found the camp.

Stansted Forest was an area of dense woodland, choked with undergrowth and young oaks. There were pathways through the almost impenetrable curtains of ancient bramble and hazel, pathways made by generations of wild creatures and used by the charcoal burners and Romanies who stayed within the safety of its heavy darkness. There were several camping areas but his nose led him to where the Lovells were established in a long dell through which a tiny stream trickled, even in the heat of this long dry summer. An almost solid roof of tree branches overhead filtered the smoke of their cooking hearths in the upper air but the delicate aroma of the hotchiwichi baked in clay in the centre of the fire drew him to them and it was with some relief that he slid down the bank into a carpet of soft leafmould and into their midst at last.

It was a curiously subdued gathering that he joined.

Callum Smith and his family: Tarsus Lovell, old and dying but still very much the Patriarch of the Clan. Around them were the wives and sons, the daughters and children, seventeen in all – and amongst them, foreign and alien, Tom Heritage and Moses. Dudie was with the women, busy over one of the cooking pots, head close to Connie Smith's as they talked softly over their cooking.

All eyes turned and watched his sliding descent into their midst. Moses stood up eagerly and waved his welcome. 'Hello there,' he called, his teeth flashing in the firelight. 'We was wonderin' about you just moments ago. How did you fare?'

Nat nodded at him and raised both thumbs before approaching Tarsus Lovell's fireside where he stood respectfully beside the old man, waiting for acknowledgement. Tom was sitting apart from the others, his head resting on his arms in an aura of dejection. He had made no move towards Nat.

Tarsus was sitting on the ground with his back against the wheel of his waggon, his lap filled with dried grasses. His fingers were knotted, the joints swollen so that movement was stiff, but they were in constant activity, picking up each strand, measuring it against three more and then plaiting the four together with neat, precise strokes.

His lined face turned towards Nat, the thin straight mouth quivered at one corner. The sightless eyes had long since shrivelled in their sockets and were now little more than cavities in the gaunt face. 'Sar shan, my son. You are welcome at our hearth.' The voice was soft and musical, the tones of one long accustomed to ruling by its influence, the voice of an actor, an orator. There were no wheezes in Tarsus Lovell's voice, no thinning of the vocal chords. There was strength there, strength and resonance of a curious beauty, coming as it did from the bloodless lips of a weary and infirm old man.

Nat, kneeling before his Elder's sense of presence, placed his hands over Tarsus' still busy fingers. 'Sar shan, Shura. My heart warms to see you again.'

The old man laid down his string and raised his hands to Nat's face. 'You are well,' Tarsus said with pleasure, feeling the bony features and warmth of his face and then sliding his hands down over his biceps, feeling the flesh on his body. 'You are fed and the bird in your jacket is rested. Did he give you success?'

'He did, Shura. He won his contests and made me ten times ten golden guineas and a chance of the Goodwood Trophy in August.' He looked round him, feeling the distraction amongst his people. 'Is there something amiss?' he asked the old man.

293

The hands were stilled and then returned to the plaiting of grasses. 'Harm has come to the high one.' The musical voice was troubled. 'The stranger who shares our blood also, it seems, now shares that Power given to so few, for it has brought Mokada with it and it is with us all now.'

Nat stared across the fireglow at Tom and Moses, hunched close together and leaning forward to hear what passed between the old man and Nat. Tom's face was ashen. He looked ill, much as he had done the first time that Nat had seen him.

Dudie came across to him and rested a hand in welcome on his shoulder. 'Our Vardo became stuck right outside Newbarn,' she said in a low voice. 'Tom and Moses climbed down to clear the other carts out of the way and we bumped straight into Charles Bayless.' She too looked white and tired. There were no tears in her eyes but the grief was there in her drooping shoulders.

'It seemed as though he had been drinken' for he was flushed and angry and he began to pester me to stay with him or else he'd bring Tom and Moses in to the Authorities. He made to strike Tom, Nat . . . and then it was as if Heaven itself struck him in retribution for he suddenly went down on the ground like a felled tree. We didn't stop to see if he was just swooned from the drink – or what. We piled into the Vardo and we fled as fast as old Pally could take us. An' we didn't let up till we got here, Bor. The din Charles had been maken' yellen' at Tom and at me – we thought everyone at Newbarn would be comen' to see what 'twas all about and then we'd have ben in trouble . . .'

'Did you see anything of this?' Tarsus asked Nat. He ignored Dudie completely and, knowing the way things would be for her, she stepped back from him with bowed head.

'No, Shura. This is the first I have heard of it.' Nat frowned, doing his best to remember the order of things before he departed from the main. 'He and I had birds fighten' together and Smokey here won the day after a lengthy battle, close run. I saw him once during the contest. He seemed all right then. He'd ben adrinken' for most of the day, I'd reckon all the same, as he was itchen' to pick a quarrel on a couple of occasions. When Smokey won, his cocker took the Duckwing's body up. I was a mite busy then, for it was a fine win an' my bird had been badly scored. I never saw 'im after that. Thought 'e must be sulken' for he'd set some store by the contest between us, you could tell. I picked up me winnen's and came away directly, for we'd a distance to cover. Stopped over at Park Farm to dress Smokey's cuts an' just kept walken' . . .'

'So who is to tell that there were no other witnesses?'

Moses' deep voice rumbled richly across the fire. 'There was coming and going up and down the lane all the time, sir, but I can't recall any one fellow who might have stopped and seen Master Bayless fall. And if they did, sir, who would identify us – for there are precious few folk who know us in these parts.'

The old man turned in the direction of the voice. His profile was skeletal, the long nose hooked. 'It is not you and our Yankee kinsman that I am concerned about, Kaulo Bor. It is those of us you leave behind who are now at risk.'

Tom, Moses and Nat slept by Callum Smith's cooling hearth. Dudie disappeared as soon as food had been taken. She had kept her distance from Tom since their arrival in the Camp as was customary for Romani women and he had resisted the urge to look for her to give her his astounding news – for here amongst her own people he felt an outsider, unfit to speak with one of their women. It was imperative to reach her somehow, for suddenly all things were possible once more for it had gone, the terrible looming monster within him. Gone completely from the instant that Charles had been struck down.

There was no time left in which to show her that he was whole again. No time for the preliminary joys of a courtship he was sure that they both wanted, as they had begun so blissfully before the Power had invaded him. She would make him a fine wife. Mother would approve of her and understand the Romani side of her nature and Dudie, wild and free, reared in the lanes and forests, Dudie would quickly feel at home in a vast land that waited, acre by acre, for youth and spirit to cultivate and develop its hidden wealth.

There was no time left for anything but the promise that

he was free from Possession and wanting her to join him. Not as Charles had done, seeking only to catch her as she caught her little songbirds, to press her into a social mould that would be acceptable to Chichester society. There were fewer social *mores* in Boston where freedom of speech and worship were now the most fought-for attributes. She would be more than acceptable in Midhurst on her own terms.

Through the auspices of Frances and Ben Chase, he would send for her. There would be ways and means of ensuring her passage over to France and from thence to Boston.

He took a scrap of paper from his pocket and cut a quill tip from a hazel twig. It seemed a little dramatic to write to her in his own blood but Romanies had no writing materials to hand. They had other ways of communicating.

Dear Dudie,
The Power has gone. I am whole and quite normal again since the meeting with Charles. It means that I can be bold enough to ask you the same question as he did for now I feel that I am no longer a danger to your precious person. I cannot go from these shores without you. Come to Boston and have the child amongst those who will love you both.

The scrap of paper took some time to cover for there was little room for all that he had to say. He wrote by the last of the embers and then sat with the paper between finger and thumb, waiting for the words to dry. Then he folded it neatly into a small square and tucked it into his belt. Sleep came easily, now that he had written to her.

Someone shook his shoulder and he reared up in confusion on one elbow. For an instant it was as though he was back in the orlop hold of 'Fortunée', waiting for another day to begin.

'Time to take a crust and be on our way,' Nat said in the darkness beside him.

There was general movement in the camp and the women were already rekindling their fires and bringing out fat round loaves of bread from their waggons.

Moses, wakening slowly beside him stretched, yawning mightily. 'These are real good people,' he said to Tom, watching the quiet figures moving about their dawn tasks. 'I'll feel a lot less guilty of risking their necks the sooner we are away from their fireside.'

Tom grunted. He watched the waggons for Dudie but she was nowhere to be seen. 'They're moving us on right away,' he said, nodding his thanks as someone offered him a thick wedge of bread and pickle. 'I daresay it'd take weeks for the Military to find this place but they'll have put a hundred miles between Stansted and themselves by that time, in any case. We just have to trust to luck that a berth can be found for us.'

Nat, leaning against a tree beside them flicked a crumb of bread into the air and watched the ravenous rush of the lurcher pack to retrieve it. 'It is all arranged,' he said. 'Whilst we slept, my cousin Shilo Smith went down into Emsworth. There's an old coal barge with hull damage, leaven' before midday, bound fer Barfleur. Cover yerself in black dust, Master Tom, and the two of ye will pass unnoticed – especially as ye are seamen by trade. The Master's an old rogue with a liver eaten away by the quantity of gin 'e puts down, so 'e walks around, more dead than alive most of the time. Did him a favour, our Shilo did, more than once, so 'e don't mind returnen' one now. Shilo'll get you down to Emsworth afore daylight an' ye can spend the hours before yer sailin' scrubben' out the coalhold an' getten yerselves blackened up. Best disguise we could think of . . .'

They left the forest camp within the hour with Shilo Smith as their guide. Farewells were brief and there was still no sign of Dudie. Tom clasped Nat's hand in both his. 'Thanks, Bor,' he said quietly, for there were no words for the kind of gratitude due to Nat and Dudie. Nat seemed to understand for he looked embarrassed at such a show of emotion, yet appreciative of the well-intended gesture.

'Thank Miss Dudie for us, if you please,' Tom said. It would not be right to ask to see her. In the eyes of the Clan, she was Mokada for she was with child and without husband. To pay court to her openly would only help to compound her guilt in the eyes of these people.

He pressed the little square of paper into Nat's palm. 'Do one last thing for me, Friend. Give her this.'

Nat looked at him. There was such anxiety in the New Englander's strong Bayless face, such controlled emotion that the refusal died on his lips. He closed his fist on the paper and nodded.

Tarsus Lovell came stiffly from his waggon just before the trio departed. Tom, with Moses at his heels, went over to say his farewell. 'I do thank you, Master Lovell, for having made Moses and myself so welcome at your hearth. There is no way that I can express our gratitude except to say that one day I pray that I may be in a position to offer you or any of your people as warm a hospitality as you have given to two strangers with a price on their heads.'

The old man was very bowed. It clearly pained him to stand but he pulled himself up onto his feet slowly and stiffly, one hand gripping Tom's arm. 'You have been welcome here because you are blood of our blood, even though you are a stranger and a gorgio. Your mother was a fine woman, a credit to our people, even though she was reared a gorgio. Your grandfather, Jess Bayless, was a true Rom, a man of his time – he used his special Gifts well, bringing benefit to all his people as well as to himself. See that you follow him, Bor . . .'

The whole Clan watched silently as the three figures slipped away from the firelight into the trees, to be swiftly engulfed in the forest.

'Bring Boudicca Smith to me,' Tarsus Lovell said to one of the children.

It was a long walk down to Emsworth through the forests of Stansted and Southleigh, keeping the river Ems well to their left side. The distance was not great – just over five miles as the crow flies but there was little open land between the sea and the Downs at this point and travelling through the network of deerpaths in the darkness proved a hazardous occupation without a lantern. They kept close together in single file and Tom, his leg beginning to ache after the first hour, was hard put to keep up with Moses and their guide. Shilo Smith moved like a shadow, disturbing few tree branches in his way. He had a strange gliding movement, like a ferret, and, stopping suddenly to identify a sound close by, seemed to melt into the darkness without moving a muscle. Their travelling companions were little forest pigs, disturbed from their slumbers by the passage of Man, and the nocturnal keepers of the woods – hedgehogs, owls, a young deer.

The trees thinned and the path widened.

'Keep close and do as I do if you see movement,' Shilo directed. Like his cousin Nat, Shilo Smith was a man of few words in the company of gorgios. It was quite clear that he wanted only to deliver them to Hugh Skillett aboard the 'Lorraine' and to be rid of them with all possible speed. As the night began to thin into predawn when the world stirred and opened its eyes to a new day, they crossed the old Roman road from Emsworth to Horndean and plunged down a long shallow incline into the first straggle of cottages. The place was still quiet, the only activity in the town coming from the quay where five fishing boats, just in with their holds filled with cascades of shimmering fish, were in the process of mooring amid shouts and curses, the fisherman's shore tongue.

The old barge was moored at the very end of the coaling jetty. There was no sign of life aboard but the rumble of casks being moved in the nearby tavern drew them into the shadow of its yard. Moses and Tom crouched down against the side of the stable block and Shilo disappeared inside.

'That leg troubling you?' Moses asked as Tom sank down onto the cobbles, rubbing his throbbing leg.

'Just a little. 'Tis the longest time I've been on it since we left "Fortunée".'

'Has it occurred to you that we're a might close to it again, too? Can't be more than a couple of miles across the marshes from here . . . I keep getting a real nasty feeling between the shoulderblades, as though that little runt, Furze, was waiting for us just the other side of this wall.' Moses rolled his eyes in the grey light and his lips moved soundlessly. He had called upon his Maker with great fervency since he had left the sanctuary of Park Farm.

'Say one for me, Friend,' Tom grinned at him. 'The company I've been keeping lately hasn't been too savoury, apart from you and Dudie, of course.'

Moses gripped his shoulder till it hurt. 'That's the first crack of good humour you've shown in days, man . . . feels like weeks! Oh my word, Master, I'm so doggonned glad to be away from that place of yours.'

'So am I, Moss.' Tom suddenly meant it with all his heart. 'By the love of my Family, so am I.'

Shilo returned. With him was Hugh Skillett, a huge shambling wreck of a man so emaciated and evil-smelling that it was hard not to recoil from the warmth of his malodorous greeting.

'Good day to ye, gents. My friend here tells me that you be requiren' passage across the water, no questions asked?'

They had risen at his approach and Tom bowed slightly, as much to escape the noxious fumes of Skillett's decaying breath as to return the greeting. 'We are in quite a predicament, sir, that is true, and would be eternally grateful to the tune of a sum of your own choosing – within reason – if you could find us a working berth aboard your vessel.'

Skillett's one good eye gleamed redly through a sea of broken veins. The other had been long lost in one of countless skirmishes. 'Well, sors . . .' he paused to rub his stubbled chin. The sound of his caress was like a ship's keel on pebbles. For a long moment he was lost in thought all too clearly torn between the decision of whether to fleece the two strangers of all their money now or put a good face on it and see whether he might not gamble it off them later. He decided on the latter.

'I'm told yer credit is good though yer coinage is small. How about a round sum of fifty guineas and work yer passages to Barfleur?' He could always get them to sign letters of credit before releasing them ashore on the other side.

Tom nodded at once and held out his hand to seal the bargain before their goodnatured villain of a captain had second thoughts. The money exchanged hands and when, within a short time, the arrangements were agreed and they turned to thank Shilo for his help he had already left them, melting into the soft airy dawn and even now making his way back to the forest.

They hurried aboard before the strengthening day brought watchful eyes to see them, stripped their good jackets off and went swiftly to work cleaning the hold of coal dust. Within the hour it was impossible to tell which was the black man for they were both encased in dust from head to foot. Three other seamen joined them while the crew was making 'Lorraine' ready for sea. By the time Master Skillett roared for the ropes to be cast off and the great brown mainsail set, their own mothers would not have recognized them.

Nat sat beside Dudie in their Vardo and patted her hand awkwardly. It was not in his nature to give her the sympathy he knew she needed. It was the custom of them all to take the punishment due to him or her if it was justly meted out. She was Mokada through her own foolishness and lack of strength. Tarsus was within his rights to direct her to leave the camp and seek the forgiveness of her own family.

'You shan't go alone, Pen,' he said to her gruffly. 'We shall go together and I'll leave you with Sarey till you're delivered. Then we'll see.'

She turned to him gratefully, huge blue eyes magnified as tears welled up in them and spilt down her cheeks. There was no complaint in her for the harsh brief words that Tarsus Lovell had poured over her bowed head were justified in the eyes of the people.

'Go from here,' he had said to her. 'Take yourself and the shameful fruit of your lusting and cast no impurity upon the women of my hearth. We want no pikies among us.'

Nat fingered the little folded square of paper in his belt. It was not yet time to give it to her.

They left the camp and only Nat said his farewells to his cousins and made his respects to the old man. He had called upon them to help and they had given it unquestioningly in the name of the blood they all shared but, with Dudie as she was, the call for their hospitality had been too much to ask. He knew that neither he nor Dudie would be welcome with the Lovells or this branch of the Smith family again. He bowed his head before Tarsus and departed.

They moved off at first light with Pally pulling gamely in her tresses, into the forest by way of a boar trail that would not have been visible to any but the sharpest eye. There was utter tiredness in all of them and Nat and Dudie sat hunched on the seat with Smokey, sleeping in his coop on his hook above their heads.

On the northwest fringes of Wickham Nat handed the little note to Dudie. He had no knowledge of reading or writing in the gorgio tongue and the scrawl meant nothing to him.

Dudie leaned against the open doorway with the paper spread out in her lap and let the movement of the waggon rock her body gently from side to side.

The contents were all that was needed to clear her mind of the aching doubts that had haunted her since she had seen the look in Tom's terrible eyes. Lavenham must have had less power over him, after all, than she had thought. He sounded in his letter like the Tom who, in the weeks since she had started to nurse him, had given her those very special feelings of complete trust that she was only half aware would shortly turn to love. Here it was now, the huge relief and tenderness returned in abundance.

But those terrible stranger's eyes of his had terrified her. Even the memory of them made her shudder, for their alien expression had turned him from an attractive, gentle lover into the kind of questing beast that she had spent her life avoiding. If he was telling her the truth – if indeed his brief possession was over and he was once more the Tom she knew, she wanted nothing more now than to go to him, to be at his side wherever he might take her. She knew that suddenly with a great burst of longing for him – but she was Romani, unused to living in bricks and mortar. It was necessary for her to be close to the wind and the rain, to breathe fresh air rather than the confined gases of other people's bodies. She had realized as soon as they had arrived at the Lovell camp that he had wanted to speak with her but custom remained stronger even than their need. And at that time, thinking him still filled with his Killing Strength, she had been mortally afraid of him for the Tom Heritage possessed by Lavenham was not the one she wanted.

She had been almost glad to feel him gone. Then. Now the dried-blood words jiggled on the scrap of paper as the waggon rumbled over uneven stones.

'I want to go to Emsworth,' she said to Nat.

He dragged his thoughts back from his silent contemplation

of Smokey's excellence. 'To that narkri gorgio, I suppose.'

She held up the letter. Her face was jubilant now. The decision had been made and suddenly time was running away from her. 'The Power has gone. He told me so here. I believe him, Nat, for he sounds so different, so like the first Tom. Stop the Vardo, Nat. Let me go with him.'

They fell silent again, swaying to Pally's comfortable amble until she said, 'Please, Pral. Let me go to him while I can. It will be better that way, with the child coming in the New Year. I shall never be anything other than Mokada to the Clan from now on. In that other place, with a great sea between us, maybe they will be kinder to us both.'

He hauled on Pally's reins and the old horse, her joints aching, was more than willing to pause and take a few mouthfuls of grass, lurched to a creaking halt.

Dudie put her hands on both of Nat's and kissed his cheek. Tears were part of it but the sadness was only for the closeness of that shared childhood between them.

'If it is really what you want,' he said eventually. 'I cannot force you to stay with the Family and I shall one day want my own woman, I daresay ... Go if you must, but you'll have to make haste for they won't wait for anythen' but the tide.'

He fumbled in his purse and took out ten gold guineas. 'Don't say I sent you away with no dowry,' he said gruffly.

She took nothing with her save her purse and the red flowered shawl. The road from Wickham market down to Fareham and the crossroads would be full of carts and hay waggons by now and she was sure to find a lift into Emsworth before noon.

She slipped down onto the road and stood looking up at him for a moment, the eager elfin face so filled with grief and hope that it hurt him to see it.

'Sar shan ...'

She turned and walked away and he gave Pally a little flick with his leather. She lifted her head with a sigh and began to move away down the road towards the forests of West Hampshire. Neither of them looked back.

Dudie set herself a steady pace and fell to daydreaming. The coal barge was not due to leave Emsworth until late in the afternoon, she knew. If only she could ride in on an empty cart there would be plenty of time to get down to the wharf and attract Tom's attention. She cast aside the small worries that did their best to push through the bursting excitement as each step brought her closer to Emsworth, the boat bound for France — and Tom.

Without any warning she had suddenly been given the chance of a bright future to be spent with the finest of men. Fine, that is, as long as the darkness did not return to his soul. It was a risk that she would have to take.

A posse of soldiers passed her by but she noticed nothing, her attention fixed firmly on the sight, the same instant, of a well-loaded waggon piled with hay on the road ahead. She quickened her pace and approached it as the six scarlet-coated horsemen clattered by on the other side of the waggon.

'Hey, master,' she called up to the driver. 'Can ye give us a lift as far as Fareham?'

The Watcher sat on the bottom stair of the old House and tried to clear the confusion in his head. He had been here before, of that he was certain, but it was as though he was getting two different incidents mixed up in his already befuddled mind.

This House was certainly Lavenham. There was so much he recognized, for the staircase was the same and the windows also. Most of the furnishings were strange, though, old to the point of decay, much damaged and dust-rotted. It was as though the House had been abandoned for a very long time . . . and yet, and yet there had recently been people here for he remembered seeing them. People involved in violence, involved with the primeval appetites of the House itself. He raised his head and did his best to focus through vision that seemed blurred and wavery as though he was staring at his surroundings through water. He forced himself to examine the few facts that he was sure of.

1. *He seemed to be in some danger of losing his sanity through the House's strange influence over him.*

2. *Frances Ayles was becoming his only anchor with reality.*
3. *He was even beginning to feel that Frances also had something to do with whatever dwelt like a putrid miasma in the ancient monolith beneath the stone floor.*
4. *There it goes again . . . Why am I so certain of that stone beneath the floor? I keep getting the feeling . . . with absolute certainty that I have been burrowing into every strata of time in this terrible Place and that I am sometimes close to reaching the vortex of the whole thing . . .*

He pulled himself up against the carved baluster.

The place stank like a midden sometimes. There must be some ancient drain blocked by mud and leaves and compressed by the winter rains. He sniffed with distaste for the odour was not of leafmould but more of enormous density of human excrement or decaying flesh for there was a sickly sweetness about the filthy stench which caught at the back of his throat and made him suddenly gag.

He tore open the front door and leaning against the weed-choked wall of the terrace, vomited into the undergrowth.

Outside in the spring sunshine the air was mellow and sweet-scented with a faint suggestion of sea salt. The stench was quite gone. He stared about him, fighting the disorientation of his mind, searching the overgrown garden for signs of life.

Overhead, a small two-seater aircraft cut across his vision as it lifted into the air from the Goodwood airfield the other side of Chichester. He stared at it in utter relief.

Fact number 5 . . . I am back in my own time at this moment.

But how do I stay that way?

The salt air ruffled Tom's hair into wispy curls that danced in and out of his eyes. He stood up for a moment and rested, leaning against the wet bulkhead. Moses, humming softly under his breath, picked up the wooden bucket and sluiced the soapy water across the decking in a wide grey arc. He grinned at Tom, his teeth flashing through the grime on his face. The grief in Tom's eyes tore at his own bounding relief to be gone from that Place.

'My word, man. You sure do make a pretty nigger. Cain't think why the Almighty made such a fool mistake as to paint you white in the first place.'

'I should be happy as you are, old friend,' he said quietly. 'But there are things in my heart that I shall never forget from these last days and nights. The sight of Charles . . . cut down by me, Moss. Cut down by just a look when, for a single moment I wished him dead. My own flesh and blood . . .'

'Goodness sake's snap out of that!' Moses said sharply. 'You was taken up by some real dreadful devil in that Place, an' don't you forget it. 'Twasn't you who floored the Snake. How could you or I do anything like that? 'Twas that House done such an act, Friend, and it was not fer the first time, either. You just happened along.'

'Drawn there as neatly as any fish on a line . . .'

The bitterness in Tom's voice made Moses shake his head.

'Mister Moses,' a voice called above them and they looked up guiltily.

A head was silhouetted against the sky beyond the open hold. A small head, wild curls whipping in the warm breeze. The face peered down at them demurely. 'Do you think your brother there would mind given' me a hand down. There's a snooper from the Customs House walken' down the jetty in this direction an' I'd rather not be seen up here.'

Dudie.

Moses bounded up the ladder in four great leaps and swung her up into the air joyfully. Then mindful of what she had just said, he ushered her down into the hold and made a nest of sacks for her to sit on while Tom took both her hands in his, shaking his head in disbelief.

'Nat gave me your letter,' she said simply. 'I knew it would be all right for us then.'

They sailed on the afternoon tide, the old barque rolling badly even in the calm waters of the fine weather sea. It was good to feel working decks beneath the feet once more, to balance the body on the soles of the feet and feel the toes doing their job of steadying their weight. Tom rocked his body gently, pivoting on one arm against the deck-rail for the other was holding Dudie close to his side. They watched the hazy green shore melt slowly into gathering sea mist. When it was quite gone they floated in pearly isolation, the oily motion of the current beneath their bows lulling them into drowsiness.

'I feel so strange.' Her voice was hushed, the awe in it as though she was beholding a miracle. 'I have never been away from the land before but now it has quite vanished and this sea is a new element to be travelling over. It has a different smell, a different feel. Even the light is different without the land, Bor. I feel as though I am floaten' up there in the clouds with all that mist around us. It's beautiful in a new way. The water with the froth on it, like the head of bubbles in a milk pail after squeezen' the last drop from the cow — but there's no cows in this world . . .'

He turned away from the rail with a sigh and tucked her hand into the crook of his arm.

'Come now, Mistress,' he said to her. 'Let us go below and have a little wager with Master Skillett. We might even win back our passage money. Moss and I learned one thing from those French *Rafales* aboard "Fortunée" — and that is how to extract money at the card table! Will you watch and be our lucky charm?'

'She's always been that since the first day.' Moses followed them down the companionway towards the Master's cabin.

The child was heavy now in Dudie. Tom put his hand under her elbow and helped her against the movement of the ship. It occurred to him that here was where he might make reparation for being responsible for such a needless death. He gave her arm a little squeeze and she glanced up at him.

'It won't be long now,' he said to her. 'We're on the first stage for home. No more trouble, no more tampering with innocent lives. We'll leave all the horrors behind us and now I only want to see Mother's face when she meets you. No more worries, my dearest. I promise you that with all my heart.'

Midhurst, so clean and rolling and goddamned wholesome — Midhurst was suddenly close over the horizon.

Bibliography

The English Prison Hulks   W. Branch-Johnson
Journal of a Young Man of Massachusetts   Benjamin Water-
    house
State of the Prisons   John Howard (1777)
Memoirs   James Hardy Vaux (1819)
Journal of the House of Commons   Public Records Office
Hansards Parliamentary Debates
Sport in the Olden Time   Sir Walter Gilbey (1975)
The Cocker   W. Sketchley (1814)
Records of Chichester   T. G. Willis

Glossary

Beng	Devil
Bok	Luck
Bor	Friend
Boshomengro	Fiddler
Chav	Child
Chiriklo	Little bird
Dadrus	Father
Dik ai!	Look out!
Dikker	Look
Dinelo	Fool
Djillia	Song
Gorgio	Non-Romani
Grauni	Gem or jewel
Gurnii	Cow
Hobben	Food
Hotchiwichi	Hedgehog
Jalling the drom	Travelling the roads
Kanni	Bird
Kaulo	Black
Kenner	House
Kushti	Fine
Mokada	Unclean
Mort	Woman
Mullo	Ghost
Mushgaying	Spying out the land
Narkri	Dark, dank or unpleasant
Pen	Sister

Pral	Brother
Pikies	Gypsies expelled from tribe
Puri Daia	Grandmother
Rawni	Lady
Rom	Romani husband
Sap	Snake
Sar shan	Good day or Hello
Scran	Food
Shura	Headman or master
Simensa	Cousin
Vardo	Waggon